George Eliot, Judaism and the Novels

George Eliot, Judaism and the Novels

Jewish Myth and Mysticism

Saleel Nurbhai

and

K. M. Newton

First published 2002 by
PALGRAVE
Houndmills, Basingstoke, Hampshire RG21 6XS and
175 Fifth Avenue, New York, N. Y. 10010
Companies and representatives throughout the world

PALGRAVE is the new global academic imprint of
St. Martin's Press LLC Scholarly and Reference Division and
Palgrave Publishers Ltd (formerly Macmillan Press Ltd).

ISBN 0–333–96381–4

This book is printed on paper suitable for recycling and
made from fully managed and sustained forest sources.

A catalogue record for this book is available
from the British Library.

Library of Congress Cataloging-in-Publication Data
Nurbhai, Saleel
    George Eliot, Judaism and the novels : Jewish myth and
    mysticism / Saleel Nurbhai and K.M. Newton.
        p. cm.
    Includes bibliographical references and index.
    ISBN 0–333–96381–4
    1. Eliot, George, 1819–1880—Characters—Jews. 2. Eliot,
George, 1819–1880—Religion. 3. Mysticism in literature.
4. Judaism in literature. 5. Jews in literature. 6. Myth in
literature. I. Newton, K.M.– II. Title.

PR4692.J48 N49 2001
823'.8—dc21
                                                        2001036488

10   9   8   7   6   5   4   3   2   1
11   10   09   08   07   06   05   04   03   02

Printed and bound in Great Britain by
Antony Rowe Ltd, Chippenham, Wiltshire

Contents

Acknowledgements		vi
Introduction: Jewish Myth, Mysticism and George Eliot's Fiction		1
1	George Eliot and Kabbalism: Historical and Literary Context	25
2	Kabbalistic Philosophy and the Novels	35
3	From Formless Matter to Matter with Form	54
4	The Relationship between Creator and Creature	69
5	Ideals of Perfection	91
6	Science, Pseudo-Science and Transgression	108
7	Investing Form with Essence	134
8	Homelessness and Speechlessness	148
9	The Messianic Potential	171
10	Conclusion: Social Critique, Education, Allegory	181
Notes		192
Bibliography		210
Index		217

Acknowledgements

The relationship that led to the writing of this book started when Saleel Nurbhai attended Dundee University to work with Ken Newton on the influence of Goethe's *Faust* on George Eliot's fiction. Eventually this developed into a study of the connections between her fiction and kabbalism. The present study is a radical reworking and development of this material. Both authors have been involved in the writing of every section of the book, though the initial research into Jewish myth and mysticism was done by Saleel Nurbhai. Material from the book has already appeared in print. We should like to thank the editor of *George Eliot–George Henry Lewes Studies* and the publisher of *The Cambridge Quarterly*, Oxford University Press, for permission to reprint.

Anyone working on the Jewish aspect of George Eliot's writings must acknowledge William Baker's work, particularly his pioneeriing book, *George Eliot and Judaism*, and his edition of her journals.

Saleel Nurbhai would very much like to thank Mina and Mustan Nurbhai for all their support, and Ken Newton would like to thank Cate, Carol, Claire and John for putting up with his devotion to George Eliot.

Introduction: Jewish Myth, Mysticism and George Eliot's Fiction

The *golem* – from the Hebrew for 'unformed mass' – is central to Jewish mythology. Its original, literal use refers to Adam, the unformed mass of clay before being shaped by God. Equally, it means the empty vessel, created and formed by God, but without the inspiriting breath which imparts life and understanding. Consequently, the golem, particularly through Jewish mystical rituals of creation,[1] has assumed a metaphorical significance that is connected with human origin, the loss of innocence, growth of human awareness, and the fall from Paradise. Considering the nature of these themes, it is understandable that this aspect of Jewish mysticism has been incorporated into Romantic literature, though one can also see its influence on certain pre-Romantic writers.[2] In the mid-nineteenth century the golem took on further significance as a consequence of various cultural developments, such as the revolutionary implications for human origins of Darwin's theory of evolution and the depiction of the proletariat as an unformed mass in the political writings of Marx and Engels. This study aims to show how the myth of the golem and Jewish mysticism were exploited artistically by George Eliot, most obviously in her final novel, *Daniel Deronda*, but also in her previous works of fiction.

Mythological content in the work of Eliot is not a new concept. In *George Eliot's Mythmaking* Joseph Wiesenfarth has identified a strong mythological current running through her works which combines her vast knowledge of classical and biblical mythology with balladic influences from, among others, Wordsworth and Sir Walter Scott. Felicia Bonaparte has, in *The Triptych and the Cross*, revealed a

1

poetic substructure in *Romola* which is based on myth and epic; and Mary Wilson Carpenter in *George Eliot and the Landscape of Time* has argued that her fiction dramatises and explores prophetic vision and history and even employs numerological symbolism. Through a further investigation of her writing we hope to demonstrate that a cohesive mythic structure is identifiable in her fiction which has its basis in Jewish mysticism and its associated mythology, the myth of the golem being particularly central.

In trying to understand why Jewish myth and mysticism figure so prominently in Eliot's writing, one needs perhaps to bear two factors in mind: her artistic ambition and her view of the novel as a genre. She clearly measured her work by the highest literary standards of the past, such as Greek tragedy and epic poetry of the quality of Milton's *Paradise Lost*. Other critics have discussed the influence of those on her work.[3] Such literary achievements, however, were dependent to a considerable degree on the fact that writers of classical tragedy and epic poetry were able to draw on myth together with its underlying metaphysical system in order to give their works layers of significance beyond the level of the narrative. Yet despite the fact that Eliot wrote poetry, including the ambitious verse drama, *The Spanish Gypsy*, her fundamental artistic commitment was to the novel, a literary form that, at least in the nineteenth century, was viewed as grossly inferior in artistic quality to tragedy or epic, partly because of the artistic limitations of realism. We shall suggest that for Eliot Jewish myth and mysticism provided the metaphorical and allegorical potential to enable the novel to compete in complexity and philosophical range with tragic drama and epic poetry.

Though Eliot is strongly associated with realism, from the beginning of her fiction there is evidence of a desire to go beyond a merely realistic representation, as one sees for example in the use she makes of ballad and gothic material in her early novels and short stories. Previous criticism and commentary have tended to see the Jewish influence on her fiction as having a significant impact only on *Daniel Deronda*. We shall argue, however, that in her final novel one sees only the culmination of her interest in and use of Jewish myth and mysticism and that throughout her fiction, at least from *Adam Bede*, one can discern a substructure shaped by kabbalistic ideas. To understand why the golem legend in particular may have been of particular use to her as a writer who aspired to extend the artistic and intellectual range of the novel one needs to discuss it briefly within the context of Jewish mystical thinking. Adam is, from a kabbalistic point of view, the original golem; he is the *Adam Kadmon* – the Primeval Element. A form of the word 'golem' is used in the Bible (Psalms 139: 16) to mean an unformed mass, as Adam was before he was shaped by the hand of God, and it can be found in this sense in Talmudic literature: 'How was Adam created? In the first hour his dust was collected; in the second his form was created; in the third he became a shapeless mass (*golem*); in the fourth his members were joined; in the fifth his apertures opened; in the sixth he received his soul; in the seventh he stood up on his feet . . .'[4] Formation of Adam from the earth establishes an important link which is discernible even in etymology:

Being the son of *Adama* ('Earth'), Man called himself 'Adam' in acknowledgment of his origin; or perhaps Earth was called Adama in honour of her son; yet some derive his name from *adom* ('red'), recording that he was formed from red clay . . .[5]

Though Robert Graves does believe the etymological links to be open to doubt, they should nevertheless be borne in mind, especially when the importance of words and letters in Jewish mystical ideas of creation is taken into account.

Connection with the earth also unites Adam with a telluric spirit said, in some ancient Hebrew traditions, to dwell in him. Through adaptations, the meaning of this spirit was widened: it was likened to the 'ruah' – the vital spirit of the golem, inherited from the earth. The pneuma, breathed into him by God, was of a more elevated principle – the 'neshamah': a spirit of intellect and understanding. Before he received the higher spirit, Adam is said to have been given a vision of future generations, related to the sentient power which is part of his clay. Linked thus with the earth, any sundering of Adam and the earth is a denial of his basic spirit. The diaspora and the continuing myth of the Wandering Jew have a profound significance, therefore, since they imply a schism that separates the Jewish people from any spirit whatsoever, divine or chthonic.

Some writings on the creation of Adam maintain that God did not create him last, but first; he left him golem so that it would not be said that Adam helped in the creation of the world.[6] This would seem to suggest an element of jealousy in the matter of creation as well as one of fear of the golem. Similar considerations lie behind the despatch of Lilith to the underworld. Originally she was said to have been the 'First Eve', created independently of Adam and also made of earth, but because she claimed to be equal to Adam she was forced to flee from God into a demonic career. God is thus shown to be protective of his own status as sole creator and also fearful of those he has created.

The formation of the Kabbalah led to different interpretations of the act of creation. Spanish kabbalists tended towards the idea that God's investment of Adam with his breath represented a marriage between heaven and earth. Medieval German kabbalism adopted a different idea: Adam was the object of a contract between God and Earth in which he was a loan from Earth for a thousand years, for which God gave Earth a receipt for 'four ells of earth'.[7] These conceptions were kabbalistic interpretations of the myth of the biblical golem. In the third and fourth centuries ideas of the magical creation of life had begun to appear, with stories of the Talmudic characters, Rava and Zera. Rava is said to have created a man who goes to Rabbi Zera, but since the man cannot speak, he is recognised as artificial. Two rabbis, Hanina and Oshaya, were purported to have created a calf one-third of the normal size by means of mysticism and magic. Eliot alludes to this in one of her notebooks when she refers to 'R. Chanina & R. Oshaja' who 'produced a calf 3 years old & ate it'.[8]

Magical and mystical creation were largely the concern of the *Sefer Yetzirah* – the 'Book of Creation'. This was an esoteric text conceived as a discourse on the deity as creator and on human attempts at emulation. It was said that one who was completely immersed in the *Sefer Yetzirah* had wisdom beyond measure, meaning it was 'comparable to the creative wisdom of God'.[9] Creation through the use of the *Sefer Yetzirah* was regarded by some – notably Yehuda Halevi, the medieval Jewish poet and mystic who has many connections with Mordecai in *Daniel Deronda*[10] – as a mystical ritual. Another story concerning Rava and Rabbi Zera, in which they create a calf – like Hanina and Oshaya – kill it and eat it, has been read as symbolising their forgetting the meaning of the *Sefer Yetzirah* and having to begin its study again. The Kabbalah scholar, Gershom Scholem, points to the ritualistic implication of this story: 'This creation of a golem is an end in itself, a ritual of initiation into the secret of creation.'[11] Beginning as a legendary figure, the golem thus became the object of a mystical ritual which was meant to enhance the awareness of esoteric knowledge, later passing back into legend. The ritual of its creation became a mystical experience, and was eventually used solely for that purpose. Eliot is likely to have been well acquainted with Talmudic stories about artificial creation. In 1867 Emanuel Deutsch had sent her proofs of an article he had written on the Talmud for the *Quarterly Review*, inviting criticism, and she had also read Giuseppe Levi's *Parabeln, Legenden und Gedanken aus Thalmud und Midrasch*.[12]

Some aspects of the golem and the legends attached to it have Faustian connotations, contained, for example, in the stories about Simon Magus. A prominent story concerning this proto-Faust is his attempt to prove his godhead.[13] He is mentioned in the New Testament as being hailed as a divine figure.[14] He is said to have come into conflict with Peter in Rome and he dies when trying to show his divinity by flying. Scholem reports that in the *Sefer Yetzirah*, Simon Magus successfully imitates the divine creator:

> Simon Magus is quoted as boasting that he had created a man, not out of the earth, but out of air by theurgic transformations (*theiai tropai*) and – exactly as later in the instructions concerning the making of the golem – reduced him to his element by undoing the said transformation.[15]

In Jewish mystical tradition the creation of a golem was taken as an indication of a human's likeness to God – though there was also an awareness that this could encourage polytheism. Simon Magus's aspirations seem to have been received with more tolerance in this tradition than do his New Testament activities of challenging Peter and using magic to try to prove his divinity. His golem resembles the homunculi of Paracelsus and of Wagner in *Faust* II, Paracelsus having based his own creative theories on esoteric kabbalistic writings about the artificial creation of life.

The method of Simon Magus's creation and disintegration is the use of, and 'undoing' of, magical transformations. This bears some resemblance to that mystical creation of the golem which involves combinations of letters – as in the creative process of letters said to be employed by Rabbis Hanina and Oshaya. The power of manipulation of letters is also prominent in popular legends of the golem (of Chelm and of Prague). Here the Hebrew word 'Emet' – meaning 'truth' – is placed on its forehead to make it live. When the first character is removed, the word 'Met', meaning 'death' is formed, so nullifying the golem.

Letters and speech are very important in golem symbolism. It was believed that the soul of all creation could be made manifest through letters. The Torah, the essential Hebrew scripture from which orthodox and esoteric philosophy developed, was looked upon by mystics as a living organism, its various parts being all the vital organs and its soul manifested in the words and their meanings. As can be seen from the above, in the story of Rava and Rabbi Zera, it was the muteness of the golem that identified it as such, and the idea of the life or death of the golem being dependent on the arrangement of letters on its forehead was also introduced in this story. Muteness, however, was not an essential aspect of the golem; the idea had come to be prevalent among kabbalists who believed that speech was the highest human faculty.

Other golem stories tend towards the idea of animation, such as the tale of Rabbi Hananel, who purportedly restored life, temporarily, to dead people by writing the name of God on a piece of parchment, which was then placed beneath the subject's tongue or sewn onto the arm. Removal of the parchment, often by pretending to kiss the creature, would make it lifeless again. Animation through alchemical or pseudoscientific methods – those said to be used by Paracelsus – was allied closely with artificial creation of a golem or homunculus. Charles Meunier's reanimation of Mrs Archer in *The Lifted Veil*, using pseudoscientific methods, links Eliot's short story to this tradition.

Animation or reanimation in golem tales is often accompanied by destruction. The story that most obviously demonstrates this is that of the golem of Chelm. This legend is about a Rabbi Elijah, a contemporary of the historical Faustus, who creates a golem in order to do good – again with letters on the forehead. One night when the Rabbi forgets to remove the all-important letter, the golem goes out of control and becomes destructive. The golem of Prague – the most commonly encountered version of the legend – is an adaptation of the golem of Chelm, but one which elevates the golem figure: 'It remained for the later legend of the *Golem of Prague* to endow the terrifying figure with moral and social grandeur.'[16] It itself has different versions, the most popular being that in which a golem is made by Rabbi Loew in order to protect the Prague Jews from pogroms. Once the danger is over, the golem is returned to dust.[17] The golem created to do good but running amuck is that aspect of the legend which can be seen most clearly in Mary Shelley's novel. With the Prague golem being portrayed as a deliverer there is a symbolic union of telluric Adam with the Messiah. In Eliot's work the role of deliverer or would-be deliverer is applied again and again to her central characters: Dinah and Adam, Romola, Felix Holt, Dorothea and Lydgate, Deronda. The ambitions of these characters are either restricted or thwarted by limitations within themselves or within their situations: the chaos of misrule – on whatever petty scale – is juxtaposed with the aspiration to deliverance, only for the conflict to be irresolvable with compromise the inevitable consequence. It is only with Deronda that the character as deliverer is most fully realised.

The destructive potential within the golem-figure itself can be seen as deriving from a tension or lack within its creator. Scholem writes:

> Golem making is dangerous; like all major creation it endangers the life of the creator – the source of danger, however, is not the golem or the forces emanating from him, but the man himself. The danger is not that the golem, become autonomous, will develop overwhelming powers; it lies in the tension which the creative process arouses in the creator himself. Mistakes in carrying out the directions do not impair the golem; they destroy its creator.[18]

This is connected to the doppelganger theme in representations of the golem, an aspect of the legend that has been identified by Byron Sherwin:

> In a sense, the human creator of the Golem confronts the human creature – himself – in his own primitive, underdeveloped and primordial form. The human creator of the golem confronts the human being – himself – as he once was, as he might have remained, as pure matter devoid of form, as a soul-less creature devoid of life and purpose.[19]

The creature as golem is both an attempt to return to a form of unsullied pre-Fall grace – a return to mythical origin of the tellurian Adam – and a crude embodiment of the basic instincts or moral weaknesses of its creator. As Sherwin puts it: 'the inability to create an intelligent Golem reflects a flaw in the creator of the Golem that becomes embodied in the Golem he creates'.[20] The responsibility for this is not the creator's in any simple sense since the creative process itself necessarily generates tensions which cannot be wholly controlled, and out of such tensions emerges a destructive potential. This implication of golem-making and the reflexive nature of the relation between creator and creature are central to Jewish mystical aspects of creation and provide a sustained and defining thematic quality which is peculiar to that particular mystical tradition.

Other implications of the golem have relevance in other literatures and beyond literature, for example in stories of statues and inanimate objects being invested with life:

> Not wholly without justification, attempts have been made to relate the notion of living statues, widespread among non-Jews, with the golem legend, though such parallels apply of course only to the purely magical and not to the tellurian aspects of the golem.[21]

Such stories, therefore, would have more to do with the golem created artificially by pseudoscientific or magical practice – as with Simon Magus or Paracelsus – than with the creation of Adam. However, it can be argued that all such stories have a tellurian aspect.

Animated statues lead to a further development of the golem legend. In 1614 one Samuel Friedrich Brenz reported that the Jews in Germany 'had a magical device "which is called *Hamor Golim*"',[22] which was used as a servant. This device was related to the creatures in medieval automaton legends; these in turn were closely associated with the 'mechanical man', much akin to the golem as servant – the theme of 'The Sorcerer's Apprentice'. This version of the legend, given literary treatment by Goethe, had important social and political implications because the servant was no longer seen as being controlled by the master. Other adaptations, originating in seventeenth-century Poland, had the servant turning on the master. By linking the golem as servant with the automaton legends, golem and mechanical device became equated. The potential of servants to turn on their masters was thus on the same level as machines reacting against their operators. The implications of this – particularly relevant in the nineteenth century given Marx's influence on political developments in the second half of the century – were such that the means of production could be interpreted as being the same as those who worked them, and the significance of this increased with the emergence of mechanisation on a large scale with the onset of the Industrial Revolution. There was now a twofold threat for those who owned machines and employed labour: both a mass of golem-like workers and industrial machinery could have a destructive potential. An eighteenth-century precedent for this was set with the 1789 Revolution in France – a partial realisation of this potential. Carlyle describes the Revolution as an abstract monstrosity which must be channelled and defined:

> To bridle-in that great devouring, self-devouring French Revolution; to *tame* it, so that its intrinsic purpose can be made good, that it may become *organic*, and be able to live among other organisms and *formed* things, not as a wasting destruction alone.[23]

By giving definition to this amorphous entity the Revolution will situate itself in the historical process, and as part of such an organic process its destructive capabilities will be negated. A sense of place in time is thus added to the concept of the golem, and we shall suggest that Eliot exploited this symbolism in various ways in her fiction, notably, with her presentation of the potential danger of the *Lumpenproletariat* which could turn on its master, provided it had sufficient awareness, as can be seen in her depiction of mob behaviour in *Felix Holt* and *Romola*, as we shall discuss later.

An increased dependence on the means of industrial production was a potential threat to the new middle class, though one should point out that Luddite machine-breaking workers perceived such a threat in more direct terms. When workers attacked machinery one had the ironical situation of one golem turning on another, as it were. Dependence upon this golem-like technology induced a fear which Eliot treated in comic mode in the essay 'Shadows of the Coming Race' in *Impressions of Theophrastus Such*: 'there rises a fearful vision of the human race evolving machinery which will by-and-by throw itself fatally out of work'.[24] The golem legend, then, came to have wider interpretations as societies transformed themselves into industrialised structures. Translated into literary terms, it was used to explore a variety of issues:

> In this literature questions are discussed which had no place in the popular legends (e.g. the *golem's* love for a woman), or symbolic interpretations of the meaning of the *golem* were raised (the unredeemed, unformed man; the Jewish people; the working class aspiring for its liberation).[25]

Almost certainly Eliot's exploitation of the golem metaphorically and symbolically would have arisen not only out of direct contact with Jewish writings but also out of her reading of literature influenced by the golem legend and Jewish mysticism more generally, especially such works as *Faust, Sartor Resartus*[26] and *Frankenstein.*[27] In *Sartor Resartus*, for example,Teufelsdroeckh is, for some part of the work, a self-confessed unformed man and an intellectual golem. He is of an indefinable substance: 'To the most, indeed, he had become not so much a Man as a Thing'.[28] There is a Faustian edge to Teufelsdroeckh, since he is associated with esoteric secrets of creation as sought after in German universities. It is in such an institution that he hopes to achieve shape. The first chapter of Teufelsdroeckh's book is said to contain 'profound glances into the *Adam Kadmon*, or Primeval Element'.[29] These can be interpreted as mystical searches, in view of the fact that Carlyle's hero has been seen as a rabbi and Kabbalah scholar.[30] According to medieval Jewish thought – that part of it which was involved with the propagation of mystical tradition – this would suggest Carlyle's character is related to both the original and messianic aspects of the biblical golem which look to the introduction of a new era: 'the Rabbinic concept of the "primordial light which is stored up for the righteous in the future world", is intimately connected with the motif of Primordial Man (*Adam Kadmon*)'.[31] One can see connections with Eliot's work, such as a link between Adam – the golem of Genesis – and Adam Bede, who is perceived by Hetty as '"something like" a man'.[32] More significantly, in *Middlemarch* Lydgate's search for the fundamental human element takes on allegorical implications. Keeping in mind the Editor of *Sartor Resartus*'s statement that the 'grand Tissue of all Tissues' is the one which enclothes the soul, Lydgate's search can be connected with a quest for the soul's shape. Moreover, since the soul's shape is the *Adam Kadmon*, there would be alignment of this primal tissue with the Primeval Element. The object of Lydgate's researches would then parallel research into the biblical creation myth. Hence, Lydgate's quest becomes more obviously paralleled with Casaubon's search for mythological origins.

As intellectual golem, Teufelsdroeckh is united with another strand of Jewish mystical thought concerning unformed matter. It was considered by some that Intellect was the first of God's creations, then the Soul, then Matter.[33] Connected with this was the idea that Matter was the result of a pairing of the Intellect with the Soul. The Soul can be compared to the ruah, and the Intellect to the neshamah.

Since pairing of the tellurian spirit with the pneuma results in the human, Teufelsdroeckh without intellectual shape is also devoid of matter and humanity. This can be compared with the mythological pairing, in classical literature, of Eros with Psyche in order to give shape to the passions. Karen Chase states: 'If eros often appears as amorphous energy, psyche is frequently pure form, and the task for any representation of personality is, as it were, to wed eros to psyche, that is, to give form to emotional life.'[34] Goethe's representation of Homunculus's attempt to achieve manifestation by joining with Galatea suggests a link between the classical and the kabbalistic: the golem in literature seeks definition through pairing with the ideal form of physical beauty. Moreover, since Galatea and Homunculus are both golem figures in being ideal characters who have been artificially endowed with life, this may have been Goethe's attempt to unite in symbolic terms the neoplatonic in the Romantic with classical creativity.

Creation in the golem legend and later versions of it, such as *Faust* and *Frankenstein*, is associated with the masculine, in that women's role in the birth process is taken over by the male through unorthodox means. With the golem, the creator is either a masculine god, the archangel Michael, or Rabbi Loew, Elijah, or another Rabbi connected with the legend. In *Faust* female creativity is denied; Gretchen and Helen must die if their offspring die; and with the poem's treatment of Pygmalion and Galatea, the perfect woman is created by a man. Victor Frankenstein's mother dies; in Victor's nightmare vision she comes to be associated with Elizabeth, who is then killed by his own creation, and he destroys the Monster's prospective mate because he does not want it to be the source of a colony of monsterlings. Females are moved to the background because they are seen to have no place in, or to inhibit, male creativity. In *Daniel Deronda*, the work by Eliot which most clearly makes use of the golem myth, masculine creation is also evident: Deronda attributes the making of his selfhood not to his mother but to the Jewish mystic, Mordecai: '"It is you who have given shape to what, I believe, was an inherited yearning"'.[35] Deronda's mother's attempt to determine his selfhood by cutting him off from his Jewish heritage ultimately fails.

Such a representation of male creativity as being more powerful than female creativity in Eliot's final novel is a golemish construction and it can be related to the passive role that is often assigned by male characters to female characters in her work. Hetty Sorrel in *Adam Bede* most readily adheres to this because of her resemblance to Gretchen in Goethe's *Faust*. Even such self-centred and wilful characters as Rosamond Vincy in *Middlemarch* and Gwendolen Harleth in *Daniel Deronda* predominantly adopt a policy of passive resistance towards the men in their lives who seek to shape and control them. Harold Transome's opinion in *Felix Holt* exemplifies the male attitude which complements this:

'Women, very properly, don't change their views, but keep to the notions in which they have been brought up. It doesn't signify what they think – they are not called upon to judge or to act.'[36]

Placed in a passive position, women, like automata and golems, are expected to act or be shaped according to the preconceptions of male creators. Consequently, like the golem and its medieval automatic counterparts, they can, merely by acting according to their own opinions, produce a reaction against the creators. Dehumanisation is often involved in this process: to escape being regarded as non-human, golem-like creatures shaped by the will of another, they can be forced to express themselves by means of a further denial of life. Through exploitation of the metaphorical implications of the golem legend in her texts, Eliot can go beyond representing male–female relations in psychological terms and add a mythic dimension that complicates and deepens that representation.

Also associated with creativity in golem literature is the achieving of godhead, and we have already mentioned the legend of Faust's forerunner, Simon Magus. Goethe's character has the same aspirations:

The hour is come, as master of my fate
To prove in man the stature of a god.[37]

The act of creation was seen as an *imitatio dei* by the Hasidim, and was advocated as such. A feature of *Daniel Deronda* is Deronda's attempts to find definition within the world. But because tension exists within the creator, which is then transferred to the golem, and because there is also tension between the creature and its environment (a similar tension is thematically incorporated in *Faust* II with the juxtaposed characters Homunculus and Euphorion who represent synthetic and natural creation respectively and who must try to establish a relationship with the world), a problem is presented to both creator and creature. This has significant implications in *Daniel Deronda*, as we shall discuss later. Considering the part played by Goethe in the artistic development of both Eliot and G. H. Lewes – she closely collaborated with Lewes in his research for and writing of his biography of Goethe and herself had written a review of *Wilhelm Meister* for the *Leader* – a brief examination of the above-mentioned tensions as they affect Homunculus and Euphorion is relevant. In *Faust* Homunculus is the product of artificial creation. He is a transcendent idea made manifest, in search of organic realisation. Were he to achieve this, however, he would be faced with an existential paradox. Physical being would deny him his own expression since he would be diffused into the world and thus sacrifice individuality. Creation by the unorthodox means employed by Wagner is depicted by Goethe as a failing in the creator, failure for the creature, and a criticism of the world. Wagner is unable to perceive that Homunculus will seek existence beyond the expression allowed him, and that this will be a danger to him. The golemish tensions are suggested by Wagner's shortsightedness. Added to this is Homunculus's inability to see the dangers to himself. To complete the imbalance, the world is unable to allow him existence without removing his individuality. Conversely, there is Euphorion (a name which Eliot used for her plagiaristic theorist in *Impressions of Theophrastus Such*[38]): ostensibly the son of Faust and Helen, he is the Byronic product of the combination of Classical Hellenism and German Romanticism. As a creature, he is of the earth, but struggling for transcendental realisation. Consequently, he is subject to a paradox similar to that of Homunculus: an urge to find expression beyond the bounds of earth is offset by an Antaeus-like necessity to be part of it. The resemblance to Antaeus and his bond to the earth has qualities similar to Adam's tellurian link: to break the bond is to bring self-destruction – to cut oneself off from life's essence. Euphorion's final leap into freedom brings an immediate Icarian demise. What is apparent in these stories from *Faust* is that the tensions are insurmountable and can only be resolved by self-destruction.

As mentioned earlier, Eliot's most obvious representation of the golem myth is in *Daniel Deronda*, and one can see that Deronda's relation to Mordecai has certain links with Goethe's treatment of golem figures in *Faust*. Deronda is for Mordecai a transcendental idea made flesh, a Platonic idea which has specific reference to the golem because it involves Deronda finding shape. Mordecai says to Deronda:

'Daniel, from the first, I have said to you, we know not all the pathways. Has there not been a meeting among them, as of the operations in one soul, where an idea being born and breathing draws the elements towards it, and is fed and grows?' (*DD*, p. 641)

The description here of an idea taking shape is reminiscent of the transformations boasted of by Simon Magus in his creation of a golem, particularly in the drawing in of elements to give the idea substance. This elemental factor is also suggestive of artificial creation and transformation in the alembics of medieval alchemists. The relationship between Deronda and Mordecai, however, differs from that between Wagner and Homunculus and Victor and the monster since Eliot's characters come to a more constructive conclusion. This is partially the result of returning the legend to its Judaic origins. Gershom Scholem emphasises its specific Jewish significance: 'The golem has been interpreted as a symbol of the soul or of the Jewish people, and both theories can give rise, no doubt, to meaningful reflections.'[39] Tellurian aspects of the *Adam Kadmon* and the golem of Prague as protector make the legend meaningful in a Jewish context by attributing to it strong messianic connotations: it saves Jews from trouble and unites them with the land from which they have been exiled. A cyclical return to the Paradise in which the golem was formed is brought to the fore, and this is re-enacted in *Daniel Deronda*.

By viewing the work of Eliot within the context of kabbalistic mysticism and the specific myth of the golem, there is an alteration in critical perception. As we have said, Eliot is widely seen as a realist writer, and her meticulous and deliberate preparation for her work would attest to such a view. Our aim is to show that her work should also be read mythically and allegorically – the mythological content being more unifying and central than simply disparate allusion – through the sustained use of golem myth and metaphor, as we shall endeavour to demonstrate more fully in the chapters that follow.

However, one needs first of all to address an obvious question raised by this study: did Eliot actually 'believe' in Jewish mysticism and kabbalistic ideas? If she did not, then why are they such a presence in her fiction – incontrovertibly in *Daniel Deronda* and, as we shall try to show, also in her other work – and why did she devote so much time to studying them? What is striking if one looks at Eliot's life as a whole is the extreme change that takes place between the anti-Semitism[40] of the earlier part of her life and her later preoccupation with and immersion in Jewish history, culture and religion – both orthodox Judaism and kabbalism – so much so that G. H. Lewes remarked that 'only learned Rabbis are so profoundly versed in Jewish history and literature as she is'.[41] It is significant, however, that she denied that there had been any fundamental change of view over the period in which she wrote fiction. She stated in a letter written in December 1876:

> It is perhaps less irrelevant to say, àpropos of a distinction you seem to make between my earlier and later works, that though I trust there is some growth in my appreciation of others and in my self-distrust, there has been no change in the point of view from which I regard our life since I wrote my first fiction – the 'Scenes of Clerical Life'. Any apparent change of spirit must be due to something of which I am unconscious. The principles which are at the root of my effort to paint Dinah Morris are equally at the root of my effort to paint Mordecai. (*Letters*, VI, 318)

This would suggest that her philosophical position remained unchanged and therefore non-metaphysical over the whole of her literary career and that she no more 'believed' in Jewish mystical ideas in any literal sense than she believed in Christianity or any other metaphysical system. Why, therefore, was she so preoccupied with them?

As we suggested earlier, Eliot's major ambition as an artist was to confront the challenge of reconciling realist fiction – the most powerful of modern literary genres but perhaps limited in its expressive power – with the scope and philosophical depth of Greek tragedy and epic poetry that were her artistic inspiration. This challenge was particularly severe for Eliot who in her early career identified herself with realism in a very narrow sense. In the first story of *Scenes of Clerical Life*, 'The Sad Fortunes of the Reverend Amos Barton', she attacked those who prefer 'the ideal in fiction' and declared her commitment to representing 'commonplace' and 'insignificant' people;[42] and in the notorious seventeenth chapter of *Adam Bede*, 'In which the story pauses a little', the narrator states that 'I turn without shrinking from cloud-borne angels, from prophets, sybils, and heroic warriors, to an old woman bending over her flower-pot, or eating her solitary dinner' (*AB*, p. 177). Yet even in her early work it is clear that realism is not completely the dominant mode. As we mentioned above, the name 'Adam' is not insignificant in *Adam Bede* and Hetty's story is clearly influenced by that of Hester Prynne in Hawthorne's *The Scarlet Letter*, as her name implies, and Hetty is also linked with Coleridge's Ancient Mariner, as we shall discuss later. Myth and literary allusion, therefore, interact with realism from very early on in her fiction.

However – perhaps looking forward to the ambitious attempt to write a novel on an epic scale with *Romola* – Eliot introduces a formal change with *Silas Marner*, a work written at the same time as she was contemplating *Romola*. It is possible to read the fiction up to that point predominantly in realist terms without concerning oneself with other layers of meaning. In *Silas Marner* and all the novels that follow the narrative is organised in terms of a double-plot in which parallelism, contrast and thematic connections are clearly present. How can this be reconciled with realism? David Cecil, at the beginning of his chapter on her in *Early Victorian Novelists*, writes of her fiction: 'They are the first novels which . . . set out to give a picture of life wholly unmodified by those formulas of a good plot which the novel had taken over from comedy and romance', yet he comments later that 'She sacrifices life to art. Her plots seem too neat and symmetrical to be true.'[43] But whereas Cecil assumes that novelists should depict life in a way that appears unmediated by artistic organisation, from *Silas Marner* on Eliot draws attention to structure and pattern. This may have been because she took the view that since form is intrinsic in literary texts and cannot be avoided, this should not be concealed from the reader. Not only could a realism based on such concealment be accused of dishonesty or bad faith, but fiction that aspired to epic scale needs the means to break beyond the limits of realism.

One of the main concerns of her short theoretical essay, 'Notes on Form in Art', is where form comes from. She argues that form as applied to art 'refers to structure or composition, that is, to the impression from a work considered as a whole. And what is a structure but a set of relations selected & combined in accordance with a sequence of mental states in the constructor, or with the precon-ception of a whole which he has inwardly evolved?' (*Essays*, pp. 433–4). Form therefore is produced by the subject and not imma-nent in the object. The use of the double-plot suggests that she chose to acknowledge this by foregrounding form rather than seek-ing to cover it up in the quest for 'mak[ing] development appear inevitable',[44] which a critic such as David Cecil would prefer.

It seems probable that the main reason Eliot decided to employ an explicit form through the double-plot was because she saw it not as creating a contradiction within realism but rather as offering an artistic opportunity to the novelist. This may be better under-stood if one bears in mind the 'story-discourse' distinction derived from Russian Formalism and developed by structuralist narratology in which 'story' represents the basic material of a narrative that can be narrated in an unlimited number of ways, and 'discourse' a particular shaping, structuring and expression of that material.[45] Since 'discourse' – or 'form' as Eliot might call it – is an inevitable element in any narrative, it can be the vehicle for incorporating the additional levels of signification such as myth and allegory which one would expect to find in epic narratives like *Paradise Lost* but which were not looked for in realist fiction because the latter was normally perceived as setting out to represent reality in as unmedi-ated a way as possible.

Silas Marner is significant because there is now no pretence at unmediated representation. The highly patterned plot, the mythic atmosphere, the obviously symbolic names of the main characters, are evidence of that. Numerous critics have had difficulty coming to terms with this text because it seems such a departure from her other fiction which is perceived as realistic in its basis. Yet in terms of 'story', we would contend, the novel remains within the con-ventions of realism; the patterning, symbolism, mythic associations belong to 'discourse'. Critics of the novel, however, have tended to confuse 'discourse' with 'story' in their readings; thus U. C. Knoepflmacher writes: 'The "mystery" previously denied to Dinah, Latimer, or Maggie is allowed to survive in this legendary tale', and he detects that 'mystery' in the style of the novel: 'In a story where obstacles come in threes, where rain and snow have affected the main events of the plot, such beliefs [as those of Nancy Lammeter] cannot be laughed away.'[46]

But *Silas Marner* is distinctive only in emphasising and thus drawing attention to the discontinuity between 'story' and 'discourse' through its use of various stylistic and formal devices associated with myth, allegory and fairy tale. Such devices, however, should not – *pace* Knoepflmacher – be identified with how reality is perceived in the novel, thus implying the acceptance of a mystical or metaphysical perspective by Eliot. In the novels that follow it, the discontinuity between 'story' and discourse' may not be foregrounded to the same extent, except possibly in the 'Jewish half' of *Daniel Deronda*, but it is equally exploited, and in works such as *Middlemarch* and *Daniel Deronda* layers of signification at the level of 'discourse' are built in to a degree that perhaps has no parallel in the history of the novel until Joyce's *Ulysses*, a text that takes the discontinuity between 'story' and 'discourse' to its limit. What makes *Ulysses* a unique text is that both realism at the level of 'story' and layers of symbolism at the level of 'discourse' were taken to an extreme unprecedented in the history of fiction. But whether there is a fundamental distinction between *Ulysses* and novels like *Middlemarch* or *Daniel Deronda* is doubtful, despite the efforts of certain critics to establish such a distinction between the work of the two authors.[47]

Of course a significant link between Eliot and Joyce is that both use the Jew as a mythic figure. At the level of 'story', however, Bloom in *Ulysses* remains on an ordinary human level, separated from the mythic and symbolic implications incorporated by Joyce at the level of 'discourse' into, for example, the culminating encounter between him and Stephen Dedalus. In *Daniel Deronda*, in contrast, Deronda appears to become finally identified with his mythic self and its symbolic meanings. Yet this is to oversimplify the novel. The mythic connotations which we will suggest are incorporated into the character belong to 'discourse' or the allegorical aspect of the novel. The human dimension of Deronda is still preserved. Though he chooses to identify himself with Mordecai's idealistic beliefs regarding himself, he never commits himself to literal belief in Mordecai's kabbalistic ideas or in Judaism as a religious system. He says to Kalonymos: '"I shall call myself a Jew ... But I will not say that I shall profess to believe exactly as my fathers have believed"' (*DD*, p. 620). Visionary idealism and Romantic irony – the latter most notably associated with Hans Meyrick and clearly evident in the letter he writes to Deronda in Chapter 52 – coexist in the novel and Deronda uses both in order to identify himself with Mordecai's idealism and at the same time maintain a metaphysical scepticism that nevertheless does not undermine that idealism.[48] It is the deep humanist content of such idealism that Deronda values but without the form supplied by Mordecai and Judaism that humanism would lack substance or focus. Deronda as a character therefore never becomes unified with the mythic and symbolic meanings Mordecai projects onto him though 'he felt at one with this man who had made a visionary selection of him' (*DD*, p. 466). His relationship is with the human being rather than with the literal content of Mordecai's idealism.[49] Myth and vision, the novel implies through the characterisation of Deronda, are of value for their form rather than for their content, and this prevents 'discourse' being completely incorporated into 'story'.

While a character like Deronda self-consciously chooses to identify himself with the mythic and symbolic role provided for him by Mordecai and the traditions of Judaism – '"it is the impulse of my feeling – to identify myself, as far as possible, with my hereditary people"' (*DD*, p. 566) – a character such as Bloom has no awareness of the myth which Joyce uses as a framework in *Ulysses*. 'Story' and 'discourse' are kept quite separate. But myth and the visionary dimension are used similarly by both writers to enlarge the significance of their narratives, Joyce utilising the *Odyssey* and various esoteric theories for this purpose whereas Eliot exploits the golem legend and kabbalism. This conscious use of myth and mysticism by both writers should be distinguished from the view, expressed for example by Northrop Frye, that all narrative is mythic in its basis, whether or not this was intended: 'In the criticism of literature . . . we often have to "stand back" from the poem to see its archetypal organisation . . . If we "stand back" from a realistic novel such as Tolstoy's *Resurrection* or Zola's *Germinal*, we can see the mythopoeic designs indicated by their titles.'[50]

Frye implies that myth is unavoidable in narrative; that even the most realistic text will have a mythic structure at some level. It is tempting to believe that Eliot no less than Joyce was aware of this and decided to exploit it rather than to ignore or repress it, as most realist novelists have done. By succumbing to the latter approach the mythic escapes authorial control and destabilises the realism such novelists set out to create. Though Eliot flirted in some aspects of her fiction with the romance tradition which incorporates myth directly within 'story', predominantly, we would contend, the mythic and symbolic in her fiction are incorporated in 'discourse' rather than 'story'. Thus though it could be argued that the Jewish characters in *Daniel Deronda* are, in narratological terms, symbolically conceived at the level of 'story', the fact that Deronda defines himself

self-consciously in terms of Mordecai's vision of him qualifies that view somewhat since a distancing effect is created between the character and the symbolism associated with him, as is also the case with the treatment of character in *Ulysses*. Another way of putting this might be that allegory is being employed rather than symbolism, adopting Paul de Man's distinction between the two: 'Whereas the symbol postulates the possibility of an identity or identification, allegory designates primarily a distance in relation to its own origin, and, renouncing the nostalgia and the desire to coincide, it establishes its language in the void of this temporal difference.'[51]

Such a view of Eliot's writing helps one resist the critique of her presented by Bryan Cheyette in his book *Constructions of 'the Jew' in English Literature and Society* in which he associates the representation of Jews in her work with that of such writers as John Buchan and Kipling by claiming that they succumbed to a 'semitic discourse' that led them construct the Jew for various ideological purposes which Cheyette seeks to expose. What distinguishes Eliot from such writers is the awareness in her Jewish novel that any literary representation of Jews will be a construction. The novel itself is preoccupied with construction. Deronda constructs his own identity as a Jew and Eliot foregrounds her own literary construction by, for example, creating a polarised relationship between Deronda as Noble Jew and Lapidoth as Evil Jew that functions allegorically, as we shall discuss later. The epigraph to Chapter 1 – 'Men can do nothing without the make-believe of a beginning' – alerts the reader to the constructed nature of narrative. Such literary self-consciousness is absent from the representation of Jews by writers such as Buchan who, it can be argued, identify their constructions with reality. Eliot recognises, as Cheyette does not appear to, that as soon as the word 'Jew' is mentioned, construction takes over and that there is no position one can adopt that is free from construction.[52] We would contend that such an awareness is implicit in the representation' of Jews in *Daniel Deronda*.

Cheyette also detects various 'unresolved tension[s]' in the novel – 'Klesmer's artistic cosmopolitanism . . . challenges the centrality of Mordecai's racial determinism'; 'The plurality of Halm-Eberstein's "lives" directly opposes Daniel's unproblematic assimilation into his Jewishness'[53] – but he fails to appreciate that *Daniel Deronda* is one of the few English novels that is genuinely dialogic. This dialogism may have its source in the tension between Eliot's philosophical sympathy for orthodox Judaism whose emphasis on tradition and authority made it highly patriarchal and the fact that she herself had rebelled against patriarchal attitudes: refusing to attend church with her father when she could no longer accept Christianity; choosing to live with a man without being married; aspiring to equality with men in her art. Although the narrative may seem to be weighted against Deronda's mother in that his point of view mediates her account of her life, she is nevertheless given scope to present a justification of her actions without her integrity being undermined by a hostile narrative commentary.[54] Even the apparently perfect Mirah, who unquestioningly accepts Judaism, is exposed to an alternative perspective. Amy Meyrick, 'who was much of a practical reformer' (*DD*, p. 305), wonders whether Mirah has ever questioned why women occupy a marginal position in the synogogue. Although Mirah has no problems with this, the narrator points out that her religion 'had never presented itself to her as a set of propositions', and Amy and her sister refrain from further questioning not because they accept Mirah's submission to religious orthodoxy but only because it would have been 'an inhospitable cruelty' to have been critical of her religion. Klesmer is also allowed to occupy a position that differs from Deronda and Mordecai and this is treated with respect. He is a liberal Jew who places art above racial considerations and chooses to marry a non-Jew, Catherine Arrowpoint, who refuses to bow to the wishes of her parents, and who chooses to live with him on a basis of equality. Even Pash, who believes in Jewish assimilation, is given space to state his case, and Hans Meyrick is allowed to write a five-page letter representing his ironic view of life.[55] Thus, though it is clear that the literary construction of the novel is directed to certain ends, notably Eliot's support for an organicist social philosophy which in the case of the Jews means Zionism, that literary construction is also able to accommodate different perspectives that are granted their own discursive space. The literary discourse of Eliot in this novel, with its self-consciousness about narrative construction, its dialogism, its employment of allegory as a literary device, exposes the limitations of Cheyette's critique.[56]

Yet when writers of the past, such as Spenser or Milton, used allegory, its meaning was underpinned by a metaphysical belief system, namely Christianity. For a post-Romantic novelist who was unable to accept metaphysical beliefs, how was it possible to enrich a narrative in the way that Spenser or Milton had done by means of such a belief system? Here the writer whom one can appropriately compare with Eliot in this context is not so much Joyce as W. B. Yeats, another writer who wished to emulate the great poets of the past but who believed he was at a serious disadvantage since he felt cut off from the levels of signification available to poets who accepted a systematic set of ideas that could provide a coherent account of the meaning and significance of human life and the universe. Faced with this deprivation, Yeats decided to create his own system and correspondent mythology, exemplified in *A Vision*, from combining a variety of elements, such as Blakean ideas and theosophy. Whether Yeats actually 'believed' in his system in any literal sense is doubtful. The important thing for him was that it provided the basis for a poetry that could compete in complexity of signification with the great poetry of the past.[57]

If it seems anachronistic to connect Eliot's practice as a novelist with Modernist writers' self-conscious approach to myth, one should bear in mind that the latter's interest in and use of myth would almost certainly have been influenced by a nineteenth-century discussion of the subject in Nietzsche's first and most famous book, *The Birth of Tragedy*, published in 1872. It is very likely that Eliot would have been sympathetic to Nietzsche's view that 'without myth every culture loses the healthy natural power of its creativity . . . Myth alone saves all the powers of the imagination and of the Apollinian dream from their aimless wanderings', but in 'the present age' one has 'the abstract man, untutored by myth' and 'the lawless roving of the artistic imagination, unchecked by any native myth'.[58] But such an awareness of the cultural need for myth inevitably changes how it can be represented in literature, thus creating the self-conscious use of it characteristic of Modernist writers and which leads a writer like Yeats to go so far as to create his own metaphysical system.

Although Eliot did not, of course, create her own metaphysical system, we shall suggest that she did something similar: she found one ready-made that would serve her purpose, namely Jewish mysticism. It seems clear that Eliot should be grouped with those writers, notably Carlyle, who felt the need for something that would act as the equivalent of a belief system such as Christianity. They therefore attempted to create 'a new Mythus', as Carlyle put it in *Sartor Resartus*, or 'a supreme fiction', to use Wallace Stevens's phrase, that could provide the benefits of a metaphysical system but which, at least for Eliot, did not need to be believed in any literal sense. Such ideas found support in neo-Kantian thought – with which Nietzsche has certain connections – exemplified most notably in Hans Vaihinger's *The Philosophy of 'As If'*, published in 1911, but which Vaihinger started as early as 1876. G. H. Lewes's *Problems of Life and Mind*, a work Eliot completed after Lewes's death, is pervaded by such neo-Kantian thinking. Thus in science he refers to the value and necessity of 'conscious fictions': 'the value of such fictions appears in the aid they furnish to calculation'.[59] He describes science as 'ideal construction' – a phrase Eliot also uses in *Middlemarch*[60] – formed out of abstractions and generalities that have only a symbolic relation to the real, and he believes such a conception of science can be applied in the spheres of morality and metaphysics.

Few writers of the Victorian period would have been more aware of the demythologising tendency of contemporary thought with its emphasis on rationalist critique than the translator of Strauss and Feuerbach. On the surface this seems to present a writer who valued the mythic and symbolic possibilities of religion and mysticism with grave problems. How was it possible to emulate writers such as Dante, Spenser or Milton, whose work relied on accepting a metaphysical system with its basis in religion? One solution to this problem – the one we believe Eliot adopted – is to accept Feuerbach's demythologising critique of religion, but then to go on to remythologise on a new foundation. Feuerbach argued that the essential content of Christianity, and by extension any other religion or set of metaphysical beliefs, was human feeling projected into objectivity:

> Religion is human nature reflected, mirrored in itself . . . Where, therefore, feeling is not depreciated and repressed, as with the Stoics, where existence is awarded to it, there also is religious power and significance conceded to it, there also is it already exalted to that stage in which it can mirror and reflect itself, in which it can project its own image as God. God is the mirror of man.[61]

It therefore became possible for a writer to use a mythology and its underlying metaphysical system without having the kind of belief in it that one would expect of writers of the past. There is ample evidence that Eliot agreed with Feuerbach that human feeling was the basis of religion, but whereas his aim was to use this to present a critique of religion she had little interest in any such critique. For her, the merit of Feuerbach was that he allowed one to value religious systems and metaphysical beliefs without sacrificing a humanist perspective. One could also choose between religions and spiritual beliefs on the basis of the human feeling that underlay them. Thus it is reasonable to assume that what attracted Eliot to Jewish mysticism and the golem myth was the power of the human truths or truths of feeling that they embodied. Yet at the same time the mystical and mythological embodiment of these human truths could be exploited artistically and enable the realist novel to take on layers of meaning in the manner of major works of the past, such as in epic poetry or tragic drama.

This study attempts to demonstrate that Eliot's novels can be read persuasively as works which aspire to alter the boundaries of realism in this way. The primary emphasis will be on those works, notably *Daniel Deronda*, which exemplify this most convincingly. But whereas in the past a work such as *Daniel Deronda* was often read inadequately by being seen as somehow failing to achieve the kind of realism displayed in *Middlemarch* or *The Mill on the Floss*, we would suggest that a reversal of this is more persuasive. Instead of *Daniel Deronda* being read in the light of *Middlemarch* and found wanting, it may be more fruitful to read a work such as *Middlemarch* in the light of her final novel. *Middlemarch* still remains a masterpiece of realism but its power is even more enhanced if one recognises its kinship with a text which clearly draws on Jewish myth and mysticism. This study does not attempt to deny that Eliot's fiction belongs to the realist paradigm, best encapsulated perhaps by her much quoted remark that her novels are 'a set of experiments in life' (*Letters*, VI, 216), but rather to suggest that one of her major achievements was to find a way of reconciling realism with an allegorical dimension which greatly extended the expressive range of realist fiction and which anticipates such Modernist developments as the self-conscious use of myth.

1
George Eliot and Kabbalism: Historical and Literary Context

George Eliot's positive identification with Jewish thought and culture, so evident in *Daniel Deronda*, is surprising given that as late as 1848 she had expressed anti-Jewish views. She wrote to John Sibree:

> My Gentile nature kicks most resolutely against any assumption of superiority in the Jews, and is almost ready to echo Voltaire's vituperation. I bow to the supremacy of Hebrew poetry, but much of their early mythology and almost all of their history is utterly revolting. Their stock has produced a Moses and a Jesus, but Moses was impregnated with Egyptian philosophy and Jesus is venerated and adored by us only for that wherein he transcended or resisted Judaism. The very exhaltation of their idea of a national deity into a spiritual monotheism seems to have been borrowed from other oriental tribes. Everything *specifically* Jewish is of a low grade. (*Letters*, I, 246–7)[1] (Eliot's emphasis)

Yet later a total shift of perspective took place and she changed from an antipathy to Jewish culture to identifying the Jews with her highest hopes for humanity. Her own awareness of this change in herself is perhaps suggested by the incorporation of some of her earlier attitudes in the critically regarded Mrs Transome in *Felix Holt* who has similar difficulties with Jewish history: 'The history of the Jews, she knew, ought to be preferred to any profane history' but 'She found ridicule of Biblical characters very amusing' (*FH*, p. 105). It is clear from the letter, however, that even at this time Eliot was vastly knowledgeable about Judaism and Jewish history. During her Evangelical stage, she was an avid reader of the Bible, Old as well as New Testament, and as early as 1838 was reading the

Jewish historian Josephus. In mapping her shift in attitude and her growing interest in Jewish thought and culture, one would need to take account of several factors: her admiration for Heine and Spinoza, whose *Ethics* she began translating in 1854, her eight-month stay in Germany with Lewes in 1854–5 which exposed her to German-Jewish culture and during which time she read widely in German literature, and her meeting with the German-Jewish polymath Emanuel Deutsch in 1866 which led to a close friendship.

As we pointed out in the Introduction, Jewish mysticism is most clearly a presence in *Daniel Deronda*, notably through Mordecai though other characters such as Joseph Kalonymos are also connected with it. It is likely that Eliot's interest in Jewish mystical thought and its influence on her arose initially out of her admiration for the work of Heinrich Heine, which drew heavily on mystical tradition, and through whom she probably encountered Yehuda Halevi,[2] himself a mystic. Eliot's use of nomenclature in the novel is acknowledgement of this. In Heine's poem, 'Jehuda ben Halevi', he refers to a friend of Halevi's called Alcharisi. The prominent Kabbalah scholar Maimonides's tract, *The Guide to the Perplexed*, had an appendix written by Rabbi Judah Charisi. Deronda's grandfather – a shadowy presence in the novel but influential nevertheless because of the Zionist tradition to which he belongs – is given the name 'Charisi' by Eliot. Thus by historical association, he is closely connected with mystical philosophy and literature. He is also important because of his relationship with Joseph Kalonymos, who recognises Deronda by his likeness to his grandfather. The family Kalonymos was at the heart of the development of kabbalistic thought in Europe.

Culturally and geographically, the mystical tradition from which kabbalism grew emerged from the Middle East, from where it spread throughout Europe:

> In so far as the historical transmission of mystical ideas can be traced, Jewish mysticism appears to have developed first in Iraq and from there to have been carried in the ninth century C.E. to Italy and thence in the tenth century to Germany. Another form coming from Iraq appears to have reached Provence in the twelfth century and from there to have spread to Spain where it became prominent in the fourteenth century.[3]

A simple division is often made between the mysticism of Spain and France, and that of Italy and Germany. The former was said to be concerned more with metaphysical speculation – indeed, two Kabbalah classics, the *Bahir* and the *Zohar*, which were written in northern Spain and Provence, were reactions to philosophic rationalism and empiricism. German and Italian kabbalism turned towards the development of mysticism in magic and experimentation. Kalonymos is a name central to this latter tradition: in the twelfth century 'Pietist texts were written by three members of the same circle who were also part of the Qalonimos family. Tracing their origins to northern Italy, the Qalonimides claimed to be descendants of the founding family of Mainz Jewry in Carolingian times and bearers of distinctive mystical traditions.'[4] Eliot was evidently aware of this history, writing of Kalonymos as 'the name of a celebrated family of scholarly Jews transplanted from Italy into Germany in mediaeval times' (*Letters*, VI, 242).[5] She also refers to the history in her Jewish novel in a more specific manner when Kalonymos informs Deronda:

> The days are changed for us in Mainz since our people were slaughtered wholesale if they wouldn't be baptized wholesale: they are changed for us since Karl the Great fetched my ancestors from Italy to bring some tincture of knowledge to our rough German brethren. (*DD*, p. 618)

The period alluded to by Kalonymos suggests a deeper understanding of the progress of Jewish mystical thought than merely its use as a historical reference point, a literary device to add authenticity. Kabbalism became a stronger force during this period of wholesale slaughter and dispossession mentioned by Kalonymos, recourse to mysticism and magic being associated with times of great tribulation for Jewish communities in Europe, as the story of the golem of Prague indicates. In *Daniel Deronda* Eliot has Kalonymos – scion of the mystic tradition – give to Deronda the key to his grandfather's chest: '"So!" said Kalonymos, returning to his seat. "And here is the curious key," he added, taking it from a small leathern bag. "Bestow it carefully"' (*DD*, p. 618). Not only is it a key to Deronda's past which unites him with a familial tradition, it is also a key to his future so that he can continue the tradition. It is, moreover, the key that includes Deronda within a wider Jewish tradition which embraces the tradition of his family and thus doubly identifies him with Zionist ideals.

The tradition to which Charisi and Deronda belong was also formed out of the extended diaspora. In 1492 and 1497 Jews, Gypsies and Moors were expelled from Spain and Portugal, and Deronda's family is traced back to Spain. This led to the movement of Jews to other countries, and thus a further spreading of mystic beliefs and teachings. In his spiritual and metaphysical outlook Mordecai is made to resemble Maimonides and Spinoza, in addition to his connections with Yehuda Halevi as mentioned in the Introduction. He is presented as something of a latter-day Spinoza – whose ethics were culled from kabbalistic metaphysics. Solomon Maimon at one point refers to the Kabbalah as 'nothing but an expanded Spinozism'.[6] Furthermore, Maimonides influenced Spinoza, who in turn influenced Maimon. Maimon is a tangible example of a member of the tradition of Central and Eastern Europe combining, through his study of Spinoza and Maimonides, with the Jewish traditions of Western Europe, as is symbolised in the coming together of Mordecai (Eastern Europe) with Deronda (Western Europe).

Maimonides and Spinoza were both affected by the expulsion of Jews from the Iberian peninsula. Maimonides had had to flee from Spain to Egypt because of persecution; Spinoza was born into a Sephardic Jewish family which was expelled from Portugal as part of the religious persecution. Certainly Eliot was well aware of this enforced movement: Deronda is shown to ponder on the fate of the Spanish Jews who were driven out in 1492:

> and among the thoughts that most filled his mind while his boat was pushing about within view of the grand harbour was that of the multitudinous Spanish Jews centuries ago driven destitute from their Spanish homes, suffered to land from the crowded ships only for brief rest on this grand quay of Genoa, overspreading it with a pall of famine and plague. (*DD*, p. 532)

Romola opens in 1492, an indication before Eliot's Jewish novel of her awareness of the significance of that date to European Jewry, and the expulsions of Spanish Jews are significant within the novel. Bratti Ferravecchi at first suspects Tito is Jewish, '"You're not a Hebrew, eh? – come from Spain or Naples, eh?"'[7] Towards the conclusion of the novel, when Romola frees herself from Tito, she encounters these Jews:

> The strongly marked type of race in their features and their peculiar garb made her conjecture that they were Spanish or Portuguese

Jews who had perhaps been put ashore and abandoned there by rapacious sailors, to whom their property remained as a prey. Such things were happening continually to Jews compelled to abandon their homes by the Inquisition (*Romola*, p. 520).

Tito's arrival in Florence and Romola's rebirth in the plague-ridden village are set against this historical background.

As stated above, this historical context of Jewish persecution accounts for a greatly increased interest in mysticism among Jewish communities in Europe. Mysticism blossomed during the late medieval period and the Renaissance because the scattered communities resorted to it as a means to combat – both physically and mentally – the persecution they suffered. One commentator writing in the 1930s pointed out a parallel with the situation of the Jews during the twentieth century: 'In the general upheaval of the fifteenth and sixteenth centuries, in many ways parallel to the present forces of destruction and reconstruction in world Jewry, it is not surprising that the imagination of the Jew should have been captured by the mysticism of the Kabalah [sic].'[8] Scholem has also written: 'mysticism as a historical phenomenon is a product of crises'.[9] Many Jews looked to kabbalistic sources to provide some form of redemption, such as the emergence of a saviour or champion – the purpose for which the golem of Prague was created. This magical-made protector was more directly associated with Messianic longings:

> It is believed he is still lying there, buried deep under a heap of torn leaves from old prayer books, and only waiting for the coming of the Messiah, or for the time when new dangers appear to menace the existence of Israel, to rise again and smite the foe.[10]

The kabbalist, Isaac Luria, connected the aims of kabbalism with a more fundamental return to creative origins, which also united the Beginning with the End:

> According to Luria, the critical movement in the process of creation consisted of the withdrawal of the all-pervading godhead into itself... This withdrawal, or contraction (*tsimtsum*), made possible the elimination of 'evil' elements inherent in the godhead... This cathartic event was followed by a series of emanations from the godhead that were intended to constitute the created world. As the emanations proceeded from their divine

source, a catastrophic event occurred – the breaking of the vessels that carried them. Sparks of the divine light fell into the material domain where they were imprisoned in shells of matter. The task of the qabbalist was to liberate the sparks in order to reconstitute the divine configuration, the primordial man (*adam qadmon*), a goal with eschatological aims.[11]

Restoration of the light to the original source implies both a return to the original primordial man, and through this return – because of the incarnation of the Messiah in the *Adam Kadmon* – a simultaneous arrival of the messianic age. A teleological cycle is formed, which unites the ultimate aim of Judaism with its origins, and the people to the earth from which they were originally formed. Luria's metaphysical interpretation of the Kabbalah has its empirical counterpart in the Jews' intention to be led back into their land by the Messiah. There is a certain sense of irony in Deronda, the descendant of Spanish Jews, being placed in the position of saviour and setting out to find a new world for the Jews. Sephardic Jews were driven out of Spain by Ferdinand and Isabella in the same year in which Columbus landed in the New World, on an expedition 'sponsored' by the same royalty. The money used to finance the expedition had, in fact, been extracted from the Jews by the Inquisition.

Separate evolution of mystical thought in Western and in Central to Eastern Europe, along philosophical as opposed to magical lines was, then, a different response to increased anti-Semitism. Such differing responses are represented in *Daniel Deronda* as vehicles through which the schisms within Judaism are trying to come together. Kalonymos and Charisi are symbols of the two main strands of these schisms and of enlightened attempts to overcome them. The arguments that take place among 'The Philosophers' in Chapter 42 indicate how divisive different responses to anti-Semitism can be. Mordecai himself incorporates divisions: as well as resembling in certain respects Spinoza and Maimonides, he shares some characteristics with Solomon Maimon – a severe critic of Judaism – in that he tries to reconcile himself to the world through philosophy. Mordecai's and his sister Mirah's union with Deronda represents a successful attempt at unification, one that has wider implications for Jewish nationhood.

As well as being aware of the effects of anti-Semitism on Jews of the fifteenth and sixteenth centuries – indicated in *Romola* – Eliot was aware of contemporary anti-Semitism. Through her characters, she illustrates prevalent attitudes towards Jews in the various times and communities she depicts. Outlined in *Romola* is the Renaissance Florence view of Jews:

> 'Many of them matriculated also to the noble art of usury before you were born,' interrupted Francesco Cei, 'as you may discern by a certain fitful glare of the eye and sharp curve of the nose which manifest their descent from the ancient harpies, whose portraits you saw supporting the arms of the Zecca.' (*Romola*, p. 88)

Jews are stereotypically identified with usury and consequently viewed with jealousy and suspicion. Such stereotypes remain in place in nineteenth-century England. In *Middlemarch* Ladislaw's grandfather is referred to derisively as a '"Jew Pawnbroker"' (*Middlemarch*, p. 707); and Gwendolen's initial anti-Semitic tendencies are voiced in the pecuniary context of gambling: 'these Jew pawnbrokers were so unscrupulous in taking advantage of Christians unfortunate at play!' (*DD*, p. 14). She is ignorant of the fact that a Jew – Deronda – has redeemed her necklace. But then, so is he.[12]

Daniel Deronda is the culmination of Eliot's change of view and of her effort to change the attitudes of others, hence her creation of a symbolically conceived Noble Jew, who wants to identify with all that is Jewish. Conceptually opposite to this is the Evil Jew, Lapidoth, an equally symbolic figure who epitomises all the worst characteristics attributed to Jews. Unlike Deronda, who wants to include himself within the Jewish heritage, Lapidoth's ultimate aim is to dissociate himself from Judaism in a manner which, as William Baker points out, is similar to Solomon Maimon: 'Common to Maimon and Lapidoth are dissipation, insecurity, gambling, dependence, continual restlessness, manic-depression, and the attempt to integrate into predominantly Gentile society.'[13] Maimon's reason for adopting this behaviour is that he finds Judaism spiritually inadequate whereas Lapidoth finds the restrictions placed on Jews by a Gentile society disadvantageous in material terms. The extreme polarisation of Deronda and Lapidoth contributes towards the allegorical aspect of this novel, which is incorporated into the work's 'discourse' or artistic structuring, as we discussed in the Introduction, and which exists in a complex interplay with the realism with which Eliot is conventionally associated. The stereotypically odious Jew is as far removed from reality as is Eliot's ideally conceived Jew. At one level, therefore, Deronda and Lapidoth function as symbols of perceptions of good and bad Jews.

In presenting the events leading up to and including the rescue of Mirah, Eliot reinterprets a common literary topic, exemplified most notably in Shakespeare and Scott, namely 'the sinister Jew deprived of his lovely daughter'.[14] Behind it lies the idea of assimilation, the topic under discussion at 'The Philosophers' in Chapter 42. Jessica, in *The Merchant of Venice*, rejects Shylock and is accepted into the Gentile world, and sinister Shylock is thus deprived of his daughter. Scott's Isaac of York is a more sympathetic character, but Rebecca does fall in love with Wilfred of Ivanhoe and is the object of love of de Bois-Gilbert. It is implied that her happiness, her rescue, or life depend on her willingness to assimilate into non-Jewish society. Eliot departs from this tradition of representation and in so doing implicitly exposes the anti-Semitic assumptions of these predecessors. Lapidoth is recognisably a 'sinister Jew', but he is the one seeking assimilation. Mirah, the 'lovely daughter', is rescued by, and falls in love with, a Jew. Leslie Fiedler describes the 'European myth of assimilation' as:

> the dream of rescuing the desirable elements in the Judaic tradition (maternal tenderness and exotic charm: the figure of Mary) from the unsympathetic elements (patriarchal rigour and harsh legalism: the figure of the High Priest and Father Abraham with a knife).[15]

Eliot revises this myth so that the desirable elements – archetypally characterised in Mirah – are rescued from assimilation as intended by Lapidoth, and returned to the recognisable figure of the High Priest: Mordecai. She is thus rescued by, and restored to, Judaism.

At the same time as she is re-inventing literary assimilation, Eliot is re-assessing those attitudes towards Jewish assimilation that were current in Victorian millenarianism. Millenarians saw the establishment of a Jewish nation in Palestine – the return of the Jews to Israel – as heralding the second coming of Christ. This would then be followed by mass conversion of the Jews. Wars and unrest at the beginning of the century, as the millenarians saw it, gave credence to their beliefs:

> In the tumultuous events of the French Revolution and the Napoleonic wars, millenarians saw the signs of the second coming, which, according to biblical prophecy, was to be preceded by the restoration of the Jews to Palestine and their conversion.[16]

Because the two were supposed to be so closely connected, efforts were made to convert the Jews – the society for the promotion and practice of this being mentioned in *Daniel Deronda*.

Eliot departs from traditional literature's views on conversion. Of the many conversionist novels of the nineteenth century, most were anti-Semitic; some, however, sought to alter perceptions of the Jews – what Michael Ragussis terms 'the revisionist novel of Jewish identity.'[17] Though *Daniel Deronda* was seen as almost the culminating example of these, there were notable predecessors: as mentioned above, Scott's *Ivanhoe* and also – more closely connected to the development of Eliot's thought – Maria Edgeworth's *Harrington*. These works examined both English anti-Semitism and the English national character by comparing the English with the Jews.[18]

Though there is a more sympathetic portrayal of Jews in literary texts such as *Ivanhoe*, the theme of assimilation was central since 'the conversion of the Jews functioned at the center of a project to reform the English nation.'[19] Eliot changed the construction of a trope already in place. Instead of the consolidation of England being reliant on the Jews being assimilated, either culturally or religiously, she emphasised the idea of separation: in 'The Modern Hep! Hep! Hep!' in *Impressions of Theophrastus Such* English national reformation is promoted by presenting Jewish strength of racial identity and aspiration to nationhood as an example to the English, but it is the very separateness of the Jews that constitutes such an example. The conflict between separateness and assimilation perhaps accounts to some extent for the polarised representations of Jews in *Daniel Deronda* – the noble-minded Deronda and the evil schemer Lapidoth, the idealistic Mordecai and the complacent Pash – though Eliot inverts the meaning of and thus defamiliarises the stereotype, with the most positive characters being opposed to assimilation. Given her literary aims in the novel, it may have been impossible to avoid representing Jews as 'types' and thus conforming with traditional representations of Jews in literature, but whereas the latter were largely anti-Semitic in intention, *Daniel Deronda* in contrast has been described variously as embodying 'hortatory philo-Semitism'[20] and being 'the most celebrated philo-Semitic novel written in England'.[21]

As mentioned above, the poet Heine may have initially stimulated Eliot's philo-Semitism. Through the work of Heine she became acquainted with Yehuda Halevi and thus with aspects of Jewish mysticism. Her journey with Lewes to Germany in 1854 introduced her to a German-Jewish intellectual circle. She knew Karl Varnhargen, who, with his Jewish wife Rahel Levin, had corresponded with Heine. Levin had also known Dorothea Mendelssohn, who was the daughter of Moses Mendelssohn – the friend and patron of Solomon Maimon – and the wife of Friedrich Schlegel.[22] Indeed, the likelihood that she drew upon Dorothea and Friedrich Schlegel in her portrayal of Dorothea and Will in *Middlemarch* suggests that she was aware of the historical characters and the tradition to which they belonged.[23] It is probable that she also knew of the kabbalistic influence on this Romantic tradition in Germany.

In addition, the 1840s and 1850s saw an influx of Jews into Britain, including Ashkenazi from Russia, Poland and Holland, who contributed to the intellectual life of Britain. Eliot, being very much at the centre of this life, undoubtedly encountered different forms of Jewish thought as a result. Emanuel Deutsch became a friend of Lewes and Eliot; his input and character feature significantly in *Daniel Deronda*. There is certainly evidence to suggest the presence of mysticism in her historical novel, for example when Maestro Vaiano is surrounded by 'yellow cabalistic figures' (*Romola*, p. 137) when he marries Tito and Tessa. Dino's reliance upon dreams as a means of prophecy resembles the belief in the revelation in dreams as practised by kabbalists in Spain, who preferred such visionary mysticism, and rejected the creative elements of central European kabbalism.[24]

Not only does mysticism appear here and, to a much greater extent, in *Daniel Deronda*, but in this last novel it is combined with more orthodox aspects of Jewish tradition. Kalonymos's enquiry of Deronda – '"Excuse me, young gentleman – allow me – what is your parentage – your mother's family – her maiden name?"' (*DD*, p. 311) – is significant for reasons other than because Deronda reminds him of Charisi. Its significance lies in the fact that Judaism is traditionally matrilinear. As if to emphasise this, Mirah identifies the religion with her mother, not her father: '"I will never separate myself from my mother's people"' (*DD*, p. 317). Thirteen is taken as the age at which Deronda's perceptions of the world begin to have meaning for him. The traditional age for the Bar-mitzvah rite of confirmation into the Jewish tradition is thirteen; it is at this age that Eliot has the young Deronda speculating – and coming to hasty conclusions – as to his origins. He is reaching for a tradition with which he can identify.

2
Kabbalistic Philosophy and the Novels

The extent to which Eliot employed ideas from Jewish mysticism in her fiction cannot be determined without a brief examination of these ideas. As stated earlier, Jewish mystical tradition originated in Iraq. This origin accounts for Jewish beliefs regarding a Messiah and duality of the human soul since both ideas can be attributed to the lasting influence of Persian Zoroastrianism on Hebrew religion. As Trevor Ling states, 'in the Persian period of Jewish history a tendency began to show itself towards a modification of Hebrew monotheism in terms of Persian dualism'.[1] This affected Jewish thinking about the ontology of good and evil. The story of Job – which, according to E. M. Butler, was the precursor of all Faust stories – addresses this issue as, indeed, does Goethe's *Faust*, and divine monopoly of moral righteousness is called into question. In these stories, the solution lies wholly in faith in the goodness of God; but a different solution lay in the acceptance of a dualistic philosophy.

Though various forms of belief incorporate dualism, it is a particularly strong feature of kabbalistic thinking and is treated in complex terms, and has perhaps been more influential on literary representations of dualism, especially in the work of Eliot, than generally thought. In kabbalism dualism expresses itself in a number of ways: good and evil; body and soul; male and female. The state of the individual is dependent upon the ability to balance or reconcile the two poles. Kabbalistic ideas on good and evil are supported by the Talmud: 'When man leaves the synagogue for his home an angel of good and an angel of evil accompany him.'[2] These two angels – obviously symbolic of human inclinations and moral ambivalence derived from the inclinations for good (*yezer tov*) and evil (*yezer ra*), with the latter being part of a more general evil inclination, the *yezer ha-ra*, which is identified with Satan – emanated from the same divine source. An influential system of belief within Jewish mysticism, devised by the scholar Luria, based its ideas on this Zoroastrian-derived dualism:

> Lurianic theology described a common source for good and evil, claiming that both emanate from the godhead; but according to Luria, evil cannot exist unless it is in close contact with good and derives sustenance from it. In order to overcome evil, the righteous must separate good from evil, thus making the latter's existence impossible.[3]

According to the Roman historian, Josephus, this kind of distinction had its roots in the garden of Eden, where, he writes, the tree of wisdom was the means 'by which might be distinguished what was good and what evil'.[4]

It was often disputed as to whether or not good and evil did come from the same source. Some opinion contradicted Lurianic doctrine:

> As far as the effect of first sin is concerned, we find two conflicting lines of thought: (1) Whereas previously good and evil had been mixed together, the sin separated evil out as a distinct reality in its own right . . . (2) Good and evil were originally separate, but the sin caused them to be mixed together.[5]

Other theological commentators equated good and evil with creation and destruction respectively. There were considered, by some, to be two aspects – or attributes – of the godhead, which were termed 'lights': 'thoughtful light' and 'thoughtless light'. Thoughtful light was directed towards creation, and manifested itself in the structures of creation. Thoughtless light was opposed to creation: it became destructive and evil. Because they were both rooted in the godhead, thoughtless light opposed all that was not actually divine. Kabbalists held that, fundamentally, evil functioned through negation, and that it was the purpose of humans to overcome the polarisation of good and evil, which they could do by balancing the positive and creative aspects of good with the negative and destructive aspects of evil. One of the principles of the Kabbalah is that 'Man is constantly engaged in the battle of the pure ("will to impart") versus impure ("will to receive").'[6]

Good angels and bad angels – the *yezer tov* and *yezer ra* of Jewish belief – have pervaded literature and culture, from the stock characters in Elizabethan drama who tease and test Marlowe's Faustus, to the little angels and demons who pop up beside characters in present-day cartoons and comics. The battle between God and Satan, in the story of Job, is little more than an extension of this Jewish idea into supreme symbols of the two inclinations. In *Faust*, Goethe explicitly internalised such conflict:

> Two souls, alas, are housed within my breast,
> And each will wrestle for the mastery there.
> The one has passion's craving crude for love,
> And hugs a world where sweet the senses rage;
> The other longs for pasture fair above,
> Leaving the murk for lofty heritage.

> (*Faust* I, p. 67)

Nineteenth-century English literature also exploited good and bad angels. Carlyle used the device in *Sartor Resartus* when commenting on the ambiguity of Teufelsdroeckh's character: he had 'the look truly of an angel, though whether of a white or of a black one might be dubious.'[7] A further reference to the duality of humans is made later in the philosophy of clothes: 'For there is a Devil dwells in man, as well as a Divinity.'[8] Eliot refers to this duality and connects it specifically with Jewish thinking: Sephardo, the Jewish astrologer in *The Spanish Gypsy* (who by his name represents the Jews living in, and expelled from, Spain at the time of the poem's setting), tells Silva,

> Two angels guide
> The path of man.[9]

These two Jewish angels, via their literary routes as well as that of Jewish tradition, are used as a device throughout Eliot's novels. For example, at the beginning of *Daniel Deronda* the question is asked of Gwendolen, 'Was the good or evil genius dominant in those beams?' (*DD*, p. 3). Deronda and Grandcourt represent the good and evil angels in Gwendolen's life. Deronda is the spirit of judgement who stands in opposition to the gambling inclination, as we see in the opening scene of the novel. Grandcourt has driven her to gamble and Deronda warns her against it, yet paradoxically it is the 'good angel' who arouses the greatest dread as he represents the force of conscience which is in opposition to her impulsive nature. The 'good angel-bad angel' characterisations established in this way at the beginning of the novel are resurrected again when Gwendolen feels the conflicting influences of Grandcourt and Deronda in their coincidental meeting in Genoa. There, Deronda appears to Gwendolen to be an awful seraphic conscience: 'He seemed to her a terrible-browed angel from whom she could not think of concealing any deed so as to win an ignorant regard from him' (*DD*, p. 577).[10] Yet this is more than a psychomachy enacted in the manner of Elizabethan drama; just as there is a soul of Judaism in the novel, there is an essence of England. Gwendolen 'becomes positioned between two masters who attempt to reinvent her, two powerful proselytizers, one attempting to master her soul, the other attempting to master her body'.[11] Whereas the latter involves rigid control – discipline in the negative sense – the former emphasises Eliot's perceptions of the role of Jews in English regeneration: Englishness is constricted and restrained from without by its own traditions and tempers; it is nurtured and enhanced from within by the effects of Judaism.

Temptation in *Daniel Deronda* is associated with Grandcourt when Gwendolen feels tempted to rid herself of him; and conscience is again represented by Deronda, by whom she feels she will be judged:

> In Gwendolen's consciousness Temptation and Dread met and stared like two pale phantoms, each seeing itself in the other – each obstructed by its own image; and all the while her fuller self beheld the apparitions and sobbed for deliverance from them. (*DD*, p. 577)

The dread is twofold. Not only does Deronda bring fear of judgement, but by forcing Gwendolen to act according to that fear he will in effect be ensuring that she remains with Grandcourt. Gwendolen comes to be faced with a tension parallel to that encountered by Goethe's Homunculus: her conscience requires that she follow her duty, but in doing so she ends up having to remain under the influence of the Temptation to which she initially succumbed.

Yet more polarisation of this kind exists in *Silas Marner*. Godfrey Cass is shown to be the object of struggle between the forces of good and evil. The good spirit is Nancy, whose influence in the house is likened to 'the voice of the good angel, inviting to industry, sobriety, and peace'.[12] Dunstan is the evil influence – an impulsive gambler who encourages the same instinct in Godfrey, who must then rely on chance to conceal both his pocketing of rent money and his first marriage. Though initially he profits from chance, the good angel in the shape of conscience proves stronger.

Again, this device of conflict and tension underlies the characterisation of Maggie Tulliver. The struggle between the demons and angels that will affect her later life is evident in her as a youngster when she pushes Lucy into a mud puddle: 'the small demons who had taken possession of Maggie's soul at an early period of the day had returned in all the greater force after a temporary absence' (*Mill*, p. 98). The isolation which results from allowing herself to be led by the demons of impulse – though they bring immediate gratification – makes her subsequently choose the angel of duty. She is later tempted by the desire for emotional gratification: choosing to maintain her friendship with Philip despite Tom's disapproval, and being persuaded to go boating with Stephen Guest. But finally her sense of duty to others proves the stronger. For Gwendolen, Godfrey and Maggie the battles between their guiding spirits result in similar conclusions: though they eventually choose the good angel, the consequence is suffering, and in Maggie's case destruction.

In *Middlemarch*, however, this conflict is given different treatment. Dorothea, like Maggie or Gwendolen, is the centre of a struggle between a good and bad genius, where one directs her to do what he regards as right, and the other to follow her impulses. Casaubon and Will compete for possession of her, but her problem is that it is not easy to decide who is the good and who the bad genius. The struggle is alluded to when she is in the room which contains the ornaments of their family relationship:

> the bare room had gathered within it those memories of an inward life which fill the air as with a cloud of good or bad angels, the invisible yet active forms of our spiritual triumphs or our spiritual falls. (*Middlemarch*, p. 367)

Here Eliot presents an embryonic form of the conflict enacted in *Daniel Deronda*: Ladislaw, the foreign interloper, descendant of a 'Jew pawnbroker', becomes the ostensible saviour of Dorothea's soul, whereas Casaubon is the controller who seeks to contain her within his own limitations.

The removal of Casaubon does not signal an immediate triumph for Will, or a state of resolution for Dorothea, and it is necessary for the evil inclination to surface again. This is projected onto the subsequently bifurcated Ladislaw, the 'bad' part of whom must be expunged before Dorothea can be reconciled with herself and with him:

> here within the vibrating bond of mutual speech, was the bright creature whom she had trusted – who had come to her like the spirit of morning visiting the dim vault where she sat as the bride of a worn out life ... And there, aloof, yet persistently with her ... was the Will Ladislaw who was a changed belief exhausted of hope. (*Middlemarch*, p. 774)

Will constitutes both angels, and thus can bring either hope or despair to Dorothea's life. The characterisation of good and bad angels is also suggestive of the polarised 'helpers' and 'dragons' encountered by the hero on a mythological quest.

The dualism is extended when Dorothea herself becomes a good angel of hope to Lydgate:

> That voice of deep-souled womanhood had remained within him as the enkindling conceptions of dead and sceptred genius had remained within him (is there not a genius for feeling nobly which reigns over human spirits and their conclusions?) (*Middlemarch*, p. 583)

Rosamond, in contrast, is the bad. Though this is readily evident in the manner in which she stifles Lydgate, the allusion to this aspect of her characterisation is given another context in the epigraph to Chapter 59:

> They said of old the Soul had human shape,
> But smaller, subtler than the fleshly self,
> So wandered forth for airing when it pleased.
> And see! beside her cherub-face there floats
> A pale-lipped form aerial whispering
> Its promptings in that little shell her ear.
>
> (*Middlemarch*, p. 589)

This carries some significance in terms of the golem: the soul possesses form and expresses itself through action. In terms of good and evil inclination – in the context of the chapter in which Rosamond tells Ladislaw of the codicil to Casaubon's will – the epigraph is ambiguous. Rosamond is guided by an evil genius who 'prompts' her to tell Will about the codicil; or she herself can be seen as the 'pale-lipped form' – again an evil genius – who suggests to Will that Dorothea likes him '"better than the property"' (*Middlemarch*, p. 591). Either way, she is associated with the evil inclination even though her act leads to good.

Polarisation within an individual as depicted in Will is also considered in kabbalistic thought to be an obstacle in the way of wholeness or perfection. The same literary device is used by Goethe to create the basis for the series of events that lead to the Gretchen tragedy. Faust has listened to Mephisto – the cartoon-like demon who has appeared to tempt him – and is unable to reconcile temptation and lust with lofty heritage. In *Romola* Savonarola becomes a Faust in that his nature is similarly divided between the spiritual and the worldly:

> Savonarola's nature was one of those in which opposing tendencies co-exist in almost equal strength: the passionate sensibility which, impatient of definite thought, floods every idea with emotion and tends towards contemplative ecstasy, alternated in him with a keen perception of outward facts and a vigorous practical judgment of men and things. (*Romola*, p. 493)

The qualifying 'almost' is significant, because it implies that one of the tendencies is stronger than the other. Romola becomes disillusioned with him because she sees in him more of the political manoeuvring that requires 'judgment of men and things' than she does passionate sensibility. This disillusionment extends to his other followers in the Trial by Fire, when he refuses to be swayed by his faith and reasons why he should not accept the challenge.

Those characters in Eliot's novels who do admit to duality of nature, but are unable to balance the two, are inclined to tragedy. Lydgate 'had two selves within him apparently, and they must learn to accommodate each other and bear reciprocal impediments' (*Middlemarch*, pp. 150–1). One of these selves is a cautious experimenting scientist; the other is the man who is impetuous in his relations with other people – particularly with women. The latter half also provokes professional animosity in Middlemarch. Lydgate's inability to reconcile the two, so that conflict within his marriage and social and professional ostracism overwhelm his questing nature, contributes towards his downfall. Gwendolen, when she contemplates killing Grandcourt, is divided between the temptation to kill him and the reasoning that such an impulse is wrong, which she describes to Deronda as being '"like two creatures"' (*DD*, p. 592). Internal division is seen by Philip Wakem to be the cause of tragic events: in his letter to Maggie he writes of '"that partial, divided action of our nature which makes half the tragedy of the human lot"' (*Mill*, p. 502). This division is at the root of Maggie's tragedy. It creates an internal struggle when she has to choose between duty and feeling – duty to her family, and feeling for Philip: 'Maggie's life struggles had lain almost entirely within her own soul, one shadowy army fighting another, and the slain shadows forever rising again' (*Mill*, p. 308).

Neither Gwendolen, Lydgate nor Maggie achieves wholeness. Deronda, who has also recognised his divided nature – he sees that there is a 'more negative spirit within him' (*DD*, p. 465) – is able to reconcile his two halves, largely because of the combined influence of Mordecai and Mirah, so that his initial snobbish dislike of the Cohens is balanced by a regard for them as part of world Jewry and consequently necessary for its completion. Deronda's completion is therefore linked with the Cohens, since his completion is a metaphor for the completion of the Jewish state.

Kabbalistic writings maintain that body and soul are separate; they are separate before life, and return to being separate after death: '. . .when a person dies, the soul and body separate from each other. The soul rises above to its abode, while the body descends to the earth, wherein it is buried.'[13] Bifurcation is thus related to the soulless aspect of the golem. And just as the soul is separate from the body, so too is the soul divided into two parts: male and female. An individual cannot be complete unless the soul is in the body; and the soul cannot be complete until its masculine and feminine parts are united. Ironically, the soul before it descends into the body is whole, but then divides as it descends – 'In its root every soul is a composite of male and female, and only in the course of their descent do the souls separate into masculine and feminine souls.'[14] They begin as one, descend into separateness, and then try to unite again. In *Adam Bede*, Dinah and Adam represent this schism: it is implied in Dinah's words that she will not be whole until she is with Adam: '"My soul is so knit to yours that it is but a divided life I live without you"' (*AB*, p. 532). Again, in *The Spanish Gypsy*, Fedalma implies that Silva is a part of her without which she will not be whole:

I will never fly!
Never forsake that chief half of my soul
Where lies my love.

(*SG*, p. 123)

These cases of duality are not as particular as in Eliot's Jewish novel, but still appear to have their origins in the same philosophy. Adam's and Dinah's union achieves a wholeness in which male and female are incorporated into a single unit.

Such unions form one category of male and female relationships within Eliot's novels. This aspect of Jewish philosophy would have helped her to explore the larger implications of unity and wholeness or disunity and separation within male–female relationships. Part of Maggie Tulliver's inability to achieve internal equilibrium is due to her estrangement from her brother Tom, who is himself a polarised character, 'strongly marked by the positive and negative qualities that create severity' (*Mill*, p. 456). Internal equilibrium is extremely difficult for both of them after childhood because of the consequences of their father's unwise decisions and impulsive actions and resulting ruin. Indeed, one of Maggie's reasons for giving up Philip is so that she can achieve this union of soul with Tom: '"But I can't divide myself from my brother for life"' (*Mill*, p. 438). It is through this union that she seeks to complete herself, having failed to do so with Philip, Thomas à Kempis and Stephen, because not only do they represent the inclination of temptation, à Kempis for example being the temptation to withdraw into martyrdom, but because they all bring division from Tom. There is a Romantic connotation to this: the ideal state, in which male and female halves are joined, is connected with childlike, paradisaic innocence. In her poem, 'Brother and Sister', Eliot regrets the passing of 'That childish world where our two spirits mingled' (*SG*, p. 411).

Fractured relationships, in Eliot's work, are those between two people who cannot achieve oneness of spirit. In Jewish mysticism this represents an inability to attain wholeness, and consequently an inability to reach God. Eliot's fiction, at the allegorical or mythic level of its 'discourse', exploits this dualism of mythological origins in her male–female relationships in order to depict the human need for form. Thus the male and female units aim to be part of a greater whole, but where an individual fails to achieve such wholeness, he or she must seek completion by other means. This is most apparent in *Romola* where the heroine is deprived of her appropriate masculine half by a series of blows: Dino leaves her, Bardo patronises her, Bernardo is executed, Savonarola disappoints her, and Tito, in whom she thought she could complete her soul through marriage, becomes estranged from her – 'They were too hopelessly alienated in their inner life' (*Romola*, p. 377) – so that their souls separate: '"I have a soul of my own that abhors your actions"' (*Romola*, p. 455). Her marriage to Tito thus becomes one of two individuals, in contrast to the mingling of souls of Dinah and Adam. Romola, however, does become harmonised with her environment through the – appropriately – Jewish infant in the plague-ridden house.

The parallel course of the Dorothea–Casaubon and Rosamond–Lydgate marriages is highlighted when they are both examined in the context of this Judaic concept of wholeness. Dorothea cannot align herself with the fruitless studies embarked upon by Casaubon, as she explains in her letter to the dead man: '"Do you not see now that I could not submit my soul to yours, by working hopelessly at what I have no belief in?"' (*Middlemarch*, p. 531). It is their souls that cannot combine. Rosamond, too, is out of alignment with her husband's aim, and theirs is a marriage of two individuals constantly in opposition to each other: 'He was always to her a being apart, doing what she objected to' (*Middlemarch*, p. 746). Such a state would not be healthy in any marriage; in the Lydgates' marriage, because their souls do not mingle, one must bow to the other. Lydgate, who does the bowing, then regards Rosamond as the cause of his destruction.

The Jewish novel sees a marriage of souls that accords with kabbalistic ideas, one which is in sharp contrast to the marriage of alienated souls in the relationship of Gwendolen and Grandcourt. Mirah, who can be – and in Baker's *George Eliot and Judaism* has been – identified with the soul of Judaism, is first united with Mordecai: 'He has recovered a perfect sister' (*DD*, p. 466). Mordecai now has the perfect soul which he wants to unite with Deronda – the perfect vessel for his ideas. When Deronda informs Mordecai and Mirah that he is a Jew, Mordecai says, '"It has begun already – the marriage of our souls"' (*DD*, p. 643). On the surface Deronda and Mordecai, through their association with one another, have a converging outlook on the future of Judaism, but with Mirah as the soul of Judaism, we are directed towards the symbolic meaning of the impending marriage between Mirah and Deronda. Both meanings imply that Deronda is included within and is a vehicle for the Jewish tradition. The latter meaning, in particular, gains strength when Mordecai continues: '"It waits but the passing away of this body, and then they who are betrothed shall unite in stricter bond, and what is mine shall be thine"' (*DD*, p. 643). The marriage of Mirah to Deronda marks the movement of the soul from Mordecai to Deronda, thus it cannot be properly fulfilled until Mordecai is dead. It also signals the final act of completion: the transition from a passive to an active hero who is able to set out to shape the lives of others and establish their nation.

Union of souls to form a whole carries with it, in the context of Jewish mystical belief, implications of a route to perfection, which in turn relates to the concept of transmigration of the soul. Ostensibly, this idea belongs to the more 'mystic' religions of the Far East, rather than to the 'prophetic' religions of the Middle East. Andrew Lang, in his discussion of J. G. Frazer, relates it to a more basic principle of ritual, from which myths and belief systems are traced. He connects transmigration of the soul to the ritual cycle of birth and death of god-kings:

> Peoples who think that all the luck depends on their king-man-god (the second sort, the superior sorcerer, with no god in him) hold, we are to believe, that his luck and cosmic influence wane with his waning forces. Therefore they kill him, and get a more vigorous recipient of his *soul* (not of a god) and of his luck. Of king-killing for this reason Mr Frazer gives, I think, one adequate example. Of the transmission of the soul of the slain divinity to his successor he 'has no direct proof,' though souls of incarnating gods are transmitted after their deaths.[15]

That metempsychosis can be linked with a rite in this way emphasises its connection with the golem, since some believed that the myth did arise from ritual practices:

> there developed among the Hasidei Ashkenaz in the 12th and 13th centuries the idea of the creation of the *golem* as a mystical ritual, which was used, apparently, to symbolize the level of their achievement at the conclusion of their studies . . . In the opinion

of the mystics, the creation of the golem had not a real, but a symbolic meaning; that is to say, it was an ecstatic experience which followed a festive rite.[16]

The Jewish interpretation of metempsychosis was of a more sophisticated variety than that of primitive birth–death ritual; it evidently had its origins in well-established and complex systems of belief. Whether it came from Indian philosophy via Manichaeism, from Platonic teachings, or from Orphic teachings, is not certain. The likelihood is that Judaism absorbed ideas from all these sources. Though such an idea was opposed by pre-kabbalistic Jewish thought, the Kabbalah was more open to mystic ideas, and metempsychosis came to be taken for granted. There were, however, modifications: 'Most of the early kabbalists . . . did not regard transmigration as a universal law governing all creatures (as in the Indian belief) and not even as governing all human beings, but saw it rather as connected with offences against procreation and sexual transgressions.'[17] Its main purpose seems to have been, then, punishment, but simultaneously an example of divine mercy by implying that transgression does not mean the individual is lost forever. As the concept became more familiar, its punitive intention became less; the righteous would continually transmigrate, not for their own benefit but for the good of the universe. In this respect it suggests the influence of Buddhism and Hinduism.

Gradually metempsychosis became enmeshed with other areas of Jewish thought. Transmigration of the soul began to be seen as a means to its perfection, thus emphasising the similarity between the Jewish concept of transmigration and transmigration within the Gypsy tradition. It is this perfection that the visionary Mordecai is trying to attain; and in order to reach it he must rely on transmigration. Because of his physical state he needs another body. Baker argues that instead of gilgul – the transmigration of a soul to another body – Eliot uses ibbur – placing one's own soul alongside the soul already inhabiting another's body. He points out that Eliot would have come across these terms in Strauss's *Das Leben Jesu*, which she translated between 1844 and 1846. Mordecai, according to Baker, sends his soul into Deronda's body while Deronda's soul is still there:

Mordecai Lapidoth for instance in *Daniel Deronda* desires to fulfil his life by transmitting his vision. He is sustained by a belief in a second soul to whom he will pass on his vision of a Jewish homeland, and refuses to give way to his physical debility and die until he discovers the soul to whom he is able to pass on his beliefs.[18]

However, one also needs to take into account that Mordecai himself is part of the ongoing process of transmigration, and the soul he possesses is not his, but that of one who has sought a Jewish nation:

> It was the soul fully born within me, and it came in my boyhood. It brought its own world – a mediaeval world, where there were men who made the ancient language live again in new psalms of exile. They had absorbed the philosophy of the Gentile into the faith of the Jew, and they still yearned toward a centre for our race. One of their souls was born again within me. (*DD*, p. 427)

Concepts of transmigration among the Gypsies, specifically among the Zincali, about whom Borrow wrote and Eliot read, play a similar part in the inherited national vision in *The Spanish Gypsy*. Zarca exhorts Fedalma not to betray her heritage and people by marrying Silva because it would be a useless appendix to her soul: 'Will you adopt a soul without its thoughts' (*SG*, p. 127). This is given added emphasis in his phrasing of the idea as one of transference of a national ideal:

> We feed the high tradition of the world,
> And leave our spirit in our children's breasts.

> (*SG*, p. 130)

The ibbur that Baker sees in *Daniel Deronda* can also be applied to *Adam Bede*. Dinah feels, when she starts preaching, that another soul has entered her body: '"I felt a great movement in my soul, and I trembled as if I was shaken by a strong spirit entering into my weak body"' (*AB*, p. 91). Similarly, and again in keeping with the Jewish idea of ibbur, Adam has his teacher's soul in his body: '"but you wouldn't have been what you are if you hadn't had a bit of old lame Bartle inside you"' (*AB*, p. 246).

Such references to metempsychosis as find their way into Eliot's work are not only from her understanding of the Gypsy and, more important, from Jewish tradition but also come from ideas expressed in Carlyle's work: 'We may say, the Old never dies till this happen, Till all the soul of good that was in it got itself transfused into the practical New.'[19] Carlyle's comment is significant because it refers to the transference of ideas in the hero, an essential concept behind the transmigration of the soul from the old hero, Mordecai, to the new one, Deronda.

As suggested above, Eliot used the idea of transmigration of the soul in a non-Jewish context before applying it to its most relevant context in *Daniel Deronda*. Primarily it indicated affinity between two individuals, and in *The Spanish Gypsy* an inherited national mission and communal obligation. Equally important is its use in *The Mill on the Floss*: the message Maggie imbibes from Thomas à Kempis – more particularly, the manner in which this message is received – has the sense of accumulated wisdom being passed down from medieval mystic to contemporary recipient, and this resembles the transmission of the message from master to pupil in Judaism:

> She knew nothing of doctrines and systems – of mysticism or quietism; but this voice out of the far-off middle ages was the direct communication of a human soul's belief and experience, and came to Maggie as an unquestioned message. (*Mill*, p. 384)

The message Mordecai passes on to Deronda is one of accumulated yearnings from the medieval Jewish mystics, which can then be transferred into a tangible reality:

> You must be not only a hand to me, but a soul – believing my beliefs – being moved by my reasons – hoping my hopes – seeing the vision I point to – beholding a glory where I behold it! . . . You will be my life: it will be planted afresh; it will grow. You shall take the inheritance; it has been gathering for ages. The generations are crowding on my narrow life as a bridge: what has been and what is to be are meeting there; and the bridge is breaking. But I have found you. You have come in time . . . you will take the sacred inheritance of the Jew. (*DD*, p. 428)

Deronda and Maggie are both part of a tradition of transmission of messages, in each case from representatives of medieval mysticism, one of whom is Christian, the other Jewish. The bridge imagery employed in *Daniel Deronda* strengthens the idea of transmission since it is the traditional place for the master to pass wisdom to the pupil. The idea receives a more sophisticated treatment in *Daniel Deronda* – perhaps because of its being an accepted part of kabbalistic belief – than it does in *The Mill on the Floss* where, in Philip Wakem's letter to Maggie, it happens through an undefined process of accumulation:

> I think nothing but such complete and intense love could have initiated me into that enlarged life which grows and grows by appropriating the life of others . . . I even think sometimes that this gift of transferred life which has come to me in loving you, may be a new power to me. (*Mill*, p. 503)

In *Daniel Deronda*, metempsychosis is supported by related, and immediately relevant, Jewish concepts which have their golemish attributes. Deronda is not just part of the transmission of the national message: he is the fruition of the growth of that idea. He is the golem in the sense that he is the ultimate vessel for that accumulated wisdom, and is thus also going to be made complete. As the heir to Mordecai's spiritual beliefs, he is in the position of creature to Mordecai's creator.

What Maggie's and Deronda's inheritances do have in common is the mythological implication: the emergence from one world of darkness into another of light. This can be interpreted as ritual rebirth for Maggie and is the ascent from the underworld for Deronda, who bears the 'elixir' with which to save the Jewish people. Deronda's characterisation as such is indicated in another passage in which Mordecai speaks of metempsychosis and which shows Eliot drawing attention to the kabbalistic meaning:

> In the doctrine of the Cabbala, souls are born again and again in new bodies till they are perfected and purified, and a soul liberated from a worn-out body may join the fellow-soul that needs it, that they may be perfected together, and their earthly work accomplished . . . It is the lingering imperfection of the souls already born into the mortal region that hinders the birth of new souls and the preparation of the Messianic time:– thus the mind has given shape to what is hidden, as the shadow of what is known . . . When my long-wandering soul is liberated from this weary body, it will join yours, and its work will be perfected. (*DD*, p. 461)

Mordecai's speech implies that Deronda is the potentially perfect soul through which the messianic era will be introduced. He is thus associated with the golem. The messianic era accompanies the establishment of the Jewish homeland: it is the means whereby Judaism stops being golem and becomes whole. By implication Deronda becomes the symbol for Israel. However, he cannot fulfil his messianic function until his soul has been perfected. He is to Judaism what Mordecai's soul is to him. Deronda needs the input of Mordecai's soul before he can become whole; once he has this, he is no longer golem, but a complete – indeed, in the novel, the supremely complete – individual who personifies what is best in Judaism. He then becomes the necessary individual who can lead the Jews to their homeland, which is a role of the Messiah. In effect, Eliot uses Deronda to represent Judaism in its perfect state and to project her future predictions for Judaism as central to world perfection. In this way, Deronda becomes not just a symbol for Israel, but a universal symbol, embodying the cosmic potential of Adam. It should be borne in mind, however, that this allegorical or mythic aspect of the novel coexists with its 'realistic' dimension in which Deronda maintains a separate identity from Mordecai and resists complete identification with his metaphysics: 'He felt nothing that could be called belief in the validity of Mordecai's impressions concerning him' (*DD*, p. 425) though he is determined to fulfil Mordecai's expectations regarding him if he can. The novel exploits the distinction between 'story' and 'discourse' so that these two aspects, the realistic and the allegorical or mythical, are not in conflict but exist in a kind of dialogical interplay with each other.

In opposition to this potentiality for perfection – which one can equate with the 'ibbur' described by Baker – is the 'dybbuk' of Jewish tradition. In contrast to passing on the soul in order to achieve spiritual perfection is degeneration of the soul. This is linked retrospectively with the two guiding spirits: 'In Jewish folklore and popular belief an evil spirit which enters a living person, cleaves to his soul, causes mental illness, talks through his mouth, and represents a separate and alien personality is called *dibbuk*.'[20] Though dybbuk was originally the term for such a demon which inhabited a human body, it came to be believed that the demons were spirits of the dead who had not been laid to rest. More modifications were introduced until the dybbuk was part of the idea of metempsychosis: 'They were generally considered to be souls which, on account of the enormity of their sins, were not allowed to transmigrate and as "denuded spirits" they sought refuge in the bodies of living persons.'[21] Eliot's initial use of the dybbuk was not in *Daniel Deronda*. She had previously used the idea in *Silas Marner* in order to show how the adverse influences of Dunstan and of Godfrey's impetuous actions have a degenerating effect on Godfrey: 'the good-humoured, affectionate-hearted Godfrey Cass was fast becoming a bitter man, visited by cruel wishes, that seemed to enter, and depart, and enter again, like demons who had found in him a ready-garnished home' (*SM*, p. 31). Though not so readily a dybbuk, an idea which bears some resemblance to it is used in *Middlemarch* to reveal the ignorance and conservatism of Middlemarch journalism. Ladislaw is likened to an 'energumen' by the Tory Keck in his leader in *The Trumpet*, when describing Will's speech on Reform. According to Keck, an energumen is, rather vaguely, '"a term that came up in the French Revolution"' (*Middlemarch*, p. 456). The word actually means one who is possessed by a demon. In this context, the reference to the French Revolution suggests that this is not merely intended to convey the ignorance of the Tory press in provincial England but alludes to a conservative fear of the French Revolution, which was regarded as something like a golem figure or Frankensteinian monster. The Revolution, it is implied, was seen by the Tories as a form of demonic possession which must be exorcised so that order can be maintained.

A surprising use of dybbuk is in *Daniel Deronda* where it is associated with Mordecai – 'The grasp was relaxed, the hand withdrawn, the eagerness of the face collapsed into uninterested melancholy, as if some possessing spirit which had leaped into the eyes and gestures had sunk back again to the inmost recesses of the frame' (*DD*, p. 327). The concept is applied more predictably to Gwendolen where it is used in juxtaposition with the idea of movement towards perfection: '"I fancy there are some natures one could see growing or degenerating every day, if one watched them"' (*DD*, p. 345). The soul can move in one of two directions: degeneration, in which case it will succumb to the spirit of negation and temptation, such as a complete reliance on the gambling principle which will result in Faustian tragedy; or growth, in which case it will improve and move towards perfection. Even Mordecai is not invulnerable to the spirit of negation.

Mordecai and Deronda have a special relationship – as a result of the transference of soul from the former to the latter – which is initiated, according to Judaism, by the connection in Mordecai's mind between Deronda and the river. Rivers occupy a special place in mythology, being associated with fecundity, and Mordecai experiences a regeneration of spirit at the river: 'The one thing he longed for was to get as far as the river, which he could do but seldom and with difficulty. He yearned with a poet's yearning for the wide sky, the far-reaching vista of bridges, the tender and fluctuating lights on the water which seems to breathe with a life that can shiver and mourn, be comforted and rejoice' (*DD*, p. 411). Bridges too are of significance in folklore, being symbolic of the journey from life to death, and they often represent the transition from this world to the next across a body of water. In Jewish belief rivers and bridges have added significance because of their association with the journey of the soul. The river is the path for the soul: 'The symbolism used to describe the descent of the souls from the world of emanation has a strongly mythical flavor. Especially prominent are the symbols of the tree of souls on which each soul blooms, and of the river which carries the soul downward from their supernal source.'[22] It marks the journey into life instead of that away from life. A bridge over a river, in mystical tradition, is the symbolic meeting place of the teacher with the pupil, where the transference of the soul takes place.[23] Mordecai sees the vision of Deronda as the ideal vessel for the perpetuation of his beliefs while standing on Blackfriars bridge, the vision becoming reality when they meet on the same bridge, and carrying deep prophetic implications for Mordecai: 'Mordecai lifted his cap and waved it – feeling in that moment that his inward prophecy was fulfilled' (*DD*, p. 422). In the novel, that particular bridge has a regenerative relevance which unites spiritual rebirth with movement of the soul from teacher to pupil:

> I have always loved this bridge: I stood on it when I was a little boy. It is a meeting-place for the spiritual messengers. It is true – what the Masters said – that each order of things has its angel: that means the full message of each from what is afar. Here I have listened to the messages of earth and sky; when I was stronger I used to stay and watch for the stars in the deep heavens. But this time just about sunset was always what I loved best. It has sunk into me and dwelt with me – fading, slowly fading: it was my own decline; it paused – it waited, till at last it brought me my new life – my new self – who will live when this breath is all breathed out. (*DD*, p. 423)

Mordecai is the spiritual messenger who will transmit the message to Deronda, his new self; Deronda will then continue to breathe and transmit the message.

Mordecai's vision of Deronda places the latter in the position of a prophetic fulfilment: he is the Messiah-figure who will see the cumulative yearnings of Masters and spiritual messengers through to fruition. In kabbalistic belief, perfection of the soul – where it has reached a spiritual state that no longer requires a physical body – heralds the arrival of the Messiah: 'The Kabbalah states that in the time of the Messiah (also known as the "age of Aquarius") there will occur a tremendous spiritual awakening, the cause of which is the violent revolt against the governing limitations of the body.'[24] Violence and spiritual awakening occur simultaneously; what is enacted is a universal rite of passage which has been adapted for literary purposes in golem stories: the simultaneous birth and death of Homunculus in *Faust* II, and the mutual destruction of Frankenstein and his creation in order that they achieve freedom from one another. What is suggested by Deronda's activities at the end of the novel – his intention to found a new land for the Jewish people – is that he is part of a creation myth, his actions being similar to the god-kings of the mythologies of Mesopotamia and ancient Egypt, beliefs which influenced early Hebrew culture, particularly in relation to the Messiah. Moreover, this intention of Deronda's places him in a position central to the Jewish conception of the Messiah: the founding of Israel will bring about a reunion with God, and 'At the core of Jewish consciousness there always lies the Messianic hope – the dream of God's Kingdom established on earth.'[25] Jewish dreams of a messianic utopia, with the intimation of its achievement through rebirth and the union of souls, are echoed in Carlyle:

> Mystical, more than magical, is that Communing of Soul with Soul, both looking heavenward: here properly Soul first speaks with Soul; for only in looking heavenward, take it in what sense you may, not in looking earthward, does what we call Union, mutual love, Society, begin to be possible.[26]

The culmination of the Jewish individual is equated with social completion and apotheosis with the creator. Through the application of principles found in Jewish mystical tradition and philosophy, Eliot is able in her Jewish novel, at an allegorical level, to predict a social cohesion which implies a return to paradise.

3
From Formless Matter to Matter with Form

As discussed previously, in kabbalistic tradition one definition of something being golem – both as noun and adjective – is that it have no shape or form. As an entity comes within bounds, or gains shape, perspective, or definition, it ceases to be golem. Such a process – from chaos to order – can be applied to many creation myths. A distinguishing feature of the golem myth is that it locates this process in the individual. Eliot's use of the paradigm is not merely the novelist's art of exploiting it for dramatic and metaphoric purposes but a more exact use of the religious and philosophic ideas that accompany Jewish mysticism. To do this, she was able to call upon precursors in literature and religious philosophy.

Mystic thought in Judaism, influenced by medieval Islamic mysticism, believed that distance from matter defined spiritual chaos since form cannot exist without matter.[1] Eliot was aware of this exchange of ideas between medieval Islam and Judaism: William Baker points out that she was reading Rabbi Munk's *Mélanges de Philosophie Juive et Arabe* (1857) on New Year's Day 1868, a work which 'deals with the Jewish mystical tradition in the medieval period'.[2] It is likely that she was also influenced by similar ideas expressed in works of more immediate literary predecessors.

Sartor Resartus emphasises the emergence of order out of chaos, not only as a common mythological theme, but with particular relevence to the idea of the golem, since Teufelsdroekh is characterised as the Wandering Jew. Chaos in this context consists in a dispersal of the kind of morality previously associated with Christianity: 'In these distracted times ... when the Religious Principle, driven out of most Churches ... wanders nameless over the world, like a disembodied soul seeking its terrestrial organisation.'[3] The Religious

Principle, like the Wandering Jew, has no home; as a result it is in a nebulous state, unable to bring itself into definite shape. If Teufelsdroeckh is indeed a Jewish mystic, the connection with the Judaic religious principle being golem because of the diaspora, becomes a distinct implication. What is needed, according to Carlyle, is the sincerity that is the primary material for all great men. In its various forms this could not be used for any benefit until it is properly channelled; that is, until it too achieves shape. This lack of organisation is an extension of Teufelsdroeckh's own lack of definition: the Editor refers to Teufelsdroeckh's book – the manifestation of thoughts and ideas – as 'an "extensive Volume," of boundless, almost formless contents'.[4] The individual, then, becomes an embodiment of the Principle, which, in turn, is a manifestation of the state of the individual. When one is incomplete so is the other; when one gains definition, so do they both.

Golem literature in Romantic fiction, too, provides examples of this concept of formlessness. In *Frankenstein* Victor tells Walton, '"we are unfashioned creatures, but half made up"'.[5] Implied by this is the necessity of another half with which to achieve completion – an aspect of kabbalism discussed in the previous chapter. Goethe's golem is also an unformed individual: Homunculus, in *Faust* II, is in an embryonic state out of which his true form must develop: 'For I myself desire to come to birth' (*Faust* II, p. 134). Though he is formed within his phial, it is an isolated environment; in the outside world he is formless:

> For birth in his case reached but life's halfway,
> No qualities he lacks of the ideal,
> But sadly lacks the tangible and real.
> Till now the glass alone has given him weight;
> But now he longs for an embodied state.
>
> (*Faust* II, p. 148)

The ideal creature initially lacking form in his life is characteristic of Deronda. This aspect of golemism – the movement of an individual character from formlessness to form – is also a significant feature of *Middlemarch*, as is the contrary theme of an individual having shape which then becomes negated and reduced to confusion.

It is not just in the later fiction, however, that there is this underlying structure to Eliot's characterisation; it can be seen as part of her artistic representation from her first full-length novel. Hetty in *Adam Bede*, for example, contemplates the idea of marriage to Arthur: 'But for the last few weeks a new influence had come over Hetty – vague, atmospheric, shaping itself into no self-confessed hopes or prospects' (*AB*, p. 99). The novel, based as it is upon the ballad formula of squire's son seducing peasant girl, emphasises the prevalent social order and its strict demarcation. Within this order, Hetty's confusion comes from her inability to reconcile her social position with her dreams. The ensuing tragedy is implied here, because when the consequence of that 'new influence' does take shape, in the form of the baby, it is negative and denies her access to her hopes. Hetty's formlessness is also related to her lack of literacy: 'Hetty had never read a novel: if she had ever seen one, I think the words would have been too hard for her: how then could she find a shape for her expectations? They were as formless as the sweet languid odours of the garden at the Chase' (*AB*, p. 136). Understanding is denied her, and the implication is that expression is also denied her; because she does not have access to either of these, Hetty remains shapeless: the future she tries to see is therefore uncertain.

A related motif applies to Mrs Holt in *Felix Holt*. She, like Hetty, is uneducated and illiterate; thus her only means of perceiving the world is through her relation to other people. When this relation becomes uncertain her perceptions become detached and she loses essential definition. When Felix – who is her focus upon the world – is imprisoned, Rufus Lyon sees her soul as correspondingly disoriented and chaotic: he speaks of it as being '"doubtless whirled about in this trouble like a shapeless and unstable thing driven by divided winds"' (*FH*, p. 294). Such shapelessness as that manifested in Hetty and Mrs Holt leads on to their small-minded selfishness, and continued shapelessness is characteristic of those who have limited vision and understanding. Their lack of education and illiteracy implies shapelessness, with their inability to perceive being related to this lack. As will be seen later, education and definition, and their centrality to the concept of golem, are themes which recur throughout Eliot's works.

In Eliot's later novels, the idea of formlessness is particularly foregrounded. Shaping and shapelessness are significant elements in *Middlemarch*, for example. Ladislaw's amorphous education and intentions are precursors of those later ascribed to Deronda. Ladislaw rejects the false shape that would be given to him by accepting conventional attitudes and values, and opts instead for an education that would not impose definition upon him:

On leaving Rugby he declined to go to an English university, where I would gladly have placed him, and chose what I must consider the anomalous course of studying at Heidelberg. And now he wants to go abroad again, without any special object, save the vague purpose of what he calls culture, preparation for he knows not what. He declines to choose a profession. (*Middlemarch*, p. 79)

Lydgate, too, goes through a cosmopolitan learning process. He does not choose to go to Oxford or Cambridge, as would be expected of a person of his social position, but attends medical schools in London, Edinburgh and Paris. In these later works, Eliot portrays Ladislaw, Lydgate and Deronda similarly in their diverse education and undirected or divided ambitions. Philip Wakem is an embryonic character of this ilk, being described not only as 'like an amorphous bundle' (*Mill*, p. 172), but also displaying an element of dilettantism in his learning: '"I'm cursed with susceptibility in every direction, and effective faculty in none. I care for painting and music; I care for classic literature, and mediaeval literature and modern literature: I flutter all ways, and fly in none"' (*Mill*, p. 327).

Lydgate and Ladislaw – eventually, through Dorothea's influence – achieve some sort of definition within their vocations; they have aims for constructing a progressive order out of their own and the surrounding chaos. This is greatly developed through the character of Deronda in her last novel in which the search for vocation and redefinition is given a kabbalistic subtext. In *Middlemarch*, Eliot also shows how the failure of that search can result in a dilettantism that is impotent and meaningless. Mr Brooke exhibits an extreme shapelessness. Though he attempts many things he accomplishes little because his mind is confused and cluttered, and he is unable to bring any discipline to his impression on anything. His attitude is summed up by Cadwallader: '"Brooke is a very good fellow, but pulpy; he will run into any mould, but he won't keep shape"' (*Middlemarch*, p. 69). Paradoxically this links him with Latimer in *The Lifted Veil* who sees visions but is unable to exert any control over them. Latimer cannot impose any definition on the formless and anonymous spectre that haunts his vision of Prague: 'I was in the midst of such scenes, and in all of them one presence seemed to weigh on me in all these mighty shapes – the presence of something unknown and pitiless.'[6] Set against the visions of Lydgate, Ladislaw and – through Mordecai – Deronda, Brooke and Latimer represent the comic and tragic aspects of lacking a shaping imagination.

Shapelessness in relation to altruistic intentions is particularly overt in a novel like *Romola* in which the mythic and allegorical are particularly foregrounded in accordance with its epic structure. Romola does not regard herself as having distinct shape, but rather is subject to having shape imposed upon her by people and circumstances. Piero di Cosimo's painting of her as a mythological character suggests this. Romola says of herself as painted, '"Ariadne is wonderfully transformed . . . She would look strange among the vines and the roses now"' (*Romola*, p. 311). While Ariadne finds shape even in surroundings not normally associated with her, Romola is not allowed to assume a shape characteristic of her nature and personality. She attempts to give her life form by acceding to imposed shapes. Firstly she adopts the stance of a dutiful daughter, criticised and condescended to by Bardo. She then becomes a wife – to Tito – and though she later rebels against this position, she is persuaded to reconcile herself to it by Savonarola. In none of these situations – by none of these characters – is she allowed to find her own shape. Romola's several encounters with Tessa and the messianic/madonna persona that she adopts during the plague, indicate that she can take charge of both herself and others; and when she is 'reborn' in the plague-ridden village she consolidates this form determined by her own feelings. At the end of the novel Romola has become a matriarch, no longer having to conform to the roles other people expect her to play.

The transition in *Middlemarch* from shapelessness to shape is achieved through a commitment to social order even if such an order is problematic for 'these later-born Theresas' who 'were helped by no coherent social faith and order which could perform the function of knowledge for the ardently willing soul' (*Middlemarch*, p. 3). The disappearance of the 'coherent social faith and order' of medieval times means that the individual finds no acceptable shape within conventional society but must discover or invent his or her own form. Eliot establishes the contrast between a shapelessness that can be challenged by an individual's goals and the amorphousness of petty dilettantism by juxtaposing Ladislaw and Brooke. She applies a similar contrast to the individual in relation to a larger social commitment – between those whose lives are defined by a clear purpose or intention in the midst of communal confusion, and those whose lives are shaped only by a social structure that is alien in human terms. The effect of this on women is particularly marked: 'Some have felt that these blundering lives are due to the inconvenient indefiniteness with which the Supreme Power has fashioned the natures of women' (*Middlemarch*, p. 4). Though the obvious reference is to Dorothea, whose character is closest to that of a would-be latter-day Saint Theresa, its relevance to Rosamond should not be ignored. In certain respects the characters of Dorothea and Rosamond parallel each other – each being a thwarting obstacle in the way of their respective husbands' researches. As golem characters Dorothea and Rosamond resemble the classical version of Pygmalion's Galatea, being chosen for their beauty and intended to fulfil the function of beautiful and decorative statues. The theme is that of women only being allowed to be shaped by surrounding situations and men, a similar situation to that of Romola, and which is alluded to in the epigraph to Chapter 10 of *Daniel Deronda*:

> What woman should be? Sir, consult the taste
> Of marriageable men. This planet's store
> In iron, cotton, wool, or chemicals –
> All matter rendered to our plastic skill,
> Is wrought in shapes responsive to demand:
> The market's pulse makes index high or low,
> By rule sublime. Our daughters must be wives,
> And to be wives must be what men will choose:
> Men's taste is woman's test.

> (*DD*, p. 81)

The implication is that women are a raw material, a commodity to be shaped and controlled by their husbands – Chapter 10 is that in which Gwendolen is introduced to Grandcourt, which leads to his decision to marry her and break her spirit; in effect, to exert his control over her.

Like a golem figure such as Frankenstein's monster Dorothea and Rosamond fight back against this control and ultimately destroy their creators and controllers. Dorothea's destruction of Casaubon is more subtle than Rosamond's of Lydgate since her character induces more sympathy in the reader, but it is equally deadly. Dorothea, in the manner of Homunculus, desires to escape from her phial and achieve shape within a larger community. This she imagines she will accomplish by marriage to Casaubon: 'Now she would be able to devote herself to large yet definite duties' (*Middlemarch*, p. 43). In doing so, she thinks she will remove herself from the influences of society which she sees controlling the existences of less strong-willed women: '"I used to despise women a little for not shaping their lives more, and doing better things"' (*Middlemarch*, p. 537). In her final act of form-finding, Dorothea is forced to accept a Faustian compromise. Homunculus is faced with a choice between form within his phial, isolated from the rest of the world, and life outside his self-possessed environment which will negate his aspirations; he can find shape outside the phial only through a self-destructive act. Dorothea must do the same: by staying within her own world she can do little acts of good and define herself as a matriarchal but potentially isolated figure. Should she decide to remove herself from that world in which she has been formed, she will be absorbed into the larger community. In Homunculus apotheosis is combined with destruction; for Dorothea the result is more creative, but by uniting with the outside world she does not achieve her ideal form in it. Though she emerges to benefit the community, she does so in a much more muted way than she had first desired. Dorothea becomes like the women she had despised, content to let her life be controlled:

> she had now a life filled also with a beneficent activity which she had not the doubtful pains of discovering and marking out for herself . . . Many who knew her, thought it a pity that so substantive and rare a creature should have been absorbed into the life of another. (*Middlemarch*, p. 819)

Comparatively, Rosamond is a success in that she shapes her own life according to her own definitions. Removed from Middlemarch where she has functioned like an automaton, though – golem-like – one possessed of a will, she finds her ideal shape elsewhere: the wife of a successful physician, accepted in London society. She revises the tenet Farebrother had applied to Lydgate – '"character is not cut in marble – it is not something solid and unalterable. It is something living and changing"' (*Middlemarch*, p. 724). Chosen to be nothing more than an ornamental statue, Rosamond is as unyielding in character as marble – a Galatea who forces Pygmalion to change, so much so that he blames her for his destruction.

The manner in which Eliot depicts these characters – the way in which they find their form – is particularly golem-like. The golem is created, becomes aware, and has to find shape for itself on the basis of its relations within a social environment. Through this process it becomes more complete. For Eliot, the 'form' of something was inseparable from its surrounding environment: how it relates to its surroundings as opposed to how it looks within its surroundings. In her fiction this is translated into the relation of characters to each other and to their society. The more intricate and varied the relations within a novel, the more complex – the higher – the form; the higher the form – the more relations in which an individual is involved – the more complete, the more whole, a person becomes. In 'Notes on Form in Art' she writes:

> And as knowledge continues to grow by its alternating processes of distinction & combination, seeing smaller & smaller unlikenesses & grouping or associating these under a common likeness, it arrives at the conception of wholes composed of parts more & more multiplied & highly differenced, yet more & more absolutely bound together by various conditions of common likeness or mutual dependence. And the fullest example of such a whole is the highest example of Form: in other words, the relation of multiplex interdependent parts to a whole which is itself in the most varied & therefore the fullest relation to other wholes. (*Essays*, p. 433)

In *Deronda*, Eliot attempts to create a character who functions – through the layers of implication built into the text at the level of its 'discourse' or artistic organisation – both mythically and in a Hegelian fashion to achieve unity out of a set of complex and varied relations. The strength Eliot came to see in the Jewish faith, as a kernel around which other faiths and nations could form, is thus highlighted, since the characters she had previously put in a similar mould – Adam Bede and, in particular, Felix Holt – are comparative failures.

In the Lurianic Kabbalah such a socio-historic individual as Deronda becomes is the kabbalist who manages to reconstitute the primordial man. As both a golem figure and the ultimate individual, Deronda enacts an apotheosis: the worshipper becomes identified with the worshipped. Such fusion is also the embodiment of an idea advocated by Carlyle when he quotes Novalis: '"There is but one temple in the world," says Novalis, "and that temple is the Body of Man. Nothing is holier than this high Form."'[7] This leads to a peripheral, but noteworthy, link. In the above context, what constitutes the body of man, for Carlyle, is clothing: 'all Forms whereby Spirit manifests itself to sense, whether outwardly or in the imagination, are Clothes'.[8] It is the manifestation of spirit out of nothingness, which will return to nothingness. Clothing as a metaphor for shape is fundamental to Old Testament creation. In Psalms, David says of the creation of light, 'He covereth himself in light as in a garment, and stretcheth out the heavens'.[9] In Jewish mystic commentary the symbolic link, with relation to the Creator, is maintained:

> It may be noted, in the first place, that R. Samuel ben Nahman speaks in another context of ten garments of God. This particular statement is based on a number of Biblical passages in which God is depicted as clothing himself in majesty, power, justice, etc.[10]

This has relevance to *Daniel Deronda*. For example, Baker writes of the images of the sky, when Mordecai imagines then sees Deronda from Blackfriars Bridge (*DD*, pp. 406–7, 422–3): 'The sky is but part of the "outer garments" where the angels reside, "simply the garment of God woven from the Deity's own substance"'.[11] More Carlylean is the use of the image of weaving to suggest shape being given to an existence, in the epigraph to Chapter 22:

> We please our fancy with ideal webs
> Of innovation, but our life meanwhile
> Is in the loom, where busy passion plies
> The shuttle to and fro, and gives our deeds
> The accustomed pattern.
>
> (*DD*, p. 202)

For Eliot the theme hearkens back to *Silas Marner*, in which the weaver resorts to the loom in an effort to recreate his life in Raveloe after the disillusionment of Lantern Yard:

> His first movement after the shock had been to work in his loom ... Every man's work, pursued steadily, tends in this way to become an end in itself, and so to bridge over the loveless chasms of his life. Silas's hand satisfied itself with throwing the shuttle, and his eye with seeing the little squares in the cloth complete themselves under his effort. (*SM*, p. 15)

There is a shift in perspective: where Marner is trying to exert some control over his own life, in *Daniel Deronda* the implication is that the loom is not under the individual's rational control. Marner's initial attempts, however, will not be successful, because all relations created by the web refer back to himself, and it is not until he gains outside signifiers that the metaphor becomes wholly applicable.

What Eliot does seem to use from *Sartor Resartus* is the formation of ideas – which is also similar to Jewish mystical ideas on form. Carlyle describes the growth of the idea in the mind of the Editor:

> Form rose out of void solution and discontinuity; like united itself with like in definite arrangement: and soon either in actual vision and possession, or in fixed reasonable hope, the image of the whole Enterprise had shaped itself, so to speak, into a solid mass.[12]

The image is, again, mythological: the realisation of a Platonic ideal, which takes on aspects of Spinoza, expressed in a golemish image. A Kabbalah text – 'The Wisdom of Solomon' – speaks of creation as an act of shaping the world '"out of unformed matter"'.[13] In this respect, the creation of humans mirrors creation of the world. The same development – from chaos to order – is, by Carlyle's reckoning, the motivation behind human attempts to make a heroic impression on the world: he states that a Great Man 'is here to make what was disorderly, chaotic, into a thing ruled, regular'.[14]

Eliot's ideas on form seem to merge with those of Carlyle in his lectures on Heroes: 'Formulas all begin by being *full* of substance; you may call them the *skin*, the articulation into shape, into limbs and skin, of a substance that is already there: *they* had not been there otherwise.'[15] Such conceptions can be traced back to Platonic ideas, influential in the philosophies of Maimonides and of Romantics, particularly Shelley, that the matter of creation must exist before there can be an act of creation. For Carlyle, form becomes more central and has its own distinctive dichotomy:

> It is meritorious to insist on forms; Religion and all else naturally clothes itself in forms. Everywhere the *formed* world is the only habitable one ... All substances clothe themselves in forms: but there are suitable true forms, and then there are untrue, unsuitable. As the briefest definition, one might say, Forms which *grow* round a substance, if we rightly understand that, will correspond to the real nature and purport of it, will be true, good; forms which are consciously *put* round a substance, bad.[16]

Corresponding to these 'good' and 'bad' forms are Eliot's differentiations between form and outline. Whereas form is in relation with the environment, outline is the manner in which the object's constitution contrasts with the surrounding environment: 'outline is the result of a nearly equal struggle between inner constitution & the outer play of forces . . . the line with which a rock cuts the sky, or the shape of a boulder, may be more due to outer forces than to inner constitution' (*Essays*, p. 434). Form suggests an organic element of growth, outline an artificial element of design; form is part of the educative process, outline the imposition of definition by another. In terms of the characters in Eliot's novels, finding form is a more natural and beneficial movement away from the state of being golem.

The representation of this dichotomy becomes apparent as part of Eliot's literary art when examining Deronda and Gwendolen. The juxtaposition of these two characters in examining form is important because they are the strongest link between the Jewish and Gentile 'worlds' of the novel. Their experiences are contrasted. Gwendolen feels that an alliance with Grandcourt would impose outline on her: 'Having come close to accepting Grandcourt, Gwendolen felt this lot of unhoped-for fullness rounding itself too definitely' (*DD*, p. 123). Nevertheless, she does marry him, and the result is constant conflict between her ideal of marriage as an entrance into society and her new immediate experience of marriage. She is unable to reconcile this conflict, or end it, without a – contemplated – destructive act.

That Deronda rejects outline in preference to form can be seen in the way he is regarded by others. He is the ultimate shapeless thing in Eliot's fiction, having no definition because he does not fit into his surroundings, into the society in which he has been raised. Deronda emphasises the constantly mutable influences which carry with them changes of emotion, because there is no correspondence with his environment: 'and round every trivial incident which imagination could connect with his suspicions, a newly-roused set of feelings were ready to cluster themselves' (*DD*, p. 142). From the point of view of Sir Hugo, Deronda is something to be shaped – in the manner of the biblical Creator – after his own image: '"I wish you to have the education of an English gentleman; and for that it is necessary that you should go to a public school in preparation for the university: Cambridge I mean you to go to; it was my own university"' (*DD*, p. 146). Since it is later stressed that 'he was not of the material that usually makes the first-rate Eton scholar' (*DD*, p. 151), it becomes apparent that Deronda would be contrasting with this environment: the shape achieved in it would not be his own, but that of Sir Hugo. His feeling of incongruity is shown to a greater extent by the need for a cosmopolitan – as opposed to English – completion of his formal education:

> In hours when his dissatisfaction was strong upon him he re-proached himself for having been attracted by the conventional advantage of belonging to an English university, and was tempted towards the project of asking Sir Hugo to let him quit Cambridge and pursue a more independent line of study abroad . . . He longed now to have the sort of apprenticeship to life which would not shape him too definitely, and rob him of the choice that might come from a free growth. (*DD*, pp. 152–3)

Growth implies a form more appropriate to his nature than being shaped by the wishes of Sir Hugo.

With Mordecai, Deronda's being a golem is more in keeping with Judaism and neoplatonism: the idea of the perfect vessel grows with Mordecai, it is part of him:

> But in the inevitable progress of his imagination towards fuller detail, he ceased to see the figure with its back towards him. It began to advance, and a face became discernible; the words youth, beauty, refinement, Jewish birth, noble gravity, turned into hardly individual but typical form and colour . . . Reverently let it be said of this mature spiritual need that it was akin to the boy's and girl's picturing of the future beloved; but the stirrings of such young desire are feeble compared with the passionate cur-rent of an ideal life straining to embody itself, made intense by resistance to imminent dissolution. (*DD*, pp. 406–7)

The formation of Deronda is the formation of an idea that is al-ready set within Mordecai's mind – a physical embodiment of a neoplatonic idea:

> But the long-contemplated figure had come as an emotional se-quence of Mordecai's firmest theoretic convictions; it had been wrought from the imagery of his most passionate life; and it inevitably reappeared – reappeared in a more specific self-asserting form than ever. Deronda had that sort of resemblance to the

preconceived type which a finely wrought individual bust or portrait has to the more generalized copy left in our minds after a long interval. (*DD*, p. 411)

In this manner it has some substance, but requires an influence which will help it to assume its innate shape from its own substance. As such, the completion of Deronda becomes the manifestation of Eliot's belief that 'the form itself becomes the object & material of emotion' (*Essays*, p. 436). The relation of a substance to its surroundings becomes in this way the relation of a substance to itself; as it finds form it becomes increasingly linked with the influential force. Goodwin, a member of the group, 'The Philosophers', to which Mordecai belongs, is made to voice this:

> For, look at it in one way, all actions men put a bit of thought into are ideas – say, sowing seed, or making a canoe, or baking clay; and such ideas as these work themselves into life and go on growing with it, but they can't go apart from the material that set them to work and makes a medium for them. (*DD*, p. 447)

Deronda and Mordecai do become increasingly linked. Their social acquaintance is the manifestation of the form that has grown within Mordecai's imagination and emotional make-up; the relation becomes intellectually and emotionally more involved. Deronda's substance finds more and more direction, which is the same as that yearned for by Mordecai. The final merging of idea, substance and 'the material that set them to work' comes in the marriage of souls – the marriage of Mirah to Deronda.

The neoplatonic nature of form as opposed to the artificial nature of outline is predominant in Mordecai's creation of Deronda from the confused mass of uncertainties and undefined intentions that constituted the substance of Deronda – he had previously 'been occupied chiefly with uncertainties about his own course' (*DD*, p. 160). There is a final fusion of the physical substance that was an unformed Deronda, and the substance of imagination which was Mordecai's conception of the ideal:

> 'Daniel, from the first, I have said to you, we know not all the pathways. Has there not been a meeting among them, as of the operations in one soul, where an idea being born and breathing draws the elements towards it, and is fed and grows?'

'It is you who have given shape to what, I believe, was an inherited yearning.' (*DD*, pp. 641–2)

This exchange implies that the shaping of Deronda is not so much the acquisition of a rigid definition, but the encouragement of fulfilment of potential to achieve a complex but unified whole: Deronda has developed into a whole person.

Eliot's social thought is also articulated in terms of form, formlessness, and wholeness. In her 'Address to Working Men, by Felix Holt', for example, she argues that the legitimate demands of the working class for social justice must be governed by wisdom in order to give them form and shape and to prevent them being taken over by more negative qualities that promote formlessness:

> Selfishness, stupidity, sloth, persist in trying to adapt the world to their desires... Wisdom stands outside of man and urges itself upon him... But while still outside of us, wisdom often looks terrible, and wears strange forms, wrapped in the changing conditions of a struggling world. It now wears the form of wants and just demands in a great multitude of British men: wants and demands urged into existence by the forces of a maturing world. And it is in virtue of this – in virtue of this presence of wisdom on our side as a mighty fact, physical and moral, which must enter into and shape the thoughts and actions of mankind – that we working men have obtained the suffrage. (*Essays*, p. 429)

Another shaping force for the working class is the cultural inheritance of the past: 'that treasure of knowledge, science, poetry, refinement of thought, feeling, and manners, great memories and the interpretation of great records, which is carried on from the minds of one generation to the minds of another', and from which the working class has 'for the most part [been] shut out from sharing' (*Essays*, p. 425). This should be transmitted to working class people through education: 'If the claims of the unendowed multitude of working men hold within them principles that must shape the future, it is not less true that the endowed classes, in their inheritance from the past, hold the precious material without which no worthy, noble future can be moulded' (*Essays*, p. 429). Social wholeness can be achieved only if people are animated by such shaping forces: 'So fellowship grows, so grow the rules of fellowship, which gradually shape themselves to thoroughness as the idea of the common good becomes more complete' (*Essays*, p. 427). But if the working class, such as members of trade unions, reject such shaping forces as education, they will unleash the social equivalent of the golem of Chelm or Frankenstein's monster on society. Such golemish imagery is clearly present in the following passage:

> ... there are numbers of our fellow-workmen who ... never use the imperfect opportunities already offered for giving children some schooling, but turn their little ones of tender age into bread-winners, often at cruel tasks ... Parents' misery has made parents' wickedness. But ... we who have some knowledge of the curse entailed on broods of creatures in human shape ... are bound to use all the means at our command to help in putting a stop to this horror ... Let us demand that [members of unions] send their children to school, so as not to go on recklessly breeding a moral pestilence among us ... (*Essays*, pp. 427–8)

4
The Relationship between Creator and Creature

Golem-tales often highlight the reflexive nature of the relation between creator and golem. If the creature is flawed, it is a reflection of the flaw in the creator: if the creature reveals itself to be monstrous, it is because the creator is essentially monstrous. The idea of monstrosity did not just limit itself to fabulous creatures, but, with the advent and establishment of the Industrial Revolution, with the 1789 Revolution in France, and with new explorations in science, monstrosity as a metaphor came to be interpreted and reinterpreted throughout the nineteenth century. At the centre of this metaphor was the subject of control – of industry, of labour, of capital, of the dissemination and understanding of new ideas. Control of these areas was as shifting and unsure as control of the golem figure in Goethe's 'Sorcerer's Apprentice'. We have already demonstrated how Eliot reconstructed (or deconstructed) previous literary representations of Jewish assimilation; in her novels and short stories she realigned and restructured the pervasive metaphors of monstrosity and control that permeated nineteenth-century writing through further exploitation of the golem myth and kabbalistic ideas.

Central to creation and control was, of course, the role of the Creator. In many mythologies the creation myth identifies the Creator with the trickster and artisan. The Kabbalah refers to the Creator in Jewish myth in these terms: 'There is an expression in the *Zohar* to the effect that "the Master struck the iron with a hammer and brought forth sparks." This refers to the Creator'.[1] Thus, the 'Master' of Jewish mythology – the supreme Creator – is characterised as a smithy. A comparative interpretation of this characterisation would align the Jewish creator with Hephaestus, the divine cripple – precursor of such artisan-tricksters as Prometheus and Daedelus, eventually of

Faust – who is associated more with his forge than with Olympus. In literatures influenced by these mythologies artisans and prophetic invalids often become – or attempt to become – creators and shapers of society. This is certainly true of the popular tales of the early nineteenth century, and is parodied in *Sartor Resartus*, where the tailor is elevated to the position of 'something of a Creator or Divinity'.[2] It can also be found at a mythic or allegorical level in Eliot's novels: characters such as Adam Bede, Felix Holt and Mordecai Cohen aspire to this position of moulder of society.

By trying to shape a community, a god or culture-hero transmits certain characteristics with regard to his creatures, which usually reflect some aspects of the creator:

> However, when we decide that the Creator, in His Supreme Perfection, is the artisan who created and designed our bodies, with all the good and evil inclinations inherent in them, it follows then that the perfect Maker can never be said to have turned out despicable, corrupt work, for every action testifies to its own quality.[3]

According to the reckoning of the kabbalists, the 'perfect Maker' cannot produce flawed work. From this it can be assumed that the human fall from grace, in the Judaeo-Christian myth – because of Adam's rejection of his creator's preconditions for life – is part of the 'Maker's' design. In this case Adam's disobedience is not a flaw but a designed characteristic which affects subsequent golems. However, in certain later versions of the golem myth the creature is imperfect because the creator is imperfect, and the creature rejects the creator, runs amuck, and is generally despicable and corrupt because of this imperfection. Literary treatments of the golem, such as the creator and creature in *Frankenstein*, conform to this version, and have their precursors in the legend of the golem of Chelm. However, when compared to the biblical creation myth, the behaviour of later golems does not differ greatly from that of Adam, though Adam's Creator is said to be perfect while the wonder-working Elijah of Chelm, Rabbi Loew of Prague, and Victor Frankenstein are flawed humans. The manner in which the golem acts – in Eden, the town of Chelm, the Prague ghetto, or Switzerland – is not wholly dependent on the relative perfection or imperfection of its creator, but on the extent to which the creature is given, or takes, charge of its own existence and how both creator and creature reconcile the creative tensions which are manifested in their relationship to one another. In this respect the problem facing the golem is similar to the dilemma confronting Homunculus in *Faust* II. The only responsibility that can be assigned to the creator, in these cases, is that he initiates creation, which in itself is merely the equivalent of a precedence for any ritual practice:

> When a God or a civilising Hero ordained a mode of behaviour – for instance, a particular way of taking food – he not only assured the reality of that behaviour (for until then the practice in question was non-existent, was not in use and so was 'unreal'), but by the very fact that this behaviour was his invention, it is also theophany, a divine creation.[4]

And it should be remembered that golem-making had its roots in ritual.

The act of creation for Rabbi Loew, Frankenstein, even Faust's toadying sycophant Wagner, is an imitation of the divine – an act which is encouraged in kabbalism. What their motives are and what their respective creations do, do not necessarily compromise morally the creator or reflect badly on the creation; rebellion is simply an inevitable consequence of the creative process based on gnostic exegesis:

> If the creator's motives in *Frankenstein* are suspect, one might at first suppose that the rebellion of the creature must be unequivocally good. One could in fact attempt a straightforward gnostic reading of *Frankenstein*. The story suggests the original creation of man was defective; therefore man owes nothing to his creator; his wisest course is then to rebel against what he has always been told is the divine order.[5]

This view is applicable to more than just Frankenstein and his creature: in terms of the reflexive relationship, a golem cannot look to a creator whose actions were – intentionally or unintentionally – flawed: intention implies lack of sympathy with the creature; absence of intention, lack of ability.

In Judaic mysticism, attitudes towards the act of creation implied a distancing of creator from creation. Indeed, the *Zohar* likens the creator's position to that of the artisan, so the creation is merely something manufactured before the creator turns to something else.

This implication can be seen in a comment on the work of the kabbalist, Maimonides:

> our teacher ... follows the opinion of Plato who said that it is impossible to assume that God produced anything from nothing; but matter has always been in existence. It stands to Him in the same relation as e.g. the clay to the potter, or the iron to the blacksmith who do with it what they please, God likewise one time forming of it heaven and earth, at another time forming of it something else.[6]

The act of creation and the object being created, then, occupy the creator's attention only for a certain amount of time. In kabbalistic thought this attitude could forfeit salvation: 'Absence of bestowal is due to the absence of love; that signifies the turning away of the Creator, God forbid, from His recipients, a condition which implies that all the gates to goodness are locked.'[7] Shelley's treatment of the Wandering Jew in 'Queen Mab' carries this denial: Ahasuerus, the Wandering Jew, berates God for the crimes committed in His name, for the malice with which He regards humans, and for the injustice of condemning Ahasuerus to an eternity of wandering. Between Ahasuerus and the Christian God there is mutual rejection, as is the case with creator and creature in *Frankenstein*. Eliot's Romantic tale, *Silas Marner*, is concerned with this sense of mutual rejection: Silas, like the Wandering Jew, sees the work of God – in particular the judgement passed on himself – as unjust, and so asserts that '"there is no God that governs the earth righteously, but a God of lies, that bears witness against the innocent"' (*SM*, p. 12).

The denigration of the Creator by Marner is akin to Romantic interpretations of mythology by inversion of accepted characteristics: God is not good; humans by acknowledging this and acting against it, are acting for the good. We see, for example, such inversion in the gnostic representation in Mary Shelley's golem story, where the creature initially displays characteristics less monstrous and more virtuous in intention than its creator. This inversion is in fact no more than adherence to Romantic interpretations of the Bible:

> The distinctive orientation of Romantic creation myths, particularly the tendency to invert gods and demons, is known in the history of religion as gnosticism. In the original Gnostic ver-

sions of the Garden of Eden story, for example, Jehovah appears as an arrogant or deluded deity, usurping dominion over Adam and Eve, striving to keep them ignorant and hence under his control by denying them the Tree of Knowledge. The villain in the orthodox version of Genesis, the serpent, becomes the hero in Gnostic versions, teaching Adam and Eve the path to divine illumination.[8]

Gnosticism had links with kabbalism, and both sought to oppose the authority of orthodoxy. As gnosticism came more into contact with Christianity, it sought to challenge the supreme authority assumed by the Christian deity: God was no longer good, and humans had the potential to re-establish a moral order.

The inverted relationship of the creator and the creature is a subject explored throughout the novels of Eliot, in the form of a person being controlled by his or her deeds. It is raised initially in *Adam Bede*, where it is connected with Classical ideas of hubris and nemesis, as in Arthur's belief both in himself as a good fellow and in his ability to control the emotional content of his relationship with Hetty that prompts him to continue seeing her. But previous actions have started to control him: 'His deed was reacting upon him – was already governing him tyrannously, and forcing him into a course that jarred with his habitual feelings' (*AB*, p. 306). More golemish is the use of the theme in later novels, where the 'deed' is presented more tangibly as a form of retribution jarring on the conscience (it could be argued that the death of Hetty's child is such a tangible form, but when this is perpetrated Arthur has no knowledge of it, or of its effect upon Hetty). Raffles appears to Bulstrode in this role as a personification of past actions: he is Bulstrode's misdeeds taking on living form, and then controlling him through blackmail. *Brother Jacob* expresses the same idea in explicitly Classical terms, referring to 'the unexpected forms in which the great Nemesis hides herself'.[9]

It is in *Romola* that monstrosity is dealt with most overtly, and Eliot inverts not only the creation myth, but Romantic interpretations of it. Tito is the being created by Baldassarre. An orphan adopted and nurtured – that is to say, shaped – by a well-meaning benefactor, Tito is eventually in a position to control his adopted father. In this aspect the relationship between Tito and Baldassarre has parallels with that of Pip and Magwitch in Dickens's *Great Expectations*, published two years before *Romola*. In Dickens's novel, Magwitch is the benefactor to Pip and enables him to rise above his boyhood station: '"I lived rough, that you should live smooth; I worked hard, that you should be above work ... Look'ee here, Pip, I'm your second father. You're my son – more to me nor any son."'[10] Baldassarre occupies a similar position with regard to Tito: he is 'a man who long years ago had rescued a little boy from a life of beggary, filth, and cruel wrong, had reared him tenderly, and been to him as a father' (*Romola*, p. 94). Like Magwitch, Baldassarre deprives himself so that Tito can have comfort: Baldassarre's 'head has lain hard that his might have a pillow' (*Romola*, p. 332).

In both novels there is anticipation of the rejection that marks the inversion. Pip rejects the classical symbol of creation – the forge and its smith – when his sense of shame about his origins alienates him from Joe Gargery. Tito's rejection of his adopted father is superimposed on to Bardo's feeling of having been betrayed by his son, Dino:

> my son, whom I had brought up to replenish my ripe learning with young enterprise, left me and all liberal pursuits that he might lash himself and howl at midnight with besotted friars ... left me when the night was already beginning to fall on me. (*Romola*, p. 51)

His recruitment of Tito to fill the role abandoned by Dino creates an even worse situation for Bardo when Tito sells Bardo's library after his death. Tito's rejection of Baldassarre is anticipated in the rejection of Bardo by Dino; and both father and father-figure are betrayed.

It is likely that Eliot's portrayal of the creature rejecting its creator was not directly influenced by Dickens despite the parallel of the use of the Frankenstein motif but was rather derived from her own specific interest in this theme. *Silas Marner* appeared in the same year as *Great Expectations*, and in this novel there is rejection of a creator which contrasts markedly with that of Magwitch by Pip and Baldassarre by Tito. In Dickens's novel, as in *Romola*, the creature has not only become more genteel and sophisticated than it was in its original state, but it has also become more elevated than its reappearing creator. It then rejects the creator whose state is now abhorrent to the new creature, or who is a reminder of an unsavoury past situation or character. Pip finds Magwitch utterly distasteful: 'If I had loved him instead of abhorring him; if I had been attracted to him . . . instead of shrinking from him with the strongest repugnance'.[11] Tito initially reasons to himself that 'his father was dead', and when confronted by this 'regenerated' man denounces him as '"*Some madman, surely*"' (*Romola*, p. 209). He then further denounces him at the supper in the Rucellai gardens as a mad, malicious former servant. Eppie, however, rejects the potential gentility offered to her by her natural father, refusing to reject her class in order to remain with Marner and the rough life which has shaped her. Tito and Pip reject those who took them away from a life of roughness and eased their lives; Eppie accepts someone who gave her a life of roughness, and rejects someone who would ease her material life. Eppie clearly hearkens back to a more Romantic, fabular ethic, where monstrosity is subjugated by feeling and community. Tito – though his story is set in the Renaissance – is shown as a monster metaphorically and allows Eliot, like Dickens in his characterisation of Pip, to satirise cynical Victorian individualism.

Even in *Silas Marner*, rejection is not a new theme, but an adaptation of one introduced in *Adam Bede*. Adam refuses to accept Arthur as his benefactor: '"I throw back your favours, for you're not the man I took you for"' (*AB*, p. 299). Adam's reason for doing this is more than just jealousy: Arthur, even more than Irwine, is a moral regulator to Adam, and therefore occupies the position of creator as much as benefactor. Adam sees Arthur's relationship with Hetty as unfair, both to Hetty and to Adam himself: it is the act of a '"double-faced man"' (*AB*, p. 300). Part of Adam's anger, therefore, is because the moral understanding he has identified with Arthur has been undermined. The relationship between Arthur and Adam can be seen as more obviously golem-like when compared with the creator–creature relationship in *Frankenstein* and *Silas Marner*. Marner rejects God because the deity has been unfair in the casting of lots, and can no longer fulfil the role of moral arbiter. The monster in *Frankenstein* regards his creator as unjust because of his unfair rejection of him:

> Oh, Frankenstein, be not equitable to every other, and trample upon me alone, to whom thy justice, and even thy clemency and affection, is most due. Remember, that I am thy creature; I ought to be thy Adam; but I am rather the fallen angel, whom thou drivest from joy for no misdeed. (*Frankenstein*, p. 101)

The role of moral arbiter or regulator is equated with that of creator, and failure to fulfil the former role results in rejection of the latter.

In *Frankenstein* there is a gnostic inversion of power; in *Romola* a similar inversion is represented in the relationship between Tito and Baldassarre. Tito is able to deny Baldassarre's freedom by withholding the stones necessary for the ransom, and thus has sway over his creator's movements. He has the power to have Baldassarre imprisoned when he denies him in the Rucellai gardens (*Romola*, Chapter 39). However, Eliot then presents a reinversion, or rereversal, of the roles, altering the power structure, as Baldassarre, rendered childlike by his loss of memory, takes on the role of destructive creature. Tito, exhausted by his escape from the mob, emerges from the Arno, and faces destruction at the hands of the creature he has formed out of his previous actions.

It is the presentation of this relationship that marks Eliot's particular reinvention of nineteenth-century monstrosity. Inversion of the creator–creature relationship, in keeping with those gnostic creation stories of Romantic literature, tended to upset traditionally assigned characteristics. Eliot, however, revises that Romantic reversal: the creator is benevolent, and the rebellion of the creature is an ungrateful act. By doing so she is aligning Tito more closely with the original golem, Adam. This is not to say she was unaware of the intentions of Romantic gnosticism; in the same novel Savonarola assumes the gnostic role of an oppressive figure of authority who can be associated with the Miltonic and Romantic ideas of an autocratic deity: 'Savonarola had that readily roused resentment towards opposition, hardly separable from a power-loving and powerful nature' (*Romola*, p. 462). The power exercised by the creature in *Frankenstein* – which enables him to re-educate Victor – is fear: Frankenstein is haunted by his creature, afraid that it will appear and kill him. Power in Eliot's revision of Romantic gnosticism functions similarly through fear; Baldassarre can unmask and disgrace Tito – a prospect from which 'Tito shrank with shuddering dread' (*Romola*, p. 212). The creator will eventually become the nemesis of the ungrateful creature. This emphasises the parallel with Pip and Magwitch in *Great Expectations*. Pip, in a clear reference to *Frankenstein*, regards Magwitch as the creator pursuing his creation: 'The imaginary student pursued by the misshapen creature he had impiously made, was not more wretched than I, pursued by the creature who had made me, and recoiling from him with a stronger repulsion.'[12] The stability of the creator–creature relation rests on the creator's ability to control the nature of the golem. When that control is lost or neglected the monstrous can be unleashed. But as Eliot suggests – and this can be seen in Dickens as well – monstrosity is confined to neither creator nor creature but can shift from one to the other.

The consequences of Tito's act of betrayal invest deeds with a life of their own beyond the control of the human will:

> But our deeds are like children that are born to us; they live and act apart from our own will. Nay, children may be strangled, but deeds never: they have an indestructible life both in and out of our consciousness; and that dreadful vitality of deeds was now pressing hard on Tito for the first time. (*Romola*, p. 156)

The imagery is related to the golem, the deeds being brought to life and acting upon their perpetrator. This idea of revivification is reinforced when Piero di Cosimo wonders whether the ghost which will account for the fear he has incorporated into his painting of Tito is '"like a dead man come to life"' (*Romola*, p. 180). In alluding to revivification, Eliot exploits a golem theme that goes back to the Old Testament. An element of irony is also contained in the above passage comparing deeds with children, not just in the fact that Tito is the child/deed pressing hard on Baldassarre. We know from Hetty's actions in *Adam Bede* that killing a child is not a means of destroying it, but another action which will increase the oppression of the original deed – in fact, the wording of the above passage is reminiscent of that from *Adam Bede*, previously quoted, in which Arthur's deeds react upon him. Eliot uses similar imagery and allusion to ensure that we realise Tito is unable to control the deeds to which he has given life, and the destructive tendencies they embody.

It is not just in the particulars of the shifting relationship between Tito and Baldassarre that Eliot restructures the nineteenth-century myth of monstrosity. She is restructuring a metaphor that has been applied to such areas as economics and industry. As the *Encyclopaedia Judaica* puts it, the golem has been used to symbolise 'the working classes' struggle for freedom'. An extension of this Marxist perspective would further interpret the myth to mean that control of the economy, and thus of society, depends on control of the means of production. Since interpretation of the golem as the servant equates means of production with the labour of workers, then it follows that should workers achieve control of the means of production, this would amount to the attainment of self-awareness and self-control. In *Romola* this is given a Renaissance context: whoever controls knowledge and scholarship possesses the means by which to control society. In an essay on *The Lifted Veil* Terry Eagleton interprets the story as signifying that knowledge equals power; therefore Latimer's inability to control his foresight signals his impotence.[13] The same is true of knowledge in *Romola*. Baldassarre has used his learning to form Tito: he has taught him and provided him with knowledge. Tito uses this knowledge to establish himself in Florence and becomes an influential figure. Baldassarre then tries to reassert his power over Tito and destroy him, but he is no longer in control of knowledge and learning as his faculties for perception, reasoning and scholarship have become dislocated – he has become a creature of emotion – and is again powerless. Bardo also loses control over knowledge as his blindness compels him to rely on others, and like Baldassarre he is betrayed by Tito who gains control of his library – the means of gaining power through knowledge and learning – and sells it for his own profit. Control of knowledge literally becomes control of capital.

The novel shows that the acquisition of knowledge for its own sake, divorced from any moral perspective, is socially dangerous. It is akin to the acquisition of money for its own sake. Without mediating moral and social factors – Eliot's 'Fellow-feeling' – knowledge and money become weapons to exert power over others. Such a warning delivered in such a manner and through the character of Tito exploits the Faustian theme that is exemplified in Goethe's use of the golem. Wagner sees knowledge and learning as a means to power, and uses them to create Homunculus in an attempt to circumvent Nature. The result is destruction for Homunculus and for Wagner, since Homunculus leaves him for Mephistopheles, the spirit of negation. In *Frankenstein* the Faustian overreacher also hopes to bypass natural creation, though the learning along mystical lines for Paracelsian ends that is implied in the creation of Homunculus is replaced by galvanism and scientific experimentation with the creation of Frankenstein's monster.

From the biblical story of Adam onwards, rejection has been an intrinsic element of the golem myth, with Romantic versions of it

– influenced by gnosticism – reversing it by having the creature reject its creator. This was a theme that is likely to have appealed to Eliot and worked its way into her fiction through her direct experience of it in her personal life. Her relationship with Lewes meant she was not only excluded from 'polite' society, but, even more important than that, she was disowned by her brother, Isaac. Hence her identification with those who were spurned, and her projection of this into her novels:

> Just as actual spinsters extracted an awareness of destiny from their culture's heroic mythology, so the century's greatest novelists lived a myth that gives shaping energy to their fiction ... assuming the role of fallen woman transfigured creator as well as character with the alchemical possibilities of the outcast.[14]

Being very much the rejected creator herself – as an author – Eliot may have recognised that the effect was as great on any individual as it was on grandiose heroes. In *Felix Holt* she places the theme in a decidedly familial setting. Mrs Transome's estrangement from her son evokes a sense of the golem in that this child-creature she had hoped to shape has developed beyond her control and understanding:

> After sharing the common dream that when a beautiful man-child was born to her, her cup of happiness would be full, she had travelled through long years apart from that child to find herself at last in the presence of a son of whom she was afraid, who was utterly unmanageable to her, and to whose sentiments in any given case she possessed no key. (*FH*, p. 94)

Like Victor Frankenstein when confronted by his 'child', she is fearful of her son, and realises that he is a product fashioned, as it has turned out, askew from her expectations and intentions; he leads an existence which is independent of her. Moreover, she is unable to control him, and says as much – '"I have no power over him – remember that – none"' (*FH*, p. 97). The repulsion she feels for him is such that she calls into question her own act of creation: 'There was a half-formed wish in both their minds – even in the mother's – that Harold Transome had never been born' (*FH*, p. 98).

The feeling of rejection is reciprocal. Harold also rejects his mother as she does not correspond to his preconceptions of her when he discovers that he is the product of an illicit relationship: 'Her son turned away his eyes from her, and left her. In that moment Harold felt hard: he could show no pity. All the pride of his nature re-belled against his sonship' (*FH*, p. 383). There is a Miltonic association in the language of the last sentence – rebellion based on pride suggesting Satan in *Paradise Lost* – which creates connotations beyond the realistic dimension of the text: the grandeur of Satan is reduced to the wilful petulance of Harold, such a reduction being a consistent theme in her fiction perhaps arising out of her lack of sympathy for Romantic gnosticism.

A significant aspect of Harold's rejection of his mother is that it enacts the Faustian denial of motherhood. In her first novel Eliot introduces this idea with a statement from Bartle Massey, the cre-ator figure with a Hephaestian limp, who is characteristically misogynistic:

> I tell you there isn't a thing under the sun that needs to be done at all, but what a man can do better than a woman, unless it's bearing children, and they do that in a poor make-shift way; it had better ha' been left to the men – it had better ha' been left to the men. (*AB*, p. 240)

This motif – present to a lesser extent in *Felix Holt* in Felix's patronising attitude towards his mother and to a greater extent in the Deronda–Mordecai relationship in her last novel – is central to the myth of the golem, where male individuals seek to usurp female creativity. Wagner and Frankenstein are more obvious usurpers of mother-hood. Wagner is particularly relevant since he sees his creation of Homunculus as an opportunity to avoid the manner of reproduction described by Bartle as a '"poor make-shift way"'.

Parallel to the familiar creator–creature conflict between Harold and Mrs Transome is the same conflict in a wider social context. Later versions of the golem legend emphasised the creature's growth in power until it threatens to overwhelm its creator, as in political interpretations of 'The Sorcerer's Apprentice'. In *Felix Holt* the mys-ticism and magic of pseudo-science are transposed on to increased industrialisation, thus placing manipulation and violent reaction of the mob within a political context appropriate to nineteenth-century history. With the development of industrialisation in nineteenth-century Europe, the workers – both urban and rural – were viewed with increasing alarm: at the same time that they were necessary for industrial and agricultural output, they came to be regarded as capable of turning on those who initiated this development and created the class. The French Revolution had already set a precedent: though it was not brought about by the rise of an industrial underclass, nevertheless a large body of rural peasantry and urban poor had turned on the aristocrats who had shaped them and attempted to control them. The golemish aspects of this Revolution cannot be overlooked, especially when it is observed that the Revolution turned upon itself and became a danger to the bourgeoisie who had subsequently seized power. The golem of the Revolution overwhelmed first the ruling class that had created the conditions – namely oppression – that led to its coming into being; then, in the Reign of Terror, it attacked the bourgeoisie who believed they had created it and were confident they could control it. In its Napoleonic manifestation, it rampaged destructively through Europe. Undoubtedly the memories of its destructive force were raised in the uprisings of 1830 and 1848, the legacy of the Revolution lying like the dust of the golem in a sealed room in the Prague ghetto, temporarily still, but potentially able to return to life. In *Impressions of Theophrastus Such*, in the chapter entitled 'Debasing the Moral Currency', Eliot's narrator fears the revival of revolutionary fervour in France, alluding in particular – through reference to Sainte-Beuve – to the 1848 Revolution and concludes: 'We have been severely enough taught . . . that our civilisation, considered as a splendid material fabric, is helplessly in peril without the spiritual police of sentiments or ideal feelings' (*TS*, p. 86).

In this interplay of violence and terror, messianic properties of the golem legend mingle with the legendary qualities that came to be attached to Napoleon: up until 1848 Napoleon was considered, by some of the rural peasantry, to be a dormant figure who would re-emerge in time of need, in the manner of King Arthur or Frederick Barbarossa. He was seen by such people as a symbol for the glory of Revolutionary France, which could rise again,[15] and simultaneously a reminder of what destruction was caused by the instigators of the 1789 French Revolution. There is evidence of a resurrection of the spectral nature of the golem legend in Marx's warnings about the latent power of the industrial proletariat and in his idea that those who sought to control the workers, the bourgeois industrialists, would be displaced in accordance with the workings of the Marxist dialectic. Significantly he draws on the story of the sorcerer's apprentice to illustrate the relation between bourgeoisie and proletariat: 'Modern bourgeois society with its relations of production, of exchange, and of property, a society that has conjured up such gigantic means of production and of exchange, is like the sorcerer who is no longer able to control the powers of the nether world whom he has called up by his spells.'[16] Contained within this is the dual threat of the golem as servant: a mass of potentially rebellious workers was a threat to the capitalists who had overthrown the traditional ruling class, and a mass of machinery was a potential threat to those who had no resource other than their labour. Instead of two sets of servants, there were now two sets of potential masters: the threat of revolutionary uprising which had become real and displaced the aristocracy could be re-enacted with regard to the relation between the middle and working classes. Manufacturers such as Vincy in *Middlemarch* were afraid of trouble from their workers, and the workers in turn, such as the Luddites alluded to in Chapter 3 of *Middlemarch*, had reason to fear machinery.

Victorian industrialists thus became aware of the danger they had formed for themselves in the creation of an industrial underclass. In *Felix Holt* the frustrations of the new industrial poor are combined with those of the established rural peasantry, who, in their political understanding, saw those who tried to shape them – no matter how benevolent the intentions (often as patronising as they were benevolent) – as an imposing influence. Consequently they turned on them: '"Ha ha! It's capital, though, when these Liberals get a slap in the face from the working man they're so very fond of"' (*FH*, p. 250). Felix sees himself as the unpatronising influence who will be able to channel the political potential of the workers away from monstrous behaviour: 'He believed he had the power, and he was resolved to try, to carry the dangerous mass out of mischief' (*FH*, p. 266). But, as with the golem, the crowd is unable to control itself, and Felix, displaying the impotence of his would-be society-shaping predecessors, cannot control it: when the destructive mob turns on Treby Manor, 'From that moment Felix was powerless' (*FH*, p. 268). In 'Address to Working Men, by Felix Holt', the monstrous potential of workers without shape is spelled out in particularly graphic terms:

> We have all to see to it that we do not help to rouse what I may call the savage beast in the breasts of our generation – that we do not help to poison the nation's blood, and make richer provision for bestiality to come. We know well enough that oppressors have sinned in this way – that oppression has notoriously made

men mad; and we are determined to resist oppression. But let us, if possible, show that we can keep sane in our resistance, and shape our means more and more reasonably towards the least harmful, and therefore the speediest, attainment of our end. (*Essays*, pp. 423–4)

Daniel Deronda places the politics of rejection – the creature–creator interplay for power and control – in a religious rather than an industrial context. Judaism is referred to in the novel as 'a national faith, which had penetrated the thinking of half the world, and moulded the splendid forms of that world's religion' (*DD*, p. 310). The implication is that Christianity has been moulded by Judaism. In a novel addressing the problems of Jews in an unsympathetic Christian society, the golem becomes applicable to the relationship between Judaism and Christianity, one which can be expressed in terms of the legend: Christianity has turned on its progenitor, and is largely responsible for the persecutions and problems suffered by Jews. The Wandering Jew is a pervasive symbol of this, Judaism being pursued, and not allowed a rest, by intolerant aspects of the religion it has created.

Mirah sees a more sinister example of the same theme when Jews mock their own religion, which she likens to abuse of one's creator: '"I have seen them mock. Is it not like mocking your parents? – like rejoicing in your parents' shame?"' (*DD*, p. 317). What makes this more sinister, in the context of the complaint, is that these views are expressed not out of dissatisfaction with the religion, but because it is necessary to be seen to reject Judaism in an anti-Jewish society. It is partially because of this that the Princess Halm-Eberstein rejects her religion; she also feels constrained within the limits of the demands of that religion, and thus believes she is denied her true nature. Ironically, her attempts to remove these constraints from her son result in his rejecting the life she has chosen for him: in answer to Mirah's complaint, quoted above, he explains, '"Some minds naturally rebel against whatever they were brought up in . . . they see the faults in what is nearest to them"' (*DD*, p. 317). His own position is an inversion of that which he is commenting on: those minds deny their religion in the hope they will be accepted into a society which excludes them; Deronda rejects what they desire and accepts what they reject.

The act of creation, by orthodox or unorthodox – that is, mystical – means, is an imitation of God, encouraged by the Talmud, which states: 'How is it possible for us to walk after God? By following his attributes and examples.'[17] As Byron Sherwin points out in his book on the golem, this applies to more than acts of goodness. Humans should try to reflect the creativity of God in their own creativity. Such activity is an attribute of God that has made its way into human nature. Just as humans have attributes of God, therefore, so do creations by humans have human attributes. Shortcomings displayed in both humans who engage in creative acts and the products of such acts are a consequence of their following the examples of their gods, as the Kabbalah makes clear: 'For whatever shortcomings of the body seems to possess [sic] they only fall back on the Creator who made us with all that is in us by nature.'[18]

Victor Frankenstein and his monster exemplify these consequences of golem-making, as Cantor points out: 'What is characteristic of Mary Shelley's creation account is that neither her creator in his creation nor her creature in his rebellion have morally pure motives.'[19] The behaviour of the monster is a displacement of the sublimated urges of Victor. Paul Sherwin writes that Victor 'conceived the Creature as a representation of the transfigured creative self, a grandiose embodiment of the creator's mind.'[20] This fits in with kabbalistic thinking, as we have already pointed out. Consequently, when the monster consigns Elizabeth to a violent death, it is a manifestation of Victor's nightmare rejection of her. The monster proposes the following pact to Victor:

> Yet you, my creator, detest and spurn me, thy creature, to whom thou art bound by ties only dissoluble by the annihilation of one of us. You purpose to kill me. How dare you sport thus with life? Do your duty towards me, and I will do mine towards you and the rest of mankind. (*Frankenstein*, p. 100)

If Frankenstein is benevolent towards the monster, the monster will act for the benefit of humans. The golems of Chelm and Prague act in accordance with similar principles. When the monster meets violence from the humans it encounters, it reacts by using violence in return. This is not merely a tit-for-tat gesture: the creature regards humans in the way his human creator regards him. Both the existence of the monster and the possibility of him perpetuating his race are anathema to Victor. By being treated in such a way, the monster becomes further associated with the Jewish golem because it is not allowed a land or rest because it is persecuted. These of course were also withheld from the Jewish people rendering them golem-like and incomplete in terms of national identity.

Romantic myth proposed its gnostic thesis in order that human creative potential could be elevated at the expense of the deity. Considered as a Romantic interpretation of *Paradise Lost*, *Frankenstein* certainly suggests this. However, in relation to human creative potential, it implies that such potential has limits: humans and their creations are necessarily flawed. Mary Shelley's treatment of the golem story implies the 'sins of the father' maxim associated with Judaism. Similar thinking is present in *The Mill on the Floss*, as in Aunt Glegg's comment on Tom: '"he's got to bear the fruits of his father's misconduct"' (*Mill*, p. 212). It also helps to establish the Dodson–Tulliver dichotomy. Not only are Mr Tulliver's sins visited on his Dodson-like son but when the creature is a Tulliver in temperament like Maggie, a reversal takes place and the sins of the creature reflect back on the creator: Mrs Tulliver says of Maggie, '"Folks 'ull think it's a judgment on me as I've got such a child – they'll think I've done summat wicked"' (*Mill*, p. 28). The influence of Feuerbach may have had an effect on this aspect of Eliot's thinking, particularly his idea that man created God after his own image. Feuerbach, in demythologising Christian theology, maintained that Christ the son and God the father were each reflections of the other:

> But at the same time, he is not yet a real finite Being, posited out of God; on the contrary, he is still identical with God, – as identical as the son is with the father, the son being indeed another person, but still of like nature with the father.[21]

This may promote a better understanding of the characterisation in *Romola*. A combination of such biblical criticism with Romantic exegesis and kabbalistic advocation of the *imitatio dei* can help explain the breaking down of the division between creator and creature. Tito acting against Baldassarre is a reflection of Baldassarre later acting against him. When Bardo tells Tito, '"For you, too, young man, have been brought up by a father who poured into your mind all the long-gathered stream of his knowledge and experience"' (*Romola*, p. 66), destructive characteristics can also be included. Baldassarre and Tito, creator and creature respectively, bring suffering and misery upon themselves and destroy each other in a re-enactment of the *Frankenstein* story. One cannot live without the other – when

Victor dies – the monster dies too. Once Baldassarre has revenged himself on Tito, he also dies.

This pattern of transposed attributes and desires which has its origins in the Kabbalah is discernible in characteristics of Deronda and his mother. She plans to use her son as a way of embodying her own desire to escape from the religious strictures that threatened to limit her existence. He has instead become an embodiment of her feelings of dissatisfaction though in reverse, and rejects the life she has tried to project on to him. His reflection of her character completes a cycle which brings Deronda back to Judaism. Such a transposition is also evident in the relationship between Lapidoth and his children. Lapidoth is one of those Jews about whom Mirah complains, who dissociate themselves from their religion as if mocking their parents. Mirah and Mordecai are unable to reconcile themselves to this, and both turn away from their father towards a deeper involvement with their religion. In the novel, this cycle of events is peculiar to the main Jewish characters, but as we have seen, such reversals are also present in her earlier fiction with Tito and Baldassarre and with Godfrey Cass's rejection of his daughter being mirrored in her later rejection of him.

In order to balance the – often mutual – rejection, there is an element of acceptance in the creator–creature relationship, since, in Judaism, rejection of the ultimate Creator would result in perdition. Josephus maintains that a destructive relationship between God and his creation – as was later posited by the Gnostics – was not what God intended: 'had He determined to annihilate mankind when made, He would not have called them into existence, for it were reasonable not to have bestowed the boon of life at all rather than having given to destroy it.'[22] Josephus maintains that the fact that time has been taken to make the human race is reason enough to assume there would be equivalent responsibility: that 'the author and creator of the human race ... would cherish it with care'.[23] The kabbalistic concept of *imitatio dei* implies that for any human undertaking creation, a similar attitude would follow. Emulation would have a constructive element as well.

As an author, Eliot would have realised she was in a position to put this constructive responsibility into practice. Indeed, in the very fiction she creates, she acknowledges the power and influence of the artist.[24] The artist as creator invests the creation with his or her own essence. This is not a new idea, and Eliot uses it again and again in her fiction: Hans Meyrick voices the opinion, ' "Every painter worth remembering has painted the face he admired most, as often as he could. It is part of his soul that goes out into his pictures. He diffuses its influence in that way"' (*DD*, p. 395); and Philip Wakem expresses his love for Maggie through a similar image: '"perhaps I feel about you as the artist does about the scene over which his soul has brooded with love"' (*Mill*, p. 502). Adam Bede is also shown to possess this characteristic, acknowledging the effort of creation, when Seth says of him: '"He'll never turn round and knock down his own work, and forsake them as it's been the labour of his life to stand by"' (*AB*, p. 45). This reflects the cherishing attitude to creation of Judaism and stands in opposition to the destructive attitude in Romanticism as portrayed in *Frankenstein*. Victor Frankenstein's positive view of his creators (parents) is contrasted with his negative response to his creation. His parents assume a position of such benevolence and care towards him that he sees his welfare as dependent on them:

> I was their plaything and their idol, and something better – their child, the innocent and helpless creature bestowed on them by Heaven, whom to bring up to good, and whose future lot it was in their hands to direct to happiness or misery, according as they fulfilled their duties towards me. (*Frankenstein*, p. 24)

Frankenstein feels it is their duty to do this, because it is 'what they owed towards the being to which they had given life' (*Frankenstein*, p. 24). His own treatment of his own creation is to abrogate responsibility completely.

In the interplay of characters in *Middlemarch* Eliot suggests that the tragedy of *Frankenstein* can be avoided. She establishes opposed principles in her representation of the shaping of Fred Vincy. Mr Vincy, in keeping with his merchant mentality, and in keeping with prevalent Middlemarch attitudes, sees his children, particularly Fred, as an investment. When Fred does not pursue the profession preferred by Vincy, he becomes a bad investment which has not paid a good return: '"I only hope, when you have a son of your own he will make a better return for the pains you spend on him"' (*Middlemarch*, p. 559). Withdrawal of his investment becomes the same as neglecting responsibility; so the son becomes alienated from his father, or the creature from his creator. The role of the father-figure or creator is then transposed on to Farebrother and Caleb Garth, who have already been acting as understudies. Garth, in particular, puts himself in the position of creative shaper: '"I say, that young man's soul is in my hand; and I'll do the best I can for him, so help me God! It's my duty, Susan"' (*Middlemarch*, p. 556): Garth accepts what Vincy rejects, partly to fulfil the responsible role towards his own offspring – Mary. It is worth noting, as an aside, and an addendum to the influence of the creative artist, that Eliot anticipates Oscar Wilde's *The Picture of Dorian Gray*. Wilde's novel incorporates the Romantic idea of the doppelganger, in that the creation – the picture – becomes a manifestation of the hero's soul.[25] In *Romola*, Eliot's novel that focuses on these destructive aspects of the golem, Piero di Cosimo invests his portrait of Tito with the same attribute: the picture displays Tito's fear and selfishness, characteristics which he had initially managed to mask.

The mutual acceptance of creator and creature is clearly manifested in *Daniel Deronda*. Depicted throughout as a prophetic figure, Mordecai does not deny the accusation that 'He feeds himself on visions' (*DD*, p. 426), but uses visionary perception to justify his expansive ideas: '"for visions are the creators and feeders of the world. I see, I measure the world as it is, which the vision will create anew"' (*DD*, p. 426). He needs visions in order to manufacture his creations – as is shown with his vision of Deronda – and in order to create his world. Mordecai takes on aspects of Carlyle's heroes, that is to say, those who are

> the modellers, patterns, and in a wide sense creators, of whatsoever the general mass of men contrived to do or to attain; all things that we see standing accomplished in the world are properly the outer material result, the practical realisation and embodiment, of Thoughts that dwelt in the Great Men sent into the world: the soul of the world's history, it may justly be considered, were the history of these.[26]

Whereas Hans Meyrick wants to diffuse his soul into inanimate paintings, Mordecai aspires towards bringing the inanimate to life, using his own soul as energy:

> But the fuller nature desires to be an agent, to create, and not merely to look on: strong love hungers to bless, and not merely to behold blessing. And while there is warmth enough in the sun to feed an energetic life, there will still be men to feel, 'I am lord of this moment's change, and will charge it with my soul.' (*DD*, p. 407)

Mordecai's feelings towards his at first imagined creation are of the type attributed by Josephus to the Jewish Creator. Sympathy accompanies the picture he forms of this intended being: 'And as the more beautiful, the stronger, the more executive-self took shape in his mind, he loved it beforehand with an affection half identifying, half contemplative and grateful' (*DD*, p. 406). This contrasts with the selfishness of the Frankensteinian creator – 'The creator is an innerness – pure, unconditioned spirit – seeking innerness – the life or light in, but not of, things. Things themselves do not exist for him except as "lifeless matter" . . .'[27] – and Mordecai's motivation brings ends that are beneficial not only to himself and Deronda, but also, potentially, to the Jewish nation, and because of the implications of Jewish nationhood in the novel, to the world.

At the end of *Daniel Deronda*, the relationship between Mordecai and the Deronda he has created is spiritually symbiotic in a manner which recalls the act of apotheosis in Jewish mysticism. The union of the hero with the father-creator at the end of his quest is present in the Kabbalah:

> the Torah commands 'cleave to your God' – and since the chasm between man and God is due to the darkness and evil inherent in man, the first step towards fulfilment of his command is service (*abodah*), by which evil is obliterated. This is the first union which gives man the power to become the perfect vessel. When he achieves total purification and becomes a perfect vessel, he is then able to unite with God for eternity . . .[28]

Two levels of apotheosis are suggested: firstly that union which enables humans to achieve perfection; secondly, that which unites the perfect vessel with the creator. Union between humans and God represents the highest spiritual achievement – *neshamah* – which brings understanding of the godhead, and is described as 'the intuitive power that connects mankind with its Creator'.[29] Moreover, since this is an aspect of the Kabbalah associated with the mystical tendencies of the Sephardi in France and the Iberian peninsula, it provides a link joining the mystical with the magical Kabbalah. This union was advocated by some celebrated kabbalists: 'even among the theurgical qabbalists the idea of a mystical union between man and God was known – as, for example, in the writings of "Ezra" of Gerona'.[30] Mordecai's other name, the one used by Mirah, is Ezra.

In this area of apotheosis of creature into creator, medieval Jewish mysticism was much influenced by Islamic teachings of the same period, which maintained that 'man could not know his Creator by himself unless a certain kinship existed between man and his Creator'.[31] This means there is an element common to both creator and creature, much in the same way that humans have attributes of God. In medieval Islam this element was similar to neshamah. Altmann goes on to say:

> Man is essentially intellect. He is created in the image of the Merciful One, which we take to signify the supernal intellect or Vicegerent. In the act of union the mystic becomes identical with this supernal intellect and, like it, by virtue of the intellect's self-knowledge knows his Lord.[32]

The Jewish mystic in *Daniel Deronda* is identified as a divine figure: Deronda regards Mordecai 'as if he had been that preternatural guide seen in the universal legend, who suddenly drops his mean disguise and stands a manifest Power' (*DD*, p. 424). Mordecai sees himself as the means whereby Deronda will become the perfect vessel. His perfect soul will unite with Deronda to achieve this:

> Nay, it was conceivable that as Mordecai needed and believed that he had found an active replenishment of himself, so Deronda might receive from Mordecai's mind the complete ideal shape of that personal duty and citizenship which lay in his own thought like sculptured fragments certifying some beauty yearned after but not traceable by divination. (*DD*, p. 437)

Deronda, the perfect vessel unites with the creator, Mordecai (the language signifying perfect union being reminiscent of the story of Pygmalion and Galatea). With imitation of God in mind, this union of creator and creature represents the union of mystic with Creator. As Deronda becomes part of Mordecai, their joining is representative of the ultimate goal of the transmigrating soul. Simultaneously, physical and spiritual perfection have been reached in union with the father-creator.

5
Ideals of Perfection

As stated in the previous chapter, the motivation behind many a creation of a golem was control – control of the self as much as control of others or of the environment. Golem making became a need to project an ideal self on to another created specifically for that purpose. For example, Homunculus in *Faust* II is intended to lack no qualities of the ideal since Wagner, his creator, is flawed. A recurrent feature of golems, however, is that they have an essential 'flaw' – despite the original intention of perfection – which is revealed through the creature becoming distanced from the creator, a distancing of the self from the ideal, and is often manifested in destructive acts. In the case of Romantic golems it is self-destruction (Homunculus) as well as destruction of others (Frankenstein's monster). However, in some instances to use the word 'flaw' is a misrepresentation of these created beings; what the creator perceives as an imperfection is in fact an assertion of the golem's self – the wish to be other than just the puppet or idol of the creator.

The idea of imperfect creation of a golem can be traced back to the paradoxical biblical creation myth with Adam as golem. Adam was meant to be God's ultimate creation – he was intended to be a flawless creature. By biting the apple, by aiming for enlightenment, however, he was perceived by God as being blemished – where apple-biting is a flaw instead of a route to enlightenment. This signals the fall from grace, and enlightenment then becomes associated with a return to Eden and consequent spiritual and physical perfection. But this return would also imply a relinquishment of the humanity – the enlightenment – that the apple-biting initiated in the first place. Kabbalism was a means of overcoming this paradox. Kabbalism differed from the divine autocracy of the Judaeo-

Christian principle in its advocation of knowledge and growth as means to spiritual perfection. Here kabbalism also borrowed from Eastern mysticism in the transmigration of souls, with its implications of accumulated wisdom in order to reach perfection. Thus physical and spiritual perfection could be successfully aligned with humanity, and all these could be applied in movement back to God.

The equation of physical with spiritual perfection was a recognised aspect of Judaic belief exemplified in the creation of Adam. Robert Graves describes the beauty of Adam before the events that resulted in expulsion from the garden of Eden:

> Moreover, he was of such indescribable beauty that though, later, the fairest of women seemed like apes when compared with Abraham's wife Sarah, and though Sarah would have seemed like an ape when compared with Eve, yet Eve herself seemed like an ape when compared with Adam, whose heels – let alone his countenance – outshone the sun! Nevertheless, though Adam was made in God's image, yet he too seemed like an ape when compared with God.[1]

So Adam was beautiful, and Eve was beautiful, but neither was as beautiful as God. Contained in this is the implication that humans are created at various distances from God, the greater the distance, the less comely the appearance, hence the greater the spiritual degeneration. And vice-versa: Josephus cites the example of Saul's claim to kingship by way of his stature and beauty, though it is stressed that this is a manifestation of his ethical and spiritual qualities: '"I make not of the kingdom a prize for comeliness of body, but for virtue of soul, and I seek one who in full measure is distinguished by this, one adorned with piety, justice, fortitude and obedience, qualities whereof beauty of soul consists."'[2]

Examples of this can be found in Romantic writings, particularly the work of both the Shelleys. In 'Queen Mab' reference is made to inner and outer beauty:

> Sudden arose
> Ianthe's soul; it stood
> All beautiful in naked purity,
> The perfect semblance of its bodily frame.[3]

This contrasts with *Frankenstein* where the 'repeated argument [of the creature] is that any ugliness in his soul is purely the result of the ugliness of his body'[4] – an argument that returns to Judaic ideas of beauty and soul because the creature contrasts Adam's beauty with his own hideousness. George Eliot employs a similar relation between the physical and the spiritual in her fiction.[5] For example, Adam Bede is presented as an ideal of rustic perfection:

> a large-boned muscular man nearly six feet high, with a back so flat and a head so well poised . . . an arm that was likely to win the prize for feats of strength; yet the long supple hand, with its broad finger-tips, looked ready for works of skill . . . jet-black hair . . . and the keen glance of the dark eyes that shone from under strongly marked, prominent, and mobile eyebrows . . . The face was large and roughly hewn, and when in repose had no other beauty than such as belongs to an expression of good-humoured honest intelligence. (*AB*, p. 6)

Adam undergoes the archetypal hero's journey, from stasis to flux to stasis. His appearance is indicative of the extent of his troubles on the journey. The above quotation describes him at the beginning of the novel. At this stage in his life his perceptions of the world are untroubled. When, however, these perceptions are disturbed – after Arthur, whom he has venerated, deprives him of his happiness and Hetty is accused of infanticide – his outward appearance deteriorates and he becomes gaunt-faced and ill-looking.

Adam's dilapidated state is a case of the fortunes of the creator paralleling, and to some extent being dependent upon, the state of the creation, for Adam is both creator and creature. He is a creator in that he has constructed an image of Hetty which denies the realities of her character: 'How could he imagine narrowness, selfishness, hardness in her? He created the mind he believed in out of his own, which was large, unselfish, tender' (*AB*, p. 354). He has invested his ideal of physical perfection with the ideal spiritual qualities he thinks should accompany it. When Hetty no longer conforms to his ideal, Adam slips from the ideal of his initial portrayal. Adam's disillusionment with his creature, Hetty, is somewhat Frankensteinian, since Frankenstein is unable to reconcile the actualities with the intention of his creation. Adam likewise is unable to reconcile the monstrous behaviour of Hetty with the image he had projected on to her. The conflict and potential danger resultant from creative tensions can be discerned here: Adam cannot overcome the imbalance between perfection and monstrosity; the equilibrium is broken, and Adam becomes unbalanced. Having himself been presented as an idealised physical specimen he is now depicted through his deteriorated physical condition. Marriage to Dinah and the establishment of his own family marks a return to stasis and the restoration of his original bearing: he 'walked with his old erectness' (*AB*, p. 534).

Daniel Deronda treats the theme of balance in creativity through the relation between the Jewish and non-Jewish worlds. Chapter 22 opens with the epigraph,

> We please our fancy with ideal webs
> Of innovation, but our life meanwhile
> Is in the loom, where busy passion plies
> The shuttle to and fro, and gives our deeds
> The accustomed pattern. (*DD*, p. 202)

Life is constructed according to ideals, but deeds have their own shape – they take on their own impetus. The specific reference is to Mr and Mrs Arrowpoint's ideas about their daughter's future being subverted by the 'busy passion' which brings Catherine and Klesmer together: Catherine is the child/deed acting apart from the intentions of the parents/creators. Thus it is implied that the British ruling class has its future in alliance not just with creativity, but, bearing in mind the history of Klesmer's nomenclature,[6] with Jewish creativity. The verse also contains the motif of weaving to create a life, one which is central to both Carlyle's *Sartor Resartus* and Eliot's own *Silas Marner*.

The preoccupation with finding an ideal of beauty is central to *Middlemarch* where it is associated with Lydgate and Casaubon. Both seek an ideal mate for their respective searches, and their choices suggest the scientific and religious idealism they proclaim is not entirely intellectual but has a physical aspect also. Lydgate's self-centred idea of perfection is significant: 'that perfect piece of womanhood who would reverence her husband's mind after the fashion of an accomplished mermaid, using her comb and looking-glass and singing her song for the relaxation of his adored wisdom alone' (*Middlemarch*, p. 573). This image has a sinister undertone, however. The mermaid is often seen as a murderous figure, seeking to take men's souls – the nixie figure of Bertha in *The Lifted Veil* being a more striking example of Eliot's use of that figure from folklore.

Mermaids derive from the folklore type of the water kelpy, a supernatural creature common in the folklore of Scotland. Kelpies themselves resembled the 'Nikr' of Iceland – the evil water-demon, from whom the term 'Old Nick', the Devil, stems. 'Nikr' is also the source for nixie, this water-sprite having, then, a demonic connotation. Scott, in his writings on demonology and witchcraft, as well as in annotations on the Scottish ballads, may well have directed Eliot towards this usage. Even if it was not from this source, the evil influence of the Nikr was also a common feature in English folklore, via Anglo-Saxon origins:

> The beautiful Nix or Nixie who allures the young fisher or hunter to seek her embrace in the wave which brings his death; the Neck who seizes upon and drowns the maidens who sport upon his banks; the river-spirit who still yearly, in some parts of Germany, demands tribute of human life, are all forms of the ancient Nicor.[7]

The song of the mermaid, then, is more akin to that of the siren. Lydgate's idea that 'he had found perfect womanhood' (*Middlemarch*, p. 348) in Rosamond is an indication that instead of bringing relaxation, she will, siren-like, cause his quest to founder. Rosamond is not the perfect woman Lydgate had constructed, but is rather 'her own standard of a perfect lady' (*Middlemarch*, p. 165); and Lydgate will not find his ideal woman because he expects an ornament, as does Casaubon. The pre-vivified figure – which resembles the statue, Galatea – of the epigraph to Chapter 43 refers to the expectations of both Lydgate and Casaubon:

> This figure hath high price: 'twas wrought with love
> Ages ago in finest ivory;
> Nought modish in it, pure and noble lines
> Of generous womanhood that fits all time.
> That too is costly ware; majolica
> Of deft design, to please a lordly eye:
> The smile, you see, is perfect – wonderful
> As mere faience! a table ornament
> To suit the richest mounting. (*Middlemarch*, p. 425)

Casaubon and Lydgate marry because they see, in Dorothea and Rosamond, their ideals of female perfection. For Lydgate this is a beautiful woman who will act as a decoration – a 'sculptured Psyche', as she is referred to (*Middlemarch*, p. 632). For Casaubon it is someone who will support, and not question, his work. Each ideal is rooted in control and is invested only with the characteristics the husbands would have them possess. This imperception and desire for control is indicative of the golem. Lydgate and Casaubon imagine that Rosamond and Dorothea have only the inclinations – the souls – that they place within them; their wives are thus in the position of Galatea. But the wives have their own inclinations, at odds with those of the husbands, upon which they will act, though action does not mean any malicious intent. Dorothea and Rosamond, by acting, contribute towards their husbands' destruction. This is the golem in historical and political form: Lydgate and Casaubon seek to control their wives; Rosamond and Dorothea resist control by displaying self-awareness and acknowledging their own desires. Their actions are those of the golem as servant whose realisation of its own potential causes the downfall of its master. At a time when social reform was making some concessions towards the underclasses who had been regarded as automata to be manipulated, women tended still to be regarded as statues. Thus the golem could be used not only to show workers breaking free from those who would control them – as in *Felix Holt* – but also to suggest the power and potential of women who refuse to submit weakly to male control.

It becomes apparent that Lydgate and Casaubon, perhaps because they are questing figures, believe in ideals, ideals which have both a mental and physical manifestation. Their tragedies stem from an inability to reconcile such ideals with a resistant reality. Once again, creative tensions arise and play their part in the potentially destructive relationship between creator and creation. In *Middlemarch* Ladislaw is responsible for the emergence of these tensions. He is the object of jealousy from Casaubon, and the potential cause of jealousy from Lydgate. More significantly, he acts as an alternative creator for Dorothea and Rosamond, and as such he embodies the extreme polarities of the creator's attitude towards the creation. On the one hand he sees Rosamond as nothing more than reality allows; she is, to him, an eminently flawed creature. On the other hand he sees Dorothea as 'a creature worthy to be perfectly loved' (*Middlemarch*, p. 359), describing her variously as a work of creative artistry – '"You *are* a poem – and that is to be the best part of a poet"'

(*Middlemarch*, p. 221) – and as a perfect but inanimate object: 'Will, we know, could not bear the thought of any flaw appearing in his crystal' (*Middlemarch*, p. 462), a crystal having cold, sharp associations, as well as the implication that for its perfection – and its flaws – to be revealed, it first requires cutting and shaping. Polarisation is then used as a basis for irony. Will's vehement attack on Rosamond causes this supreme egotist for once to break the boundaries of her own ego when she tells Dorothea the truth about Ladislaw, acting against her own interest: '"He said yesterday that no other woman existed for him beside you"' (*Middlemarch*, p. 785). Yet Dorothea eventually allows her own aims to be subordinated to those of Will, while at the same time helping to shape his life. In effect she exchanges places with Will. He had been described by Brooke as 'a young man capable of putting ideas into form' (*Middlemarch*, p. 289) – a creator who can bring some definition to the nebulous mass of ideas which Brooke is: '"I have plenty of ideas and facts, you know, and I can see he is just the man to put them into shape"' (*Middlemarch*, p. 325). The lofty ambitions of both come to be reduced: Will, the creator, needs Dorothea, whom he had described in terms of a work of art, to bring him shape; and Dorothea, who helps give form to Will, takes a subordinate role to him and is willing to be shaped.

The projection of ideals on to their wives has significant implications for both Lydgate's and Casaubon's intellectual quests. Their blindness to any presence or attribute of soul within the humans closest to them – Dorothea and Rosamond – suggests their attempts to reveal the fundamental biological and mythological structures of humanity will be characterised by a similar lack of perception, and fail correspondingly.

When Eliot introduced the idea of physical perfection in *Daniel Deronda*, it was not only with Deronda as golem, but also with Gwendolen. Rex sees Gwendolen as 'the most perfect creature in the world' (*DD*, p. 47). Her statuesque appearance and marble-like complexion point to her being a sculptured beauty – a Pygmalionesque theme which is emphasised by the tableau scene from *The Winter's Tale*, in which she plays Hermione, whose 'vitalised' statue parodies the story of Galatea. There is then the implication that she, like Deronda, requires an injection of essence. This is reliant upon the 'hidden' Jew, Deronda, who in turn is reliant upon the 'open' Jew, Mordecai – Eliot thus emphasising her subversion of ideas of conversion of Jews since it is the Jews who are the converters rather than the converted. One of her early letters shows her awareness of Victorian efforts to convert the Jews: 'So much for bad news. For good, I have nothing better than that the "Society for the Conversion of the Jews" has converted *one* Jew during the past year and has spent £4400' (*Letters*, II, 102), and in her essay 'Silly Novels by Lady Novelists' she refers derisively to a plot development in a 'silly novel' in which there is a conversion to Christianity 'after the shortest and easiest method approved by the "Society for Promoting the Conversion of the Jews"' (*Essays*, p. 321). Her later attitude to Jews and Judaism rejected any need for conversion to Christianity: '[T]owards the Hebrews we western people who have been reared in Christianity, have a peculiar debt and, whether we acknowledge it or not, a peculiar thoroughness of fellowship in religious and moral sentiment (*Letters*, VI, 301–2).

In individual terms, Deronda fits readily into the category of golem: his appearance is presented in a manner which, though it invites admiration, does not suggest activity but rather promotes and encourages the creative urges of others. He is compared to the Mallingers and 'was handsomer than any of them, and when he was thirteen might have served as a model for any painter who wanted to image the most memorable of boys' (*DD*, p. 141); when he is older, the Meyrick sisters 'so thoroughly accepted Deronda as an ideal, that when he was gone the youngest set to work, under the criticism of the two elder girls, to paint him as Prince Camaralzaman' (*DD*, p. 156).[8]

It is this movement, the ideal influencing and shaping the real, that makes him golem to Mordecai's creator. Mordecai envisages an ideal person to be the vessel for his ideas:

he imagined a man who would have all the elements necessary for sympathy with him, but in an embodiment unlike his own: he must be a Jew, intellectually cultured, morally fervid – in all this a nature ready to be plenished from Mordecai's; but his face and frame must be beautiful and strong, he must have been used to all the refinements of social life, his voice must flow with a full and easy current, his circumstances be free from sordid need: he must glorify the possibilities of the Jew, not sit and wander as Mordecai did, bearing the stamp of his people amid the signs of poverty and waning breath. Sensitive to physical characteristics, he had, both abroad and in England, looked at pictures as well as men, and in a vacant hour he had sometimes lingered in the

National Gallery in search of paintings which might feed his hopefulness with grave and noble types of the human form, such as might well belong to men of his own race. (*DD*, p. 405)

As well as characterising Deronda as an ideal figure, this passage also has significance in Mordecai looking for his ideal among paintings. This refers back to an earlier discussion in the novel about the ideal model looked for by painters – and painted by Mab Meyrick. Mordecai assumes the role of creative artist, seeking a model into whom he can – as Hans maintains artists do – place his soul. He enacts a form of *imitatio dei* since he wants a beautiful golem into whom he can breathe a soul. Klesmer's acknowledgement of Mirah as an artist is relevant here: he tells Gwendolen that the life of an artist '"is out of the reach of any but choice organizations – natures framed to love perfection and to labour for it"' (*DD*, p. 217). Mordecai's search for perfection is combined with Mirah's artistic quest for perfection, and both quests are successful in Deronda, the artist's model and the physically perfect Jew.

Connected to human perfection is the idea of duality in humans. By viewing these two Judaic concepts in conjunction, the reference to Gwendolen as 'the most perfect creature in the world' (*DD*, p. 47) is linked with the struggle of the good and bad angels – Deronda and Grandcourt respectively – for her soul. The Kabbalah refers to the bad angel as a hindrance to human perfection: 'In order that the children of Israel might earn their reward by fulfilling the law and the commandments, God created in them an evil *yezer* (inclination) as an obstacle to their execution of perfect deeds.'[9] The superseding of Grandcourt's influence over Gwendolen by that of Deronda means the defeat of the evil *yezer*: he is removing an obstacle from her – as well as his – movement towards perfection. Eliot's use of such characterisation shows how an essentially Judaic model governs an aspect of the novel's structure and also promotes allegorical interpretation. The 'Deronda half' and the 'Gwendolen half' of *Daniel Deronda* are related through the struggle – both literal and symbolic – between Grandcourt and Deronda, with Gwendolen as the factor in common.

Perfection carries with it the aim of maintaining universal balance. The Zoroastrian origins of Jewish duality bring an interplay of good and evil forces which ultimately induce ideal perfection by suppression of evil:

It was the Creator's desire to fashion two distinct creations: one of deficiency and one of perfection, so that the cycle of deficiency shall have sole sway at times. But His final intention is to perfect that which is imperfect. Hence the supervision of ... perfection operates in a concealed manner: the hidden governing power of completeness underlies those processes which operate secretly towards the goal of perfecting all things, freeing them from evil, and bringing them to a condition of total goodness.[10]

By triumphing over evil, by overstepping the hurdle of the evil *yezer*, humans achieve perfection. This aspect of Judaic belief can be applied specifically to *Daniel Deronda*, which shows the evil inclination being defeated and spiritual wholeness attained. Deronda's symbolic defeat of Grandcourt – the embodiment of a purely egotistic will to power – is juxtaposed with his own spiritual completion: his discovery of his Jewish heritage. This enables him to be united with Mordecai in spiritual and bodily perfection. The whole cycle has a kabbalistic base:

Under the present supervision in which the body is given dominion the soul remains debased. This condition exists in order that man be subject to the evil *yezer*. But at the end of this era of choice, the soul will be empowered to rise from its low estate to triumph over the body, to purify it in successive stages, until its transformation is so complete that the two may unite as one. At this perfect union, all possible bodily defects will vanish.[11]

Union and completion in *Daniel Deronda* are symbolised by the marriage of Deronda and Mirah. In Jewish mysticism, humans are created as androgynous beings – in a state of perfection. Their descent is marked by a separation into male and female; the rejoining of male with female is a return to perfection, as the following Jewish mystical passage shows, which Joseph Campbell cites in his examination of the hero of mythology:

'Each soul and spirit,' we read in the Hebrew *Zohar*, 'prior to its entering into this world, consists of a male and female united into one being. When it descends on this earth the two parts separate and animate two different bodies. At the time of marriage, the Holy One, Blessed be He, who knows all souls and spirits, unites them again as they were before, and they again constitute one body and one soul, forming as it were the right and left of one individual . . . This union, however, is influenced by the deeds of man and by the way in which he walks. If the man is pure and his conduct is pleasing in the sight of God, he is united with that female part of his soul which was his component part prior to his birth.'[12]

A similar expression of this coming together can be found in the mystical interpretations of Jewish scripture. In the *Zohar* the Torah is seen to resemble a beautiful woman; a scholar who became familiar with the Torah was termed 'perfect', a 'Master', a 'bridegroom of the Torah'.[13] In *Daniel Deronda* Deronda's increasing knowledge of the Jewish scriptures parallels his familiarity with Mirah; his perfection occurs simultaneously with his marriage to Mirah, and he inherits the mantle of 'Master' which Mordecai had received from previous Jewish mystics.

The dual aspect of Judaism is present in Romantic literature, for instance in Blake's *The Marriage of Heaven and Hell*, where sexual love is seen as an attempt to reintegrate the feminine into the masculine psyche.[14] In Eliot's work, male and female uniting to form a whole is a factor which is present not just in *Daniel Deronda*; in *Adam Bede* Dinah and Adam are shown as having the sense that they are complete when they unite:

> What greater thing is there for two human souls, than to feel that they are joined for life – to strengthen each other in all labour, to rest on each other in all sorrow, to minister to each other in all pain, to be one with each other in silent unspeakable memories at the moment of the last parting? (*AB*, p. 532)

This, though, is expressed in humanist terms. The union of Deronda and Mirah is formulated in mystical terms. Before their marriage there is an indication that they are already complete. Gwendolen says of Mirah, '"she is such a complete little person"' (*DD*, p. 480), and Deronda is described as being possessed of both masculine and feminine aspects of character:

> This state of feeling was kept up by the mental balance in Deronda, who was moved by an affectionateness such as we are apt to call feminine, disposing him to yield in ordinary details, while he

had a certain inflexibility of judgment, an independence of opinion, held to be rightfully masculine. (*DD*, p. 271)

The relationship between Mordecai, Mirah and Deronda corresponds to the principles of the *Zohar*: Deronda is the male part, Mirah the female, and Mordecai the Holy One who has the power to unite male and female. After he has finished his work on Deronda – when Deronda is a sufficiently perfect vessel for him – Mordecai encourages the marriage which results in Mirah and Deronda 'meeting so fully in their new consciousness' (*DD*, p. 679). In contrast with the union between the Jewish couple is the disunity between Grandcourt and Gwendolen. Their marriage is destructive because of their inability to synthesise, represented by their barren relationship, which testifies to that tenet of the Kabbalah which states, 'For as long as they remain separate entities, created beings will remain subject to corruption and destruction.'[15]

The soul's journey, after it has descended and bifurcated, is back towards God; the Jewish concept of *gilgul* – transmigration of the soul – is part of this journey. Talmudic as well as kabbalistic lore recognises this: the Kabbalah states that 'Perfection, or emendation, is the offspring, or result of the appropriate ascents upward on the ladder of being',[16] and the Talmud that 'in all nature death is but a transformation; with the soul it is the portal to a new and higher realm'.[17] The journey is central to the Kabbalah which views it as a means to self-improvement: 'Lengthy discussions on various types of metempsychosis (gilgul), or the transmigration of souls, are found in Qabbalah from the very beginning. Metempsychosis was regarded mainly as an opportunity given to a sinner to amend his former sins and rarely as a purgative period.'[18] As we have suggested before, its eventual intention was not to punish, but to give people the opportunity to improve their souls by working towards God, that is, to try to achieve perfection by suppressing the selfish urge and making oneself an instrument of God. In his autobiography, Solomon Maimon equates this with the imitation of God: he says to his friend, Lapidoth, '"Our destination is merely the *attainment of perfection through the knowledge of God and the imitation of his actions*"'[19] (original emphasis).

Maimon's argument is supported by the mystical traditions of the medieval Middle East, which maintained that 'A man will not be perfect unless he recognizes the work of God in the supernal and lower worlds and knows his ways.'[20] According to this tradition, in order to recognise the work of God, it is necessary to know oneself, self-knowledge being the first stage of the soul's purification.[21] This Jewish belief seems to presage the Arnoldian idea of humanity moving towards culture by 'the study and pursuit of perfection',[22] an idea in keeping with the Judaic beliefs expressed by Mordecai: '"I believe in a growth, a passage, and a new unfolding of life whereof the seed is more perfect, more charged with the elements that are pregnant with diviner form"' (*DD*, p. 449). Although this would seem to indicate a movement away from Gnostic tendencies of Romantic creation – and particularly the intention in *Frankenstein* to recreate the human race in the mould of the Noble Savage, which would amount to regeneration through degeneration[23] – when examining Mordecai and Deronda in the context of Jewish mysticism, the movement towards perfection does become linked with Romantic Gnosticism in the combination of innocence (the 'newborn' Deronda) with perfection. Where Eliot's idea in *Daniel Deronda* differs from Romanticism is in movement towards the Divine instead of towards Nature.

The growth of Deronda into a more complete person is supported by kabbalistic and mystic concepts, particularly in his relationship with Mordecai in which there is an intimation of mutual perfection. As we discussed previously, Baker suggests that the form of metempsychosis which unites them is ibbur – placing one's soul alongside the soul within another's body[24] – so that Mordecai's impregnation of Deronda with his soul can be seen therefore as a form of ibbur. Other aspects of the relationship also imply a movement towards the creator through Deronda's spiritual improvement. This rests on the peculiar relationship of the human with the deity since Man is seen as the perfecting agent in the structure of the cosmos.[25] Deronda's role, at an allegorical level, becomes more fully realised: he represents the coming together of the Jewish nation; by extension, and in keeping with Eliot's ideas, he represents the coming together of all nations. As a representation of perfection in Jewish mystical terms, he is a human figure who symbolises a perfect structure in the universe, and is thus linked back to the cosmic proportions of the perfect *Adam Kadmon*, hence back to the pre-Fall paradise which can be associated with the 'Age of Aquarius'.

Various mystical tenets equate movement towards perfection with acquisition of a soul and with a sort of apotheosis. There is 'a distinction between the "speaking soul" . . . and the "rational soul" . . . the latter alone possessing the supernal power which can bring man to perfection and which is identical with the true soul or *neshamah*[26] – that is, the intellectual soul that unites the human with God: '"By corporeality man is an existing being; by spirituality he is a more noble being; and by intellectuality he is a divine and virtuous being."'[27] If by ibbur Mordecai achieves true perfection of soul and by association passes this on to Deronda, then it follows that the joining of Deronda and Mordecai is an enactment of the human becoming divine in terms of Deronda's immediate apotheosis with the creator figure, as well as movement back towards a pre-Fall sense of grace and reconciliation with God. This utopianism is part of the messianic complex of ideas which envisaged a state of perfection as an indication of the new age. Solomon Maimon in his autobiography writes that some of the Hasidim formed a sect which believed that

> The true service of God ... consists in exercises of devotion ... and annihilation of self before God; for they maintain that man, in accordance with his destiny, can reach the highest perfection only when he regards himself, not as a being that exists and works for himself, but as an organ of the Godhead.[28]

The joining of Mordecai and Deronda means that Deronda reaches perfection, and at the same time begins to do the work of Mordecai, his creator and representative of the deity.

It would seem that Christian interpretations of the Messiah are also implied here, in the combination of the human with the divine. In *Romola* a similar mystical combination is made in a Christian context when Dino tells Romola, '"Before I knew the history of the saints, I had a foreshadowing of their ecstasy. For the same truth had penetrated even into pagan philosophy: that it is a bliss within the reach of man to die to mortal needs, and live in the life of God as the unseen Perfectness"' (*Romola*, p. 212). Such connections in *Romola* between Christian and Jewish thought – similar to those encountered in *Daniel Deronda* – can be explained through the contact and exchange between Jewish, Christian and Islamic mysticism from medieval times, partly as a result of the Crusades. Dino's reference to pagan philosophy also has additional significance, since medieval Judaism was influenced by neoplatonic ideas. This surfaced in both the association with magical observances and, more relevant to this context of joining the human with the divine, its advocation of the ascension of the soul until it merged with the 'One'. There was also a revival of Platonism during the Renaissance, which particularly stressed the use of physical beauty to portray and manifest spiritual perfection.

The use of Platonic philosophy by Romantic poets, especially Shelley, was no doubt an influence on this aspect of Eliot's thought. Such Romantic thinking has a strong relationship with Mary Shelley's interpretation of the golem in *Frankenstein* as Cantor suggests when he writes that 'Frankenstein's physical attempt to construct the human frame serves as an image for the goal of Romantic artists: the spiritual regeneration of man.'[29] For the many Romantics who had been influenced by Rousseau, spiritual regeneration was manifested in the concept of the Noble Savage. The desire for a return to a state of grace which incorporates a pre-Fall innocence implies a movement closer to the deity, though ironically, this is in conflict with their gnostic rebellion against the deity and parallels the paradox mentioned at the opening of this chapter. Romanticism comes to be subverted by such insurmountable irony, and faced with this irresolvable contradiction succeeds in deconstructing itself. Eliot acknowledges such ironies – Hans Meyrick, in his letter to Deronda, is shown to be a Romantic ironist[30] – and clearly draws attention to them, not only in *Daniel Deronda* but in *Middlemarch* in the concluding characterisations of Rosamond and Dorothea as discussed above.

It has been mentioned earlier that some Jewish mystical teachings equate the achievement of perfection with apotheosis. Kabbalists trace the completion of an individual back to its creator: 'the offspring must still attain completion. But its completion comes to it from none other than the very origin which gave it birth.'[31] This idea gains emphasis in Jewish folklore. A Hasidic story, 'How the Rabbi of Kelev Freed a Song' begins: 'Every soul comes to the earth to accomplish a purpose, the Rabbi from Kelev taught his Hasidim. It is the duty of every man to strive to "release the holy spark" from the lower creations and bring that spark back to the Godhead.'[32] Eliot expressed a similar belief – she maintained that the ultimate Form was made up of the synthesised connections of its previously disparate parts: 'The highest Form, then, is the highest organism, that is to say, the most varied group of relations bound together in a wholeness which again has the most varied relations with all other phenomena' (*Essays*, p. 433). An associated idea, that the individual is the sum of various parts, is expressed similarly in the Kabbalah and in her writing; the Kabbalah states, 'The completion of creation calls for a synthesis of all its parts to be the point where individual units are all transformed into a single assemblage of complementary forces',[33] and Eliot writes, 'the outline defining the wholeness of the human body is due to a consensus or constant interchange of effects among its parts' (*Essays*, p. 435). Eliot's ideas converge with Judaic belief in the views attributed to Mordecai, which combine completion, the joining of separate parts, and union with a creator:

> for the divine Unity embraced as its consequence the ultimate unity of mankind ... Now, in complete unity a part possesses the whole as the whole possesses every part: and in this way human life is tending toward the image of the Supreme Unity. (*DD*, p. 628)

It is significant that individual completion is inseparable from communal completion. For society to be complete, it is reliant upon the actions of its constituent members. The collective development of society and its intention and movement towards perfection had been implied by Carlyle: 'For not Mankind only, but all that Mankind does or beholds, is in continual growth, re-growth and self-perfecting vitality.'[34] For Carlyle society had to develop new forms if it was to achieve communal completion, as forms based on traditional Christian beliefs were worn out. Carlylean ideas interacting with imagery associated with the golem legend and *Frankenstein* can be seen in Eliot's essay on R. W. Mackay in which she states:

> Our civilization, and, yet more, our religion, are an anomalous blending of lifeless barbarisms, which have descended to us like so many petrifactions from distant ages, with living ideas, the offspring of a true process of development ... for succeeding ages to dream of retaining the spirit along with the forms of the past, is as futile as the embalming of the dead body in the hope that it may one day be resumed by the living soul. (*Essays*, pp. 28–9)

The fact that kabbalistic ideas had some similarities with Comtean thinking would also have appealed to Eliot. Humanity, for Comte, was 'the continuous whole formed by the Beings which converge',[35] and kabbalism saw the world as arising out of the constant interaction of its constituent parts, as it 'consists of a hierarchy of created things, which, when they properly act and react upon each other, together form one organic body'.[36]

Though a complete humanity was the ultimate aim and necessary for the completion of the individual, Eliot believed that initially the individual should be attached to a national centre of consciousness as a step towards completion, and only through the joining together of national centres of consciousness would a complete humanity be possible. In 'The Modern Hep! Hep! Hep!' the narrator states : 'A common humanity is not yet enough to feed the rich blood of various activity which makes a complete man' (*TS*, p. 147). This sentiment is in continuity with that voiced by Mordecai, who sees nationhood as a necessary part of completion: ' "I say that the effect of our separateness will not be completed and have its highest transformation unless our race takes on again the character of a nationality" ' (*DD*, p. 456). What is implied in the words 'highest transformation' is articulated later when he tells Mirah that completion is perfection.[37] Eliot uses the Jewish people as a religio-historic core for the rest of the human race, their development being central to that of the world, and their consolidation being a precursor to universal salvation, a view which is recognised by Jewish commentators on *Daniel Deronda*:

> the ultimately noble Jew makes his appearance in George Eliot's Zionist novel, *Daniel Deronda* (1876). This shows the Jews not merely as worthy of sympathy, but as having within them a spiritual energy through which mankind may one day be saved and made whole.[38]

Here, Deronda comes to represent the idea of a complete individual representing not just a complete nation but a centre of universal perfection. He is the messianic individual assuming macrocosmic proportions, and embodiment of the kabbalistic idea that totality could be manifest in a perfect individual.[39]

6
Science, Pseudo-Science and Transgression

Certainly throughout her life with G. H. Lewes – partly as a result of it – Eliot was in active dialogue with the contemporary scientific debate. Though the theme of the ideal organic society, which runs through her work, may seem remote from science, it has its foundation in scientific theories of natural history and experimental psychology. Underlying such theories one can detect a metaphysic based in Jewish mysticism and its relation to scientific and pseudo-scientific creation and experimentation, aspects of which are discernible throughout the varied worlds created in her novels, from fifteenth-century Florence to contemporary England.

Kabbalistic creation of an artificial person was rooted in alchemical experimentation. Since orthodox Judaism viewed the Kabbalah as occult teachings, alchemical practices associated with it were viewed with suspicion. Alchemy could also be regarded as suspect because of its transgressive nature, but nevertheless it had significant repercussions for scientific experimentation and technological advances. Alchemy was, in some ways, a metaphor for legitimate scientific investigation, since it sought to reveal chemical, physical and biological secrets; but this meant, in turn, that legitimate scientific investigation came to be seen as alchemical – a mysterious and occult practice associated with negative impulses.

In terms of the golem, this perceived association between science and alchemy contained implications of control. Alchemy, as the search for the philosopher's stone, was associated with the Faustian quest: as an attempt to manufacture gold, it suggested a desire for economic mastery; as science it suggested control of nature. Legends of mechanical golems and the connotations of golem as servant suggested control of both labour and the means of production. Thus control of these areas of economy, science and industry are linked with each other and with creativity, and all are associated with transgression. Such interplay can be seen both in Romantic golem literature and in Eliot's fiction where there are further connections with more recent perceptions of scientific and industrial developments, and their consequent effects upon people.

Although at first Faust is characterised as the questing scientist, his role as such is soon abandoned. He represents the questing soul, but to pursue his quest he replaces science with occult practice, and his lesser shade, Wagner, assumes the scientific mantle. Where Faust transgresses religiously, Wagner, through his synthetic creation of human life, does so scientifically. This dichotomy, however, is a simplification of the actions of the two characters. Wagner's creation of Homunculus is a way of squeezing the essence out of Nature and avoiding the natural method of procreation which he considers too lowly:

> Now hope may be fulfilled,
> That hundreds of ingredients, mixed, distilled –
> And mixing is the secret – give us power
> The stuff of human nature to compound.
>
> . . .
>
> The thing in Nature as high mystery prized,
> This our science probed beyond a doubt;
> What Nature by slow process organized,
> That have we grasped, and crystallized it out.
>
> (*Faust* II, p. 100)

Moreover, his action has associations with Romantic notions of biblical creation when Homunculus abandons his creator and seeks existence in the world of Greek myth. In this world Christian understanding of good and evil does not apply, as is indicated by Mephisto's impotence until he infuses himself into the Phorkyads. Faust's decision to resort to the occult leads to his use of kabbalistic ritual, and since Wagner's making a homunculus was part of a pseudo-scientific practice, advocated by the Kabbalah and with its origin in ritual, the paths of Faust and Wagner cross. There is still polarisation of the characters, however. Goethe transposes unsavoury aspects of

Faust on to Wagner, thus ennobling the Faust of the second part and distancing him from the somewhat decadent character of part one. In keeping with the theme of experimentation, Goethe has distilled Faust, making him more pure, the impurities having attached themselves to Wagner.

The history of the Kabbalah is closely connected with the growth of mystical applications of science during medieval times. In his autobiography, Solomon Maimon refers to this aspect of the Kabbalah: 'In the narrower sense of the term, however, Kabbalah means only the tradition of occult sciences.'[1] In the broader sense of the term, he acknowledges that the Kabbalah is synonymous with a Faust-type quest:

> I knew that there was a so-called science, which was somewhat in vogue among Jewish scholars of this district, called the Kabbalah, which professes to enable a man, not merely to satisfy his desire for knowledge, but also to reach an uncommon perfection and closeness of communion with God.[2]

Thus through the desire to reach perfection, it also connects the Faustian search with the philosophy behind transmigration of the soul.

Judaism had its own Faustian figures. The *Encyclopaedia Judaica* states that 'Tubal-Cain, who lived before the Flood, was considered the father of alchemy since it was said of him that he was "the forger of every cutting instrument of brass and iron"'.[3] In Eliot's poem 'The Legend of Jubal' this link is acknowledged. She describes Tubal-Cain as having a Faustian urge which he seeks to assuage by fashioning the world after his own imaginings:

> But strength that still on movement must be fed,
> Inspiring thought of change, devices bred,
> And urged his mind through earth and air to rove
> For force that he could conquer if he strove,
> For lurking forms that might new tasks fulfil
> And yield unwilling to his stronger will.
> Such Tubal-Cain.

(SG, p. 293)

Phrased in this way, the originator of Jewish alchemy belongs to the same mythological type as Hephaestus and Prometheus. It is also said of the Old Testament that 'All the patriarchs, as well as Judah, wore the philosopher's stone on their bodies',[4] this stone being the object of the quest of the mythological hero in Joseph Campbell's *The Hero with a Thousand Faces*, and being specifically associated with Faust.

Other Jewish figures associated with the Kabbalah are historical, from the period that produced the historical Faustus. Yehuda Loew ben Betsal'el of Prague, celebrated as a legendary wonder-worker among Jews and in Czechoslovakia, was deeply involved in both the rabbinic and kabbalistic traditions, and considered mysticism to be the only path to truth. Rabbi Loew united the prominent magical tradition from Central Europe with mystical tradition. Sephardic mysticism also recognised such union in the person of Yosef della Reina:

> An interesting blend of qabbalistic and Neoplatonic theurgies with magical practices was evident in late fifteenth-century Spain where Yosef della Reina, a Faustian figure, attempted to facilitate the arrival of the messianic aeon by means of theurgico-magical practices.[5]

In *The Spanish Gypsy* Eliot placed the magical Kabbalah alongside the mystical Kabbalah in the character of Sephardo. His name and place imply he belongs to the mystical tradition; his occult trappings suggest he has involved himself with the experimental and magical, even down to the philosopher-like stone around his neck:

> here and there
> Show books and phials, stones and instruments.
> In carved dark-oaken chair, unpillowed, sleeps
> Right in the rays of Jupiter a small man,
> In skull-cap bordered close with crisp grey curls,
> And loose black gown showing a neck and breast
> Protected by a dim-green amulet. (*SG*, p. 148)

The formation of the Kabbalah encouraged the development of alchemical ideas from the Talmud, which would link them with pseudo-scientific ideas that had gained prevalence. Some of these were concerned with the synthetic creation of human life. Central to the propagation of these ideas was the family of Kalonymos – suggesting a link with Joseph Kalonymos in *Daniel Deronda* who has the key to Deronda's heritage. The Kalonimides were closely connected to the tradition of esoteric writings, which descended from the oral tradition of eighth-century Italy, in which there were mystical elements:

> This tradition was carried mainly by the Kalonymos family, which was transferred in the ninth century from Italy to Germany by one of the Carolingian emperors. Most of the prominent leaders of the Hasidei Ashkenaz were members of this family... The Kalonymos family represents the central group of the Hasidei Ashkenaz, authors of esoteric literature.[6]

In particular, El'azar of that family edited a text called *Sodei razayya*, a work of esoteric secrets, part of which 'dealt with the manipulation of the Hebrew alphabet and of the divine names to achieve mystical results, including the fabrication of a homunculus or *golem*'.[7] The Hasidim of Germany came to look upon the collection of kabbalistic literature, the *Sefer Yetzirah*, as magical writings connected with traditions about making a golem.[8]

These kabbalistic ideas found their way into Gothic romance in the story of Frankenstein. In his narrative, Frankenstein cites Paracelsus as one of the medieval authors whose mystic ideas excite his own enthusiasm for the creation of life. Paracelsus had based his theories on the use of alchemy in the creation of a homunculus or golem on the Kabbalah.[9] In Mary Shelley's novel, Victor's experimentation and its consequences unite three major elements of the legend of the golem: the idea of resurrection of the dead; mainly Paracelsian ideas concerning the creation of an alchemical man or homunculus; and the creature's tendency to become uncontrollable and destructive, as with the golem of Chelm. Frankenstein attempts the first, having become interested in this by his knowledge of the second, which results in the third.

Besides such a basic use of golem themes, the novel invests the use of electricity in scientific experimentation with the aura of occult mystery that surrounded the alchemy of medieval practitioners. Frankenstein's desire for revivification comes from his studies of Cornelius Agrippa, Paracelsus and Albert Magnus, but instead of employing the mystical means advocated by the alchemists, Mary Shelley substituted more modern scientific, and pseudo-scientific, methods, making Victor use 'electricity and galvanism' (*Frankenstein*, p. 32). The character of Victor Frankenstein is in the Faustian mould, and in his methods of questing, Mary Shelley has united the disparate elements of Goethe's Faust and Wagner. She merged religious with social and scientific transgression and incorporated them into one character. Eliot built into her novels this aspect of the golem and associated themes, with sufficient and appropriate adaptation to highlight contemporary scientific advances and inadequacies, and also – eventually – to reunite them with kabbalistic origins.

That there are numerous references to scientific experimentation in Eliot's work can be attributed as much to her acknowledged debt to other writers, such as Goethe, as to her own interest in and knowledge of such practices, though it is clear that she was well acquainted with Lewes's work in this area. This scientific knowledge coexisted with her intensive and extensive study of Jewish history and culture,[10] with her particular interest in kabbalism, and her own literary representation emerges out of this interaction between science, mysticism and literature. The early nineteenth century produced many 'stories of doomed experimenters and obsessive chemists',[11] and popular short stories of the time involved tales of scientific and artistic transgression which led to self-destruction. The fantasy-tales of German Romantics, such as Hoffmann and von Arnim, and stories by Hawthorne were similarly peopled: 'we find in these stories a gallery or arcade of watchmakers, jewellers, goldsmiths, architects, opticians, and assorted experimenting doctors or professors'.[12] For instance, Aylmer, in Hawthorne's 'The Birthmark', takes on creative characteristics of the proportions of Prometheus or the Biblical deity: 'In his grasp, the veriest clod of earth assumed a soul.'[13] In this tradition the artisan was placed alongside the experimenting scientist. Even in Carlyle it is suggested that the ironically presented tailor requires the dead cast-offs of Nature – evoking the morgues and graveyards frequented by experimenting scientists in literature – in order to supply humans with a living shape:

> While I – good Heaven! – have thatched myself over with the dead fleeces of sheep, the bark of vegetables, the entrails of worms, the hides of oxen or seals, the felt of furred beasts; and walk abroad a moving Rag-screen, overheaped with shreds and tatters raked from the Charnel-house of Nature.[14]

While there seems to be little doubt that Eliot was influenced by the scientific magic of this literature – and refined it by placing it within a world neither magical nor improbably scientific – Nina Auerbach suggests her fiction was affected by a deeper and more personal alchemical process. Auerbach has Eliot forged from the crucible into which Marian Evans had fallen, as part of the myth of the 'fallen woman':

> Hettie and Maggie had to be destroyed for the transformations their sins and sorrows caused, but the transforming power of the myth brought gladness and grace to George Eliot. Whether deliberately, unconsciously, or accidently, she seems to have composed her own life so that its fitful, rudderless, and self-doubting first half was alchemized into gold when the austere bluestocking became the fallen woman ... George Eliot was formed out of the mistakes of Mary Ann Evans.[15]

From the start of her life with Lewes, who has been termed her 'benign Pygmalion',[16] Eliot underwent a literary revivification.

As well as this suggestion that her life underwent this alchemical metamorphosis from within, Eliot was also influenced by pseudo-scientific factors from without. Before she became George Eliot, Marian Evans was interested in practices which posed as sciences. She was temporarily attracted to phrenology, so much so that in 1844 she had a phrenological cast made of her head, and later became acquainted with the Edinburgh phrenologist, George Combe. In the same year she had been mesmerised 'to the degree that she could not open her eyes'.[17] While not persuaded as to the scientific basis for its procedure, she was nevertheless interested enough to follow the exploits of William Gregory, Professor of Chemistry at Edinburgh, whose experiments in mesmerism included recording subjects' supposed clairvoyant ability while in a trance. Both of these interests made their way into *The Lifted Veil*, her short story which most obviously belongs to the early nineteenth-century tradition of fantasy and transgression, where Latimer is subjected to a phrenological study:

> Mr Letherall was a large man in spectacles who, one day took my small head between his large hands, and pressed it here and there in an exploratory, suspicious manner – then placed each of his great thumbs on my temples, and pushed me a little way from him. (*LV*, p. 6)

Latimer's view of Prague is a mesmeric one, pointedly resembling the clairvoyant accounts of European cities given by one of Gregory's subjects.[18]

Clairvoyance, mesmerism and second sight are the devices of Eliot's macabre short story. The themes she deals with – the attempt to extricate oneself from social and spiritual isolation, the equation of blood with violent emotion, and mesmeric trances – have been identified as occupying an important thematic position in *Middlemarch*. Karen Chase claims that 'a motif that runs through the novel and unifies Dorothea's aspirations' is 'the overcoming of boundaries around the self and the release of emotion as a vital fluid. It is almost a case of possession along mesmeric lines.'[19] Thus the experimental science of Meunier and the visionary aspect of Latimer are combined into one theme and one character in her later novel.

As a theme on its own, clairvoyance is a significant one which recurs throughout the novels. It implies an understanding above and beyond that of other humans – the kind of perception attributed to Teufelsdroeckh, when the Editor says of him, 'The secrets of man's Life were laid open to thee; thou sawest into the mystery of the Universe'[20] – or it implies a fatalistic attitude. This latter implication suggests passivity, the willingness to be shaped by events, situations and people; it is characteristic of Adam Bede who 'believed in dreams and prognostics' (*AB*, p. 50). Latimer becomes a more complete version of this fatalistic type, content to live through his visions. Where one might expect Deronda to follow this pattern, the novel's narrator specifically states otherwise: 'Deronda's was not one of those quiveringly-poised natures that lend themselves to second-sight' (*DD*, p. 403).

While Deronda's own character is shown to be thus, there is a certain amount of ambiguity as to just how much credence he would give to second-sight in Mordecai. When he first encounters the realisation of his own vision – Mordecai's resemblance to the type of Master he had imagined – Deronda is sceptical, adding to the ambiguity of his character; he does not completely discount visions, and such is the strength of Mordecai's belief in their prophetic value – regarding Deronda – that he happily transcends his tendency towards doubt, and accepts that visions possess a validity despite their psychological origins.

Prophetic visions themselves can be categorised as either idealistic or warning. Mordecai's belong to the former category. As a man guided by visions, he has predecessors in earlier novels. Felix Holt is guided by dreams: '"Because I am a man who am warmed by visions. Those old stories of visions and dreams guiding men have their truth: we are saved by making the future present to ourselves"' (*FH*, p. 222). Felix is a watchmender – a skilled artisan who is akin to the Faustian overreachers who populate German Romantic fiction,[21] and who himself is shown to possess Faustian ambitions: '"I want to be a demagogue of a new sort"' (*FH*, p. 223), he admits. He aims to change the world so that it is in correspondence with his vision, and though this larger aim fails he succeeds in transferring his visions to Esther, who, like Deronda, had been initially resistant to such idealism: '"I think I am getting that power Felix wished me to have: I shall soon see strong visions"' (*FH*, pp. 384–5).

While Mordecai has this visionary predecessor in Felix, Mordecai is a mystic where Felix is not. In this respect, Mordecai's predecessor is in *Romola*. Dino, Romola's brother, is a religious mystic who is subject to clairvoyant visions. When he tells Romola, '"I have had a vision concerning thee"' (*Romola*, p. 148), it is a combination of foreknowledge and prophetic warning:

> I saw my father's room ... and I saw you ... And at the *leggio* stood a man whose face I could not see ... And my father was faint for want of water and fell to the ground; and the man whose face was a blank loosed thy hand and departed: and as he went I could see his face; and it was the face of the Great Tempter. (*Romola*, pp. 152–3)

As a dream which bodes ill for the future, Dino's prophecy has a similar effect to Maggie Tulliver's dream while on the boat with Stephen Guest, which portends her isolation from Tom (*Mill*, p. 470). Dino's is also a vision of ecstasy, of a type associated with medieval mystic monks, and is characterised by fantastic and dream-like, as well as by apocalyptic images. His vision takes on this character in the following passage:

> And the bronze and marble figures seemed to mock thee and hold out cups of water, and when thou didst grasp them and put them to my father's lips, they turned to parchment. And the bronze and marble figures seemed to turn into demons and snatch my father's body from thee, and the parchments shrivelled up, and blood ran everywhere instead of them, and fire upon the blood, till they all vanished. (*Romola*, p. 153)

Dino's visions suggest a somewhat limited second-sight, concerned mainly with what will affect his family. While it could be argued that Dino's is a Christian mysticism, such aspects of Renaissance Christianity were influenced by Jewish and pagan mysticism. Eliot's use of imagery is certainly suggestive of both pagan automata (those created by Hephaestus) and the *hamor golim*: the message of danger is symbolised by the actions of 'bronze and marble figures' – ornamental figures come to life in the manner of golem-like creatures, which carry portents of menace.

Savonarola, who displays a much more pragmatic mysticism than Dino, has wider-reaching ambitions which are reflected in the greater breadth of his clairvoyant vision:

> While in others the gift of prophecy was very much like a far-thing candle . . . in Savonarola it was like a mighty beacon shining far out for the warning and guidance of men. And to some of the soberest minds the supernatural character of his insight into the future gathered a strong attestation from the peculiar conditions of the age. (*Romola*, p. 198)

However, what is suggested by Savonarola's fate is that the visions exceed the potential of the man, as pragmatism cannot be reconciled with mysticism. Since Felix Holt's prophetic views of the future are also brought to an abrupt and violent end, it would appear that Eliot is warning against the use of visions to shape the future in concrete terms. They are shown in the novels to have an element of worldly wish-fulfilment and thus may bring the visionary to grief. Initially this warning is suggested in *Romola*. The implication in Bardo's question to Tito, '"You see no visions, I trust, my young friend?"' (*Romola*, p. 70), is that they are a suspect method of prediction, which is most strongly borne out in relation to Savonarola. This negative aspect of the visionary recurs in *Daniel Deronda*. Second-sight is associated with Lush – an odious sidekick, rather like Dickens's Littimer in *David Copperfield*: 'Having protested against the marriage, Lush had a second-sight for its evil consequences' (*DD*, p. 267). Gwendolen also comments unfavourably on clairvoyance: '"Clairvoyantes are often wrong: they foresee what is likely"' (*DD*, p. 56).

With Mordecai, however, clairvoyance is seen in a more positive light: '"Second sight" is a flag over disputed ground. But it is a matter of knowledge that there are persons whose yearnings, conceptions – nay, travelled conclusions – continually take the form of images which have a foreshadowing power' (*DD*, p. 404). Significantly, Mordecai's belief that his vision of the ideal Jew has been realised – when he meets Deronda while standing on Blackfriars Bridge – is likened to that of the experimental scientist: 'His exultation was not widely different from that of the experimenter, bending over the first stirrings of change that correspond to what in the fervour of concentrated prevision his thought had foreshadowed' (*DD*, p. 422). It is suggested that the vision is a projection on to and therefore a construction of reality rather than a metaphysical experience of the future in a literal sense though the visionary, of course, has to believe in the reality of his visions. Mordecai's visionary experiences can be linked with the theme Karen Chase has identified in *Middlemarch* and associated with Dorothea's aspirations – as mentioned above – in that they unite scientific experimentation with mesmeric clairvoyance.

The warning Eliot attached to Savonarola's prophetic visions is illuminated if we bear in mind the relation between the visionary and the scientist. The experimental scientist and the visionary both start with an initial idea or hypothesis which requires to be tested against a subsequent set of events. Sally Shuttleworth posits a more active parallel between the scientist – specifically the scientist seeking to explore the secrets of organic life – and the prognosticator:

> Vitalist theories had insisted that organic life was indivisible, and that experimentation was thus impossible; but Comte and Bernard, in breaking through the traditionalist split between vitalism and materialism, laid the foundations of a new experimental science. The role of the scientist was not simply to record and observe, but actively to construct experiments ... [T]he scientist not only creates the appearance of these phenomena, he also actively constructs in his mind's eye the potential results.[22]

The connection between science and vision is first adumbrated in *The Lifted Veil* in the relationship between Meunier and Latimer, who are experimental natural philosophy and clairvoyance united in a 'community of feeling' (*LV*, p. 8). The shortcomings of both are seen when Meunier's experiment uncovers secrets which neither scientist nor visionary had expected: the revivification of Mrs Archer signals simultaneous clarification and horror for both Latimer and Meunier:

Even Meunier looked paralysed; life for that moment ceased to be a scientific problem to him. As for me, this scene seemed to be of one texture with the rest of my existence: horror was my familiar, and this new revelation was only like an old pain recurring with new circumstances. (*LV*, p. 42)

This indicates that experimentation does not always go as planned – it can recoil upon the scientist. So it is for visionaries such as Savonarola and Felix Holt, who suffer in consequence. The initial vision, like the scientist's hypothesis, may not always be fulfilled in reality. This is not necessarily because reality is recalcitrant; the visions may be suspect in the first place. Vision also cannot be dissociated from character: Lydgate's failure as a scientist is not unconnected with his 'spots of commonness'; he is singularly lacking in any visionary capacity in his life outside science.

Providing excessive expectations are not invested in them, seeing visions and having clairvoyant experiences are unlikely to be harmful. They suggest mysticism rather than transgression. Mordecai's visions are riskier, however, since they entail a transgression from orthodox Judaism into the Kabbalah, which invokes the occult. Because he has been unable to find in reality (before he meets Deronda) the ideal vessel for his vision, he turns to contemplation of the unorthodox, which involves dabbling with, even exceeding the limits of, the Kabbalah: 'and hence it was that his imagination had constructed another man who would be something more ample than the second soul bestowed, according to the notion of the Cabbalists, to help out the insufficient first' (*DD*, p. 406). The vision is of another human: a human being constructed. Kabbalistic pseudo-science becomes allied to kabbalistic mysticism in the realisation of Mordecai's vision.

Scientific transgression of the sort associated with Faust and Frankenstein can be easily identified in Eliot's fiction. George Levine places this sort of breaking of boundaries within an archetypal tradition:

[Victor] is one of the first in a long line of fictional overreachers, of characters who seem to act out the myth of Faust in modern dress, and who transport it from the world of mystery and miracle to the commonplace ... Frankenstein is the indirect father of lesser, more humanly recognizable figures, like Becky Sharp or

Pip or Lydgate, who reject the conventional limits imposed upon them by society and who are punished, more or less, for their troubles.[23]

Lydgate is most obviously an heir to this tradition because he is a questing scientist (Pip, as discussed in a previous chapter, is better identified with the created than with the creator). From one point of view he is a medical innovator who, as Brooke puts it, '"has lots of ideas, quite new, about ventilation and diet, that sort of thing"' (*Middlemarch*, p. 90). For the people of Middlemarch, his new ideas are in opposition to accepted tradition: '"Hang it, do you think that is quite sound? – upsetting the old treatment, which has made Englishmen what they are?"' (*Middlemarch*, p. 91). As a medical practitioner, his attack upon contemporary medical practice is as condemning as any accusation of unethical experimentation. That Lydgate's transgression is intended to be beneficial to humanity is intrinsic to the nineteenth-century adaptation of the mythical archetype of the questing scientist: 'Faust has become Prometheanized; and in the nineteenth-century world of industrial development, transgression and damnation have become identified less with devilry than with production.'[24] Felix Holt voices this view, seeing the type of thinking which results in machines and mechanism – that which the Luddites saw as a threat – as a means of furthering human progress:

The men who have had true thoughts about water, and what it will do when it is turned into steam and under all sorts of circumstances, have made themselves a great power in the world: they are turning the wheels of engines that will help to change most things. (*FH*, p. 248)

But with Felix Holt and Lydgate, what inhibits beneficial transgression is the limited perception of the would-be transgressor.

Viewed with suspicion by his colleagues because he refuses to be constrained by professional taboos, Lydgate is also distrusted by people in Middlemarch generally, partly for the same reason but predominantly because his researches involve experimentation. The suspicion surrounding creative experimentation – of which Eliot was aware, some such suspicion having been directed at Lewes during his scientific studies – can be traced back to alchemy and the occult significance attached to it.[25] Lydgate is seen as a necromancer. What people feared about medieval magic – manipulation of the living and the dead – they now feared in science.

The late eighteenth and early nineteenth centuries saw a literary change take place as medieval alchemy with its associations with mystery and the occult was replaced by scientific experimentation. It is significant that Victor Frankenstein and Lydgate have similar fundamental aims: Victor wants to '"pioneer a new way, explore unknown powers, and unfold to the world the deepest mysteries of creation"' (*Frankenstein*, p. 40); Lydgate aims to find 'the primitive tissue' (*Middlemarch*, p. 147) – a modest term for an ambitious task. Ironically the modern scientist is not only linked with Frankenstein but shares the metaphysic of Casaubon, the religious idealist who seeks the 'Key to all Mythologies'. While Casaubon is looking for the original creation myth from which all other myths have evolved or devolved, Lydgate applies similar thinking to science in seeking 'to demonstrate the homogeneous origin of all the tissues' (*Middlemarch*, p. 449). The connection with alchemy is suggested when he engages in experiments involving galvanism: 'when he was studying in Paris . . . he was occupied with some galvanic experiments' (*Middlemarch*, p. 149). The narrator is even more explicit about the relationship between science and alchemy in a comment on the great chemist Lavoisier: 'Doubtless a vigorous error vigorously pursued has kept the embryos of truth a-breathing: the quest of gold being at the same time a questioning of substances, the body of chemistry is prepared for its soul, and Lavoisier is born' (*Middlemarch*, p. 472). The latter image links alchemy with the body waiting for a soul – a kabbalistic reference and an essential element of the golem legend. Since Lavoisier, the natural philosopher, is associated with the body awaiting a soul, the division between the scientist as creator and creation is broken down, Lavoisier as scientist being golem-like since the state of science at any given time creates the conditions that necessarily will generate such an individual. Thus both creator and creation are versions of the golem.

Eliot sees this aspect of science as having a metaphoric application to the nineteenth century at a more general level: just as the workforce and the mechanics of industry both came to be associated with the golem, so did the practitioner and object of scientific investigation. The processes of biological research and industrial expansion are homologous. Shuttleworth, in writing about the position of humans in nineteenth-century science, quotes from Walter Buckley: 'Man was regarded as a physical object, a kind of elaborate machine, whose actions and psychic processes could be analyzed in terms of the principles of mechanics.'[26] Both Lewes and Herbert Spencer had followed Comte in applying scientific theories to society and humans as physiological constructs alike.[27] Thus science and industry – both separately and together – could be seen as part of a process of dehumanisation in that human sensibilities and emotions were left out of account. This linked science and industry with the former view of magical circumvention of nature by alchemical means: as finally entailing a contempt for life itself.

It is an association with pseudo-scientific magical practices that leads to this ultimate accusation against Lydgate. One of the reasons that Lydgate's experiments are viewed with suspicion is the contemporary preoccupation with charlatanism and quackery. An example of such practice is directly alluded to in *Middlemarch*: 'In those days the world was agitated about the wondrous doings of Mr St John Long, "noblemen and gentlemen" attesting his extraction of a fluid like mercury from the temples of a patient' (*Middlemarch*, p. 448). Eliot gives her own fictional example of pseudo-scientific practices in *The Lifted Veil* in Meunier's intention to experiment on Mrs Archer: '"I want to make an experiment on this woman, if you will give me permission . . . I want to try the effect of transfusing blood into her arteries after the heart has ceased to beat for some minutes"' (*LV*, p. 39). The people of Middlemarch have only a vague and generalised idea of the nature of Lydgate's research. This ignorance is what leads to him being seen as something of a charlatan. The Middlemarch populace is not capable of distinguishing science from magic: what cannot be explained in rational terms, and is not religion, is magic and ought not to be trusted. Lydgate is thus not trusted: '"if you like him to try experiments on your hospital patients, and kill a few people for charity, I have no objection. But I am not going to hand money out of my purse to have experiments tried on me"' (*Middlemarch*, p. 91). The events of the novel begin at the same time that Burke and Hare achieved infamy for their notorious exploits, and the medical profession as a whole was tainted – in the eyes of the ignorant – by the post-mortem investigations that instigated the actions of such 'resurrection men'. Lydgate is associated with these doctors:

> Mrs Dollop became more and more convinced by her own asseveration, that Dr Lydgate meant to let the people die in the Hospital, if not to poison them, for the sake of cutting them up

without saying by your leave or with your leave; for it was a known 'fac' that he had wanted to cut up Mrs Goby . . . but there was a prevalent feeling in her audience that her opinion was a bulwark, and that if it were overthrown there would be no limits to the cutting-up of bodies, as had been well seen in Burke and Hare with their pitch-plaisters – such a hanging-business as that was not wanted in Middlemarch! (*Middlemarch*, p. 436)

Thus Lydgate's experimentation leads to monstrous allegations that he practises vivisection and might even resort to murder to serve his purposes.

Mary Shelley had modified golem creation in *Frankenstein*. The golems of Chelm and Prague had been made from mud and clay, but Victor Frankenstein's golem is reanimated tissue. His initial intention had been to control his creation; Lydgate is perceived in *Middlemarch* as attempting to shape people for his own ends. This perception makes the people of Middlemarch fear him not only for the crimes they fancy he does, but because they think he will be able to control them while they are still living.

This aspect of *Middlemarch* – with Lydgate seen as a potential controller by ignorant people fearful of being controlled – places Lydgate firmly within the myth of monstrosity that pervaded the nineteenth century and suggests a link between science and industrialism. Predominant in the nineteenth-century fear of monstrosity is the idea that what is created is potentially dangerous – the warning behind the golem of Chelm and 'The Sorcerer's Apprentice'. As Cantor puts it, 'while creativity can be exhilarating, it can also be dangerous, and passes over easily into destructiveness'.[28] This point of view was influenced by social and economic developments where previously powerless workers could now exert control – in a golem-like manner – over their former controllers, since they operated the industrial means of production, though, as we have mentioned earlier, the means of production also had the potential to become a type of golem that was a threat to workers. Industrialisation thus destabilised the relation between controller and controlled. As Baldick writes, the 'running wild of the huge productive energies of the nineteenth century, particularly in the unprecedented conquests of nature going forward in Britain and America, is a recurrent nightmare for the mid-century writer.'[29]

Middlemarch parallels the fear of Lydgate's anatomical research with the fear of new industrial developments. References to the

Luddism of machine-breaking and to the violent opposition to railways which is interrupted by Caleb Garth represent worries that the growth of technology and industry will ultimately constitute a threat to humanity. At the forefront of the translation of this fear into twentieth-century science fiction was Karel Capek's golem story, *R.U.R.*, which coined the word 'robot'. Eliot anticipated this concern about humanity being superseded by machines in her last published work, *Impressions of Theophrastus Such*, in the essay 'Shadows of the Coming Race':

> Am I already in the shadow of the Coming Race? and will the creatures who are to transcend and finally supersede us be steely organisms, giving out the effluvia of the laboratory, and performing with infallible exactness more than everything that we have performed with a slovenly approximateness and self-defeating inaccuracy? (*TS*, p. 138)

But this theme was one which she had already treated in various ways in her novels. Nancy Lammeter's attitude towards adopted children in *Silas Marner* possesses such connotations. She cannot accept them because they are not a natural creation: 'the adopted child, she was convinced, would never turn out well, and would be a curse to those who had wilfully and rebelliously sought what it was clear that, for some high reason, they were better without' (*SM*, p. 151). Transgression is also implied here. Nancy fears that an 'unnatural' orphan, obtained through a transgressive rebellion against what God has ordained, will react against its unnatural parents. In *The Mill on the Floss* golem imagery is used to suggest that even a mill can resemble a machine-like monster that can take on a life of its own beyond the control of humans: '. . . the great vertical millstones with their scythe-like arms, roaring and grinding and carefully sweeping as if an informing soul were in them' (*Mill*, p. 118). *Felix Holt* depicts the rural proletariat as golem-like when it collectively turns on its masters, breaking free of the control of those, such as Felix Holt, who believe they can channel its power for particular ends. As we mentioned in the Introduction, the idea of the golem as servant was derived from the mechanical golem. Eliot's description of the millstones as animated machinery is related to the mechanical golem while her depiction of the mass of workers in *Felix Holt* relates to the golem as servant.

Associated with the investment of mechanical objects with souls is the golemish effect of industrialisation and the fear that it could lead to a dehumanisation of society. This danger is implied in 'The Legend of Jubal'. Eliot's description of the feats and accomplishments of Tubal-Cain contains a warning both alchemical and economic:

> Thus to mixed ends wrought Tubal; and they say,
> Some things he made have lasted to this day;
> As, thirty silver pieces that were found
> By Noah's children buried in the ground.
> He made them from mere hunger of device,
> Those small white discs; but they became the price
> The traitor Judas sold his master for;
> And men still handling them in peace and war
> Catch foul disease, that comes as appetite,
> And lurks and clings as withering damning blight.
>
> (*SG*, p. 296)

Capital, and the means of accruing it, are shown to result in debilitude and death. Another poem, 'A College Breakfast-Party', asserts that if economics achieves control over human beings the result will be regression to an animal-like state – another form of dehumanisation:

> Do Boards and dirty-handed millionaires
> Govern the planetary system? – sway
> The pressure of the Universe? – decide
> That man henceforth shall retrogress to ape,
> Emptied of every sympathetic thrill
> The All has wrought in him?
>
> (*SG*, p. 433)

Eliot was of course writing at a time when industrialism had created fundamental social and economic change. This had led to a struggle for control over the means of production, both mechanical and human, with socialism emerging to challenge capitalism and the domination of the bourgeoisie, Robert Owen's co-operative experiment being an obvious example of a proto-socialist form of industrial organisation. For Eliot, associating industry with alchemy was a way of warning against both the dangers it could present to society and the monstrous behaviour it could generate, just as Mary

Shelley had warned against the dangers of scientific experimentation by drawing attention to the links between science and alchemy. Both industry and science are attempts at achieving control, a control that is at its root economic. Thus Lydgate's view of himself as an outsider in Middlemarch, pursuing scientific truth for its own sake, may be deluded since he may have more in common with Middlemarch and its bourgeois industrialists than he thinks.

The question of control was central, not merely because of the fear that it could create social struggle on a scale hitherto unknown; it was also feared that the controllers of machinery could lose their souls and become more like the inanimate things they used. Eliot was not alone in her concern about this. Matthew Arnold came to see industrialism as a machine which, if misused, would oppose culture.[30] But it was Carlyle who took the most extreme view:

> For Carlyle the nineteenth century was to be defined not just as the Machine Age – as if technology were the end of the problem – but more fully as a Galvanic world in which the inward sanctuary of organic human authenticity has been abandoned to the rule of the corpse.[31]

In *Sartor Resartus* industry is seen as the means whereby people lose their humanity:

> And now the Genius of Mechanism smothers him worse than any Nightmare did; till the Soul is nigh choked out of him, and only a kind of Digestive Mechanic life remains. In Earth and in Heaven he can see nothing but Mechanism; has fear for nothing else, hope in nothing else: the world would indeed grind him to pieces.[32]

This reduction of humanity is also commented upon in *Impressions of Theophrastus Such*, but it is viewed from a different angle. In 'Shadows of the Coming Race', machines are seen as being elevated to the status of living beings. More than being anthropomorphised, they are animated after the manner of mechanical golems:

> What I would ask you is, to show me why, since each new invention casts a new light along the pathway of discovery, and each new combination or structure brings into play more conditions than its inventor foresaw, there should not at length be a machine

of such high mechanical and chemical powers that it would find and assimilate the material to supply its own waste, and then by a further evolution of internal molecular movements reproduce itself by some process of fission or budding. (*TS*, pp. 140–1)

By elevating machines to the level of living beings, the beings they will supplant – humans – are simultaneously reduced to the merely mechanical. Eliot's ironic comment on the imaginative excesses to which the power of machines can lead contains an implicit understanding of the golem as machine: it can take control of itself and its actions, and ultimately exert control over others.

Following on from Carlyle's warning there is a question which is also relevant to the golem legend. He ends the above passage by asking, 'but cannot he fathom the Doctrine of Motives, and cunningly compute these, and mechanise them to grind the other way?'[33] The controller loses control, then regains it, turning the destructive influences back on the creature. Simon Magus reduces his golem to air by reversing the transformations he used to make it; the golem is destroyed by the manipulation of the letters on its forehead or removal of the parchment which gave it life. The rabbi uses the mechanics of creation to bring the golem to death. *Romola* provides an example of such a reversal when Tito is pursued and destroyed by his creator, Baldassarre.

The aspect of dehumanisation still remained, however. Human attempts at creation resulted in flawed and unnatural products, it was assumed, so that human productivity could be a movement away from humanity. With the mass production of the Industrial Revolution, the distance between creator and product lessened, and the creator became identified less with the human and more with lifeless mechanism, dead material, and consequently the inhuman products of industry. Lydgate's medical practice is not dissociated from this. Although people in the town are irrational in their fear that he may turn them into corpses to serve his own purposes, this fear is not without some philosophical foundation, since progress in medical science was dependent on mechanising the body, that is, seeing it as a machine that can be understood through dissection, concentrating on the part rather than the whole, viewing the human being as purely material and discarding metaphysical concepts such as the soul. It could thus be claimed that the price of medical progress would be dehumanisation unless scientists proceeded with great human tact, a quality Lydgate signally lacks.

Daniel Deronda reveals a different form of dehumanisation, Grandcourt in particular being the major dehumanising influence. The imagery in the following passage, when Gwendolen considers refusing his offer of marriage, should be noted: 'She would have expressed her resolve as before; but it was a form out of which the blood had been sucked – no more a part of quivering life than the "God's will be done" of one who is eagerly watching chances' (*DD*, p. 252). The reference is of course to vampirism, but in this, Eliot's 'Jewish' novel, and for one who had read Josephus, the equation of blood and soul is significant as, indeed, it is in *The Lifted Veil*, in which the animating essence of blood is a feature. Also included in this passage is the implication that gambling and chance are also dehumanising in their effect. The opening scene of *Daniel Deronda*, with Gwendolen at the gaming table, suggests the same inhuman state: 'There was deep stillness, broken only by a light rattle, a light chink, a small sweeping sound, and an occasional monotone in French, such as might be expected to issue from an ingeniously constructed automaton' (*DD*, p. 3). Chance and Grandcourt are already identified with the 'Spirit of Negation' and the negative impulse. Here negativity is extended by use of the golem as a metaphor for dehumanisation. Vampirism also recurs in the manner in which Gwendolen regards Mrs Glasher: '"Why did you put your fangs into me and not into him?"' (*DD*, p. 384). In having the blood sucked out of her, she loses her soul and therefore her humanity, and becomes a golem-like creature.

In *Felix Holt* dehumanisation is also associated with the mechanical. Initially it is used with reference to Harold's outlook which tends to see others as mechanisms, so much so that a faithful family retainer is reduced to the level of an automaton: '"I'll have old Hickes. He was a neat little machine of a butler; his words used to come like the clicks of an engine. He must be an old machine now, though"' (*FH*, p. 21). Harold's general attitude is thus encapsulated: other people are machines which he intends to set in motion, or puppets he intends to manipulate. By regarding others as machine-like, he himself becomes a mechanical man, as the epigraph to Chapter 14 suggests:

> This man's metallic; at a sudden blow
> His soul rings hard. I cannot lay my palm,
> Trembling with life, upon that jointed brass.

I shudder at the cold unanswering touch;
But if it press me in response, I'm bruised.

(*FH*, p. 131)

The unintentional harm caused by the metallic man is not a new image in Eliot's fiction. It had been used in *The Mill on the Floss* in the supposed animosity of Wakem to Tulliver which is explained in terms of the imagined animosity of a machine:

> It is still possible to believe that the attorney was not more guilty towards him, than an ingenious machine, which performs its work with much regularity, is guilty towards the rash man who, venturing too near it, is caught up by some fly-wheel or other, and suddenly converted into unexpected mince-meat. (*Mill*, p. 247)

Attributing human emotions and reason to the movements of an object or the behaviour of a non-human belongs to monstrosity in nineteenth-century fiction: Ahab in *Moby-Dick* – which has been described as a Frankensteinian novel[34] – sees human rationality and animosity behind the behaviour of the whale, whereas it is a displaced vehicle for his own emotions. The malice which Tulliver perceives in Wakem has a similar quality: it is the malice with which an inanimate machine is invested in order to satisfy the imagination of those it affects. An evil potential is invented which replaces the actual innocence or ignorance of a mechanical function in order to justify, in Tulliver's case, the irresponsibility of the person who is injured. Wakem, in fulfilling the function of the law, is not carrying out a deliberate vendetta against Tulliver, but the latter character, in being worsted, chooses to see it in that way.

Investing inanimate objects with life is a powerful golemish theme, and it is a recurrent one in Eliot's fiction as can be seen from examining particular images. Religious revivification is implied in Savonarola's intention to regenerate the Church:

> sometimes he saw himself taking a glorious part in that revolt, sending forth a voice that would be heard through all Christendom, and making the dead body of the Church tremble into new life, as the body of Lazarus trembled when the Divine voice pierced the sepulchre. (*Romola*, p. 415)

Savonarola's messianic view of himself adds to the golem aspect of this dream: the reanimation of the golem of Prague was said to be a simultaneous occurrence with the arrival of the Messiah. Since the messianic millennium is supposed to herald the return of Jews to their homeland, the Christian dream of Savonarola becomes linked with the Zionist dream of Mordecai and Deronda. The reanimation theme is also enacted by Romola. Her actions during the plague epidemic earn her the title 'Madonna', and she is thus associated with the Messiah. It is she who brings Baldassarre back to life: '"He was lying lifeless in the street from starvation . . . I revived him with bread and wine"' (*Romola*, p. 392). Not only does she raise Baldassarre, but to do so she uses the food and drink of the Last Supper – a specific reference to Christ as Messiah. The character she brings back to life is the 'deed' returning to haunt Tito; she is reanimating a golem who will accelerate Tito's destruction – the creator who will destroy the wayward creature.

Although it is not until *Middlemarch* that revivification and reanimation constitute a major theme as part of Eliot's concern with science and pseudo-science and their metaphoric implications, they are mentioned throughout the novels.[35] In *Silas Marner*, Marner is seen as a revivified corpse: 'and it was soon clear to the Raveloe lasses that he would never urge one of them to accept him against her will – quite as if he had heard them declare that they would never marry a dead man come to life again' (*SM*, p. 6). Grandcourt is given the air of a corpse, whom people attempt to galvanise: 'Lady Flora, coming back charged with news about Miss Harleth, saw no good reason why she should not try whether she could electrify Mr Grandcourt by mentioning it to him at table' (*DD*, p. 133). This may not seem an overt reference, but the mention of electrification in application to Grandcourt – a character presented as being almost completely lacking in animation – suggests such connotations. Similar imagery is used in relation to Gwendolen when she thinks that by turning down Grandcourt she will be exercising control over her own life and his: 'Meanwhile, the thought that he was coming to be refused was inspiriting: she had the white reins in her hands again; there was a new current in her frame, reviving her from the beaten-down consciousness in which she had been left by the interview with Klesmer' (*DD*, pp. 253–4).

In contrast with Gwendolen's spiritual death by marriage to Grandcourt – so that she has 'visited the spirit world' (*DD*, p. 892) – is the revivifying influence of Deronda on her. She is brought back to life by the attention of Deronda: 'Mingled emotions streamed through her frame with a strength that seemed the beginning of a new existence, having some new powers or other which stirred in her vaguely' (*DD*, p. 659). This is indicative of the new role of Deronda as creator, who transcends the division between Judaism and Christianity, and whom Gwendolen identifies with her revived self: 'She identified him with "the struggling regenerative process in her which had begun with his action' (*DD*, p. 660). He has become a messianic creator who is able to invest life into the spiritually inanimate.

The presentation of the golem theme, with a new human being built out of parts of old ones, is suggested in a comment of Maggie in *The Mill on the Floss*: '"It's foolish work ... tearing things to pieces to sew 'em together again"' (*Mill*, p. 14). This seems hardly like the golem when viewed in its immediate context – Maggie is talking about a patchwork quilt. When viewed in a larger context it contains elements of Carlyle which are open to golemish interpretation: the comparison of the threads and cloths which make up the outer shell of clothing with the parts that are joined together to constitute the human form. A more pointed Carlylean reference is made in *Middlemarch* in connection with Lydgate's research: 'have not these structures some common basis from which they have all started, as your sarsnet, gauze, net, satin and velvet from the raw cocoon?' (*Middlemarch*, p. 146). Primal human tissue is here likened to the primal element of cloth. The idea of one thing formed out of bits of other things is, moreover, not just golemish in its implications, but also Faustian. Mephisto refers to the Lemures as ill-constructed creatures:

> Cobbled from sinew, bone, and skin,
> You patched-up, shambling, demi-creatures.
>
> (*Faust* II, p. 267)

Aunt Pullet's description of Philip as 'mismade' (*Mill*, p. 339) is a connected image. It suggests a flawed attempt at creation, a badly constructed individual instead of God's highest creation.

In *Middlemarch* references to revivification have more significance. These are surrounded by allusions to electricity, often inducing restoration to life: Will and Dorothea in particular are susceptible to feeling the thrill of – or something like – electric shocks; Fred is brought back to life by the magnanimous gesture of Farebrother: 'Some one highly susceptible to the contemplation of a fine act has said, that it produces a sort of regenerating shudder through the frame, and makes one feel ready to begin a new life. A good degree of that effect was just then present in Fred Vincy' (*Middlemarch*, p. 728). When Bulstrode is forced to look after Raffles, the description contains direct allusion to *Frankenstein*:

> This delicate-looking man, himself nervously perturbed, found the needed stimulus in his strenuous circumstances, and through that difficult night and morning, while he had the air of an animated corpse returned to movement without warmth, holding the mastery by its chill impassibility, his mind was intensely at work thinking of what he had to guard against and what would bring him security. (*Middlemarch*, p. 692)

Subsequent events in the novel bear out the golem – of Chelm – qualities of this passage. At this point in *Middlemarch* Lydgate, who is already regarded as having the 'power of resuscitating persons as good as dead' (*Middlemarch*, p. 436), like the Frankensteinian creator, finds that the corpse returned to life has become the controller, with Lydgate having to turn to Bulstrode to overcome his financial difficulties. The subsequent death of Raffles is significant in this context because Lydgate's disgrace is primarily the result of his association in the matter with Bulstrode, the 'animated corpse', and Lydgate is perceived as a scientific experimenter eager, as Mrs Dollop puts it, '"for cutting up everybody before the breath was well out o' their body"' (*Middlemarch*, p. 712).

That Lydgate's downfall is related to what is seen as his meddling in science emphasises the fear of such investigation by the middle-marchers of industrial England. The irony is, it is not his engagement in medical experimentation that brings about Raffles's death. At the time that he accepts defeat by Middlemarch, he has virtually ceased to be a questing scientist and has abandoned his previous ideals. The people of Middlemarch fear him because they see him as someone who can use science to exercise control over them, and thus to dehumanise them; it is a perceived fear at the level of the imagination. There is little danger of his gaining that dehumanising power through science, but Middlemarch is right to see Lydgate as one who desires to control people. He initially regards Rosamond as merely an ornament who should be subject to his will. Her resistance to his control by the exercise of her will parallels Middlemarch's resistance to his scientific aims. There may be perversity in this resistance, but the fault is partly Lydgate's for failing to humanise science for Middlemarchers, and for failing to appreciate his wife's 'equivalent centre of self' (*Middlemarch*, p. 208).

7
Investing Form with Essence

Related to the idea of inspiriting a being by way of supposedly scientific methods is the concept of endowing something with a soul or essence. But this too, it is implied, is the source of jealousy, as can be seen in gnostic interpretations of biblical creation:

> The hour at which God created Adam's soul has been much disputed: whether at dawn on the Sixth Day (his body being made a little later), or whether on the Fifth Day before the appearance of sea-beasts; or whether this precious thing was the very first of God's handiworks. Some held that the creation of Adam's inert clod preceded not only his soul, but even Light itself. They say that God, when about to breathe His spirit into it, paused and reminded Himself: 'If I let Man live and stand up at once, it may later be claimed that he shared My task... He must stay as a clod until I have done!' At dusk on the sixth day, therefore, the ministering angels asked: 'Lord of the Universe, why have You not yet created Man?' He made answer: 'Man is already created, and lacks only life.' Then God breathed life into the clod, Adam rose to his feet, and the work of creation ended.[1]

The inspiriting of a being, then, is also the cause of some creative tension: God's intention to complete the ultimate creation is set against jealousy of the creature's potential.

According to Josephus, however, the soul is identified with the blood.[2] Hence there is specific Judaic significance in Meunier's act, in *The Lifted Veil*, of infusing the dead maid's body with his own blood. He is investing the body with a new soul – with his soul. The tension, therefore, arises from incompatibility of the soul and its vehicle. In Jewish myth golem refers to more than one state of being: it can be the absence of shape or form to matter or substance; it can also be the lack of a guiding spirit or soul within a formed individual. It is tempting to believe that Eliot may have thought of her fiction in analogous terms in that it exploited a similar tension between soul and vehicle for artistic purposes. Though well aware of the power of demythologisation in modern approaches to biblical exegesis, as in the work of Strauss, her own fiction suggests that she valued the power of myth and desired to get beyond the limiting conception of fiction in the nineteenth century in which myth and realism are seen as incompatible, since for her both were necessary if prose fiction were to be elevated into an art form comparable with epic poetry or classical tragedy. Her fiction, therefore, can be seen as having an inspiriting aspect in that a mythic 'essence' under-lies the narrative and exists in creative tension with the vehicle of that narrative, realism; or in narratological terms, a mythic dimension is incorporated into narrative at the level of 'discourse' – literary organisation and expression – creating layers of implication that go beyond the 'realistic' meanings which are present at the level of 'story'.

Kabbalistic thought took lack of essence or soul as a sign of im-perfection. The Kabbalah refers to ten divine aspects which make a supernatural man. These aspects are: thought; understanding; wisdom; stern judgement; greatness/mercy; grandness; splendour; eternity; foundation; and kingdom.[3] Without all of these aspects, the super-natural man, who represents the bridge to God, is incomplete. Since the soul consists of various aspects, to lack any one which en-hances moral judgement and understanding is a serious limitation. Carlyle is aware of this idea: 'Can a great soul be possible without a conscience in it, the essence of all souls, great or small?'[4] To have no soul is to be undeveloped and crude, and this is as relevant to the community as it is to the individual. As an example, Carlyle cites Scotland before the reforming zeal of Knox: 'It is a country as yet without a soul; nothing developed in it but what is rude, external, semi-animal.'[5]

For Eliot, to have no soul is to be merely mechanical, an automa-ton. In her essays it is striking that she often uses the word 'animate' in a positive sense and creates an implicit opposition with that which functions only mechanically or automatically. The theology of Dr Cumming is attacked for not being 'animated . . . by the spirit of fidelity to his fellow men' (*Essays*, p. 186); in contrast to Cumming's mechanistic doctrine she values the idea of a God 'who will pour new life into our too languid love' (*Essays*, p. 188). Reviewing Tennyson's *Maud*, she regrets that 'the finest sentiments that animate his other poems are entirely absent' (*Essays*, p. 92). Carlyle is a major force because of his power to animate: 'He does not, perhaps, convince you, but he strikes you, undeceives you, animates you' (*Essays*, p. 213). Harriet Beecher Stowe's *Dred* is praised for showing that 'Hebraic Christianity is still a reality, still an animating belief' (*Essays*, p. 327). In 'Leaves from a Note-Book' an author for her is 'remarkable' and contributes to 'the spiritual wealth of mankind' if the following question can be answered affirmatively: 'Did he animate long-known but neglected truths with new vigour...?' (*Essays*, p. 442). In contrast the mechanistic is treated negatively. In an essay on Heine she selects a passage for praise that contains the following:

> The mass – the English blockheads, God forgive me! – are hateful to me in my inmost soul; and I often regard them not at all as my fellow men, but as miserable automata – machines, whose motive power is egoism. In these moods, it seems to me as if I heard the whizzing wheel-work by which they think, feel, reckon, digest, and pray: their praying, their mechanical church-going ... (*Essays*, p. 211).

In her essay on W. H. Riehl, she refers to 'the evils resulting from a bureaucratic system which governs by an indiscriminating, dead mechanism' (*Essays*, p. 284). While Dr Cumming views his fellow-men 'as automata through whom Satan plays his game upon earth' (*Essays*, p. 180), for her 'the great end of the Gospel is not merely the saving but the educating of men's souls' (*Essays*, p. 181).

It is apparent that the acquisition of a soul is a matter of achieving some balance. It signals development into a more complete individual or a more complete society (or a more complete artistic form), and hence is a sign of progress. Too much development in the wrong area, however, will have a dehumanising effect. As is implied in Eliot's ideas on artistic form and her emphasis on animation, the natural is not dissociated from the soul, but is an essential part of it. In *Sartor Resartus*, a society which moves closer and closer to mechanised industrialism becomes artificial, so that it is threatened with a disharmony that leads to soullessness. Eliot exploits such ideas in her work. For example, the following passage from *Silas Marner*, which concerns Raveloe's response to Silas's cataleptic fits, suggests that the soul can become over-developed and thus separated from the body:

> But there might be such a thing as a man's soul being loose from his body, and going out and in, like a bird out of its nest and back; and that was how folks got over-wise, for they went to school in this shell-less state to those who could teach them more than their neighbours could learn with their five senses and the parson. (*SM*, p. 7)

An example from the opposite end of the social spectrum is Grandcourt, a man who takes notions of class and property to such a degree that he becomes almost lifeless: 'it was perhaps not possible for a breathing man wide awake to look less animated' (*DD*, p. 91). Like Browning's Duke in 'My Last Duchess' his sense of class position and status is so rigid that it has drained him of any natural spontaneity and leads him to crush it in others.

Though the acquisition of a soul or essence is necessary for a truly human identity, to develop the soul to such a degree that one is cut off completely from natural innocence and spontaneity is dangerous. As Cantor puts it: 'In Eden, man is morally innocent and happy, but comparatively ignorant and undeveloped in his faculties.'[6] Yet to gain knowledge and understanding one must forsake innocence and risk loss of a natural happiness. Eliot, like the Romantics, exploits these tensions to serve her artistic purposes. For example, in *Middlemarch* the careers of Lydgate and Casaubon are relevant to the soul–nature relation. Casaubon has taken learning and scholarship to such an extreme that he is alienated from any sense of natural self; Chettam asks about him, '"Now, Cadwallader, has he got any heart?"' (*Middlemarch*, p. 67). He is singularly lacking in animation or an 'enthusiastic soul': 'his soul was sensitive without being enthusiastic . . . it went on fluttering in the swampy ground where it was hatched' (*Middlemarch*, p. 277). Lydgate, before he discovers medicine, was driven by purely natural vitality, but when medicine arouses his intellectual passion, the development of soul becomes possible: until he discovered medicine he was 'a vigorous animal, with a ready understanding, but no spark had yet kindled in him an intellectual passion' (*Middlemarch*, p. 141). Yet what we can see from the development of the two characters is that the intellectual passion that inspires them is not sufficient to create a soul in balance with the natural.

Kabbalistic thought sees the soul as going through different stages of development: the Zohar refers to three parts of the soul that go from low to high, these being, nefesh, ruah and neshamah – as we have discussed earlier. Lydgate, as a 'vigorous animal' has the first part, the natural vitality with which each person is born; his 'ready understanding' is the potential for the second part. With the intellectual fulfilment he finds in medicine, he hopes to achieve transcendence. However, his lack of some of those aspects of soul mentioned earlier, which lead to his dismissing Mary Garth because of her plainness or idealising Rosamond because of her looks, indicate that he will not achieve the highest development of soul.

The kabbalistic conception of the soul clearly recognises the potential for tension and conflict within human beings and one can understand its appeal to a novelist interested in complexity of character. But why, it might be asked by those who see Eliot as a conventional realist, does she need to draw on kabbalism in representing character? Can character not be represented directly in psychological terms without the need for a mythic approach? We would suggest that Eliot was increasingly drawn to Jewish myth and mysticism because it allowed her to integrate character more fully into the artistic fabric of her fiction. As a writer she was clearly particularly aware of and interested in the question of form in art, most obviously in her short essays 'Notes on Form in Art' and 'Notes on the Spanish Gypsy and Tragedy in general' but also in letters she emphasises that her works should be seen as structures: 'if I have ever allowed myself in dissertation or in dialogue [anything] which is not part of the *structure* of my books, I have sinned against my own laws' (*Letters*, V, 459, Eliot's emphasis), and she commented on *Daniel Deronda*, 'I meant everything to be related to everything else there' (*Letters*, VI, 290). The attraction of myth and mystical ideas for a writer who thinks in such formalist terms, therefore, would have been that they were a means of giving form to fiction, particularly in creating certain boundaries and controls in relation to characterisation. Again one might compare her with Joyce. Why did Joyce in *Ulysses* relate his narrative of a day in the life of various Dubliners to Homer's *Odyssey* if not because of a need to create a framework of control over his material? Arguably such frameworks are particularly necessary with regard to the novel as a genre because it embodies no intrinsic controls in the way that genres such as epic or tragedy do. A purely psychological representation of character, it can be argued, tends to allow characters to take on a kind of independent existence, as if they were real people, and thus potentially to break free from literary form and structure. This encourages the reader to identify with them in direct terms, and inhibits the kind of artistic expression to which Eliot aspires. A more mythic presentation allows the author greater artistic control over the representation of character and thus restricts the reader from having too much imaginative freedom through identifying with characters. One can therefore understand its appeal to a novelist like Eliot who complained, for example, that readers of *Daniel Deronda* 'cut the book into scraps and talk of nothing in it but Gwendolen' (*Letters*, VI, 290).

As well as the idea of soul or essence within a character and within a novel as a mythic dimension that functions as allegory, Eliot would surely have been aware that the relationship between writer and reader parallels in some ways that between creator and creature, which we have discussed previously, as the text remains lifeless unless animated by the reader. In both cases a balance needs to be struck; with regard to the writer–reader relation the success of the work of art depends on writer and reader taking a responsible attitude to the text. It would be as bad for the writer to exercise too great a control over the reader as for the reader to take control of the text for his or her own purposes. Perhaps Eliot's interest in the golem myth was influenced by an awareness in herself of the attractions of control for the artist-creator and the dangers of taking it too far so that the reader has too little freedom of response. Thus allegory has to be handled with tact.

One can see how Eliot may have intended myth and mysticism to work, even if readers remained recalcitrant, by looking at characters such as Gwendolen Harleth and Lydgate. Both these characters – particularly Gwendolen – are among Eliot's most psychologically complex, but there is a strongly kabbalistic element to their representation. Their human reality for the reader is powerful but not at the expense of their integration into the artistic organisation of the text. For instance, both characters compromise their moral nature by acting in a way that is not reconcilable with their sense of what is right. Thus Gwendolen, despite having promised Mrs Glasher that she will not marry Grandcourt, does marry him mainly for financial reasons. Her true soul then comes to be disguised by her outward appearance, sartorial or otherwise, as Deronda says:

> Strange and piteous to think what a centre of wretchedness a delicate piece of human flesh like that might be, wrapped round with fine raiment, her ears pierced for gems, her head held loftily, her mouth all smiling pretence, the poor soul within her sitting in sick distaste of all things! (*DD*, p. 354)

Gwendolen's miserable soul being clothed in finery has further Jewish implications, since it incorporates the idea of zelem. In Jewish thought, 'the zelem is the principle of individuality with which every single human being is endowed, the spiritual configuration or essence that is unique to him and him alone'. It is also described as a 'garment for the soul' woven from good deeds.[7] Gwendolen is dressed in a false garment, since it belies her soul as reflected in her deed; by extension, she has undermined her individuality and spiritual essence.

Following his supposed involvement in the death of Raffles, Lydgate faces a dilemma since he must either stand by his sense of moral responsibility and remain in Middlemarch despite his social and professional ostracism, or desert it and settle for a life based on materialistic considerations:

> I must do as other men do, and think what will please the world and bring in money; look for a little opening in the London crowd, and push myself; set up in a watering-place, or go to some southern town where there are plenty of idle English, and get myself puffed – that is the sort of shell I must creep into and try to keep my soul alive in. (*Middlemarch*, p. 756)

To do so, however, would be a compromise which would be contrary to his earlier ideals. To become a society physician at the expense of his vocation in medical research would be to exist in a false garment. Both characters are thus dehumanised by the choices they make, Lydgate to a drastic extent. Without the soul-making intellectual zeal that inspired him, it is no surprise that he has an early death, since his soul has already died.

As we mentioned previously, not only individuals have soul but so do communities of people. At a time when industrialisation was transforming the British economy, the workers were becoming a potentially powerful entity which could either be kept down by being denied a collective soul or could rise up having been inspirited. Eliot is interested in both of these possibilities.

In *Felix Holt* the workers are regarded as a single entity. To Harold and the landowners they are a body waiting to be imbued with an essence, and that essence is the leadership of the landed classes. Harold's uncle Lingon tells him, '"If the mob can't be turned back, a man of family must try and head the mob"' (*FH*, p. 31). A similar attitude is expressed by Mrs Cadwallader in *Middlemarch*, with the addition that she regards everybody who is not a member of the gentry as monstrous. Without landlords to control them, the farmers are monsters: '"They are quite different from your uncle's tenants or Sir James's – monsters – farmers without landlords"' (*Middlemarch*, p. 322). Whereas the farmers are monsters because they have no soul, in the shape of landlords, she regards the manufacturing classes as monsters because they, vampire-like, extract the blood – which in Judaism is the soul – from their workers; she says of Vincy that he is '"one of those who suck the life out of the wretched handloom weavers in Tipton and Freshitt"' (*Middlemarch*, p. 323).

Chris Baldick comments on the representation of the Manchester workers in *Mary Barton*: 'a class at first represented as suffering passively now "rises up into life" in protest, and has therefore to be distanced and reinterpreted as a monster, strong but childishly misguided'.[8] Eliot depicts Felix Holt as seeing the workers in such a manner. Felix regards the workers as having no direction. He divides them into two parts: the first is the uneducated mass of workers who form the childish body; the second is the educated few who provide the soul which will inspirit the first – the 'dim political consciousness' (*FH*, p. 42). Without the educated soul, the others are liable to degenerate, dybbuk-like, and become monstrous:

> That's how the working men are left to foolish devices and keep worsening themselves: the best heads among them forsake their born comrades, and go in for a house with a high door-step and a brass knocker. (*FH*, p. 55)

However, Felix's viewpoint is not dissimilar from that of Harold, since they both see the workers as a body to be led, with themselves as leaders supplying the soul. Felix, like Harold, sees them as 'ignorant numbers' capable of 'Ignorant power [which] comes in the end to the same thing as wicked power; it makes misery' (*FH*, p. 247). Ignorant power results in monstrosity: the undirected destruction associated with the soulless golem of Chelm. Felix feels that he possesses the power to educate the workers out of their weak ignorance. That this conviction is a foolish one is suggested by the fact that Mr Brooke in *Middlemarch* holds a similar view; he plans to enliven the rural workers by educating them: '"the freemen are a little backward. But we shall educate them – we shall bring them on, you know"' (*Middlemarch*, p. 380). However, to gain power over workers is less easy than they think.

When the mob does rise up, it is presented as something inhuman, likened to 'oxen and pigs' (*FH*, p. 262). Its collective destructive behaviour is like that of the uncontrollable mob in *Romola* which turns on Tito. This presentation is reminiscent of Marx's idea in the *Communist Manifesto* of the monster of the proletariat emerging as a retributive force.[9] Instead of Felix giving soul or essence to the workers, he is seen as part of its destructive power: he looks 'to undiscerning eyes, like a leading spirit of the mob' (*FH*, p. 265). The mob itself is happy to accept his leadership: 'A man with a definite will and an energetic personality acts as a sort of flag to draw and bind together the foolish units of a mob' (*FH*, p. 266), but only because they see in him the possibility of being led to do the mischief he abhors. The destructive potential of elements within the working class is more fully spelled out in Eliot's essay, 'Address to Working men, by Felix Holt' in which she refers to 'the multiplying brood begotten by parents who have been left without all teaching save that of a too craving body . . . the hideous margin of society, at one edge drawing towards it the undesigning ignorant poor, at the other darkening imperceptibly into the lowest criminal class' (*Essays*, p. 423).

The mob in *Felix Holt* is in a literal sense more like the golem of Chelm than, say, the aids to labour in 'The Sorcerer's Apprentice'. Eliot's representation of the mob in *Felix Holt* suggests that she views the application of the golem myth to industrialised societies in more traditional terms than Romantic versions of it that are more influenced by gnosticism. This may be related to political conservatism on her part, particularly her fear, most clearly expressed in *Impressions of Theophrastus Such*, that the values and institutions that are identified with civilisation are extremely fragile. When Felix falls and any potential for the mob to take on a shape or form imbued with soul disappears, it returns to a shapeless mass of separate parts: 'Felix fell. The rioters ran confusedly, like terrified sheep' (*FH*, p. 269). When the name of God – it is that which had given it life – is removed from the head of the golem of Chelm, it too disintegrates and returns to dust.[10]

The novel is sympathetic to Felix's belief that the workers need an idealistic leader. In effect Felix aspires to be a Carlylean hero who takes the lead in the formation of a community and whose aim is to inspirit others, to be responsible for 'the awakening for them from no-being into being'.[11] It was Eliot's aim as a writer to encourage communal unity, and thus give some sort of collective direction and shape to people in her society:

> the inspiring principle which alone gives me courage to write is, that of so presenting our human life as to help my readers in getting a clearer conception and a more active admiration of those vital elements which bind men together and give a higher worthiness to their existence; and also to help them in gradually dissociating these elements from the more transient forms on which an outworn teaching tends to make them dependent. (*Letters*, IV, 472)

As an individual moves towards identification with a communal existence, both the individual and the community will be more fulfilled with the individual becoming less important and human unity more important. An individual needs a wider community in which to become complete, just as the wider community needs individuals invested with community spirit. Society is golem without such individuals, and the individual is golem without society.

Silas Marner shows how an individual does not have true existence while isolated, Marner only being drawn into a fuller life by Eppie, who also forms the bridge between him and Raveloe. Where *Silas Marner* indicates the importance of society for the individual, *The Spanish Gypsy* goes further and emphasises the idea of nationhood superseding the wants of the individual. Zarca informs Fedalma that her life within Spanish society, where she is appreciated but at the same time regarded as behaving in a way not acceptable to Spanish ladies, is one that does not provide her with an essential spirit which will give her direction: 'Your life is all a fashion without law' (*SG*, p. 127). Fedalma is consequently faced with the paradox of Homunculus: she must sacrifice part of her individuality in order to reintegrate herself with that aspect of community which she had previously been without. What is lost in individuality is gained in community and by becoming part of the Gypsy heritage Fedalma is helping to make her people whole, and providing herself with a 'tribal' identity which may be a better alternative than self-realisation.

This idea receives fuller treatment in *Romola*. Romola becomes part of Florence through the influence of Savonarola:

> His special care for liberty and purity of government in Florence, with his constant reference of this immediate object to the wider end of a universal regeneration, had created in her a new consciousness of the great drama of human existence in which her life was a part; and through her daily helpful contact with the less fortunate of her fellow-citizens this new consciousness became something stronger than a vague sentiment. (*Romola*, p. 367)

Growth into a community is here united with the individual gaining essence and thus spiritual regeneration. Romola's regeneration begins to be manifest in her movement away from empty scholarship into activity within and towards a community. She becomes part of a wider regeneration when she is responsible for the 'rebirth' of the village into which she drifts. This also marks a movement away from Savonarola's influence – from his conception of a universal regeneration – into her own existence within humanity; she becomes the figure who inspirits the village.

In 'The Modern Hep! Hep! Hep!' Eliot expresses the idea that the national spirit of the Jews is what elevates them above common humanity:

> The eminence, the nobleness of a people depends on its capability of being stirred by memories, and of striving for what we call spiritual ends – ends which consist not in immediate material possession, but in the satisfaction of a great feeling that animates the collective body as with one soul. (*TS*, p. 146)

Again the connection between animation and soul-making is apparent. The conclusions she reached in this essay have their origins in *Daniel Deronda*. National consciousness has a very significant place in this novel because of the centrality of the Jewish nation to completion. Judaism needs to gather together all its disparate elements before it can achieve nationhood and reach God. Deronda is the disparate element who must be drawn into the Zionist cause before he can be made whole, and through him the Jewish nation can be established, thus making it whole. A human gaining shape and direction through acquisition of a spirit symbolising a wider-reaching awareness of a community had been postulated in the philosophical poem 'A College Breakfast Party' where Guildenstern maintains,

> All sacred rules, imagined or revealed,
> Can have no form or potency apart
> From the percipient and emotive mind.
> God, duty, love, submission, fellowship,
> Must first be framed in man, as music is,
> Before they live outside him as a law.
> And still they grow and shape themselves anew,
> With fuller concentration in their life
> Of inward and of outward energies
> Blending to make the last result called Man.

(SG, pp. 432–3)

In her Jewish novel, Eliot does not make Deronda aware of his need to belong to his Jewish heritage until he encounters the heart of Judaism in Mirah: 'Deronda himself, with all his masculine instruction, had been roused by this apparition of Mirah to the consciousness of knowing hardly anything about modern Judaism or the inner Jewish history' (*DD*, p. 306). Such a sense of being part of a community and a tradition Eliot saw as the basis for the 'living force of sentiment in common which makes a national consciousness' (*TS*, p. 147). Through Mirah, Deronda realises that Judaism can be a shaping force in people's lives: 'But Mirah, with her terrified flight from one parent, and her yearning after the other, had flashed on him the hitherto neglected reality that Judaism was something still throbbing in human lives, still making for them the only conceivable vesture of the world' (*DD*, p. 306).

For Deronda, Mirah is the spark that ignites his Jewish consciousness, but Mordecai is the one who places him within the whole:

> The world grows, and its frame is knit together by the growing soul; dim, dim at first, then clearer and more clear, the consciousness discerns remote stirrings. As thoughts move within us darkly, and shake us before they are fully discerned – so events – so beings: they are knit with us in the growth of the world. You have risen within me like a thought not fully spelled: my soul is shaken before the words are all there. The rest will come – it will come. (*DD*, p. 430)

Deronda is incomplete as the world is incomplete. For Mordecai's soul's yearnings to be realised, Deronda must be complete. Mordecai's yearnings require Deronda to be invested with a soul, and it is implied that this will be the process necessary for a complete world; each one is dependent on the other. Since Eliot's reinvention of nineteenth-century millenarianism advocated Jewish nationhood as an inspiration for other nations to seek a similar sense of national identity, the Jewish nation must come together first. It is implied that Deronda's acquiring a soul is part of the process of Israel finding its soul. Mordecai expresses the idea that Jewish nationalism is vital for the world: '"But it is true, as Jehuda-ha-Levi first said, that Israel is the heart of mankind, if we mean by heart the core of affection which binds a race and its families in dutiful love"' (*DD*, pp. 452–3). Israel needs a heart which can bind the Jews together, and then will act as the spirit which binds the world together. The whole world will remain golem, unless it has the soul of Judaism to guide it.

The phrase 'dutiful love' in this process of national and international consolidation needs to be qualified. We have already mentioned the paradoxical situation faced by Fedalma, where she is forced to relinquish some individuality in having to sacrifice her love for Silva in order to serve the needs of the Gypsy nation. Deronda is faced with a similar conflict: he must sacrifice a potentially passionate relationship with Gwendolen in order to become part of Jewish nationalism and commit himself to Mordecai and his legacy. The relationship with Mirah is, in this sense, not the joining of two individuals, but a binding to the heart of Judaism so that the individual can become communally whole; it is 'dutiful love' as opposed to 'passionate love'; agape instead of eros.

It becomes clear that Eliot does acknowledge a Romantic debt in these situations of irony. Romantic golems, in *Faust* II and *Frankenstein*, either dissolve, or degenerate and die. However, though Eliot's golems do make sacrifices, these are for ultimately constructive ends: Fedalma moves towards establishing a Gypsy nation, and Deronda becomes a symbol of world consolidation. Before the world becomes a universal human community, however, Israel must come together. The world lacks a heart to bind it, and without that central feature, it is merely a set of separate elements, just as the mob in *Felix Holt* is in confusion without Felix to lead it, or the golem is a pile of dust without the word of God to animate it. The heart is in the manifestation of a prophet, who will embody the wisdom of the Jews, and once this heart is established, '"Then our race shall have an organic centre, a heart and brain to watch and guide and execute"' (*DD*, p. 456). Mordecai sees himself as the prophet who has inherited the wisdom of Israel, and this he passes on when his soul travels to Deronda.

8
Homelessness and Speechlessness

In Josephus's chronicles of Old Testament history, the patriarch Jacob says to his father-in-law, Laban, that love of one's country is 'innate in all'.[1] A sense of patriotism is particularly central to Judaism since its religious history is based on exile. Also, to be denied a home is to be denied salvation. This idea is reinforced by the Kabbalah scholar Gershom Scholem: 'Absolute homelessness was the sinister symbol of absolute Godlessness, of utter moral and spiritual degradation.'[2] It is this same reasoning that influences the legend of the Wandering Jew – that eminently Christian rendering of the theme – which equates spiritual degradation with homelessness, relating it specifically to the denial of Christ as Messiah. The spiritual and historical movement of Jews and Judaism is towards the establishment and consolidation of a Jewish nation; among Jewish legends are 'stories about the eternal longing for and aspiration to get to the Promised Land'.[3] In kabbalistic philosophy homelessness, and therefore Godlessness, is linked with incompletion of form:

> The kabbalists of Gerona held that for as long as the exile continues the *Sefirot* do not function normally; as they are withdrawn toward the source of the original emanation, Israel lacks the power to adhere to them truly by means of the Divine Spirit, which has also departed for above.[4]

Moreover, in one strand of kabbalistic thinking, nationalism has a wider implication in keeping with the use of myths to symbolise supposedly universal cycles: 'In the final analysis, national and even nationalistic motifs blend with cosmic ones in the Lurianic Kabbalah to form a single myth of exile and redemption.'[5] As a people, then,

Jews are unformed until they have a nation. The Wandering Jew legend incorporates this by not allowing Ahasuerus a rest or home until he accepts Christ as Messiah, or until Judgement Day. The legend of the golem has strong messianic themes, not least of which are the connections of the golem with both the Jewish saviour and the simultaneous establishment of a homeland.

At the end of Faust's life, in the second part of Goethe's poetic drama, he works towards his own salvation by establishing a free land for a free people:

> I work that millions may possess this space,
> If not secure, a free and active race.
> . . .
> Such busy, teeming throngs I long to see,
> Standing on freedom's soil, a people free.

> (*Faust* II, p. 269)

Uniting the Faustian and the Judaic ideas, homelessness, rootlessness or wandering characterise unease of soul, an unformed individual or society, or exclusion from society.[6] The establishment of some sort of centre around which a nation can shape itself, or an individual can orient himself or herself, is equivalent to national or individual unity and salvation. Coming home is coming to God.

George Eliot's eventual acceptance of the centrality of nationhood to Jewish identity – having rejected her earlier views on this subject, and having come to appreciate the contribution of Jewish thought to European culture, partly through her contacts with Jewish intellectuals such as Emanuel Deutsch – is apparent in her belief that what evoked a spirit in Jews which enabled them to choose death over conversion was this commitment to their nation, which she identified as 'the continuity of that national education (by outward and inward circumstance) which created in the Jews a feeling of race, a sense of corporate existence, unique in its intensity' (*TS*, p. 150). She also placed Jewish national identity at the centre of a larger human movement – reflecting her ideas on form – the constituent members of the Jewish race contributing towards the formation of the whole, which will then take its place as another constituent part of a more substantial whole:

Every Jew should be conscious that he is one of a multitude possessing common objects of piety in the immortal achievements and immortal sorrows of ancestors who have transmitted to them a physical and mental type strong enough, eminent enough in faculties, pregnant enough with peculiar promise, to constitute a new beneficent individuality among the nations. (*TS*, p. 164)[7]

Implicit in this is Jewish nationalism as a positive force, and it seems to echo the opinion of Geiger's *Judaism and its History* – which Eliot had read and taken notes from in preparation for *Daniel Deronda* – that once Judaism had achieved nationhood, its people would transcend nationalism in the narrow, particularist sense.

In her writing, Eliot shows how nationalism and homelessness affect both the individual and a people. *Daniel Deronda* marks the culmination of both dimensions. It develops ideas that can be found in her dramatic poem *The Spanish Gypsy* in which the Gypsies occupy a position much akin to the Jews in history, the Gypsies like the Jews being a dispossessed people – a view supported by George Borrow in his writings on the Zincali with which Eliot was well acquainted.[8] The reputed reason for the Gypsies' nomadic lifestyle was as a result of Christian animosity and prejudice: in her 'Commonplace Book' she wrote, 'One story (said to be told by the Gypsies themselves) was that their wandering from Egypt was inflicted on them as a punishment for the sin of their ancestors in refusing an asylum to the Infant Jesus.'[9] This idea is expressed in the poem:

> ... [God] sent the Gypsies wandering
> In punishment because they sheltered not
> Our Lady and Saint Joseph.
>
> (*SG*, p. 38)

Borrow, in his writing on the Gypsies, makes a comparison between Gypsies and Jews:

There are certainly some points of resemblance between the children of Roma and those of Israel. Both have had an exodus, both are exiles and dispersed among the Gentiles, by whom they are hated and despised.[10]

He is less definite about the reasons for the Gypsies being home-less. One reason he gives is virtually the same as that proposed by Eliot: the Gypsies were dispossessed Egyptians who had been banished because they refused hospitality to the Virgin Mary, but another cause for their banishment is said to be that they persecuted the Israelites in Egypt. It is ironic, therefore, that like the Jews they should be deprived of a homeland.

Both *The Spanish Gypsy* and *Daniel Deronda* have as one of their central themes the hope of establishing nationhood for Gypsies and Jews. Mordecai voices nationalist ideas at the meeting of 'The Philosophers'.[11] Deronda's views on nationalism are clearly influ-enced by kabbalistic thinking: he sees the inspiration behind national identity as one which evolves in cycles, suggesting a mythic basis similar to the Lurianic Kabbalah's cycle of exile and redemption: '"A sentiment may seem to be dying and yet revive into strong life ... Nations have revived"' (*DD*, p. 448). Nations go through cycles of death and revivification. The use of the metaphor of re-vivification calls to mind *The Lifted Veil*, especially in Deronda's implication that a nation's lifeblood is its people: '"We may live to see a great outburst of force in the Arabs, who are inspired with a new zeal"' (*DD*, p. 448).

Of course, we know that Arab nationalism, of which Deronda speaks, and Jewish nationalism have created what appears to be irreconcilable conflict in the Middle East, but this is a historical irony and the novel itself gives no indication of anticipating the problem of competing nationalisms. Is it fair to criticise it for failing to do so? Edward Said claims that the novel displays an indifference to Eastern peoples: 'The few references to the East in *Daniel Deronda* are always to England's Indian colonies, for whose people – a people having wishes, values, aspirations – Eliot expresses absolute silence', and goes on to complain about 'the total absence of any thought about the inhabitants of the East, Palestine in particular'.[12] This may be a weakness of *Daniel Deronda*'s treatment of the theme of nationalism, but the fact that Said fails to mention Deronda's comment on the Arabs suggests that he is reading the novel with a certain partiality. Said might also have taken note of the following com-ment in a letter on her aims in writing the novel. After saying that the 'usual attitude' of Christians towards Jews urged her 'to treat Jews with such sympathy and understanding as my nature and knowledge could attain to', she went on:

Moreover, not only towards the Jews, but towards all oriental peoples with whom we English come into contact, a spirit of arrogance and contemptuous dictatorialness is observable which has become a national disgrace to us. There is nothing I should care to do, if it were possible, than to rouse the imagination of men and women to a vision of human claims in those races of their fellow-men who most differ from them in customs and beliefs. (*Letters*, VI, 301–2)

There is perhaps a failure of historical understanding on Said's part in his not being able to see beyond the present impasse and comprehend a different perspective on the Middle East, one in which support for Jewish nationhood was clearly not seen as irreconcilable with support for non-Jewish peoples and their aspirations. Eliot may have been idealistic in believing that different peoples could live together harmoniously but this is surely not intrinsically impossible and there is also a lack of historical perspective in Said's implication that Eliot should have foreseen the present conflict as an inevitable one when it was the consequence of specific historical forces and circumstances that conceivably might not have happened or have happened differently.

It should also be borne in mind that Eliot represents Jewish nationalism idealistically as a supra-national development; Mordecai asserts: '"I cherish nothing for the Jewish nation . . . but the good which promises good to all the nations"' (*DD*, p. 458). Since the establishment of a Jewish nation would be an initiatory influence on liberal nationalism elsewhere, the cohesion of the Arabs into a national force would, in this case, be dependent on the establishment of Israel. It was Eliot's view that nationalism, based on the Jewish formation of Zion, would not incite antagonism but would bring about the formation of interdependent societies, which in turn would culminate in the achievement of a global community. The zeal which would inspire the Arabs would be inextricable from the foundation of Israel.

Thus nationalism in this context does not have the negative connotations it has taken on in the twentieth century. However, it can be argued that certain passages in *Impressions of Theophrastus Such* suggest that she associated nationalism with racial purity; the narrator asserts that 'A common humanity is not yet enough to feed the rich blood of various activity which makes the complete man' and that 'it is a calamity to the English, as to any other great historic people, to undergo a premature fusion with immigrants of alien blood' (*TS*, pp. 147, 158). Citing these passages, Marc E. Wohlfarth claims that 'Like so many of her contemporaries, Eliot is obsessed by the possibility of miscegination.'[13] This reading ignores the words 'yet' and 'premature' in the passages quoted which indicate that it is not miscegination that is the issue. The fear of 'alien blood' is not racial *per se* but cultural since the 'distinctive national characteristics [of the historic people] should be in danger of obliteration by the predominant quality of foreign settlers' (*TS*, p. 158). In *Daniel Deronda* there is no suggestion that Klesmer's marriage to Catherine Arrowpoint is undesirable on racial grounds. Indeed, according to Catherine, Klesmer 'looks forward to a fusion of races' (*DD*, p. 206).

Eliot was a supporter and advocate of the Risorgimento philosophy of Italian unification, the prominent proponents of which – Cavour, Mazzini, and latterly, Garibaldi – presented a decidedly liberal front. The form of nationalism favoured by Eliot was of an anti-imperialist nature. It was associated with the desire to replace domination with self-determination – a similar motivation to that which provoked the struggles of the working classes and which could be interpreted in kabbalistic terms as the golem's search for self-awareness.

In kabbalistic thinking, there is an organic quality to ideas of form. As with Eliot's own views on the subject in 'Notes on Form in Art', which may have been influenced by kabbalism, parts of a form or entity should combine to constitute an organic whole. It is in such terms that Mordecai expresses his ideas of national identity: the nation is a body; its life-force is its people:

> The life of a people grows, it is knit together and yet expanded, in joy and sorrow, in thought and action; it absorbs the thought of other nations into its own forms, and gives back the thought as new wealth to the world; it is a power and an organ in the great body of the nations. (*DD*, p. 449)

This carries within it Eliot's conception of the Jewish nation as finally transcending nationalism. Once the Jewish homeland is founded and its potential realised, it forms the central part of an organic whole. Her reading of Jewish mystical poets would have contributed to this view, as is evident in Sephardo's declaration in *The Spanish Gypsy*:

Israel
Is to the nations as the body's heart:
Thus writes our poet Jehuda.

(*SG*, p. 164)

It is not only in the context of *Daniel Deronda* and *Impressions of Theophrastus Such* that the significance of these lines becomes apparent. They show clearly that Eliot was interested in Jewish issues and was knowledgeable about Jewish aspirations to nationhood long before she started working on her Jewish novel. To refer to Jehuda (Judah/Yehuda) Halevi is to name a poet whose aim was to see the return of Jews to Israel: 'Juda ha-Levi believed that the redemption of the Jews would be accomplished by their return to the Holy Land. He himself determined to go on pilgrimage and settle there.'[14] The themes of return from exile and redemption informed his work, as can be seen from the following extracts from translations of two of his poems:

'Jerusalem'
How shall I kiss and cherish your stones. Your earth will be sweeter than honey to my taste.

'Longing for Zion'
The air of your land is the soul's very life . . .
The souls of your companion are bound to you.
They delight in your peace, mourn

Your desolation, bewail your destruction.
From the pit of captivity they aspire towards you,
Bow, each in his place, towards your gates.
They are the flocks of your people, exiled, scattered
Through hill and valley, and yet they remember your folds.[15]

In addition to yearning, the latter extract emphasises the disunity of exile, hence the implications of redemption. This brings together homelessness with political golems, as suggested by Eliot for example in *Felix Holt*: the collective force of the workers when they are inspired contrasts with their being scattered like sheep when the uniting influence is gone. Similarly the Jewish people are described as being scattered and thus rendered lifeless and ineffectual when they are apart from the binding influence of their homeland.

As for citizenship, it is apparent in *Daniel Deronda* that in order for there to be a Zion, Jews must adhere to the vision of a shared identity shaped by their heritage and tradition: citizenship rests on the centrality of that concept to all Jews, since, according to the voice of Mordecai, Jews cannot find a home in any country but their own. Whereas Pash is shown to advocate the assimilationist argument and thinks that Jews should integrate themselves into separate societies, Mordecai argues that this is a betrayal of the nationhood that binds Jews together:

> Can a fresh-made garment of citizenship weave itself straightway into the flesh and change the slow deposit of eighteen centuries? What is the citizenship of him who walks among a people he has no hearty kindred and fellowship with, and has lost the sense of brotherhood with his own race? It is a charter of selfish ambition and rivalry in low greed. He is an alien in spirit, whatever he may be in form; he sucks the blood of mankind, he is not a man. (*DD*, p. 450)

The imagery used suggests something inhuman – indeed, something monstrous and vampire-like – about separating oneself from one's nation (not to mention the evocation of the theme of clothing from *Sartor Resartus*). Tito in *Romola* is the type of the alienated individual conjured up by Mordecai: '"he's not made of the same clay as other men, is he?"' (*Romola*, p. 183). Lapidoth is the Jewish equivalent. In terms of the golem, Mordecai's argument would mean that a Jew who remains separate from the rest of his people is incomplete – is deprived of the essence of Jewishness. More important, it is an act that deprives Judaism of its wholeness, so that Judaism is golem-like, and therefore Godless.

In contrast with that, should all Jews unite in forming a nation, the result would be a rebirth of Judaism:

> The degraded and scorned of our race will learn to think of their sacred land, not as a place for saintly beggary to await death in loathsome idleness, but as a republic where the Jewish spirit manifests itself in a new order founded on the old, purified, enriched by the experience our greatest sons have gathered from the life of the ages. (*DD*, p. 458)

Mordecai's vision ironically echoes that of the millennialists whose new order would entail the conversion of all Jews. His belief that the renewal of the Jewish spirit can create the basis for nationhood reinforces the view put forward by Deronda that there is something mythical in the founding of a nation. Manifestation of the spirit of Judaism also suggests the golem, since Deronda, characterised as the potential embodiment of that spirit, achieves wholeness at the same time as he sets out to establish the nation that is essential to the manifestation of the collective Jewish spirit. National and individual completion are in this way complementary.

As well as expressing the aspirations of a nation in seeking a home-land, Mordecai is also representative of homelessness, his character being associated in many ways with the Wandering Jew. In legend, this figure, Ahasuerus, is doomed to roam the world until the Day of Judgement, because he mocks Christ when he stops to rest on his way to be crucified, and tells him to keep walking. He is characterised by his great age, his great wisdom, often by his knowl-edge of medicines and ability to cure illness, and, of course, by his wandering – his mysterious appearances and disappearances. Some versions of the legend have him repenting and accepting Christ; in some he remains a Jew; some imply that he has a non-doctrinal affinity with Judaism, Christianity and Islam, which is a further interpretation of his rootlessness.[16] Literary treatment of the char-acter has included Shelley's use of him in 'Queen Mab', and even Teufelsdroeckh is said to be sometimes referred to as the *'Ewige Jude*, Everlasting, or as we say, Wandering Jew'.[17] Probably the most notable representation of the character is in the 'gray-beard Loon' in 'The Rime of the Ancient Mariner'. Coleridge's poem was clearly influential on Eliot's early work; there seems little doubt that Hetty Sorrel is associated with the Ancient Mariner as certain obvious parallels exist between the two: she feels her baby as a great weight about her neck when she contemplates killing it: '"I don't know how I felt about the baby. I seemed to hate it – it was like a heavy weight hanging round my neck"' (*AB*, p. 453) – a referral to her guilt feelings just as the albatross is to the Ancient Mariner:

> Ah well-a-day! What evil looks
> Had I from old and young!
> Instead of the Cross the Albatross
> About my neck was hung.[18]

Her lonely travels through a bleak countryside link her with the Mariner's solitary wanderings in uninhabited and harsh areas, as does the lack of water; Hetty tells Dinah: '"But I went on to the wood, and I walked about, but there was no water"' (*AB*, p. 453) which alludes to the following well known lines:

> Water, water, every where,
> And all the boards did shrink;
> Water, water, every where,
> Nor any drop to drink.[19]

In both contexts water is associated with death – an image which Eliot maintains throughout her fiction: it is associated with death in *The Mill on the Floss*, in *Romola* – in Dino's mystical and prophetic vision – and in *Daniel Deronda* when Mirah tries to drown herself.

But the most powerful use of water imagery – again derived from Coleridge – is in relation to Grandcourt's death by drowning in *Daniel Deronda*. The epigraph which introduces Chapter 56 is a stanza from 'The Ancient Mariner':

> The pang, the curse with which they died,
> Had never passed away;
> I could not draw my eyes from theirs,
> Nor lift them up to pray.[20]

This again refers to the Mariner's feelings of guilt at the deaths of his shipmates because of his actions, and testifies to his sense of isolation. The chapter focuses on Gwendolen's feelings of guilt after Grandcourt's drowning. She explains to Deronda her intent to kill her husband '"was as strong as thirst"' (*DD*, p. 592). She is in danger of being driven further into a moral isolation similar to that of the Mariner, an isolation exacerbated by her fear that Deronda will reject her: '"will you forsake me?"' (*DD*, p. 592). For both Hetty and Gwendolen the fear of isolation leads to admission of guilt.

This, then, is a more pointed revival of the theme as Eliot used it in her first novel. Hetty's likeness to the Mariner is reinforced by moral isolation combined with wandering: her 'great dark eyes wander blankly over the fields like the eyes of one who is desolate, homeless, unloved' (*AB*, p. 364), which is later emphasised:

Poor wandering Hetty, with the rounded childish face, and the hard unloving despairing soul looking out of it – with the narrow heart and narrow thoughts, no room in them for any sorrows but her own, and tasting that sorrow with the more intense bitterness! My heart bleeds for her as I see her toiling along on her weary feet, or seated in a cart, with her eyes fixed vacantly on the road before her, never thinking or caring whither it tends, till hunger comes and makes her desire that a village may be near.

What will be the end? – the end of her objectless wandering, apart from all love, caring for human beings only through her pride, clinging to life only as the hunted wounded brute clings to it? (*AB*, p. 389)

At the novel's conclusion, Hetty's tragedy of solitude is epitomised when Dinah calls her '"the poor wanderer"' (*AB*, p. 538).

A still more obvious allusion to the Ancient Mariner is to be found of course in *Silas Marner*, as the title of the novel indicates. Weavers are also at the beginning of the novel associated with Jews and Gypsies:

there might be seen in districts far away among the lanes, or deep in the bosom of the hills, certain pallid undersized men, who, by the side of the brawny country-folk, looked like the remnants of a disinherited race. (*SM*, p. 3)

Marner's connection with the Wandering Jew is reinforced by the fact that he feels forsaken by God, so rejects the deity himself. His physical aspect is certainly golemish. His homelessness is both physical and spiritual. Only a miserly hoarding of gold provides him with something to which he can attach his soul. Without this surrogate soul, Marner again becomes spiritually dispossessed: when the gold is stolen it 'left his soul like a forlorn traveller on an unknown desert' (*SM*, p. 42).

A further link between Marner and the Wandering Jew is his knowledge of medicinal herbs and their efficacy, to which is added an atmosphere of mystery about the remedy and about his origins: 'Silas Marner could cure folk's rheumatism if he had a mind'; 'when a weaver, who came from nobody knew where, worked wonders with a bottle of brown waters, the occult character of the process was evident' (*SM*, pp. 4, 17). The Wandering Jew was also associated with unusual remedies:

The Stranger desired a Cup of Beer; the Lame Man desired him to take a Dish and draw some, for he was not able to do it himself. The Stranger asked the poor Old Man how long had he been ill? The poor Man told him. Said the Stranger I can cure you. Take two or three Balm Leaves steeped in your Beer for a Fortnight, or three Weeks, and you will be restored to your Health; but constantly and zealously serve God. The poor Man did so, and became perfectly well. This Stranger was in a Purple-shag Gown, such as was not known in these Parts.[21]

This is, in fact, a version of a common episode in the legend.[22] Since Marner has such associations with the Wandering Jew and since his Romantic counterpart is the Ancient Mariner, it would appear that for Eliot the two characters were linked.

Homelessness, both for the individual and for a people, has a distinctive place in Eliot's novels. Although not always directly linked with Judaism, the dispossession of soul and spirit associated with it suggest the Jewish experience. In *Daniel Deronda* the connection is overt, but in the preceding novels those characters who aim to establish a social or communal centre (perhaps influenced by Fourier's phalansteries), or those who find themselves without a home because of religious or social transgression, owe much to the aspirations of nationless Jews and Gypsies. Maggie Tulliver's homelessness belongs to the latter category, and it is significant that she is associated with Gypsies, her spiritual exile paralleling their physical homelessness. She is out of place – the 'ugly duckling' or Cinderella who is still rejected once her beauty is realised – deprived of a sense of belonging. She has 'a blind, unconscious yearning for something that would link together the wonderful impressions of this mysterious life, and give her soul a sense of home in it' (*Mill*, p. 235). Her exile, like Marner's, results from perceived rather than actual transgression. After she has 'fallen' she is no longer considered to be part of St Ogg's, and the town wants her to be elsewhere: 'It was to be hoped that she would go out of the neighbourhood – to America, or anywhere' (*Mill*, p. 492). Again, as with Marner, place and time are connected; to be banished from the mill and St Ogg's is to be cut off from her past: '"O, if I could but stop here ... I have no heart to begin a strange life again. I should have no stay. I should feel like a lonely wanderer – cut off from the past"' (*Mill*, p. 496). Her contemplation of her future suggests a fall from Grace, the situation of the Wandering Jew, and the purported history of the Gypsies,

exiled because she has trangressed: 'She must be a lonely wanderer ...
There was no home, no help for the erring' (*Mill*, p. 513).

In contrast with transgressors being banished by others, Eliot also
depicts those who choose a life of exile. They transcend boundaries
instead of being forbidden boundaries, and Eliot often chooses to
depict them as creative artists; for example, Klesmer in *Daniel Deronda*
who, in answer to the statement from Bult – his rival suitor for
Catherine Arrowpoint – that he is a Panslavist, says, '"No; my name
is Elijah. I am the Wandering Jew"' (*DD*, p. 206). The Yiddish word
'klezmer' – from the Hebrew 'klei-zemer' ('musical instruments') –
refers to Jewish itinerant musicians of Eastern Europe, whose music
'reflected the patchwork quilt of national cultures in which Jewish
life was lived'.[23] Eliot may have been influenced here by Carlyle,
who in *Heroes and Hero Worship* describes Dante as 'An unimpor-
tant, wandering, sorrowstricken man',[24] and goes on to say that
'The great soul of Dante' was 'homeless on earth'.[25]

Latimer and Mordecai reflect this influence, but not being artists,
the Wandering Jew then has more negative connotations. Latimer,
whose visions allowed him to travel in spirit, becomes 'a wanderer
in foreign countries' (*LV*, p. 42) after Bertha's intentions are revealed.
Before his illness, Mordecai is a wanderer who deprives himself of
a fixed abode so that he can find knowledge:

> England is the native land of this body, which is but as a breaking
> pot of earth around the fruit-bearing tree, whose seed might make
> the desert rejoice. But my true life was nourished in Holland, at
> the feet of my mother's brother, a Rabbi skilled in special learn-
> ing; and when he died I went to Hamburg to study, and afterwards
> to Göttingen, that I might take a larger outlook on my people,
> and on the Gentile world, and drink knowledge at all sources.
> (*DD*, p. 426)

This implies that a lack of knowledge is equivalent to Godlessness.
Since Mordecai will not rest in spirit until he has drunk this knowledge and has helped establish a Jewish homeland, and since to be
without a homeland is to be without God, he will not be with God
– that is, he will be golem – until he has this knowledge. Furthermore Mordecai cannot be considered whole until he finds the ideal
vessel for his spirit, until which event he considers himself to be
in 'spiritual banishment' (*DD*, p. 406).

Mordecai is one of a group of wandering characters who want to shape people (Daniel specifically) and establish an Israelite nation. Kalonymos, who first approaches Deronda, and eventually hands him his heritage, tells him, '"I choose to be a wanderer"' (*DD*, p. 618). Closer to Mordecai in spirit is Deronda's grandfather, Daniel Charisi, from whose Zionist ambitions Deronda's mother seeks to remove him. Kalonymos states '"He travelled to many countries, and spent much of his substance in seeing and knowing"' (*DD*, p. 619). All three characters are like the Wandering Jew: they are all travellers who look to return to a Jewish homeland; and they choose to belong to no particular country in order to increase the intensity of desire to create a nation for Jews.

Another Wandering Jew figure is Ladislaw in *Middlemarch*, an artist, though less committed to the role than Klesmer. Will's alienation from Middlemarch society, his rootlessness, and his descent from an Eastern European patriot as well as, reputedly, a 'Jew pawnbroker', combine to associate him with the character of legend. His artistic inclination is stressed throughout *Middlemarch* – he is introduced sketching, and travels in Europe to increase his experience of and in art. Middlemarch regards him as a social, artistic and intellectual dilettante, his mind wandering as his body does. Lydgate recognises the wanderlust in Will, and says: '"Ladislaw is a sort of gypsy"' (*Middlemarch*, p. 430). It is only in relation to Dorothea that Will feels any sense of belonging; his indeterminate origins and expansive education deny him a home and perpetuate his roaming, but this is brought to an end when he sees in Dorothea someone around whom he can centre himself; wanderlust vanishes: '"He has made up his mind to leave off wandering at once"' (*Middlemarch*, p. 222). Will admits that his home is where Dorothea is, and that she is the only reason he would stay in Middlemarch:

'... And here is something offered to me. If you would not like me to accept it, I will give it up. Otherwise I would rather stay in this part of the country than go away. I belong to nobody anywhere else.'
   'I should like you to stay very much,' said Dorothea ...'
   'Then I *will* stay,' said Ladislaw ... (*Middlemarch*, p. 364)

By allowing Ladislaw a geographic location, Dorothea becomes his shaper and creator.

Almost as foils to Ladislaw are wanderers in the novel who have no or low aims. The most obvious is Mr Brooke, who sets himself up as Ladislaw's patron because he imagines he sees his younger self in Ladislaw. However, his Grand Tour has left him mentally and spiritually homeless. He does little even to improve his land. Raffles is also characterised by his homelessness, and lack of home is related to his lack of a moral sense. The relationship between these two attributes is explored in other novels besides *Middlemarch*. In *Romola* Bernardo del Nero equates Tito's unscrupulousness with his lack of roots: '"It seems to me he is one of the *demoni*, who are of no particular country"' (*Romola*, p. 184). Eliot contrasts this deracinated individual with the Jews expelled from Spain in the same year in which the novel begins, and with whom Tito is at first associated. The Jews are deprived of their adopted home and robbed of their possessions, as is shown in Romola's encounter with them after their misfortunes. Tito, arriving in Italy also dispossessed, proceeds to rob his benefactors and exploit his adopted state to further his position and ambitions because he feels no affinity with the place or the people – such selfishness and betrayal being one of the charges levelled by the anti-Semites at the Jews in Spain. Lapidoth – Mordecai's and Mirah's father – is this kind of stereotypical Jew. Whereas Tito is a study of egotism and ambition beneath a veneer of culture and scholarly sophistication, Lapidoth, whose characterisation is similar, connects such qualities with Jews dissociated from any value or ideal that can restrain self-interest. While other Wandering Jews are victims of homelessness or are, like Klesmer, committed to an ideal of art that stands in place of it, Lapidoth the actor chooses and exploits a wandering role because he is continually seeking self-gratification. He thus stands in opposition to other Wandering Jews in the novel.

To show that Lapidoth-like behaviour does not necessarily result from Jewish homelessness, the novel contrasts his response to homelessness with that of Mordecai and Deronda, who has a sense of not belonging anywhere. Mordecai claims his wandering is as a result of his father's actions: '"Mine was the lot of Israel. For the sin of the father my soul must go into exile"' (*DD*, p. 463). His penance is partly of his own choosing, since it is a means of working towards the ideal of a Jewish homeland.

The success of Mordecai and ultimately Deronda in being able to transcend the negativity of Jewish exile can be related to kabbalistic ideas on the feminine potency of God, the division of Israel, and masculine and feminine halves of the individual. Mirah represents the soul of Judaism. She is identified with the kabbalistic concept of 'Shekhinah' or feminine potency, which derived from 'Talmudic interpretations of the Song of Songs about the Community of Israel as daughter and bride'.[26] Her departure from her father's influence is symbolic of exile and thus in keeping with the 'Shekhinah', which is also seen as going into exile. Scholem writes: 'This exile is sometimes represented as the banishment of the queen or of the king's daughter by her husband or father.'[27] Forced to part from her father because of his actions, Mirah is, in a sense, banished, thus signalling the disintegration of the community of Israel which must then seek reconciliation. The desire for such reconciliation culminates in the marriage of Mirah and Deronda. Exile of the 'Shekhinah' is also seen as the separation of those feminine and masculine principles which constitute God. Reunion of the two principles – marriage – not only indicates a return to wholeness but a restoration of Israel and an act of redemption.

Deronda's homelessness is represented in his being stranded between two cultures, and his golem state is connected to having no home to which he can attach himself:

> But how and whence was the needed event to come? – the influence that would justify partiality, and make him what he longed to be yet was unable to make himself – an organic part of social life, instead of roaming in it like a yearning disembodied spirit, stirred with a vague social passion, but without fixed local habitation to render fellowship real? (*DD*, p. 308)

Absence of purpose to Deronda's life is a kind of spiritual exile. It means he is unable to find form or shape and contributes to the sense that he lacks essence, which renders him golem-like. A sense of being an exile creates the urge to wander and links him with the Wandering Jew: 'The germs of this inclination had already been stirring in his boyish love of universal history, which made him want to be at home in foreign countries, and to follow in imagination the travelling students of the middle ages' (*DD*, pp. 152–3).

Deronda's inability to control his destiny – part of his lack of definition – again manifests itself in lack of abode. Although accepted as part of the Mallinger family, and treated as a son by Sir Hugo, he is unable to inherit Ryelands, the house in which he has grown up. When Gwendolen asks whether he will live at Diplow, he replies, '"I am quite uncertain where I shall live"' (*DD*, p. 600). While he lacks essence – before he discovers his heritage and ascertains his

Jewishness – he is unable to predict his abode or be sure of his home; once he inherits a soul from Mordecai, his plans are definite: he will travel to Palestine to make a home there.

Deronda's commitment to founding a nation of Israel is part of the messianic aspect of the golem. Before being given a specifically Jewish rendering, the idea of a free land for a free people was used in *Middlemarch*. The theme of national identity is introduced in the prologue: St Theresa and her brother possess 'human hearts, already beating to a national idea' (*Middlemarch*, p. 3). The character in the novel most associated with St Theresa is, of course, Dorothea. However, there is a Faustian connection, since Faust also possessed a national idea, based on land reclamation: the building of dykes, and the drainage of a 'noisome bog':

> Thus toil my people for me without cease;
> They make, that earth may find itself at peace,
> A frontier for the billows of the sea,
> Committing ocean to a settled zone.
>
> (*Faust* II, p. 268)

Dorothea has similar aims: '"I should like to take a great deal of land, and drain it, and make it a little colony"' (*Middlemarch*, p. 542).

Dorothea shares this aim with Ladislaw, but his plan is to go out and establish a colony in the New World, inspired by the opening up of new territories in North America. This national fervour has been inherited from his grandfather who '"was a patriot"' (*Middlemarch*, p. 362). Exploration and settlement of North America is also used as a metaphor for Lydgate's scientific research: 'about 1829 the dark territories of Pathology were a fine America for a spirited young adventurer' (*Middlemarch*, pp. 145–6). Such a comparison of exploration of the New World with biological exploration of humans had been a common image since the Renaissance. When viewed alongside Will's utopian ambitions in America, Lydgate's medical ambitions become somewhat messianic. Instead of leading people to a new land and new freedom, he will use science to save and enlighten them. Will's and Lydgate's Americas, however, come to nothing, as do Dorothea's plans.

In Deronda, the Faustian idea expressed through Dorothea and the utopian idea expressed through Ladislaw are combined to form the Zionist ideal, but while this provides him with a political aspiration, the two elements create tension at an individual level. As mentioned previously, Deronda the individual must forsake a personal relationship with Gwendolen that potentially offers passionate love. His commitment to Jewish self-determination and national consolidation is in conflict with such a personal affirmation. He chooses instead to restore his people to their land: '"The idea that I am possessed with is that of restoring a political existence to my people, making them a nation again, giving them a national centre"' (*DD*, p. 688). By doing so he will be fulfilling his messianic role and restoring his people to God. Deronda's Zionism, as well as being a Victorian orphan's search for his origins, becomes symbolically the golem's attempt to return to Eden – to reforge the telluric link and, through his identification with Judaism, to rediscover the *Adam Kadmon*, the primal tissue. This, of course, suggests a parallel with Lydgate, another orphan in search of origins, in his case the 'primitive tissue' that underlies bodily organs. There is a kabbalistic connection here as Scholem shows in his discussion of the Kabbalah text which unites the essence of learning, the body and the land, the *Tikkune Zohar*, and expresses it with an organic metaphor:

> The Torah has a head, a body, a heart, a mouth and other organs in the same way as Israel . . . The mystical organism of the Torah . . . is thus correlated with the mystical body of the Community of Israel.[28]

Land and language are linked by Mordecai in his description of what it means to be Jewish:

> In the multitudes of the ignorant on three continents who observe our rites and make the confession of the divine Unity, the soul of Judaism is not dead. Revive the organic centre: let the unity of Israel which has made the growth and form of its religion be an outward reality. Looking towards a land and a polity, our dispersed people in all the ends of the earth may share the dignity of a national life which has a voice among the peoples of the East and the West – which will plant the wisdom and skill of our race so that it may be, as of old, a medium of transmission and understanding. (*DD*, p. 454)

Upon realisation of the national ideal, Judaism will be given a means of expression in the world: to return to God by reclamation of Israel is to be given a national voice. Union of nation and language is part of the socio-historic development of a people:

> Every human being at every stage of history or pre-history is born into a society and from his earliest years is moulded by that society. The language which he speaks is not an individual inheritance, but a social acquisition from the group in which he grows up. Both language and environment help to determine the character of his thought; his earliest ideas come to him from others. As has well been said, the individual apart from society would be both speechless and mindless.[29]

Judaism states that an individual apart from society would be speechless, without soul and god. In the story of the golem of Prague, speechlessness has a particular significance: 'the Golem could not speak, for the power of speech is God's alone to give'.[30] This inability to speak is also mentioned in connection with the Talmudic golem story of Rabbi Rava, and the tale about the golem created by Rabbi Samuel.[31]

The centrality of speech to the golem results from language and speech in Jewish mystical experience. Language is the manner in which mystical experience is given form: it takes the shape of the language and symbols imposed on the mystic as a means of expression. In an additional sense, words and language have more profound implications, which have their roots in divine creativity:

> The secret world of the godhead is a world of language, a world of divine names that unfold in accordance with a law of their own. The elements of the divine language appear as the letters of the Holy Scriptures. Letters and names are not only conventional means of communication. They are far more. Each one of them represents a concentration of energy and expresses a wealth of meaning which cannot be translated, or not fully at least, into human language.[32]

According to this philosophy, divine perfection relies on the interpretive complexity of the letters of the Torah.

Mary Shelley's monster, when it is first formed, has no speech; it can only make 'uncouth and inarticulate sounds' (*Frankenstein*, p. 105). As such it is very much apart from society: it cannot talk, has no developed mind, and has been forsaken by its god. It is a complete golem (requiring an oxymoronic description). As it acquires language it becomes less monstrous. Articulation is the difference between the popularised dumb, lurching figure of Boris Karloff, and the often sensitive, imaginative creature of the novel.

Dumbness implies menace as one sees in the legend, 'The Golem of Chelm', where the monster runs amok. The influence of the Romanticised creature in *Frankenstein* meant the menace had wider implications: 'What wells up in the inarticulate hero and the dumb mass alike is the transcendent Truth of history; both are signs of, in the traditional and semi-allegorical sense, monsters.'[33] The connection is between an inarticulate and illiterate populace and a monster, but both can be shaped by education, grow from illiteracy into literacy, and by the movement from inexpression to articulation can turn subservience into control of themselves. What was particularly threatening to nineteenth-century rulers was that when these monsters became articulate they threatened to control their creators and thus become controllers themselves. There is even a suggestion of this education away from monstrosity in *Adam Bede* in Bartle Massey's school when Bill, 'Brimstone' and the dyer are trying to learn how to read: 'It was almost as if three rough animals were making humble efforts to learn how they might become human' (*AB*, p. 235).

For Carlyle, language was the force that bound together the nebulous thoughts of humans: 'Language is called the Garment of Thought: however, it should rather be, Language is the Flesh-Garment, the Body of Thought.'[34] In *Heroes and Hero-worship* this view is discussed at greater length, and can be seen to resemble the golem-like and Frankensteinian equation of lack of language with monstrosity. Not only does language enable people to form their thoughts, it becomes a protective carapace by which thoughts gain credence: 'Hardened round us, encasing wholly every nation we form, is a wrappage of traditions, hearsays, mere words.'[35] It is also a means by which a people can be invigorated and vitalised. When Deronda speaks of an outburst of nationalistic zeal from the Arabs, it is an echo of Carlyle's idea that 'a Hero-Prophet was sent down to [the Arabs] with a word they could believe',[36] and through which they can stop being a disparate group of people, and form themselves into a unified nation.

Another Carlylean use of speechlessness connects land and language more fully and again there is a link with Deronda. Carlyle contrasts genius and articulation with dumbness and monstrosity. The Tsar of Russia, he says,

> does a great feat in keeping such a tract of Earth politically together; but he cannot yet speak. Something great in him, but it is a dumb greatness. He has had no voice genius, to be heard of all men and times. He must learn to speak. He is a great dumb monster hitherto.[37]

What divides a politically bound 'tract of Earth' from a nation is that which divides the monstrous from the human: the inability of its king to speak. In his role of potential Messiah, Deronda is prevented from realising his potential – he is still golem – until he has learned Hebrew. Only then can he work towards the establishment of a Jewish nation in the manner of the Carlylean Hero-Prophet.

One aspect of the golem's lack of speech which is used in golem literature is the alienation it causes. Frankenstein's monster believes he will not be accepted until he learns to communicate, so he sets out to acquire language.[38] In *The Lifted Veil*, the gothic world of Prague's Jewish quarter is at the root of Latimer's visions and these are associated with a lack of linguistic understanding:

> But, as I stood under the blackened, groined arches of that old synagogue, made dimly visible by the seven thin candles in the sacred lamp, while our Jewish cicerone reached down the Book of the Law, and read to us in its ancient tongue – I felt a shuddering impression that this strange building, with its shrunken lights, this surviving withered remnant of medieval Judaism, was of a piece with my vision. (*LV*, p. 22)

Latimer's inability to become integrated into society is symbolised by his withdrawal into visions; when his vision becomes real, it is still shown to be separate from the world because of the use of Hebrew, a language of which Latimer has no understanding. He is thus still alienated from his immediate surroundings and the specifically Jewish Prague which constitutes his visions. William Baker has discussed Judaism's role in *The Lifted Veil* in representing the importance of a community as a force that can negate the state of being an outcast, and goes on to suggest that human ambition and aspiration must not become divorced from human contact.[39] Eliot uses separation from Judaism and its society and tradition to stress

Latimer's exclusion both from the community in which he exists, and from that of which he dreams.

Dorothea understands language to be indicative of several ideals. Her idea of a perfect husband is someone who 'could teach you even Hebrew, if you wished it' (*Middlemarch*, p. 10). She regards Hebrew, Latin and Greek as links with the past, with knowledge, and above all with her husband: these languages are the epitome of understanding; through them she will find the origins of her religious zeal. Ironically, as she acquires an ability to read ancient languages, her previous ideas are thwarted, and she finds herself distanced from Casaubon and his work. Casaubon had not envisaged that Dorothea would demand to be treated as fully human and refuses relationship with her. Language is also involved in Maggie Tulliver's sense of isolation in *The Mill on the Floss*. When a child, Maggie identifies herself with a dispossessed race, the Gypsies, as a response to her feeling of being rejected by her family. But when she tries to become a Gypsy, she is excluded because their speech is alien to her: 'It was a little confusing, though, that the young woman began to speak to the old one in a language which Maggie did not understand' (*Mill*, p. 108).

For Deronda isolation comes from speechlessness, which in the novel is translated into linguistic ignorance. Deronda's first meeting with his future Master is marked by his inability to speak Hebrew: Mordecai asks him, '"Perhaps you know Hebrew?"' to which Deronda replies, '"I am sorry to say, not at all"' (*DD*, p. 338). In Jewish tradition Hebrew was considered to be the language of God, therefore that of creation:

> The words of this language are antecedent to the universe; they are its spiritual form and support. Hence, in their study one approaches the truth and being, reality and power, of divinity itself.[40]

Deronda, by learning Hebrew, brings himself closer to Mordecai, his creator. This strengthens the eventual apotheosis as well as indicating Deronda's journey to perfection by union with the creative force of language and the creator.

That Mordecai assumes the active, creative role, and Deronda the passive, shaped one (an inversion of their superficial characterisation since Mordecai is obviously physically inactive, and Deronda physically dynamic) is indicated in Mordecai being the reason for Deronda's attempts to learn the language: 'for somehow, in deference to Mordecai, he had begun to study Hebrew' (*DD*, p. 353). Their relationship as creator and golem is put into clearer perspective when Mordecai actively instructs Deronda in the language necessary for him to understand his heritage: 'Deronda was reading a piece of rabbinical Hebrew under Ezra's correction and comment' (*DD*, p. 677). Mordecai's intention is to put the final preparations to Deronda for his journey to Palestine as heroic saviour, and language signifies this completion.

It is clear that there is a similarity between Eliot's use of homelessness and speechlessness and their meaning in terms of the golem as both character and metaphor. In Jewish belief land and God are linked: if Jews are without one they are without the other. Hence the movement of Jewish history – biblical or otherwise – is towards Zion. Similarly, the original golem of the Bible is connected with the land: while Adam is still golem he is given a vision of future generations, 'as if there were in the *golem* a hidden power to grasp or see, bound up with the element of earth from which he was taken'.[41] Part of the essence of the golem is the earth from which he was formed, and severance of the connection means loss of essence. The suggestion is that while separated from their home, Jews are not whole; they are without essence, which is to be without God. The isolation this conveys – which becomes intrinsic to the archetype of the Wandering Jew – is used to show spiritual estrangement, typified in the manner in which Savonarola admonishes Romola when she leaves her home: '"My daughter, you are fleeing from the presence of God into the wilderness"' (*Romola*, p. 339).

The connection is not only with land, it is with language. The kabbalistic idea of golem is based on 'ideas of the creative power of speech and of letters'.[42] Thus Deronda, initially ignorant of Hebrew, unable to name his mother, unaware of his origins, is transformed into a consummate Jew, able to act for himself and others, which is symbolised through his learning the ancient language of Judaism, and exemplified in his intention to form a Jewish homeland. He is the most complete example of Eliot's interpretation of Kabbalah philosophy and of the golem, with lack of speech and land indicating lack of essence and God, which leads to isolation as a consequence of exile and non-communication. The shedding of these two characteristics denotes a completion of character.

9
The Messianic Potential

George Eliot's attitude towards Jews and Judaism can almost be enclosed parenthetically between statements concerning a Messiah figure. In her letter to John Sibree in 1848, detailing her criticisms of Disraeli, she sees messianic figures as separate from or at odds with Judaism: the Jews may have 'produced a Moses and a Jesus, but Moses was impregnated with Egyptian philosophy and Jesus is venerated and adored by us only for that wherein he transcended or resisted Judaism' (*Letters*, I, 247). Twenty-eight years later, when her composition of *Daniel Deronda* was well under way, her view was wholly different:

> But towards the Hebrews we western people who have been reared in Christianity, have a peculiar debt and, whether we acknowledge it or not, a peculiar thoroughness of fellowship in religious and moral sentiment. Can anything be more disgusting than to hear people called educated making small jokes about eating ham, and showing themselves empty of any real knowledge as to the relation of their own social and religious life to the history of the people they think themselves witty in insulting. They hardly know Christ was Jewish. (*Letters*, VI, 301–2)

Eliot has replaced a perceived philosophical division with continuity of thought and tradition. There is no record of her acknowledging the irony of her change of attitude, and, indeed, any such acknowledgement would be overwhelmed by the absoluteness of her *volte face*. Rather than separation, there was a debt owed by 'western people' to the Jews for producing a Messiah who, rather than transcending the teachings of Judaism, was the product of them, thus undermining any radical separation between Judaism and Christianity. As we have discussed previously, this change of view on Eliot's part was largely a result of her growing contact with Jews and Jewish thought throughout her life. In particular this led her to sympathise with the Jewish view that the Messiah was still awaited.

During the middle ages and the Renaissance, Jewish mysticism grew in response to massive oppression and persecution in Europe. One mystical measure was invocation of the Messiah who, by tradition, would bring about the redemption of the people of Israel at a time of great need. Kabbalistic means were used to hasten the arrival of this saviour 'by prompting Elijah the Prophet to herald the Messiah'[1] whose arrival would be accompanied by a new paradisaical era.

Such utopian ideals can be seen underlying the acts of certain of Eliot's characters. To Mordecai especially, the coming of the Messiah will be contemporaneous with the establishment of a Jewish nation: '"The Messianic time is the time when Israel shall will the planting of the national ensign"' (*DD*, p. 459). This is consistent with kabbalistic interpretations of messianism, in which the 'Age of Aquarius' and return to the Promised Land are simultaneous. However, the idealism of other characters is treated more ironically. Though a utopian impulse underlies Savonarola's desire to promote '"what will further the coming of God's Kingdom"', he also claims: '"The cause of my party is the cause of God's Kingdom"' (*Romola*, p. 464), and Dorothea's ambition '"to make life beautiful – I mean everybody's life"' (*Middlemarch*, p. 216) is scarcely achieved. Even Lydgate has connections with utopian idealism: 'He was an ardent fellow, but at present his ardour was absorbed in love of his work and in the ambition of making his life recognized as a factor in the better life of mankind' (*Middlemarch*, p. 163), but his ardour leads to nothing.

Such aims as Eliot places within her aspiring individuals are reflected in her poetic treatment of Old Testament mythology in her poem 'The Legend of Jubal', with specific reference to the original alchemist and his predilection for creative and metallurgical production. Tubal-Cain's aims are to improve society and work for 'The social good, and all earth's joy to come' (*SG*, p. 295). As such, he embodies a synthesis of messianism with alchemical experimentation and symbolises technological progress – one of the channels through which humans must work in order to remove the mark of

Cain and regain God. Allegorically he can be seen to represent Britain's industrial development in the nineteenth century. Reaching God, however, is shown as a Faustian aim:

> He was the sire of swift-transforming skill,
> Which arms for conquest man's ambitious will.

> (*SG*, p. 296)

Messianism, then, could be connected with selfish undercurrents which may produce destructive tendencies and thus lead to a movement away from humanity. Both the positive and negative tendencies exist within the messianic figures in Eliot's fiction: whereas Mordecai wants to bring the messianic era into being through the identification of the messianic in another, characters such as Savonarola, Dorothea and Lydgate see themselves more dangerously as Messiah-like figures.

In Jewish tradition, the individual who constitutes the Messiah is made up of two parts, one priestly, the other royal. A combination of the spiritual Mordecai and the aristocratic Deronda (through identification) corresponds to these two aspects. Messianic characterisation relies as much on recognition by others as it does on self-proclamation, some strands of belief advocating the idea that 'in every generation there is one righteous man who has the disposition to receive it if only the age is worthy'.[2] Deronda's mother quotes her father as adhering to this view: '"Every Jew should rear his family as if he hoped that a Deliverer might spring from it"' (*DD*, p. 568).

Would-be deliverers can be discerned in several of Eliot's novels; they fail because they proclaim themselves but ultimately are not regarded as such by others. Felix Holt sees himself as a potential leader: '"I should like well enough to be another sort of demagogue, if I could"' (*FH*, p. 55). But his outlook is limited: '"I have the blood of a line of handicraftsmen in my veins, and I want to stand up for the lot of the handicraftsman as a good lot"' (*FH*, p. 223). By identifying with a single group within society, he signifies an inability to relate to a more inclusive humanity. In *Middlemarch* Bulstrode represents a misplaced, self-proclaimed messianism: 'He believed without effort in the peculiar work of grace within him, and in the signs that God intended him for special instrumentality' (*Middlemarch*, p. 606). He is thus likened to the Carlylean hero: 'There needs not a great soul to make a hero; there needs a god-created soul which will be true to its origin; that will make a great soul!'[3] But because Bulstrode sees God's grace in extreme Calvinist terms, any act which benefits him is interpreted as God's grace, and any act carried out for his own benefit is taken as a sign of special instrumentality. This contradiction undermines any comparison to Carlyle's hero, rendering it superficial. Savonarola has a more substantial claim to messianic status since he is regarded as a spiritual leader and saviour by others as well as himself: 'Savonarola appeared to believe, and his hearers more or less waveringly believed, that he had a mission like that of the Hebrew prophets' (*Romola*, p. 198). Savonarola's failure lies in the belief that he will lead the new age he intends to herald, whereas Hebrew prophets in such contexts are more associated with preparations for the coming of the Messiah; and despite his demagogic powers of rhetoric, he is spiritually inadequate.

The Messiah is personified, appropriately enough, in Eliot's Jewish novel, in Deronda. Deronda's tradition in Spanish Jewry is thus apt, because among Spanish kabbalists in Gerona were those most strongly associated with mystic exhortation of the Messiah: '[it was] in these same Spanish circles that there first arose the belief in the mystical nature of the Messiah, who was supposedly a harmony of all levels of creation from the most rarified to the most gross'.[4] Prominent among these kabbalists was the Faustian Yosef della Reyna who tries, in legend, to hasten the arrival of the Messiah but is eventually thwarted.[5] The tale concerns his attempt, and is a warning against untimely summoning of the Messiah, just as golem tales warn against aspects of human creation. Deronda becomes a scion of this tradition, conjured up, as it were, by Mordecai. In his formative years – when he is of Bar-mitzvah age, seeking to find his place within the community and rejecting the artistic 'Jewish' path of singing – he identifies with Columbus, and wants to '"be a greater leader, like Pericles or Washington"' (*DD*, p. 147). His models are those who have shaped nations: they are seen as leaders in their own time, and historically represented as creators of nations.

There is still an air of vacillation about Deronda, however, which is apparent in his indecisiveness. In order for him to fulfil Mordecai's messianic vision he must be Jewish, but until he receives his heritage he can rely on nothing more than Mordecai's enthusiasm. Though his aspirations are those of a deliverer, his conviction needs the backing of a Jewish ancestry. This vacillation is a point raised by Nina Auerbach, who casts Deronda as an 'ineffectual angel' who is 'full of vaporously right intentions, but lacking the actual power to save'.[6] This is valid up to a point, but it needs some qualification. From the opening of the novel Deronda is shown to be a redeemer. His initial act is to redeem Gwendolen's necklace, pawned for gambling, an act with messianic implications since he is leading her from the temptation for which gambling is a metaphor. His first encounter with Mirah is to save her from drowning. The Meyricks, among whom he places Mirah, regard Deronda as a talisman and object of worship:

> 'Kate burns a pastille before his portrait every day,' said Mab. 'And I carry his signature in a little black-silk bag round my neck to keep off the cramp. And Amy says the multiplication-table in his name. We must all do something extra in honour of him, now he has brought you to us.' (*DD*, p. 191)

Amy's act functions ironically to undercut the deification of Deronda, but this produces a kind of double irony since Deronda's position as a messianic figure has been reinforced through his initial encounters with Gwendolen and Mirah.

Deronda does exhibit initially, however, a lack of perception and imagination. It should be remembered that realism and the allegorical or mythic coexist in this novel through the interplay of 'story' and 'discourse' and that Deronda is both a human being with weaknesses and a messianic figure. In particular, he is depicted as imperceptive of creativity among Jews. Firstly there is his vehement rejection of life as a musician – '"I should hate it!"' (*DD*, p. 143). Only in retrospect is the reader aware that this is a denial of his mother who saw her son as a hindrance to her art. Bearing in mind Jewish matrilinearity, Deronda's rejection of the essence of his mother is an initial and unconscious denial of his heritage, but on a basic human level it arises from class prejudice. And considering the historical restrictions on Jewish professions, he is rejecting a role which offers an opportunity to shape the world and contradicts Klesmer's proclamation of the creative potential of the artist:

> A creative artist is no more a mere musician than a great statesman is a mere politician. We are not ingenious puppets, sir, who live in a box and look out on the world only when it is gaping for amusement. We help to rule the nations and make the age as much as any other public men. We count ourselves on level benches with legislators. And a man who speaks effectively through

music is compelled to something more difficult than parliamentary eloquence. (*DD*, p. 206)

Implicit in Klesmer's rebuff of Bult is the creative artist as world shaper and not a mere puppet – that is, a mechanical and soulless golem-like creature – subject to the control of society. Deronda's marriage to Mirah – joining with a performing artist – coincides with his ceasing to be golem. He becomes a national shaper like those with whom he previously identified.

Deronda's perceptions are sharpened upon contact with Mordecai. He immediately classifies Mordecai: 'the thought glanced through Deronda that precisely such a physiognomy as that might possibly have been seen in a prophet of the Exile, or in some New Hebrew poet of the mediaeval time' (*DD*, p. 326). Prophet and creative artist are placed alongside each other; Deronda identifies them as the same type. Since the 'New Hebrew poet' is a reference to Yehuda Halevi whose physical and spiritual yearnings were for a return to Israel, both these types are identified with the Kabbalah mystic. Klesmer's speech on the importance of the creative artist should also be recalled at this point as he sees the artist as creating society, recalling Shelley's claim that 'Poets are the unacknowledged legislators of the world.' But more significant than that, Klesmer's speech has implications for the relationship between Mordecai and Deronda. Before meeting Mordecai, Deronda is merely an 'ingenious puppet' manipulated and shaped by the will of others. In his incarnation as a potential Messiah, Deronda needs a prophet to pave the way and prepare people for his coming and Mordecai is identified as this prophet; Mirah tells Lapidoth, '"To stand before him, is like standing before a prophet of God"' (*DD*, p. 633). The relationship between the two becomes more symbiotic: while Deronda is the golem to Mordecai's creator, Mordecai is the prophet to Deronda's Messiah.

There must, though, be evidence in Deronda's actions and character that he is a messianic figure, that he is golem (incomplete individual) and Messiah (ultimate individual) in one, so that the teleological link is established which ties the *Adam Kadmon* – created in, then cast out of Paradise – to the saviour who had been incarnated in him, and who brings about a return to a paradisaical state. Certain aspects of Deronda's life do coincide with anticipations of the Messiah. The awaited Messiah of the Old Testament and his New Testament embodiment are saviours who are characterised together in the decidedly mythic path they follow:

A mysterious birth is followed by an epiphany or recognition as God's son; symbols of humiliation, betrayal, and martyrdom, the so-called suffering servant complex, follow, and in their turn are succeeded by symbols of the Messiah as bridegroom, as conqueror of a monster, and the leader of his people into their rightful home.[7]

Northrop Frye's description of Old and New Testament messianic signs can easily be applied to Deronda in order to identify him as a Messiah, though the novel, of course, aims to integrate these with its realistic dimension. Those signs that do apply to him are: mysterious birth (who are his parents?); recognition (by Mordecai); humiliation (his assumption of illegitimacy); his becoming the bridegroom (of Mirah); conquering the monster (Grandcourt); and his eventual departure to establish a rightful home for the Jews. Though the defeat of Grandcourt may seem tenuous, since he has nothing to do with Grandcourt's death, Deronda and Grandcourt are polarised characters in their conflict over Gwendolen. According to Frye, such polarised characterisation has strong romantic connotations:

> A quest involving conflict assumes two main characters, a protagonist or hero, and an antagonist or enemy . . . The enemy may be an ordinary human being, but the nearer the romance to the myth, the more attributes of divinity will cling to the hero and the more the enemy will take on demonic mythical qualities . . . the hero of the romance is analogous to the mythical Messiah or deliverer who comes from an upper world, and his enemy is analogous to the demonic power of the lower world.[8]

The conflict in *Daniel Deronda*, translated into these terms, shows a divinely associated hero battling a demonically associated antagonist. It resolves itself in a mythic manner, with the death of Grandcourt, and thus the triumph of Deronda.

Central to Deronda's triumph is the Zionist aim, which has golem implications. Restoration of the Jewish state is completion of the Jewish people. It is also a return to the Promised Land, which in turn is analogous with the return to Paradise which signals the messianic 'Age of Aquarius'. Origins for these ideas derived from the Near East, where a messianic king assumed the ritual role of saviour of his people, the rite including symbolic death and resurrection, which would purify the land. This ritual office was attached to the Jewish Messiah – with a few alterations – so that the term 'ultimately . . . acquired the connotation of a saviour or redeemer who would appear at the end of days and usher in the kingdom of God, the restoration of Israel, or whatever dispensation was considered to be the ideal state of the world'.[9] Eliot came to see the restoration of Israel as the dispensation which would lead to the ideal state for the world. By giving Mordecai the other name 'Ezra', she associates him with this restoration of Israel in a historical as well as messianic context, which is emphasised when viewed in retrospect from 'The Modern Hep! Hep! Hep!', in which she writes of

> the hope that among its finer specimens there may arise some men of instruction and ardent public spirit, some new Ezras . . . who will know . . . how to triumph by heroic example, over the indifference of their fellows and the scorn of their foes, and will steadfastly set their faces towards making their people once more one among the nations. (*TS*, p. 163)

Foundation of a nation representing a people's ideal had already been tested in *The Spanish Gypsy*, with strong messianic connotations. In this poem, Zarca's aim is to unite the Gypsies into a nation and place its disparate parts into a definite order:

> And make a nation – bring light, order, law,
> Instead of chaos.
>
> (*SG*, p. 128)

The language used to express his intentions suggests the actions of a divine creator. As such, his daughter – his child and creation – becomes a messianic counterpart who will fulfil the creator's ambitions and unite the people with their land. Fedalma enacts a Gypsy version of the Jewish messianic act of reforging the link between the telluric and the divine.

A connection between the golem and the Messiah stems from the ushering in of an ideal state. Traditionally the Messiah would appear when the Jews were in greatest need of a deliverer. The story of the golem created by Rabbi Loew of Prague emerged during a period of severe tribulations, when pogroms, originating in the false accusations of the 'Blood-libel', were encouraged – such acts and accusations being symptomatic of attitudes towards Jews from medieval times. Loew's golem was created as a deliverer, to protect the Jews of the Prague ghetto. In this way the golem can be identified with the Messiah through action rather than belief. Extending this to *Daniel Deronda*, the trials suffered by Mirah become the trials of Judaism, her intended suicide being the nadir of its fortunes. Deronda emerges as her saviour, and through his act of saving her, golem and Messiah are again amalgamated into one.

Eliot does present Deronda as a saviour to a greater degree than related characters in the previous novels – Romola, for instance, who is hailed as 'the Holy Mother' by the plague-ridden villagers whom she has helped (*Romola*, p. 522), or Dorothea, who is said, by Lydgate, to have '"a heart large enough for the Virgin Mary"' (*Middlemarch*, p. 757). These are messianic by association only, Eliot identifying them more with the Mater Dolorosa and the 'eternal feminine' of Goethe's *Faust*. Deronda is referred to as a saviour and deliverer by Mirah:

> She lifted her eyes to his and said with reverential fervour, 'The God of our fathers bless you and deliver you from all evil as you have delivered me. I did not believe there was any man so good. None before have thought me worthy of the best. You found me poor and miserable, yet you have given me the best.' (*DD*, pp. 170–1)

The messianic aspect is strengthened by Deronda's acceptance by both Gentiles and Jews. Eliot portrays Deronda as a saviour within both worlds – uniting both halves of the novel – which is apt, since Frye shows the Messiah's characteristics are common to both the Old and the New Testament. This is suggested in Deronda's self-sacrifice: helping Hans Meyrick with his classical scholarship, at the expense of his own studies. His position as Gentile saviour is even more in evidence with Gwendolen. Deronda's initial relationship with her is that of redeemer – of the pawned necklace. After Grandcourt's death his position becomes even more associated with the New Testament Messiah since she regards him as having delivered her from a more sinful life:

> 'You have saved me from worse,' said Gwendolen, in a sobbing voice. 'I should have been worse, if it had not been for you. If you had not been good, I should have been more wicked than I am.' (*DD*, p. 601)

Gwendolen sees herself as something of a 'prodigal-daughter', repenting and returning to a more righteous existence. Deronda's role as deliverer is emphasised when Gwendolen receives his advice to use her suffering to start anew: 'The words were like the touch of a miraculous hand to Gwendolen' (*DD*, p. 659). The efficacious nature of this advice suggests the healing power of Christ in the Gospels.

It is significant that Deronda's Christ-like status is enhanced at this point, because he too has undergone a rebirth, into Judaism – irony again – which includes the meeting with his mother and the restoration of his past by Kalonymos. Whereas his philanthropy was previously expressed only through a general inclination to 'take care of the fellow least able to take care of himself' (*DD*, p. 152), it now has a more definite sense of purpose, directed towards aiding the Jewish people: '"I hold that my first duty is to my own people, and if there is anything to be done towards restoring or perfecting their common life, I shall make that my vocation"' (*DD*, p. 620). Restoration and perfection are the pivotal aims. The former implies returning the land of Israel to its people – or the people to their land. The latter incorporates wide-ranging aspects of Jewish mysticism: not only does it imply the return to God, with the individual and communal perfection this assumes, but it also suggests the advent of a utopian era. Deronda's proposed actions, then, are messianic.

10
Conclusion: Social Critique, Education, Allegory

This study has tried to demonstrate that there is a discernible Jewish background to George Eliot's fiction, in particular that ideas derived from Jewish mysticism become increasingly prominent in her work. As we have discussed, mysticism and kabbalistic practice grew as a result of increased persecution of the Jews and both *Romola* and *The Spanish Gypsy* are set at a time when such persecution existed, the Jewish character Sephardo in the latter having connections with kabbalism. Although there is little direct Jewish reference in *Middlemarch*, there is evidence of anti-Semitism, and as suggested earlier it is possible that Dorothea may have been partly based on the Jewish Dorothea Schlegel, daughter of Moses Mendelssohn. In *Daniel Deronda*, the culmination of the Jewish presence in her work, both anti-Semitism and Jewish mysticism are crucial elements. Even Deronda, before his involvement with Mirah and Mordecai, has some anti-Jewish prejudice and Mordecai is clearly in a tradition of Jewish mystics, one to which Maimonides, Maimon and Moses Mendelssohn belonged and which significantly influenced Dorothea Schlegel even though she converted to Christianity.

While this background of Jewish mysticism is certainly present, Eliot does employ more specifically golem themes in her fiction through which she dramatises her ideas. The golem legend had emerged from the literary and philosophical tradition which made use of kabbalism and its derivatives. Goethe's use of the Homunculus and Mary Shelley's *Frankenstein* both warn against empty creation which, through insufficient understanding, results in destruction. In *Faust* and *Frankenstein* science and technology are associated with the dangers of the occult, and because there is insufficient understanding, Faust's recourse to classicism and the sensibilities inherent in Mary Shelley's interpretation of Rousseau's Natural Man are not able to redress selfish knowledge. Eliot wrote at a time when the dangers to which society was exposed were changing in significant ways. As well as the threat posed by social and industrial developments of the past hundred years, new threats derived from these developments were emerging. Even before she became an established writer of fiction – a creative artist in her own right – Eliot had identified some of these problems, and had already begun to formulate responses to them. In her fiction, the golem as myth and metaphor allowed her to engage artistically with such problems.

In particular she was concerned at the threat presented by two types of social tendency. In her discussion of W. H. Riehl in 'The Natural History of German Life', written for the *Westminster Review* in 1856, she argues that modern industrialised societies rely too much on the workings of bureaucracy on the one hand and unthinking tradition on the other. To illustrate the first of these, she distinguished between the enlightening and inspiriting influence of communal organic life and the dispiriting effects of imposed enlightenment through social control:

> Instead of endeavouring to promote to the utmost the healthy life of the Commune, as an organism the conditions of which are bound up with the historical characteristics of the peasant, the bureaucratic plan of government is bent on improvement by its patent machinery of state-appointed functionaries and off-hand regulations in accordance with modern enlightenment. (*Essays*, p. 282)

Her use of the word 'machinery' implies that what passes for enlightenment actually reduces the humanity of people: the process is one that has little regard for the individual and is concerned only with fulfilling its own prescribed function. Here one can see the beginnings of an application of the golem myth to modern social developments. People are seen only as part of the workings of the social machinery and as such they become like machines. Forced to comply with the inhuman regulations that surround them, they are likely to turn into automata.

However, should this in turn imply that merely by following a communal approach to life and tradition such inhuman tendencies will be negated, Eliot in the same essay points to the danger if these are adhered to without understanding. She records the monstrous activities of the German peasantry in their reactionary rebellion against bureaucratic structures:

> they set their faces against the bureaucratic management of the communes, deposed the government functionaries who had been placed over them as burgomasters and magistrates, and abolished the whole bureaucratic system of procedure, simply by taking no notice of its regulations, and recurring to some tradition – some old order or disorder of things. In all this it is clear that they were animated not in the least by the spirit of modern revolution, but by a purely narrow and personal impulse towards reaction. (*Essays*, p. 285)

Again, the use of language – the idea of the peasantry being animated – suggests the golemish concept of a monstrous mass of people, an image which belongs to derivatives of the story of the golem of Chelm or 'The Sorcerer's Apprentice' and which finds expression in *Felix Holt*. At the same time, she emphasises her progress from Romantic ideas, dispelling the myth of the 'natural man' and its implications of the 'noble savage'. The peasants, left to themselves, will not revert to some inherent moral sensibility – a Rousseau-based state of grace; they revert instead to inapplicable tradition, one which does not allow growth and maturation. The peasant tradition in itself is not the subject of Eliot's criticism but she suggests that tradition, which has been distorted by the imposition of a more mechanical social system, has been provoked into rebellious reaction. Here, empty tradition results in an undirected mass. If bureaucratic machinery produces inhuman attributes by false progress, reaction has a similar effect by applying false tradition. Both dehumanise: the former through reduction of people to automata; the latter through reduction of them to brutes.

Contained within Eliot's critique was an implicit criticism of social systems which do not take into account differences of culture and tradition – those aspects of communities which give them individuality and continuity. Thus, generally applied social systems will not take into account, for instance, the differences between the rural peasantry and the urban proletariat; and while they will give shape to certain parts of society, they will merely impose outline on others – and here her ideas on form in art can be seen as having ramifications beyond art which are applicable to individual and society alike. And what is true of social systems is also true of religious systems which generalise, and therefore negate the individual. That Eliot saw these social developments as having a reductive affect upon women in particular, can be seen in another of her essays, her review of the works of Margaret Fuller and Mary Wollstonecraft, written for the *Leader* in 1855. Women are seen as objects, not as people, who adorn and are to be adorned on the outside, not animated from within (a distinction which has repercussions in her 'Notes on Form in Art'). This Pygmalionesque view is described thus:

> and so men say of women, let them be idols, useless absorbents of precious things, provided we are not obliged to admit them to be strictly fellow-beings, to be treated, one and all, with justice and sober reverence. (*Essays*, p. 205)

Eliot agreed with some of the ideas advocated by Mary Wollstonecraft, and it should be noted that her attack on this ornamental view of women, though it superficially belongs to the story of Pygmalion and Galatea, is clearly related to the golem myth. For one who was immersed in the works of Goethe – and this review was written shortly after her journey to Germany with Lewes in order that he could research his biography of Goethe – the Pygmalion allusion, and consequently the connection between Galatea and the Paracelsian Homunculus as it occurs in *Faust* II, would have had such implications. The question of control is central to both.

Monolithic doctrines of social organisation and generalisations applied to an entire sex take away people's humanity. Eliot's criticism went further, however, since a similar critique was directed at religious belief. In her article for the *Westminster Review* entitled 'Evangelical Teaching: Dr Cumming', she openly criticised this form of religious doctrine, which she saw as socially regressive: 'we do *not* "believe that the repeated issues of Dr Cumming's thoughts are having a beneficial effect on society", but the reverse' (*Essays*, p. 162). Evangelical Christianity was a regressive force in its view of both humanity and the individual. It denied humanity to a generalised large mass of people because they were not 'Christians' – Christianity in any case being restricted to Cumming's own particular brand of Calvinistic Protestantism. At the individual level Evangelicism led to a dulling of the intellect and a deadening of the faculties: 'they do not search for facts, as such, but for facts that will bear out their doctrine . . . It is easy to see that this mental habit blunts not only the perception of truth, but the sense of truthfulness (*Essays*,

p. 167). This religious attitude 'unmans the nature' (*Essays*, p. 168), and again golem implications are present in the language she uses to describe this type of religious practice:

> A man is not to be just from a feeling of justice; he is not to help his fellow-men out of good-will to his fellow-men; he is not to be a tender husband and father out of affection: all these natural muscles and fibres are to be torn away and replaced by a patent steel spring – anxiety for the 'glory of God'. (*Essays*, p. 187)

Those attributes which would ordinarily make a person human – such as compassion and sensibility – are dismissed and instead there is the mechanism which is evangelical teaching. The doctrines advocated by Dr Cumming thus reduce people to the mechanistic, with human tissue being replaced by a 'patent steel spring', a continuation of the metaphor used in 'The Natural History of German Life'.

These were problems identified by Eliot the critic, and, as we have argued, were addressed also by Eliot the writer of fiction. Thus we can see the negativity of generalised social and political systems and their brutalising or dehumanising effects in *Felix Holt*; women being regarded as statues or objects in *Middlemarch*; and the parochial and life-denying attitudes of organised evangelical religion in *Silas Marner*. To combat these debilitating forces, Eliot turned to education, which she saw as a means of inspiriting people. She held Carlyle to be 'the most effective educator', one who 'inspires [men's] souls with courage and sends a strong will into their muscles' and thus 'animates you' (*Essays*, p. 213); education, to continue the golemish imagery, was therefore an energising process and the educator – Carlyle – one who gave life. Since education is synonymous with animation, the educator becomes the creator. But there are resultant tensions between creator and creature, for example the conflict between individual passion and the social idealism urged by the creator that demands the sacrifice of such passion, as experienced by Fedalma and Deronda. Educators are also flawed. In *Adam Bede*, Bartle Massey tries to bring his pupils – described by the narrator as being animal-like – out of ignorance, but the educator is also mysogynistic; Felix Holt wants to educate the workers, but fails to see that he has romanticised them. Consequently the ideals of these educators are affected by such flaws: Bartle sees his prize pupil Adam Bede disintegrate because of Hetty, and Felix sees the workers act with monstrous violence.

Eliot saw, too, that as a creative artist she herself could educate:

she could use her fiction to animate people. It is here that her ideas on form in art and poetry become relevant. Shape, or form, is a central element of the legend of the golem. Through its literary interpretation, the golem represents both the form of an individual and wider ideas of form, such as those which encompass a society or nation. In her fiction Eliot stresses the importance of a 'whole' community, and especially the 'complete' individual within a community, and suggests a contrast with those forces which reduce humanity to a mass of entities who act and react like automata. She did not merely confine herself to modern industrial society, for the same themes are present in her portrayal of fifteenth-century Florence in *Romola* and the Spain of *The Spanish Gypsy*. However, failure is much in evidence for characters seeking completeness in integrated communities, as we have discussed previously.

Silas Marner is a notable exception. Marner transcends the dehumanising tendencies of Lantern Yard – which are a result of both religious and industrial forces. We have already discussed Marner's connection with the golem and the significance of homelessness and wandering in the novel, as well as its Romantic links. Marner achieves connection with Raveloe, with the land and the people and thus gains wholeness as an individual. Gold, as a symbol of capital, loses its value after having threatened humanity with loss of value. A character such as Dunstan who lives for gold and who dies after stealing Marner's gold is dehumanised by such materialism. Silas Marner himself, during his period of alienation when he is cut off from human contact, identifies with his gold. Godfrey tries to buy back his child and thus reduces her to a material possession. But for Marner meaningless gold is transformed, as Sandra Gilbert points out, into a meaningful child,[1] in what amounts to inverse alchemy. The arrival of Eppie suggests both the telluric link and the messianic potential of the golem myth. Gilbert writes:

> 'Hephzibah', or 'Eppie,' was the name of both Silas' mother and his sister: in gaining a new Hephzibah, he has regained the treasure of all his female kin. Even more significantly, the name itself, drawn from Isaiah, refers to the title Zion will be given after the coming of the Messiah. Literally translated as 'my delight in her', 'Hephzibah' magically signifies both a promised land and a redeemed land.[2]

It is after Marner is fully integrated into society, and is educated and enlightened through being connected with Eppie, that the gold is restored to him. With the change that has taken place in Marner, it is no longer a threat to human value.

The idea of community was of great importance to Judaism, since it was part of the return to Zion. Eliot's ideas of community had taken shape along more decidedly kabbalistic lines as she had developed her ideas on form in art. Her essay, 'Notes on Form in Art', argued that form was essentially organic and was composed of an interdependent collection of individual parts, this idea being related to the image of the web which is a dominant metaphor in *Middlemarch*. These ideas have their parallel in Jewish thought: in kabbalistic doctrine, Jewish teachings and Jewish people were interdependent and symbiotic parts of a whole that was the essence of Israel and the body of tradition that was the Torah.

Mysticism was an essential element in this way of thinking about the world. Eliot came to prefer the metaphysics of mystical Christianity to the evangelicalism to which she adhered in her early life; and one of her criticisms of Dr Cumming was that 'There is not the slightest leaning towards mysticism in his Christianity' (*Essays*, p. 162). However, mysticism can be embraced in an improper spirit. For Maggie Tulliver the Christian mysticism of Thomas à Kempis leads to inauthentic renunciation and misdirected duty, the acceptance of outline as opposed to form. Similarly Romola, following the example of Dino, succumbs to the influence of Savonarola, and the result is as constricting as her life as Bardo's daughter or Tito's wife. Savonarola, in compelling her to accept duty by denying her emotions imposes outline rather than form on her existence. Form only comes into her life when duty and feeling are fused in the plague-stricken village.

As Eliot's knowledge of Jewish mythology and mysticism grew, they played an increasingly important role in her ideals of social reconstruction. The manner in which she came to use them, shedding her previous distaste for Jewish mythology and poetry, may be attributed, in part, to her journey to Germany with Lewes, where she came into contact with those influenced by the tradition of Romantic Jewish intellectualism and its kabbalistic base. The influence of her friend, Emanuel Deutsch, may also have been particularly significant.

It is in her final novel that Eliot fully united her ideas of form with those of kabbalism, and through this expressed her ideas of

nationhood. Her ideas on determinism in the scientific sphere resembled kabbalistic ideas in which individual and universal were
inextricably linked, the form of one only being complete in the
completion of the other, with the completion of the individual also
depending on the relation to and connection with other individuals.[3] Biblical Adam, as the original golem, was intended to be the
embodiment of this in a single symbol of splendour and power
which would again be manifested in the Messiah. Deronda, as golem
and Messiah, came to embody the same thing. The myth of the
golem thus came to play a central role in Eliot's fiction, with the
novels being connected to the myth in different ways from *Adam
Bede* on.

Though the 'Deronda' part of Eliot's last novel has often been
seen as an artistically flawed departure from the realism that found
its greatest expression in *Middlemarch*, the two novels are much
more closely related than is generally thought when one considers
them in relation to Jewish myth and mysticism. Eliot suggests, for
example, that science is not the completely rationalistic enterprise
that it is conventionally thought to be, but shows that it has maintained rather dubious links with alchemy. Lydgate represents forward-
looking science: he has had the best education, he is inspired by
great medical minds, and he has his own mind set on supposedly
important research. But he becomes distracted by Rosamond, his
ideal of a perfect woman, who is herself a golem figure trying to
express herself, and not an ideal. He dehumanises her by reducing
her to a manufactured ornament, 'a table ornament/To suit the richest
mounting' (*Middlemarch*, p. 425). His ultimate aim – the search for
the 'primitive tissue' – is not only similar to Casaubon's, but is
equally unsuccessful. Instead, then, of offering a progressive alternative to the creationist theories of Casaubon, he becomes linked
with them. He is also linked with reactionary religious ideas through
seeking the support of Bulstrode and then having to borrow money
from him, and with Vincy's dehumanising economics through marrying into the Vincy family. All of this has a reductionist effect on
him. Golem-like in being an orphan, a searcher for origins, and an
outsider in the community, he completely fails to overcome the
negative aspects of being golem through finding definition as an
individual and integration in a community, in contrast to Deronda.
Like other characters in the novel – Bulstrode, Featherstone,
Casaubon, Vincy – he is associated with the desire to control people,
in effect, to make them golem-like. Opposing these characters with

their negative golemish connections are characters such as Dorothea, Ladislaw and Mary Garth who rebel against or try to escape control. In *Daniel Deronda* Eliot overcomes the destructive tendencies and existential ironies of previous literary golems – such as those of Goethe and Mary Shelley – as well as her own use of the golem as a predominantly negative metaphor in her previous novel. Instead she provides a positive rendering of the legend and its metaphoric implications. What she presents is a promise for the future. Israel is seen as the heart of the world's nations and its chief advocate is Mordecai, who is in the mould of kabbalists and Old Testament prophets. He is connected with alchemy but positively in that he is associated with progress in the form of a complete Jewish nation. Once this is complete, by which is meant the establishment of a Jewish homeland to which Jews can return in order to build their own community, the world's nations will grow around it. The final essay in *Impressions of Theophrastus Such* suggests that for Britain to regain its national shape or identity, it should learn from the example of the solidarity of Judaism and the Jewish nation in forming itself.

As was suggested in the Introduction, the 'discourse' or literary organisation of her fiction operates in such a way as to allow it to embody different levels of meaning, and this is particularly evident in *Daniel Deronda*. The psychomachy or struggle for the soul en-acted by Grandcourt and Deronda in relation to Gwendolen is, true to its resemblance to morality plays, an allegorical representation of a larger conflict at the national level. Deronda certainly has an allegorical dimension. While he is golem Judaism is incomplete; once he acquires a soul he sets out to found a Jewish homeland, thus indicating that Judaism has returned to God. Like him it can become complete. In another sense, Deronda represents the coming together of the different Kabbalah traditions in Judaism: he is a product of the mystical tradition of Spain and Provence, and his spiritual tutor belongs to the magical tradition of Central and Eastern Europe. Moreover, his 'heart' – Mirah – has travelled from Prague, the city most associated with the legend of the golem. In personify-ing Judaism, he is an inspiriting influence on Gwendolen, who represents at this allegorical level the potential of Britain.[4] In order to educate Gwendolen – to imbue her with the spirit to shape and take control of herself – Deronda has to defeat the major dehumanising influence on her. Grandcourt is representative of a 'dead' aristocracy – as the references to his lifelessness attest: he is empty tradition whose only aim is to control, which he does by dehumanising others. What is implied in this allegorical battle is that Britain, left to itself, will not just become stagnant, but – dybbuk-like – regress and self-destruct. Only by looking to the energising influence of Judaism and its implications of nationhood, can it and other nations recreate themselves. In this, her final novel, Eliot has combined all predominant elements of the golem – completion of the individual by gaining a soul, the founding of a land, thereby completing the telluric link and simultaneously returning both to God and messianically to paradise – to act as a counter-force to contemporary dehumanising influences by turning instead to ideals of organic harmony in a harmonious future.

What is particularly significant is Eliot's use of the golem to present progress. Although her advocation of the 'organic' principle to oppose the mechanical tendencies of modern society resembles Romantic perspectives, there are significant differences. She came to recognise the self-defeating limits of Romanticism – the paradox whereby a return to an idyllic, pre-Fall state of grace would be, in the gnostic terms epitomised in Shelleyan discourse, a movement towards the Creator against whom the Natural Man rebelled. As can be seen in *Daniel Deronda*, in the relationship between Deronda and Mordecai – creature and creator – it was necessary for the two to be joined in order that the organic principle be upheld.

One of the major implications of this study is that Eliot's fiction should not be seen as limited to realist representations of life, a basic assumption in much critical discussion of her work and one which has been reinforced by its association – on the part of critics influenced by structuralism, particularly the writings of Roland Barthes – with the 'classic realist text'.[5] Though some recent criticism has called into question the identification of her fiction with realism, as mentioned in the Introduction, this study takes an even more radical view. Realism is not directly undermined by the use of the golem myth and kabbalistic thought in the novels but it functions only at one level. At another level the novels need to be read allegorically. Beneath the realist surface there is a unifying sub-structure founded upon the central myth of the golem, around which are literary interpretations of Jewish mysticism related to this myth. Her view of the relation between the individual and society is ultimately golemish. The individual remains golem if he or she fails to become integrated into society, since it is only when the individual is a part of society that wholeness is possible. But equally, societies that deny certain individuals integration risk suffering the revenge of the golem. And only when there are whole societies can they interact to become composite parts of a larger whole. The golem in Eliot's work becomes a metaphor not only related to the completion of the individual and the individual's immediate community, as in the specific Jewish context of the legend, but it also – in accordance with kabbalistic thinking where it merged with her own ideas on form – becomes a symbol of the need for national and international completion.

Notes

Introduction

1 See below in the text for discussion of the legend of Rava and Rabbi Zera.
2 Writers well known to George Eliot who utilised Jewish mysticism were Milton, Coleridge, Shelley, Goethe and Carlyle. Milton exploited it not only in the nomenclature of his angels, but in his use of gnostic ideas in the portrayal of God and Satan. This portrayal was one which appealed to Shelley, as can be seen in *Prometheus Unbound*, notably in his reference to the nature of Satan in the prologue to that work. Shelley combined it with neoplatonic ideas of form and beauty – ideas which in their origin had interacted with kabbalistic ones, as indeed had Platonic philosophy. Coleridge, Goethe, Carlyle and Mary Shelley made more specific use of the golem myth: Coleridge in the characterisation of the Ancient Mariner, Goethe in the Paracelsian Homunculus in the second part of *Faust* (he had used kabbalistic references in the first part of this poetic drama when Faust conjures up the Spirit of the Earth and Mephisto), Carlyle in *Sartor Resartus*, and Mary Shelley in her novel *Frankenstein*. Carlyle's use of the myth would have been of special importance to George Eliot, because of her regard for him as an educator, and her belief that literature should be an educative force. One of the prime ideas underlying the golem myth – that knowledge should be used to enlighten and inspirit – was one that was particularly well suited to serve George Eliot's purposes in her fiction.
3 See, for example, on Greek myth, Joseph Wiesenfarth, *George Eliot's Mythmaking* (Heidelberg, 1977) and for the influence of Milton, Diana Postlethwaite, 'When George Eliot Read Milton: the Muse in a Different Voice', *ELH*, 57 (1990), pp. 197–221.
4 Passage from the Talmud cited in *A Treasury of Jewish Folklore*, ed. Nathan Ausubel (New York, 1954), p. 603. On the golem as *Adam Kadmon* see Gershom Scholem, *On the Kabbalah and its Symbolism*, trans. Ralph Manheim (New York, 1969), p. 97.
5 Robert Graves and Raphael Patai, *Hebrew Myths* (London, 1989), p. 63.
6 See Scholem, p. 162. He quotes from a fragment of Midrash Abkin:

> When God wished to create the world, He began His creation with nothing other than man and made him as golem. When He prepared to cast a soul into him, He said: If I set him down now, it will be said that he was my companion in the work of Creation; so I will leave him as a golem ... until I have created everything else.

7 See Scholem, p. 165.
8 See *Some George Eliot Notebooks: an Edition of the Carl H. Pforzheimer Library's Holograph Notebooks*, ed. William Baker (Salzburg, 1976–85), I, 114.

9 See Scholem, p. 170.

10 Part of a poem by Halevi is quoted by Mordecai in Chapter 38 of *Daniel Deronda*. In the notes to her edition of the novel (Harmondsworth, 1967) Barbara Hardy writes of Halevi: '... he is the inspiration behind the novel's insistence on "separateness and communication", and also behind Mordecai's poetry, his ideals and his language ... A study of Halevi (even in translation) shows that he is the source not only of this poem but of many images and expressions in Mordecai's speech' (*Daniel Deronda*, ed. Barbara Hardy, Harmondsworth, 1967, p. 896). See also William Baker, *George Eliot and Judaism* (Salzburg, 1975), pp. 170–80.

11 Scholem, p. 177.

12 This was published in 1863 and is to be found among George Eliot's and G. H. Lewes's books in Dr Williams's library. See William Baker, *The George Eliot–George Henry Lewes Library: an Annotated Catalogue of Their Books at Dr Williams's Library, London* (New York, 1977). It is certain that George Eliot had read Levi's book. Baker comments on it: 'Contains G.E's pencilled marginal linings and markings' (p. 118). The connections between the Jewish interpretive practice of midrash and kabbalism are suggested by the following passage from Deborah L. Madsen's *Rereading Allegory: a Narrative Approach to Genre* (London, 1996):

> Primarily midrash was used to renovate the sacred book by giving account of its ongoing relevance and 'newness', and to provide a medium through which new ideas could be introduced to the book, religion, and culture without taint of heresy, schism or any loss of authority. The early Cabbalists made use of midrash in this way, to present new ideas in the guise of traditional, authoritative exegesis. Joseph Dan, describing the relationship between Cabbalist symbols and their midrashic interpretations, writes: 'The midrash thus becomes a necessary tool for a religion based on divine revelation, once actual [physical] revelation no longer takes place' ... Indeed, Judaic midrash presents a unique blending of classical and patristic, metaphorical and metonymic, allegorical methods. (pp. 38–9)

Mordecai refers to midrash at the end of Chapter 51 of *Daniel Deronda*. Emanuel Deutsch's *Quarterly Review* article, together with other relevant discussion of the Talmud, can be found in *Literary Remains of the Late Emanuel Deutsch with a Brief Memoir* (London, 1874).

13 For a detailed study of Simon Magus as a proto-Faust, see E. M. Butler, *The Myth of the Magus* (Cambridge, 1979).

14 See 'Acts of the Apostles', Chapter 8, verses 9–24.

15 Scholem, p. 172. Scholem quotes from the account in the Sefer Yetzirah as follows:

> First, he says, the human pneuma transformed itself into warm nature and sucked up the surrounding air like a cupping glass. Then he transformed this air that had taken form within the pneuma into water, then into blood ... and from the blood he made flesh.

When the flesh had become firm, he had produced a man, not from earth but from air, so convincing himself that he could make a new man. He also claimed that he had returned him to the air by undoing the transformations. (pp. 172–3)

This can be compared with the description of Paracelsus's method of creation, also cited by Scholem:

> According to Jacoby, Paracelsus's homunculus was an 'artificial embryo, for which urine, sperm, and blood, considered as vehicles of the soul-substance, provided the materia prima'. At the end of forty days the homunculus began to develop from the putrefaction of this raw material. (p. 197)

Jewish mysticism did not advocate this use of body effluvia but used clay or mud.

16 *A Treasury of Jewish Folklore*, ed. Nathan Ausubel, p. 605.
17 *A Treasury of Jewish Folklore*, pp. 605–12. Ausubel writes: 'So in its despair, the folk-mind, fed by sickly cabalistic dreams and myths, created the figure of the *golem* to protect the Jews' puny weakness with his enormous physical strength' (p. 605).
18 Scholem, pp. 190–1
19 Byron L. Sherwin, *The Golem Legend: Origins and Implications* (Lanham, New York, 1985), p. 8.
20 Sherwin, p. 40.
21 Scholem, pp. 181–2.
22 Scholem, p. 199.
23 Thomas Carlyle, *On Heroes, Hero-worship and the Heroic in Literature* (London, 1896), p. 283 (Carlyle's italics).
24 George Eliot, *Impressions of Theophrastus Such*, ed. Nancy Henry (London, 1994), p. 137. All subsequent references will be to this edition and will be cited parenthetically in the text by the abbreviation *TS* and the page number.
25 *Encyclopaedia Judaica* (Jerusalem, 1971), Volume VII, p. 756.
26 George Eliot had read *Sartor Resartus* in 1841 and its effect on her is suggested in the following comment in an essay on Carlyle published in 1855: 'The character of his influence is best seen in the fact that many of the men who have the least agreement with his opinions are those to whom the reading of *Sartor Resartus* was an epoch in the history of their minds.' See *Essays of George Eliot*, ed. Thomas Pinney (London, 1963), p. 214. All subsequent references to this volume will be cited parenthetically within the text by the abbreviation *Essays* and page number.
27 Though there is no reference to *Frankenstein* in Eliot's letters or essays it is almost inconceivable that the author of *The Lifted Veil* would not have been acquainted with at least the basic story. U. C. Knoepflmacher argues that *Frankenstein* significantly influenced *The Lifted Veil*. See *George Eliot's Early Novels: the Limits of Realism* (Berkeley, 1968), pp. 140–3. *Frankenstein* contains elements of Jewish mysticism and experimental

natural philosophy that can be found in German Romantic writers – in addition to Goethe – such as Chamisso and von Arnim. For example, Chamisso's Faust story, 'Peter Schlemihl', in which the hero sells his shadow to the devil, employs an archetypical character from Jewish folklore, the 'Schlemiel'. *Frankenstein* combines these elements with Gnostic influences drawn from the work of Shelley, Byron and Coleridge's 'The Ancient Mariner'. It has been suggested that Mary Shelley was influenced by the golem legend. Peter Haining writes:

> What seems more likely still is that an important influence [on *Frankenstein*] was the real-life man of clay, the Golem, who had been spoken of in Jewish folklore for over 300 years. An account of this monstrous creature who had been brought to life in medieval times by Rabbi Judah Loew in order to protect the Jews in the Prague ghetto from a pogrom was to be found in the collection of ghost stories, *Fantasmagoriana* read around the fire in the Villa Diodati. Peter Haining (ed.), *The Frankenstein Omnibus* (London, 1995), p. 597.

Whereas Victor represents the Faustian questing scientific over-reacher, trying to shape the world, the creature and its subsequent relationship with *Frankenstein* embody more of the scientific and Judaic influences. The creature represents the ability to shift the reader's responses within the text; as Paul Sherwin puts it in '*Frankenstein*: Creation as Catastrophe' (*PMLA*, 96 [1981], p. 891): 'A kind of wandering signifier, the Creature proceeds through the text triggering various signifying effects.' Some of these signifying effects operate allegorically – particularly the dangerous servant aspect of the legend. Gnosticism, a philosophy with strong appeal to those drawn to a Romantic ethos, is significant in the texts mentioned above, since it had interacted greatly with kabbalistic mysticism, and had developed as a reaction against the increasingly literal tendencies of orthodox Judaism: 'for gnosticism itself, or at least certain of its basic impulses, was a revolt, partly perhaps of Jewish origin, against anti-mythical Judaism'. See Scholem, p. 98.

28 *Sartor Resartus*, p. 17.
29 *Sartor Resartus*, p. 36.
30 See John Hruschka, *Carlyle's Rabbi Hero: Teufelsdroeckh and the Midrashic Tradition* (Bloomington, 1992).
31 Alexander Altmann, *Studies in Religious Philosophy and Mysticism* (London, 1969).
32 George Eliot, *Adam Bede*, ed. Valentine Cunningham (Oxford, 1996), p. 97. All subsequent references will be to this edition and will be cited parenthetically in the text by the abbreviation *AB* and the page number.
33 Altmann, p. 98.
34 Karen Chase, *Eros and Psyche: the Representation of Personality in Charlotte Brontë, Charles Dickens and George Eliot* (New York and London, 1984), p. 2.

35 George Eliot, *Daniel Deronda*, ed. Graham Handley (Oxford, 1988), p. 642. All subsequent references will be to this edition and will be cited parenthetically in the text by the abbreviation *DD* and the page number.

36 George Eliot, *Felix Holt*, ed. Fred C. Thomson (Oxford, 1988), p. 35. All subsequent references will be to this edition and will be cited parenthetically in the text by the abbreviation *FH* and the page number.

37 J. W. von Goethe, *Faust Part One*, trans. Philip Wayne (Harmondsworth, 1986), p. 54. All subsequent references will be to this edition and will be cited parenthetically in the text by the abbreviation *Faust* I and the page number. References to *Faust Part Two*, trans. P. Wayne (Harmondsworth, 1986) will also be cited in the text, by the abbreviation *Faust* II and the page number.

38 See the essay, 'The Wasp Credited with the Honeycomb'.

39 Scholem, p. 204.

40 In using the term 'anti-Semitism' to characterise George Eliot's early attitudes to Jews and Judaism one should bear in mind, however, that this term has certain modern connotations that are not appropriate in discussing her views, as 'anti-Semitism' did not yet exist as a concept. As Nancy Henry has pointed out, 'anti-Semitism' was first used in German only in 1879 and in English translation three years later. See her essay, 'Ante-Anti-Semitism: George Eliot's *Impressions of Theophrastus Such*', in *Victorian Identities: Social and Cultural Formations in Nineteenth-Century Literature*, ed. Ruth Robbins and Julian Wolfreys (Basingstoke and London, 1996), pp. 65–80.

41 The *George Eliot Letters*, ed. Gordon S. Haight (New Haven and London, Volumes I–VII, 1954; Volumes VIII–IX, 1978), VI, 196. All further references will be cited as *Letters* and included parenthetically in the text.

42 George Eliot, *Scenes of Clerical Life*, ed. Thomas A. Noble (Oxford, 1988), p. 36.

43 David Cecil, *Early Victorian Novelists: Essays in Evaluation* (Harmondsworth, 1948), pp. 218, 244.

44 Cecil, p. 244.

45 See Seymour Chatman, *Story and Discourse: Narrative Structure in Fiction and Film* (Ithaca, New York and London, 1978).

46 Knoepflmacher, pp. 240, 247. Other critics have shared Knoepflmacher's view. Walter Allen states that it is 'essentially a myth of spiritual rebirth'. See *George Eliot* (London, 1965), p. 120; F. R. Leavis thinks that 'the atmosphere precludes too direct a reference . . . to our everyday sense of how things happen'. See *The Great Tradition* (London, 1966), p. 59. Mario Praz states: '*Silas Marner* is simply an allegorical fairy-tale: Silas finds the gold of the little girl's hair instead of the material gold he had been longing for.' See *The Hero in Eclipse in Victorian Fiction*, trans. Angus Davidson (Oxford, 1956), p. 352.

47 See, for example, Colin MacCabe's discussion of George Eliot in relation to Joyce in *James Joyce and the Revolution of the Word* (London, 1978).

48 In his book *Shadowtime: History and Representation in Hardy, Conrad and George Eliot* (London and New York, 1993), Jim Reilly is troubled

by apparent contradictions in George Eliot: 'She seems to be able to express scepticism and yearning simultaneously towards an object that is more contradictory the more one examines it' (pp. 56–7). Reilly perhaps fails to appreciate George Eliot's links with Romantic irony which holds such contradictions in balance without resolving them. Reilly also does not see the point of her use of myth and asserts: '. . . myths are required to mask social tensions and oppressions for which they offer purely illusory solutions' (p. 95). Such a view of myth is clearly reductive and it leads to Reilly's failure to appreciate how George Eliot uses it to escape some of the limitations and contradictions within realism that Reilly discusses so powerfully.

49 Amanda Anderson has argued that Deronda's relationship with Mordecai represents a dialogical encounter with tradition: '. . . there are significant tensions within [Eliot's] own conception of Jewish nationalism. Commonly, the Jewish plot is cast as romance and the English as realism, but through Daniel's encounter with Judaism a complex tension is generated within the Jewish plot itself. Indeed, only after reconstructing Daniel's reflective and dialogical relation to his cultural heritage can we see the stark contrast between his form of nationalism and Mordecai's.' 'George Eliot and the Jewish Question', *Yale Journal of Criticism*, 10 (1997), pp. 48–9.

50 Northrop Frye, *Anatomy of Criticism: Four Essays* (Princeton, NJ, 1957), p. 140.

51 Paul de Man, *Blindness and Insight: Essays in the Rhetoric of Contemporary Criticism* (London, 1983), p. 207.

52 The power of Jewish stereotypes which any novelist who creates Jewish characters will have to contend with is demonstrated forcibly by Frank Felsenstein in *Anti-Semitic Stereotypes: a Paradigm of Otherness in English Popular Culture, 1660–1830* (Baltimore and London, 1995). Because of this power of the Jewish stereotype George Eliot may have concluded that the kind of realistic representation she normally employed in characterisation would not be viable for her Jewish characters and that therefore she would have to some extent to work with various Jewish stereotypes, but undermining their anti-Semitic content.

53 Bryan Cheyette, *Constructions of 'the Jew' in English Literature and Society: Racial Representations, 1875–1945* (Cambridge, 1993), pp. 48, 51, 52.

54 A recurrent motif in George Eliot's fiction is the importance of choice and this may account for the novel's implied negative view of the Princess's behaviour with regard to Deronda. To deprive someone of choice is to deprive him or her of freedom and thus to undermine their human identity. When Deronda accusingly asks his mother, '"How could you choose my birthright for me?"' she responds, '"I chose for you what I would have chosen for myself"' (*DD*, p. 538). Whereas she had a choice, she has tried to deny him one, thus reducing him to a golem-like creature under her control. Similarly in *The Mill on the Floss*, Stephen Guest deprives Maggie Tulliver of choice in their drift down river: '"I couldn't choose yesterday"' (*The Mill on the Floss*, ed. Gordon S. Haight [Oxford, 1996], p. 474. All subsequent references will be to this edition and will be cited parenthetically in the

text by the abbreviation *Mill* and the page number). Even such a rigid moralist as Tom Tulliver gives Maggie a choice as to whether she continue to meet Philip Wakem – 'Choose!' (*Mill*, p. 342) – though the terms of the choice make it for Maggie a choice of evils. Rosemarie Bodenheimer, however, sees this as 'a parody of choosing'. See *The Real Life of Mary Ann Evans: George Eliot, Her Letters and Fiction* (Ithaca and London, 1994), p. 107.

55 Related to this point is Graham Handley's argument in his introduction to the World's Classics edition of the novel that George Eliot does not overprivilege Mordecai at the expense of those who disagree with him: 'the critical error is to read him as self-consciously embodying his author's views and unqualified sympathy. He embodies what George Eliot intended he should – a realistic Jew of mystical obsessiveness born out of his time and turned back upon himself and his visions until the fortuitous advent of Deronda' (*DD*, p. xvii).

56 Cheyette's use of *Impressions of Theophrastus Such* is open to similar objections to those that can be levelled at his discussion of *Daniel Deronda*. He refers to 'Eliot's persona' in that text but passages are quoted as if they give unmediated access to George Eliot's thought without any necessity to take account of the narration and literary aspects of the text. As Nancy Henry has argued, one cannot ignore the interplay beween the mock-Theophrastian mode that George Eliot adopts and the 'content' of the essays. Cheyette ignores this in order to embed her in a rigid ideology. See Henry's introduction to *Impressions of Theophrastus Such*: 'The verbal tricks that characterise *Impressions* – contorted sentences, ambiguous quotations, incessant puns – destabilise the identification of sources, the fixed meaning of words, and the readers' expectations' (*TS*, p. xiii).

57 For a discussion of Yeats's relation to 'belief', see Richard Ellmann, *The Identity of Yeats* (London, 1975), Chapter 3.

58 See *Basic Writings of Nietzsche*, ed. and trans. Walter Kaufmann (New York, 1968), p. 135.

59 G. H. Lewes, *The Foundations of a Creed* (London, 1874), p. 329.

60 See *Middlemarch*, Chapter 27: 'The reveries from which it was difficult for him [Lydgate] to detach himself were ideal constructions of something else than Rosamond's virtues' (*Middlemarch*, ed. David Carroll (Oxford, 1997), p. 270). All subsequent references will be to this edition and will be cited parenthetically in the text by the title *Middlemarch* and the page number.

61 Ludwig Feuerbach, *The Essence of Christianity*, trans. George Eliot (New York, Evanston, and London, 1957), p. 63.

1 George Eliot and Kabbalism: Historical and Literary Context

1 William Baker thinks the roots of Eliot's anti-Jewish views when young may have been shaped by such works as Defoe's *The Political History of the Devil*. See *George Eliot and Judaism*, pp. 12–13.

2 See Baker, *George Eliot and Judaism*, p. 10. See also Baker's essay 'The Kabbalah, Mordecai, and George Eliot's Religion of Humanity' in *The Yearbook of English Studies*, 3 (1973), 216–21 in which he discusses Mordecai's connections with kabbalism. In both this article and his book Baker argues that the major source of Eliot's knowledge was C. D. Ginsburg's *The Kabbalah: its Doctrines, Development and Literature* (1863): 'George Eliot's notebooks indicate that the main source of her Kabbalistic ideas is the work of the Anglo-Jewish scholar Christian David Ginsburg' (p. 217). As we have suggested, however, it is likely that she had knowledge of kabbalism before reading Ginsburg. The influence of kabbalism in England between the Renaissance and Blake is discussed in Désirée Hirst's *Hidden Riches: Traditional Symbolism from the Renaissance to Blake* (London, 1964). It is possible Eliot had some awareness of this tradition through her study of, for example, the Bible and Milton.

3 Trevor Ling, *A History of Religion East and West: an Introduction and Interpretation*, p. 281.

4 *Encyclopedia of Religion*, editor-in-chief M. Elaide (New York, 1987), Volume 1, p. 458.

5 For a discussion of Kalonymos, see Baker, *George Eliot and Judaism*, pp. 226–30.

6 Solomon Maimon, *The Autobiography of Solomon Maimon*, trans. J. Clark Murray (London, 1954), p. 77.

7 George Eliot, *Romola*, ed. Andrew Brown (Oxford, 1994), p. 14. All subsequent references will be to this edition and will be cited parenthetically in the text with the title and page number.

8 *The Jewish Caravan*, ed. Leo M. Schwarz (New York, 1935), p. 187.

9 Scholem, p. 32.

10 'The Golem of Prague', in *A Treasury of Jewish Folklore*, p. 612.

11 *Encyclopedia of Religion*, Volume 12, pp. 118–19.

12 Similar stereotypical attitudes towards Gypsies are also expressed in the novels – as with the assumption that the passing Gypsy pedlar has stolen Marner's gold – or they conform to type, as in *The Mill on the Floss*. Traditional stereotypes of Gypsies and Jews often merge, with their nationless states being open to charges of Gypsy cannibalism cited by George Borrow or the 'blood libel' directed at Jews.

13 Baker, *George Eliot and Judaism*, p. 120.

14 Leslie Fiedler, *Waiting for the End: the American Literary Scene from Hemingway to Baldwin* (London, 1965), p. 73.

15 Fiedler, p. 73. Fiedler recognises the archetypal representations of Jews in *Daniel Deronda*, attributing the '"little Jew," ... enduring and forgiving under abuse – a kind of Semitic version of "Uncle Tom"' to 'a spreading out and down of George Eliot's hortatory philo-Semitism', pp. 73, 74.

16 Michael Ragussis, *Figures of Conversion: 'the Jewish Question' and English National Identity* (Durham, NC and London, 1995), p. 4. Conversion is also discussed in Frank Felsenstein, *Anti-Semitic Stereotypes: a Paradigm of Otherness in English Popular Culture, 1660–1830* (Baltimore and London, 1995), pp. 90–122. Perhaps one of the major reasons for Eliot's attraction

to Judaism was its opposition to conversion which could be taken to mean that literal belief in its theology was not essential. Emanuel Deutsch in a lecture discussing the Talmud, given in 1868, writes: 'There was no occasion for conversion to Judaism, as long as a man fulfilled the seven fundamental laws. Every man who did so was regarded as a believer to all intents and purposes' (*Literary Remains of the Late Emanuel Deutsch*, p. 147).

17 Ragussis, p. 8.
18 Ragussis, pp. 12–13.
19 Ragussis, p. 1.
20 See Note 15 above.
21 Ragussis, p. 234.
22 See Baker, *George Eliot and Judaism*, p. 35.
23 See K. M. Newton, 'Historical Protoypes in Middlemarch', *English Studies*, 56 (1975), pp. 403–8.
24 Baker believes that there is a relationship between Dino and Yehuda Halevi. See Baker, *George Eliot and Judaism*, p. 96.

2   Kabbalistic Philosophy and the Novels

1 Ling, p. 115.
2 *The Talmud*, trans. H. Polano (London and New York, n.d.), p. 270.
3 *Encyclopedia of Religion*, 6, p. 208.
4 Josephus, *Jewish Antiquaries*, I–IV, trans. A. St J. Thackeray (Cambridge, Mass., 1961), p. 19.
5 *Encyclopaedia Judaica*, X, p. 617.
6 Rabbi Moses C. Luzzatto, *General Principles of the Kabbalah*, trans. The Research Centre of Kabbalah (New York, 1970), p. xxv.
7 *Sartor Resartus*, p. 15.
8 *Sartor Resartus*, p. 232.
9 George Eliot, *The Spanish Gypsy, The Legend of Jubal and Other Poems, Old and New* (Edinburgh and London, n.d.), p. 169. All subsequent references will be to this edition and will be cited parenthetically in the text with the abbreviation *SG* and page number.
10 This image of conscience as a haunting dread is one which is also seen in *The Mill on the Floss*: after Maggie's boat trip with Stephen it appears as a phantom figure of Lucy which gains more definition as the conscience pangs become more painful: 'And as the days passed on, that pale image became more and more distinct; the picture grew into more speaking definiteness under the avenging hand of remorse' (*Mill*, p. 508).
11 Ragussis, p. 270.
12 George Eliot, *Silas Marner*, ed. Terence Cave (Oxford, 1996), p. 30. All subsequent references will be to this edition and will be cited parenthetically in the text with the abbreviation *SM* and page number.
13 Luzzatto, p. 50.
14 *Encyclopaedia Judaica*, X, p. 610.
15 Andrew Lang, *Magic and Religion* (New York, 1969), p. 94.

16 *Encyclopaedia Judaica*, VII, p. 754.
17 *Encyclopaedia Judaica*, VII, p. 574.
18 Baker, *George Eliot and Judaism*, p. 62.
19 Thomas Carlyle, *On Heroes, Hero-worship and the Heroic in History* (London, 1840), p. 162.
20 *Encyclopaedia Judaica*, VI, p. 19.
21 *Encyclopaedia Judaica*, VI, pp. 19–20.
22 *Encyclopaedia Judaica*, X, pp. 610–11.
23 E. S. Shaffer writes:

> The mystical basis of the I–thou unity is the gnostic-cabbalistic notion of Adam as the soul that contained all souls ... The moral task of man in the Jewish cabbala is to restore his primordial spiritual structure, and so contribute to the restoration of the spiritual structure of mankind ... In *Daniel Deronda*, the mystical substratum is expressed directly through the fraternal relation of the master and his disciple. (See *'Kubla Khan' and 'The Fall of Jerusalem': the Mythological School in Biblical Criticism and Secular Literature 1770–1880* [Cambridge, 1975], p. 255.)

24 Luzzatto, p. xxvi.
25 Luzzatto, p. xxxiv.
26 *Sartor Resartus*, pp. 207–8.

3 From Formless Matter to Matter with Form

1 Altmann, p. 80.
2 Baker, *George Eliot and Judaism*, p. 152. Emanuel Deutsch particularly stressed the links between Talmudic Judaism and both Christianity and Islam, arguing that the essence of the latter religions is contained within Talmudic Judaism. See his essays on the Talmud and Islam in his *Literary Remains*.
3 *Sartor Resartus*, p. 265.
4 *Sartor Resartus*, p. 9.
5 Mary Shelley, *Frankenstein*, with an introduction by R. E. Dowse and D. J. Palmer (London, 1985), p. 17. All references will be to this edition and will be cited parenthetically in the text with the page number.
6 George Eliot, *The Lifted Veil; Brother Jacob*, ed. Helen Small (Oxford, 1999), p. 36. All subsequent references will be to this edition and will be cited parenthetically in the text with the abbreviation *LV* and page number.
7 *Sartor Resartus*, pp. 231–2.
8 See *Sartor Resartus*, pp. 255–60.
9 'Psalms', Chapter 104, verse 2.
10 Altmann, p. 134.
11 See Baker, *George Eliot and Judaism*, pp. 189–90 in which he argues that kabbalism is very influential on this scene in the novel.
12 *Sartor Resartus*, p. 11.

13 Altmann, p. 128.
14 *Heroes and Hero-worship*, p. 241.
15 *Heroes and Hero-worship*, p. 213 (Carlyle's emphasis).
16 *Heroes and Hero-worship*, pp. 243–4 (Carlyle's emphasis).

4 The Relationship between Creator and Creature

1   Luzzatto, p. 153.
2   *Sartor Resartus*, p. 279.
3   Luzzatto, pp. xiii–xiv.
4   Mircea Eliade, *Myths, Dreams and Mysteries*, trans. Philip Mairet (London, 1960), p. 15.
5   Paul A. Cantor, *Creature and Creator: Myth-making and English Romanticism* (Cambridge, 1984), p. 105.
6   Altmann, p. 138.
7   Luzzatto, p. 163.
8   Cantor, p. x.
9   George Eliot, *The Lifted Veil; Brother Jacob*, ed. Helen Small (Oxford, 1999), p. 87.
10 Charles Dickens, *Great Expectations*, ed. Angus Calder (Harmondsworth, 1979), p. 337.
11 *Great Expectations*, p. 340.
12 *Great Expectations*, p. 354.
13 See Terry Eagleton, 'Power and Knowledge in *The Lifted Veil*' in *George Eliot*, ed. K. M. Newton (London and New York, 1991), pp. 53–64.
14 Nina Auerbach, *Women and the Demon: the Life of a Victorian Myth* (Cambridge, Mass. and London, 1982), p. 184.
15 See A. Reville, *Prolégomènes de l'Histoire des Religions* (Paris, 1886), p. 163.
16 Karl Marx and Friedrich Engels, 'Manifesto of the Communist Party', in *Basic Writings on Politics and Philosophy*, ed. Lewis R. Feuer (London, 1969), p. 54.
17 *The Talmud*, p. 241.
18 Luzzatto, p. xiv.
19 Cantor, p. 106.
20 Sherwin, *PMLA* 96 (1981), p. 896.
21 Ludwig Feuerbach, *The Essence of Christianity*, trans. George Eliot (New York, 1957), p. 80.
22 Josephus, I–IV, p. 49.
23 Josephus, V–VIII, p. 197.
24 In *Adam Bede: a New Edition* (London and Edinburgh, n.d.) Chapter 17 has been revised, and emphasises authorial imprint and creative influence to a greater extent than in the 1st edn. The narrator says: 'I might fashion life and character after my own liking' (p. 149).
25 See Baldick, *In Frankenstein's Shadow* (Oxford, 1987), pp. 148–52.
26 *On Heroes and Hero-worship*, p. 3.
27 Sherwin, *PMLA*, 96 (1981), p. 895.
28 Translator's note, Luzzatto, p. 214.
29 *Encyclopaedia Judaica*, X, p. 609.

30 *Encyclopedia of Religion*, 12, p. 122.
31 Altmann, p. 8. The sentiment is attributed to Al-Ghazali.
32 Altmann, p. 13.

5 Ideals of Perfection

1 *Hebrew Myths*, p. 65.
2 Josephus, V–VIII, p. 247.
3 See *The Complete Works of Percy Bysshe Shelley* (London, n.d.), p. 3, 'Queen Mab', ll. 130–3.
4 Cantor, p. 128.
5 The idea also appears in 'The Birthmark', the short story by Hawthorne, an author who influenced Eliot. In 'The Birthmark', Aylmer, a scientist and natural philosopher, intends to remove this blemish from his wife's cheek. He tells her: '"There is no taint of imperfection on thy spirit. Thy sensible frame, too shall be perfect."' Hawthorne, *Mosses from an Old Manse*, Centenary Edition, Volume X (Ohio, 1974), p. 53. For discussion of Hawthorne's influence on Eliot, see Edward Stokes, *Hawthorne's Influence on Charles Dickens and George Eliot* (Queensland, 1985).
6 See below in the chapter on 'Homelessness' for the Hebrew origin of 'Klezmer' as an itinerant musician.
7 J. M. Kemble's *Saxons in England*, quoted by J. M. Mackinlay, *Folklore in Scottish Lochs and Springs* (Glasgow, 1893), p. 163.
8 Prince Camaralzaman is the hero of a tale from *The Thousand and One Nights*. He is a beautiful but misogynistic youth who will not marry until, after the actions of an angel and a genie, he sees Princess Barouda, a beautiful but misanthropic girl. There is great mutual attraction, and after various complications and diversions common to folktales, they marry. Eliot's purpose in citing this character in particular would seem to be to indicate the attraction between Deronda and Gwendolen, since Gwendolen's attitude towards men resembles Barouda's, and Mirah's does not.
9 Luzzatto, p. 1.
10 Luzzatto, p. 138.
11 Luzzatto, p. 146.
12 Joseph Campbell, *The Hero with a Thousand Faces* (London, 1979), p. 239.
13 Scholem, pp. 55–6.
14 See Cantor, p. 50. Cantor also discusses the male–female aspect of *Los-Enitharmon*.
15 Luzzatto, p. 161.
16 Luzzatto, p. 133.
17 *The Talmud*, p. 222.
18 *Encyclopedia of Religion*, 12, p. 122.
19 Maimon, p. 88.
20 See Altmann, p. 26. He quotes the mystic writer, Ibn Ezra. When Mordecai is telling Deronda about the mystic soul he has inherited, he says that '"it debated with Aben-Ezra"' (*DD*, p. 427).

21 See Altmann, p. 31. He refers to Proclus's theory of the ascent of the soul.
22 Matthew Arnold, *Culture and Anarchy*, ed. J. Dover Wilson (Cambridge, 1986), p. 72.
23 Eliade maintains that the myth of the 'Noble Savage' is the result of a wish to return to a paradisaical state, by imagining humans to have been in a state of Homeric heroism with a pe-Fall naivety, instead of having evolved from troglodytes.
24 *Encyclopaedia Judaica*, VII, p. 577.
25 See discussion in Chapter 2.
26 *Encyclopaedia Judaica*, X, p. 610.
27 Altmann, p. 81: he quotes the commentator, Ibn Bajjo.
28 Maimon, p. 166.
29 Cantor, p. 108.
30 See Cynthia Chase's deconstructive reading of *Daniel Deronda*, 'The Decomposition of the Elephants', which focuses on Hans Meyrick's letter, and K. M. Newton's discussion of Romantic irony, in *George Eliot*, ed. Newton, pp. 198–217 and 229–30.
31 Luzzatto, p. 176.
32 Manasseh Unger, 'How the Rabbi of Kelev Freed a Song' in *The Jewish Caravan*, p. 391.
33 Luzzatto, p. 161.
34 *Sartor Resartus*, p. 138. A similar idea is present in Matthew Arnold's concept of culture, in which perfection can only be reached collectively and individual perfection is only part of the collective: 'It is not satisfied till we all come to a perfect man; it knows that the sweetness and light of the few must be imperfect until the raw and unkindled masses of humanity are touched with sweetness and light' (Arnold, p. 69).
35 See Baker, pp. 166–7.
36 Scholem, p. 46.
37 See in the text above the quotation from *Daniel Deronda*, p. 628.
38 *Encyclopaedia Judaica*, VI, p. 780.
39 See Scholem, p. 2.

6   Science, Pseudo-Science and Transgression

1 Maimon, p. 71.
2 Maimon, p. 70.
3 See *Encyclopaedia Judaica*, II, pp. 542–3.
4 See *Encyclopaedia Judaica*, II, p. 543.
5 See *Encyclopedia of Religion*, 12, p. 121.
6 See *Encyclopaedia Judaica*, VII, pp. 1377–8.
7 See *Encyclopedia of Religion*, 1, p. 461.
8 See *Encyclopaedia Judaica*, VII, p. 755.
9 See *Encyclopaedia Judaica*, II, p. 544.
10 See, for example, Baker, *George Eliot and Judaism*, Chapter 7.
11 Baldick, p. 63.

12 Baldick, p. 64.
13 Hawthorne, *Mosses from an Old Manse*, p. 49.
14 *Sartor Resartus*, pp. 53–4.
15 *Women and the Demon*, p. 183.
16 *Women and the Demon*, p. 184.
17 For an account of this see *Letters*, I, p. 180.
18 As well as following his experiments, Eliot was acquainted with Gregory's accounts as given in *Letters to a Candid Inquirer on Animal Magnetism*. See Beryl Gray's 'Afterword' to her edition of *The Lifted Veil* (London, 1987). It is interesting to note that the narrative recollection of Gustav Meyrink's novel, *The Golem*, is a clairvoyant one induced by wearing the wrong hat.
19 Chase, p. 182.
20 *Sartor Resartus*, p. 16.
21 See Baldick, Chapter 4.
22 Sally Shuttleworth, *George Eliot and Nineteenth-Century Science: the Make-Believe of a Beginning* (Cambridge, 1994), p. 22.
23 Bloom (ed.), *Mary Shelley's* Frankenstein, p. 17.
24 Baldick, p. 81.
25 'Even in the development of ancient belief systems, alchemical-type activities and creativity – particularly human creativity – are linked. In the myths of ancient Babylon, Sumeria and Egypt, all of which influenced Hebrew mythology, there was a creative relationship between metallurgy and obstetrics' (Eliade, pp. 169–70) so that the production of metal was likened to the production of children. This idea may be alluded to in *Silas Marner* when Silas's gold is stolen and apparently magically replaced by a child, an ironical version of alchemy in which gold is the base metal transformed into the golden hair of Eppie whose value for Silas is eventually beyond material calculation.
26 Shuttleworth, p. 8 quotes Walter Buckley, *Sociology and Modern Systems* (New Jersey, 1967).
27 Shuttleworth, p. 6.
28 Cantor, p. 109.
29 Baldick, pp. 72–3.
30 '... the idea of perfection as an inward condition of the mind and spirit is at variance with the mechanical and material civilisation in esteem with us, and nowhere, as I have said, so much in esteem with us.' See Arnold, *Culture and Anarchy*, p. 49.
31 Baldick, p. 105.
32 *Sartor Resartus*, p. 214.
33 *Sartor Resartus*, p. 214.
34 See Baldick, pp. 75–84. See also K. M. Newton in *George Eliot: Romantic Humanist*, p. 102 for reference to the Ahab-like qualities of Tulliver.
35 Even in her essays this kind of imagery is used, indicating her preoccupation with the subject. In 'Silly Novels by Lady Novelists' she writes: 'The finest effort to reanimate the past is of course only approximative' (*Essays*, p. 320), and discussing story-telling in 'Leaves from a Notebook' she creates a link between the power of language

and vivification: 'to see a word for the first time either as substantive or adjective in a connection where we care about knowing its complete meaning, is the way to vivify its meaning in our recollection' (*Essays*, pp. 444–5).

7 Investing Form with Essence

1 *Hebrew Myths*, pp. 64–5.
2 See Josephus, I–IV, p. 50.
3 See *Encyclopedia of Religion*, 12, p. 120.
4 *Heroes and Hero-worship*, p. 250.
5 *Heroes and Hero-worship*, p. 170.
6 Cantor, p. 3.
7 *Encyclopaedia Judaica*, X, pp. 611, 612.
8 Baldick, p. 86.
9 '[The workers] direct their attacks not against the bourgeois conditions of production, but against the instruments of production themselves; they destroy imported wares that compete with their labour, they smash to pieces machinery, they set factories ablaze...' See Karl Marx and Friedrich Engels, *Basic Writings on Politics and Philosophy*, p. 57.
10 See *A Treasury of Jewish Folklore*, p. 604.
11 *Heroes and Hero-worship*, p. 26.

8 Homelessness and Speechlessness

1 Josephus, I–IV, p. 153.
2 Quoted in Baker, *George Eliot and Judaism*, p. 165.
3 *Encyclopaedia Judaica*, VI, p. 1382.
4 *Encyclopaedia Judaica*, X, p. 618. The Sefirot are divine emanations through which God's power is carried.
5 *Encyclopaedia Judaica*, X, p. 619.
6 Bernard Semmel, in *George Eliot and the Politics of National Inheritance* (New York, Oxford, 1994) emphasises the Romance myth as the motivation behind the 'disinherited one'.
7 Semmel contends that the centrality of nationalism in the nineteenth century was not just European, but was also a force in America, the Middle East and in parts of the British Empire.
8 Deborah Epstein Nord acknowledges the similarities between the Gypsies and Jews in nineteenth-century England, but also mentions the differences in their perception at that time: 'Unlike... the Jew, who, though outsider, functioned within English Society, the gypsy hovered on the outskirts of the English world, unassimilable, a domestic and visible but socially peripheral character.' See '"Marks of Race": Gypsy Figures and Eccentric Femininity in Nineteenth-Century Women's Writing', *Victorian Studies*, 41 (1998), p. 189.
9 See Baker, *George Eliot and Judaism*, p. 113.
10 Borrow, p. 123.
11 Amanda Anderson suggests that Mordecai may represent a threat to

a certain concept of modern national identity: '. . . the figure of the Jew in Victorian culture became the charge site for underlying anxieties forming nationalist discourse, which is always trying to negotiate the challenges or disruptions caused by traditions or subcultures perceived to be particularist, alien, or, to adopt a recent term, transnational. As two extremes, the tradition-bound Jew and the cosmopolitan Jew figured threats to, and defined the limits of, modern national identity, which, however civic minded, was never articulated wholly apart from a notion of shared ethnic or cultural heritage.' 'George Eliot and the Jewish Question', *Yale Journal of Criticism*, 10 (1997), p. 44. We can see a relation between this and characters from *Daniel Deronda*, where Mordecai is the tradition-bound Jew and Klesmer the cosmopolitan one.

12 Edward W. Said, *The Question of Palestine* (London, 1980), pp. 63, 65. Graham Handley also comments in the Introduction to the World's Classics edition of *Daniel Deronda*: 'It is one of the tragedies of our century, which George Eliot could not foresee, that separate nationalisms have destroyed positive communication for good: the part is often no longer part of the whole but a separate power entity serving itself, not serving others' (*DD*, p. xix).

13 Marc E. Wohlfarth, 'Daniel Deronda and the Politics of Nationalism', *Nineteenth-Century Literature*, 53 (1998), p. 210. For a fuller discussion of this question see Newton, *George Eliot: Romantic Humanist*, pp. 92–4.

14 *Jewish Poets of Spain*, trans. and introduced by David Goldstein (Harmondsworth, 1971), p. 117.

15 *Jewish Poets of Spain*, pp. 129, 132.

16 See S. Baring-Gould, *Curious Myths of the Middle Ages* (London, Oxford and Cambridge, 1877), Chapter 1, pp. 1–31; and Appendix, pp. 637–40. See also the chapter on the Wandering Jew in Frank Felsenstein, *Anti-Semitic Stereotypes: a Paradigm of Otherness in English Popular Culture, 1660–1830* (Baltimore and London, 1995), pp. 59–89.

17 *Sartor Resartus*, p. 17.

18 See *Lyrical Ballads*, 2nd edn, ed. Derek Roper (London, 1976), p. 119, ll. 135–9 from 'The Ancient Mariner'. In Roper's notes to the text, he writes of the cross, 'This visible emblem of guilt connects the Mariner with the Wandering Jew and with Cain, two figures which were in Coleridge's mind at about this time' (p. 343).

19 'The Ancient Mariner, ll. 115–19.

20 'The Ancient Mariner, ll. 431–5.

21 Aubrey's *Miscellanies*, quoted by Jennifer Westwood in *Albion: a Guide to Legendary Britain* (–, 1985), p. 224. The version of the legend from which this extract was taken was said to have originated in Staffordshire, but found its way around the Midlands.

22 See S. Baring-Gould, *Curious Myths of the Middle Ages*.

23 Leo Rosten, *The Joys of Yiddish* (Harmondsworth, 1971), pp. 186–7. See also Baker, *George Eliot and Judaism*, p. 234, for a discussion of the name 'Klesmer'.

24 *Heroes and Hero-worship*, p. 101.

25 *Heroes and Hero-worship*, p. 105.

26 Scholem, p. 106.

27 Scholem, pp. 107–8.
28 Scholem, p. 47.
29 E. H. Carr, *What is History?* (Harmondsworth, 1972), p. 31.
30 *A Treasury of Jewish Folklore*, p. 608.
31 *A Treasury of Jewish Folklore*, pp. 603–4. As always with folk stories which have several versions, there are golem stories in which it does speak. See *Encyclopaedia Judaica*, VII, p. 755.
32 Scholem, p. 36.
33 Baldick, p. 101.
34 *Sartor Resartus*, p. 70.
35 *Heroes and Hero-worship*, p. 11.
36 *Heroes and Hero-worship*, p. 90.
37 *Heroes and Hero-worship*, p. 134.
38 See *Frankenstein*, p. 118.
39 See Baker, *George Eliot and Judaism*, pp. 83–4.
40 Joseph Campbell, *Occidental Mythology*, p. 113.
41 *Encyclopaedia Judaica*, VII, p. 754.
42 *Encyclopaedia Judaica*, VII, p. 753.

9 The Messianic Potential

1 *Encyclopaedia Judaica*, VI, p. 1382.
2 *Encyclopaedia Judaica*, X, p. 619.
3 *Heroes and Hero-worship*, p. 171.
4 *Encyclopaedia Judaica*, X, p. 618.
5 See *A Treasury of Jewish Folklore*, pp. 206–15: 'Joseph della Reyna Storms Heaven'.
6 *Women and the Demon*, p. 64.
7 Northrop Frye, *Anatomy of Criticism* (Harmondsworth, 1990), p. 316.
8 *Anatomy of Criticism*, p. 187.
9 *Encyclopedia of Religion*, 9, p. 472.

10 Conclusion: Social Critique, Education, Allegory

1 See Sandra Gilbert, 'Life's Empty Pack: Notes toward a Literary Daughter-onomy (*Silas Marner*)' in K. M. Newton (ed.), *George Eliot*, p. 104.
2 *George Eliot*, ed. Newton, pp. 105–6. Gilbert refers the reader to Isaiah 62, verses 4 and 5.
3 George Levine argues that it was Eliot's acceptance of a deterministic universe that made her believe that 'nothing is really isolable':

> George Eliot saw a deterministic universe as a marvelously complex unit in which all parts are intricately related to each other, where nothing is really isolable, and where past and future are both implicit in the present. Nothing in such a universe is explicable without reference to the time and place in which it occurs or exists. This suggested that one can never make a clear-cut break with the society in which one has been brought up, with one's friends and relations,

with one's past. Any such break diminishes a man's wholeness and is the result of his failure to recognize his ultimate dependence on others, their claims on him, and the consequent need for human solidarity. ('Determinism and Responsibility in the Works of George Eliot', *PMLA*, 77 [1962], p. 270)

This is well put, but in our view it is misleading to see scientific determinism as being at the root of Eliot's thinking about connectedness in the human sphere. It derives rather from a wider range of ideas, particularly kabbalism.

4 'Gwendolen' is the name of a legendary queen of Britain, who is also a prominent character in an early version of the Midlands legend of 'Fair Rosamond'. Joseph Wiesenfarth points out that the 'name Gwendolen itself came from [Eliot's] reading in Charlotte Yonge's History of Christian Names'. See *George Eliot: a Writer's Notebook 1854–1879* and *Uncollected Writings*, ed. Joseph Wiesenfarth (Charlottesville, 1981), p. xxxvi. In a notebook Eliot writes that 'Gwen is considered as the British Venus' and that 'Gwendolen, or, the Lady of the bow, or perhaps from Gwendal, white browed, was, it seems, an ancient British Goddess, probably the moon.' See *Some George Eliot Notebooks*, ed. William Baker, I, 101.

5 See Introduction to *George Eliot*, ed. Newton.

Bibliography

Allen, Walter, *George Eliot* (London, 1965).

Altick, R. D., 'Anachronisms in *Middlemarch*: a Note', *Nineteenth-Century Fiction*, 33 (1978), pp. 366–72.

Altmann, Alexander, *Studies in Religious Philosophy and Mysticism* (London, 1969).

Anderson, Amanda, 'George Eliot and the Jewish Question', *Yale Journal of Criticism*, 10 (1997), pp. 39–61.

Arnold, Matthew, *Culture and Anarchy*, ed. J. Dover Wilson (Cambridge, 1986).

Ashton Rosemary, *George Eliot* (Oxford, New York, 1983).

—— *The German Idea: Four English Writers and the Reception of German Thought* (Cambridge, 1980).

Auerbach, Nina, *Women and the Demon: the Life of a Victorian Myth* (Cambridge, Mass. and London, 1982).

—— 'The Power of Hunger: Demonism and Maggie Tulliver', *Nineteenth-Century Fiction*, 35 (1980), pp. 29–52.

Ausubel, Nathan (ed.), *A Treasury of Jewish Folklore* (New York, 1954).

Baker, William, *George Eliot and Judaism* (Salzburg, 1975).

—— *The George Eliot–George Henry Lewes Library: an Annotated Catalogue of their Books at the Dr Williams's Library, London* (New York, 1977).

—— (ed.), *Some George Eliot Notebooks: an Edition of the Carl H. Pforzheimer Holograph Notebooks*, Volumes I–IV (Salzburg, 1976–85).

—— 'The Kabbalah, Mordecai, and George Eliot's Religion of Humanity', *The Yearbook of English Studies*, 3 (1973), pp. 216–21.

Baldick, Chris, *In Frankenstein's Shadow: Myth, Monstrosity and Nineteenth-Century Writing* (Oxford, 1987).

Baring-Gould, Sabine, *Curious Myths of the Middle Ages* (London, Oxford and Cambridge, 1877).

Beer, Gillian, *Darwin's Plots: Evolutionary Narrative in Darwin, George Eliot and Nineteenth-Century Writing* (London, 1983).

—— *George Eliot* (Brighton, 1986).

Blamires, D., 'The Challenge of Fairytales to Literary Studies', *Critical Quarterly*, 21 (1979), pp. 33–40.

Bloom, Harold, *The Kabbalah and Criticism* (New York, 1975).

—— *Modern Critical Interpretation: George Eliot's 'Middlemarch'* (New York, 1987).

—— (ed.), *Mary Shelley's 'Frankenstein'* (New York, 1987).

Bodenheimer, Rosemarie, *The Real Life of Mary Ann Evans: George Eliot, Her Letters and Fiction* (Ithaca and London, 1994).

Bonaparte, Felicia, *The Triptych and the Cross: the Central Myths of George Eliot's Poetic Imagination* (New York, 1979).

—— *Will and Destiny: Morality and Tragedy in George Eliot's Novels* (New York, 1975).

Borges, Jorge Luis, with Geurrero, Margarita, *The Book of Imaginary Beings*, trans. Norman Thomas di Giovanni in collaboration with the author (Harmondsworth, 1987).

Borrow, George, *The Zincali: an Account of the Gypsies in Spain* (first published 1841) (London, 1907).

Bullen, J. B., *The Sun is God: Painting, Literature and Mythology in the Nineteenth Century* (Oxford, 1989).

Butler, E. M., *The Myth of the Magus* (Cambridge, 1979).

—— *The Fortunes of Faust* (Cambridge, 1979).

Campbell, Joseph, *The Hero with a Thousand Faces* (London, 1979).

—— *Occidental Mythology* (Harmondsworth, 1987).

Cantor, Paul, *Creature and Creator: Myth-making and English Romanticism* (Cambridge, 1984).

Carlyle, Thomas, *On Heroes, Hero-worship and the Heroic in Literature* (London, 1896).

—— *Sartor Resartus* (London, 1896).

Carpenter, Mary Wilson, *George Eliot and the Landscape of Time: Narrative Form and Protestant Apocalyptic History* (Chapel Hill, North Carolina, 1986).

Carr, E. H., *What is History?* (Harmondsworth, 1972).

Carroll, David (ed.), *George Eliot: the Critical Heritage* (London, 1971).

—— *George Eliot and the Conflict of Interpretations: a Reading of the Novels* (Cambridge, 1992).

Cecil, David, *Early Victorian Novelists: Essays in Evaluation* (Harmondsworth, 1948).

Chase, Karen, *Eros and Psyche: the Representation of Personality in Charlotte Brontë, Charles Dickens, and George Eliot* (New York and London, 1984).

Chatman, Seymour, *Story and Discourse: Narrative Structure in Fiction and Film* (Ithaca, 1978).

Cheyette, Bryan, *Constructions of 'the Jew' in English Literature and Society: Racial Representations, 1875–1945* (Cambridge, 1995).

Creeger, G. R. (ed.), *George Eliot: a Collection of Critical Essays* (New Jersey, 1987).

Cross, John W. (ed.), *George Eliot's Life*, Vols I–III (Edinburgh and London, 1885).

Dale, Peter, 'Symbolic Representation and the Means of Revolution in *Daniel Deronda*', *Victorian Newsletter*, 59 (1975), pp. 25–30.

De Man, Paul, *Blindness and Insight: Essays in the Rhetoric of Contemporary Criticism* (London, 1983).

Deutsch, Emanuel, *Literary Remains of the late Emanuel Deutsch with a Brief Memoir* (London, 1874).

Dickens, Charles, *Great Expectations*, ed. Angus Calder (Harmondsworth, 1979).

Eliade, Mircea, *Myths, Dreams and Mysteries*, trans. Philip Mairet (London, 1960).

Eliot, George, *Adam Bede*, ed. Valentine Cunningham (Oxford, 1996).

—— *Adam Bede: a New Edition* (London and Edinburgh, n.d.).

—— *Daniel Deronda*, ed. Graham Handley (Oxford, 1988).

—— *Daniel Deronda*, ed. Barbara Hardy (Harmondsworth, 1967).

—— *Felix Holt*, ed. Fred C. Thomson (Oxford, 1988).

——— *Impressions of Theophrastus Such*, ed. Nancy Henry (London, 1994).
——— *The Lifted Veil*, ed. Beryl Gray (London, 1987).
——— *The Lifted Veil and Brother Jacob*, ed. Helen Small (Oxford, 1999).
——— *Middlemarch*, ed. David Carroll (Oxford, 1997).
——— *The Mill on the Floss*, ed. Gordon S. Haight (Oxford, 1996).
——— *Romola*, ed. Andrew Brown (Oxford, 1998).
——— *Scenes of Clerical Life*, ed. Thomas A. Noble (Oxford, 1988).
——— *Silas Marner*, ed. Terence Cave (Oxford, 1996).
——— *The Spanish Gypsy, the Legend of Jubal and Other Poems, Old and New* (Edinburgh and London, n.d.).
——— *Essays of George Eliot*, ed. Thomas Pinney (London, 1963).
——— *The George Eliot Letters*, Volumes *I–VII* (New Haven and London, 1964), Volumes VIII–IX, ed. Gordon S. Haight (New Haven and London, 1978).
——— *The Journals of George Eliot*, ed. Margaret Harris and Judith Johnston (Cambridge, 1998).
Ellmann, Richard, *The Identity of Yeats* (London, 1975).
Encyclopaedia Judaica (Jerusalem, 1971).
Encyclopedia of Religion, The (M. Eliade Editor in Chief) (New York, 1987).
Feldman, David, *Englishmen and Jews: Social Relations and Political Culture 1840–1914* (New Haven and London, 1994).
Felsenstein, Frank, *Anti-Semitic Stereotypes: a Paradigm of Otherness in English Popular Culture, 1660–1830* (Baltimore and London, 1995).
Feuerbach, Ludwig, *The Essence of Christianity*, trans. George Eliot (New York, Evanston and London, 1957).
Fiedler, Leslie, *Waiting for the End: the American Literary Scene from Hemingway to Baldwin* (London, 1965).
Frye, Northrop, *Anatomy of Criticism: Four Essays* (Harmondsworth, 1990).
Ginsburg, C. D., *The Kabbalah: its Doctrines, Development and Literature* (London, 1863).
Goethe, J. W. von, *Faust Part One*, trans. Philip Wayne (Harmondsworth, 1986); *Faust Part Two*, trans. Philip Wayne (Harmondsworth, 1986).
Goldstein, David (ed. and trans.), *Jewish Poets of Spain* (Harmondsworth, 1971).
Graver, Suzanne, *George Eliot and Community: a Study in Social Theory and Fictional Form* (Berkeley, California, 1984).
Graves, Robert and Patai, Raphael, *Hebrew Myths* (London, 1989).
Gray, Beryl, 'Pseudoscience and George Eliot's *The Lifted Veil*', *Nineteenth-Century Fiction*, 36 (1982), pp. 401–23.
Haight, Gordon S., *George Eliot: a Biography* (Oxford, 1968).
——— and Vanarsdel, R. J. (eds), *George Eliot: a Centenary Tribute* (London, 1982).
Haining, Peter (ed.), *The Frankenstein Omnibus* (London, 1995).
Handley, Graham, Introduction to *'Daniel Deronda'* by George Eliot (Oxford, 1988).
Hardy, Barbara, *The Novels of George Eliot* (London, 1959).
Harvey, W. J., *The Art of George Eliot* (London, 1961).
Hawthorne, Nathaniel, *Mosses from an Old Manse*, Centenary Edition, Volume X (Ohio, 1974).

Heine, Heinrich, *The Complete Poems of Heinrich Heine: a Modern English Version by Hal Draper* (Boston, Suhrkamp/Insel, Oxford, 1982).

Henry, Nancy, Introduction to *Impressions of Theophrastus Such* by George Eliot (London, 1964).

—— 'Ante-Anti-Semitism: George Eliot's *Impressions of Theophrastus Such*', in *Victorian Identities: Social and Cultural Formations in Nineteenth-Century Literature*, ed. Ruth Robbins and Julian Wolfreys (Basingstoke and London, 1996).

Higdon, D. L., 'The Iconographic Backgrounds of *Adam Bede* Chapter 15', *Nineteenth-Century Fiction*, 27 (1972), pp. 155–70.

Hirst, Désirée, *Hidden Riches: Traditional Symbolism from the Renaissance to Blake* (London, 1964).

Hruschka, John, *Carlyle's Rabbi Hero: Teufelsdroeckh and the Midrashic Tradition* (Bloomington, 1992).

Hull, E., *Folklore of the British Isles* (London, 1928).

Idel, Moshe, *Golem: Jewish Magical and Mystical Traditions on the Artificial Anthropoid* (New York, 1990).

Irwin, Jane (ed.), *George Eliot's 'Daniel Deronda' Notebooks* (Cambridge, 1996).

Josephus, *Jewish Antiquaries*, Volumes I–IV trans. A. St J. Thackeray, Vols V–VIII, also trans. Ralph Marcus (Cambridge, Mass. and London, 1961).

Kaufmann, David, *George Eliot and Judaism: an Attempt to Appreciate 'Daniel Deronda'*, trans. J. W. Ferrier (Edinburgh, 1877).

Kirk, G. S., *Myth: its Form, Function and Analysis in Ancient and Other Cultures* (Cambridge, 1986).

Kissane, J., 'Victorian Mythmaking', *Victorian Studies*, 6 (1962), pp. 5–28.

Knoepflmacher, U. C., *George Eliot's Early Novels: the Limits of Realism* (Berkeley, 1968).

—— *Religious Humanism and the Victorian Novel: George Eliot, Walter Pater and Samuel Butler* (London, 1965).

—— 'The Balancing of Child and Adult: an Approach to Victorian Fantasies for Children', *Nineteenth-Century Fiction*, 37 (1983), pp. 497–530.

Lang, Andrew, *Magic and Religion* (New York, 1969).

Leavis, F. R., *The Great Tradition: George Eliot, Henry James, Joseph Conrad* (London, 1966).

Levine, George, 'Determinism and Responsibility in the Novels of George Eliot', *PMLA*, 77 (1962), pp. 268–79.

Lewes, George Henry, *The Foundations of a Creed* (London, 1874).

Ling, Trevor, *A History of Religion East and West: an Introduction and Interpretation* (London, 1983).

Luzzatto, Moses C., *General Principles of the Kabbalah*, trans. the Research Centre of the Kabbalah (New York, 1970).

MacCabe, Colin, *James Joyce and the Revolution of the Word* (London, 1978).

Mackinlay, J. M., *Folklore of the Scottish Lochs and Springs* (Glasgow, 1893).

Madsen, Deborah, *Rereading Allegory: a Narrative Approach to Genre* (London, 1996).

Maimon, Solomon, *The Autobiography of Solomon Maimon*, trans. J. Clarke Murray, with an essay on Maimon's philosophy by Hugo Bergman (London, 1954).

Marx, Karl and Engels, Friedrich, *Basic Writings on Politics and Philosophy*, ed. Lewis R. Feuer (London, 1969).

Mason, Michael Y., '*Middlemarch* and Science: Problems of Life and Mind', *Review of English Studies*, 22 (1971), pp. 151–69.

McLaverty, J., 'Comtean Fetishism in *Silas Marner*', *Nineteenth-Century Fiction*, 25 (1981), pp. 318–36.

Merivale, P., 'Learning the Hard Way: Gothic Pedagogy in the Modern Romantic Quest', *Comparative Literature*, 36 (1984), pp. 146–61.

Meyrink, Gustav, *The Golem*, trans. M. Pemberton (Sawtry and New York, 1991).

Milton, John, 'Paradise Lost' in *The Complete Poems*, ed. B. A. Wright (London and Melbourne, 1986).

Myers, William, *The Teaching of George Eliot* (London, 1984).

Newton, K. M., 'Byronic Egoism and George Eliot's *The Spanish Gypsy*', *Neophilologus*, 57 (1973), pp. 388–400.

―――― (ed.), *George Eliot* (London and New York, 1991).

―――― 'George Eliot, George Henry Lewes and Darwinism', *Durham University Journal*, 66 (1974), pp. 278–93.

―――― *George Eliot: Romantic Humanist* (London, 1981).

―――― 'Historical Prototypes in *Middlemarch*', *English Studies*, 56 (1975), pp. 403–8.

Nietzsche, Friedrich, *Basic Writings of Nietzsche*, ed. and trans. Walter Kaufmann (New York, 1968).

Pinion, F. B. (ed.), *A George Eliot Miscellany* (London and Basingstoke, 1982).

Postlethwaite, Diana, 'When George Eliot Read Milton: the Muse in a Different Voice', *ELH*, 57 (1990), pp. 197–221.

Pratt, J. C. and Neufeldt, V. A. (eds), *George Eliot's 'Middlemarch' Notebooks* (Berkeley and Los Angeles, 1979).

Praz, Mario, *The Hero in Eclipse in Victorian Fiction*, trans. Angus Davidson (Oxford, 1956).

Ragussis, Michael, *Figures of Conversion: 'The Jewish Question' and English National Identity* (Durham, N.C. and London, 1995).

Redinger, Ruby, *George Eliot: the Emergent Self* (London, 1976).

Reed, J. R. and Heron, J., 'George Eliot's Illegitimate Children', *Nineteenth-Century Fiction*, 40 (1985), pp. 175–86.

Reilly, Jim, *Shadowtime: History and Representation in Hardy, Conrad and George Eliot* (London and New York, 1993).

Reville, A., *Prolégomènes de l'Histoire des Religions* (Paris, 1886).

Rosten, Leo, *The Joys of Yiddish* (Harmondsworth, 1971).

Said, Edward W., *The Question of Palestine* (London, 1980).

Schneewind, J. B., 'Moral Problems and Moral Philosophy in the Victorian Period', *Victorian Studies*, 9, Supplement (1965), pp. 29–46.

Schneiderman, L., *The Psychology of Myth, Folklore and Religion* (Chicago, 1981).

Scholem, Gershom, *On the Kabbalah and its Symbolism*, trans. Ralph Manheim (New York, 1969).

Schwarz, Leo M. (ed.), *The Jewish Caravan* (New York, 1935).
Scott, Walter, *Minstrelsy of the Scottish Border*, Volumes I–IV, revised and ed. T. F. Henderson (Edinburgh and London, 1932).
―――― *Letters on Demonology and Witchcraft Addressed to J. G. Lockhart, Esq.* (London and Edinburgh, 1832).
Shaffer, Elinor S., *'Kubla Khan' and 'The Fall of Jerusalem: the Mythological School in Biblical Criticism and Secular Literature* (Cambridge, 1975).
Shah, Idries, *The Secret Lore of Magic: Books of the Sorcerers* (London, 1972).
Shelley, Mary, *Frankenstein* (London, 1985).
―――― *Collected Tales and Stories*, ed. Charles E. Robinson (Baltimore and London, 1976).
Shelley, Percy Bysshe, *The Poetical Works of Percy Bysshe Shelley* (London, n.d.).
Sherwin, Byron L., *The Golem Legend: Origins and Implications* (Lanham, New York and London, 1985).
Sherwin, Paul, *'Frankenstein*: Creation as Catastrophe', *PMLA*, 96 (1981), pp. 883–903.
Shuttleworth, Sally, *George Eliot and Nineteenth-Century Science: the Make-Believe of a Beginning* (Cambridge, 1984).
Sidgwick, F., *Ballads of Scottish Tradition and Romance* (London, 1906).
Spinoza, *Ethics*, trans. Andrew Boyle, revised by G. H. R. Parkinson (London, 1989).
Stange, G. R., 'The Voices of the Essayist', *Nineteenth-Century Fiction*, 35 (1980), pp. 312–30.
Stokes, Edward, *Hawthorne's Influence on Charles Dickens and George Eliot* (Queensland, 1985).
Stone, Harry, 'Dickens and the Jews', *Victorian Studies*, 2 (1959), pp. 223–53.
Sullivan, W. J., 'Piero di Cosimo and the Higher Primitivism in *Romola*', *Nineteenth-Century Fiction*, 26 (1972), pp. 390–405.
―――― 'Music and Musical Allusion in *The Mill on The Floss*', *Criticism*, 16 (1974), pp. 232–46.
―――― 'George Eliot and Goethe's *Faust*', *George Eliot Fellowship Review*, 6 (1975), pp. 15–22.
Swann, Brian, '*Middlemarch* and Myth', *Nineteenth-Century Fiction*, 28 (1973), pp. 210–14.
―――― '*Silas Marner* and the New Mythus', *Criticism*, 18 (1976), pp. 101–21.
Talmud, The, trans. H. Polano (London and New York, n.d.).
West, R. H., *Milton and the Angels* (Athens, USA, 1955).
White, D. A., 'Northrop Frye: Value and System', *Criticism*, 15 (1973), pp. 189–211.
Wiesenfarth, Joseph, *George Eliot's Mythmaking* (Heidelberg, 1977).
―――― (ed.), *George Eliot: a Writer's Notebook, 1854–1879 and Uncollected Writings* (Charlottesville, 1981).
Wohlfarth, Marc E., '*Daniel Deronda* and the Politics of Nationalism', *Nineteenth-Century Literature*, 53 (1998), pp. 188–210.
Wolfreys, Julian, 'The Ideology of Englishness: the Paradoxes of Tory-Liberal Culture and National Identity in *Daniel Deronda*', *George Eliot–George Henry Lewes Studies*, 26–7 (1994), pp. 15–33.

Wordsworth, William, *The Poetical Works of William Wordsworth*, ed. E. de Selincourt (Oxford, 1952).

—— and Coleridge, Samuel Taylor, *Lyrical Ballads*, ed. Derek Roper (London, 1976).

Zipes, Jack, *Breaking the Magic Spell: Radical Theories of Folk and Fairy Tales* (London, 1979).

Index

Adam Bede, 2, 7, 9, 16, 28–9,
    30–1, 34, 41, 44, 58, 59, 73–8,
    85–6, 88, 104, 116–17, 118,
    119, 127, 129–30, 142, 144,
    155, 157, 162, 170, 172, 173,
    174, 179, 181, 186, 187
'Address to Working Men, by Felix
    Holt', 67–8, 82–3, 142
Agrippa, Cornelius, 112
Allen, Walter, 196n
Altmann, Alexander, 10, 62, 71,
    90, 102, 104, 203n, 204n
Anderson, Amanda, 197n, 206–7n
Armin, Achim von, 113, 195n
Arnold, Matthew, 103, 126, 204n
    Culture and Anarchy, 204n, 205n
Auerbach, Nina, 79, 113–14, 174–5
Ausubel, Nathan, 6, 194n

Baker, William, 31, 44, 46, 50, 54,
    103, 168, 192n, 198n, 199n,
    200n, 201n, 207n
Baldick, Chris, 113, 120, 123, 126,
    141
Barbarossa, Frederick, 81
Barthes, Roland, 190
Bernard, Claude, 118
Blake, William, 22, 101
    'The Marriage of Heaven and
    Hell', 101
Bodenheimer, Rosemarie, 198n
Bonaparte, Felicity, 1
Borrow, George, 150–1, 199n
Brenz, Samuel Friedrich, 8
'Brother and Sister', 43
Brother Jacob, 73
Browning, Robert, 137
    'My Last Duchess', 137
Buchan, John, 20
Buckley, Walter, 121
Burke and Hare, 122
Butler, E. M., 35
Byron, Lord, 13, 195n

Campbell, Joseph, 100, 110, 169
Cantor, Paul, 72–3, 84, 93, 123,
    137, 203
Capek, Karel, 124
Carlyle, Thomas, 8, 10, 22, 37, 48,
    53, 55, 61, 62, 63, 88, 94, 106,
    113, 126, 131, 135, 136, 143,
    167–8, 173–4, 184, 192n, 194n
    *On Heroes, Hero-worship and the
    Heroic in Literature*, 9, 48,
    63, 88, 135, 143, 167–8,
    173–4
    Sartor Resartus, 10, 22, 37, 53,
    54–5, 61–2, 63, 70, 94, 106,
    113, 115, 126, 127, 136, 155,
    156, 192n, 194n
Carpenter, Mary Wilson, 2
Carr, E. H., 166
Cavour, Camillo Count, 153
Cecil, David, 16, 17
Chamisso, Adelbert von, 195n
Charisi, Rabbi Judah, 26
Chase, Cynthia, 204n
Chase, Karen, 11, 115, 118
Cheyette, Bryan, 20, 21, 198n
Coleridge, Samuel Taylor, 192n,
    195n
    The Rime of the Ancient Mariner,
    156–8, 192n, 195
'College Breakfast Party, A', 125, 145
Columbus, Christopher, 30, 174
Combe, George, 114
Comte, Auguste, 106, 118, 122
Cumming, Dr John, 135, 136, 184,
    185, 187

Dan, Joseph, 193
Daniel Deronda, 2, 4, 7, 11, 12,
    13–4, 15, 18–21, 24, 25, 26,
    27, 28, 30, 31–2, 33, 34, 37–8,
    39, 42, 44–7, 48–52, 55, 56,
    57, 59, 61, 62–7, 70, 83,
    86–90, 94, 97–107, 111, 115,

Daniel Deronda – *continued*
117–18, 119, 128, 130–1, 137,
138, 139–40, 144, 145–7, 150,
151, 153, 154–6, 157, 159,
160–5, 167, 169–70, 171–80,
181, 185, 188, 189–90, 197n,
201n, 203n, 207n
Dante, 23
Darwin, Charles, 1
De Man, Paul, 20
Della Reina, Yosef, 111, 174
Deutsch, Emanuel, 5, 26, 34, 149,
187, 192n, 200n, 201n
Dickens, Charles, 73, 117
David Copperfield, 117
Great Expectations, 73–7
Disraeli, Benjamin, 171

Eagleton, Terry, 78
Edgeworth, Maria, 33
Harrington, 33
Eliade, Mircea, 71, 204n, 205n
Engels, Friedrich, 1, 206n
'Evangelical Teaching: Dr
Cumming', 135–6, 184–5, 187
Evans, Isaac, 79
Ezra, Ibn, 203n

Felix Holt, 7, 9, 12, 25, 56, 61, 70,
79, 80, 82, 96, 115–16, 117,
119, 120, 124, 128–9, 141–3,
146, 154, 173, 183, 185
Felsenstein, Frank, 197n, 207n
Feuerbach, Ludwig, 23, 85
Fiedler, Leslie, 32, 33, 199n
Fourier, F. M. C., 159
Frazer, J. G., 45
Frye, Northrop, 19, 177, 179
Fuller, Margaret, 184

Garibaldi, Giuseppe, 153
Gaskell, Elizabeth, 141
Geiger, Abraham, 150
Gilbert, Sandra, 186, 208n
Ginsburg, C. D., 199
Goethe, J. W. Von, 8, 11, 12, 35,
37, 55, 69, 78, 109, 113, 149,
179, 181, 184, 189, 192n,
195n

Faust, 10, 11, 12, 13, 14, 35, 37,
41, 53, 55, 59, 60, 71, 78,
80, 91, 108–10, 115, 116,
119, 131, 143, 146, 149, 164,
173, 174, 179, 181, 184,
192n, 195n
'The Sorcerer's Apprentice', 8,
69, 80, 123, 142
Wilhelm Meister, 13
Graves, Robert, 3, 92
Gray, Beryl, 205n
Gregory, William, 114

Haining, Peter, 195n
Halevi, Yehuda, 4, 26, 28, 33, 146,
154, 176, 193n, 200n
Handley, Graham, 198n, 207n
Hardy, Barbara, 192n
Hawthorne, Nathaniel, 16, 113, 203n
'The Birthmark', 113, 203n
The Scarlet Letter, 16
Hegel, G. W. F., 61
Heine, Heinrich, 26, 136
Henry, Nancy, 196n, 198n
Hirst, Désirée, 199n
Hoffmann, E. T. A., 113
Homer, 138
The Odyssey, 138

Impressions of Theophrastus Such, 9,
13, 33, 81, 107, 124, 126–7,
142, 144, 145, 149–50, 152–3,
154, 178, 189, 198n

Josephus, 36, 86, 92, 128, 134, 148
Joyce, James, 18, 19, 22, 138
Ulysses, 18, 19, 20, 138

Karloff, Boris, 167
Kipling, Rudyard, 20
Knoepflmacher, U. C., 17, 18,
194n, 196n
Knox, John, 135

Lang, Andrew, 45
Lavoisier, A. L., 121
'Leaves from a Notebook', 136,
205–6n
Leavis, F. R., 196n

'Legend of Jubal, The', 110, 125,
172–3
Letters of George Eliot, 15, 24, 25,
27, 98, 138, 139, 143, 152, 171
Levi, Giuseppe, 5
Levin, Rahel, 33
Levine, George, 119, 208–9n
Lewes, G. H., 13, 15, 23, 26, 33,
34, 79, 108, 113, 114, 122,
184, 192n
Lifted Veil, The, 6, 17, 57, 78, 94,
114, 118–19, 122, 128, 134,
151, 160, 168–9, 194n
Ling, Trevor, 35
Loew, Rabbi Yehuda, 6, 11, 70, 71,
111, 178
Luria, Isaac, 29, 36, 148
Luzzati, Moses C., 36, 42, 69, 72,
84, 99, 100, 102, 105–6

Mackay, R. W., 106
Madsen, Deborah L., 193n
Magnus, Albert, 112
Magus, Simon, 5, 7, 12, 14, 127
Maimon, Solomon, 28, 30, 31, 34,
102, 104, 110, 181
Maimonides, Moses, 26, 28, 30,
63, 72, 181
Marlowe, Christopher, 37
Marx, Karl, 1, 8, 77, 81–2, 142,
206n
The Communist Manifesto, 142
Mazzini, Giuseppe, 153
Melville, Herman, 129
Moby-Dick, 129
Mendelssohn, Moses, 34, 181
Meyrink, Gustav, 205n
Middlemarch, 7, 10, 12, 18, 23, 24,
31, 34, 39–42, 44, 51, 55,
56–7, 58–60, 82, 87–8, 94,
95–7, 105, 115, 118, 119,
120–4, 126, 127, 130, 131–3,
137–8, 139–40, 141, 161–2,
164, 169, 172, 173, 179, 181,
185, 187, 188–9, 198n
Mill on the Floss, The, 17, 24, 39,
42, 43, 48, 49, 57, 84, 87, 116,
124, 129, 131, 157, 159–60,
169, 187, 197–8n, 199n, 200n

Milton, John, 2, 21, 23, 76, 80,
192n, 199n
Paradise Lost, 2, 17, 80, 85
Munk, Rabbi Salomon, 54

Napoleon, 81
'Natural History of German Life,
The', 136, 182
Nietzsche, Friedrich, 22
The Birth of Tragedy, 22
Nord, Deborah Epstein, 207n
'Notes on Form in Art', 61, 64,
66, 105, 138, 184, 187
'Notes on the Spanish Gypsy and
Tragedy in General', 138
Novalis, 61

Owen, Robert, 125

Paracelsus, Philippus, 5, 6, 7, 78,
112, 194n
Pericles, 174
Praz, Mario, 196n

Ragussis, Michael, 32, 33, 38
Reilly, Jim, 196–7n
Riehl, W. H., 136, 182
Romola, 2, 7, 9, 16, 28–9, 30–1,
34, 41, 44, 58, 59, 73–8, 85–6,
88, 104, 116–17, 118, 119,
127, 129–30, 142, 144, 155,
157, 162, 170, 172, 173, 174,
179, 181, 186, 187
Roper, Derek, 207n
Rousseau, Jean-Jacques, 105, 182, 183

Said, Edward W., 151–2
Sainte-Beuve, Charles, 81
Scenes of Clerical Life, 15–16
Schlegel, Dorothea, 34, 181
Schlegel, Friedrich, 34
Scholem, Gershom, 4, 7, 8, 14, 29,
101, 106, 148, 163, 166,
193–4n
Scott, Walter, 1, 32, 33, 95
Ivanhoe, 32, 33
Semmel, Bernard, 207n
Shaffer, E. S., 200n
Shakespeare, William, 32

Shakespeare, William – *continued*
  The Merchant of Venice, 32
  The Winter's Tale, 97
Shelley, Mary, 6, 11, 55, 72, 85,
  92, 105, 112, 123, 126, 166,
  181, 182, 189, 192n, 195n
  Frankenstein, 6, 10, 14, 55, 59,
  68, 70, 71, 72, 74, 75–6, 78,
  79–80, 84–6, 87, 89, 93, 103,
  105, 106, 112, 119, 121, 123,
  129, 132, 146, 166–7, 181,
  192n, 194n, 195n
Shelley, Percy Bysshe, 63, 72, 92,
  105, 156, 176, 190, 192n, 195n
  Prometheus Unbound, 192n
  Queen Mab, 72, 92, 156
Sherwin, Byron, 7, 84
Sherwin, Paul, 84, 89, 195n
Shuttleworth, Sally, 118, 121
Sibree, John, 25, 171
Silas Marner, 16, 17, 38–9, 62, 63,
  72, 74, 75, 94, 124, 130, 137,
  143, 158–9, 185, 186–7, 205n
'Silly Novels by Lady Novelists', 98, 205n
Spanish Gypsy, The, 2, 37, 43, 47,
  48, 111, 143, 150, 151, 153–4,
  178, 181, 185, 186

Spencer, Herbert, 122
Spenser, Edmund, 21, 23
Spinoza, Baruch, 26, 28, 30, 63
Stevens, Wallace, 22
Stowe, Harriet Beecher, 136
  Dred, 136
Strauss, David, 23, 46, 135

Tennyson, Alfred, 132
  Maud, 136
Tolstoy, Leo, 19

Vaihinger, Hans, 23
Varnhargen, Karl, 34
Voltaire, 25

Washington, George, 174
Wiesenfarth, Joseph, 1, 209n
Wilde, Oscar, 88
  The Picture of Dorian Gray, 88
Wohlfarth, Marc E., 153
Wollstonecraft, Mary, 184
Wordsworth, William, 1

Yeats, W. B., 22

Zola, Emile, 19